Trial by Fire

A Spiritual Warfare Novel

The Fire Series

Eric M. Hill

Published by SunHill Publishers
P.O. Box 17730
Atlanta, Georgia 30316
www.ericmhill.com
ericmhillauthor@yahoo.com
www.twitter.com/EricMHillATL
www.facebook.com/ericmhillauthor

ISBN-13: 978-1519726193
ISBN-10: 1519726198

Cover design by Cora Graphics

A Note from the Author

Hello! If this is your first time reading one of my stories, I welcome you and thank you for choosing my book to read among the millions that are available. If you have read at least one of my stories and have returned for more, that says it all! I can't think of a greater compliment and vote of confidence than for someone to read one of my books and ask for more. ☺

May I ask you a favor?

Once you read the book, if you find that you enjoyed the story, would you mind going online to Amazon.com, iTunes, Kobo, Barnes and Noble, or wherever you purchased the book and writing a review? Many people determine from book reviews whether or not a story is worth their time. Your review (even a short one!) can help convince others to join the fun!

Let's Stay In Touch!

Readers who sign up for my mailing list receive and/or do the following:

Receive advance news of stories I'm working on.

Receive ***free*** portions of stories before they are published.

Receive whatever wonderful written ***freebie*** I can come up with.

Provide me with feedback on what they liked or disliked about a story.

Share their ideas about what they'd like to see in future stories. (*Trial by Fire* was written in part because a fan of *Bones of Fire* strongly encouraged me to turn the book into a series!)

Join my newsletter at www.ericmhill.com/newsletter. Here's my contact info: ericmhillauthor@yahoo.com or Twitter.com/ericmhillatl.

God bless you!

Other Books by the Author

Spiritual Warfare Fiction

The Fire Series
Book 1: Bones of Fire
Book 2: Trial by Fire
Book 3: Saints on Fire

The Demon Strongholds Series
Book 1: The Spirit of Fear
Book 2: The Spirit of Rejection

Other Fiction

Out of Darkness Series
Book 1: The Runaway: Beginnings
Book 2: The Runaway: Endings

Non-Fiction

Deliverance from Demons and Diseases
What Preachers Never Tell You About Tithes & Offerings
You Can Get Can Answers to Your Prayers

Chapter 1

The Mighty Bashnar.

The legendary warrior demon watched him in contempt. He hated the preacher and had been trying to destroy him for over a year. He hated weak adversaries. If he could even be called an adversary.

Great demons were recognized as such because of great conquests. Reverend Edwin Styles wasn't great. He wasn't strong. He wasn't worthy of the attention of a demon as great as the Mighty Bashnar. Yet, the obvious question that dogged the great warrior's reputation was, If Bashnar was so great and if Edwin was so weak, why had he not destroyed him yet?

The great strategist seethed as he observed this meeting of the three enemies. His failure wasn't hidden in some dark mystery. The reason he hadn't destroyed this worm of a man *yet* was because of the two people who carried him like the spiritual cripple he was.

Jonathan the dagger.

Sharon the thorn.

Without these two crutches, the worm would fall on his face!

He watched the worried preacher. "You should be troubled, Reverend Worm," said the Mighty Bashnar.

*****

Edwin couldn't shake the troubling thought. *What if someone or something worse than Anthony Righetti popped out of nowhere? What would I do?*

No one had ever accused Reverend Edwin Styles of being strong, or better yet, of not being weak. *Weak.* That was the word. The word that described his sorry self to a T. He groaned inwardly, as though his mental conversation with himself was on speaker phone and Jonathan and Sharon could hear his self-recriminations.

It didn't make sense. He had seen absolutely spectacular things in the past year since that warlock maniac, Anthony Righetti, had been killed by the police. Incredible healings and miracles. He shook his head as he thought in awe, in almost disbelief actually. Yet he had to believe. He had seen these things with his own eyes. His own eyes! But even more astounding than what he had witnessed was what he had done. He had actually worked miracles with his own hands. He had commanded diseases to leave and they had. Edwin's racing thoughts slowed down. He settled on one of the many miracles he had done. He thought of the lady with the rolling air canister and the face mask. The one with the lung disease.

She had needed a lung transplant. A *lung* transplant. He hadn't even known there was such a thing. One command of faith (from him no less!) and the lady had been healed. She had taken that mask off her face and thrown it to the floor like it was a skunk with his tail raised. The movie in Edwin's mind of this woman running up and down the aisles screaming, "Thank you, Jesus!" was as vivid now as when it had happened.

Her shouts were joined by several others in his mind who had received outstanding miracles of healing or deliverance from demons. The parade of triumph was endless. He literally couldn't remember all of the people who had been mightily touched by God when he had prayed for them. Some of them he hadn't even prayed for. He had simply touched them.

And yet...

Weakness reverberated in his soul. Not an inch of his being was under the slightest illusion that he was anything other than what he had always been.

Weak.

A failure.

And now, a fraud.

Edwin knew that as wonderful as this move of God was, and that even though he was the face of the revival (what a joke!) and had become a celebrity of sorts—He was embarrassed, but celebrity was the only word that seemed to fit—it was a make-believe world. Not that it wasn't real. It was. But it was real like a good movie is real. No matter how good the movie, it ends. And the person watching has to inevitably leave the movie in the theater and go back to the real world. Unfortunately for him, his *real* world after the movie's end would be worse than before it began.

He couldn't go back to the emptiness of dead religion. Especially now that he had tasted the thrilling powers of God. *Jesus Christ really was alive!* To go back would be worse than death. And yet he was going back and he knew it. For he wasn't in control of, of whatever this was that Jonathan had gotten him into. He was simply riding a powerful wave. And like all powerful waves, they make the ones who ride them look good until they inevitably die out. The problem with waves was they couldn't be controlled.

Edwin thought regretfully that his problem wasn't simply that the wave was destined to die, but that he couldn't surf. He didn't know how he had been so lucky to stay on the miracles and healings board this long.

Jonathan.

Yep, he agreed with himself. The only reason he had not yet been exposed as a fraud was Jonathan. Edwin's face barely concealed the tipping point of terror that this thought brought with it. Jonathan was the true power behind this revival. He was the one who had made such a fool of that warlock that he had gone crazy in front of everyone and started shooting into the crowd. Where would Atlanta be today if Jonathan had not challenged that nut?

Edwin knew the answer to this and it wasn't good. *What if something happens to Jonathan?* he asked himself with alarm. What if a greater threat arises and Jonathan's not here? What if he simply leaves? What if? What if? What if? Edwin was a grown man with a family, and his total well-being depended upon how well another man could cover for him. This was sickening. He could've thrown up all over himself.

Jonathan says you've chosen me, Edwin prayed. *Why would you choose someone like me? If you did choose me, you've made a big mistake.* Edwin wasn't expecting a response. He was simply doing what he regularly did—questioning God's wisdom in choosing him. But immediately a strong thought pressed itself forcefully upon his mind.

I don't make mistakes.

*****

There were no relatives among demons, but if there were, Krionina would've been the nephew of Prince Krioni. He had been assigned to watch Edwin's every movement, and to record anything of consequence. This was a task that could've been performed by any one of a nearly innumerable host of regular familiar or observer spirits. Yet he had been chosen above them all for this high visibility assignment. He knew the rumors. He sneered inside his dark soul. He didn't care what they said about him. They were just jealous. Any one of those who criticized him as being the prince's lap dog would gladly trade places with him if they could. He wasn't in the least bit ashamed. Yes, he was the prince's lap dog, and there wasn't room enough on the prince's lap for anyone but him. He was going to milk this special relationship for all he could get. And he would put a dagger in the back of anyone who tried to stop it. He had killed demons before, and he would do it again.

But there was one rumor that did bother him. Word was out that the real reason he had been assigned to watch Edwin was to watch the Mighty Bashnar. Krioni-na was reluctant to buy into this. It was much more flattering to believe he was assigned to Edwin to watch Edwin. This would mean his sponsor, the prince, had been impressed with his accomplishments. There had been many, and any one of them qualified him for the prestigious task of being assigned to the number two revival threat in Atlanta.

Yet he had to admit to himself that it was odd of the prince to require private face-to-face meetings to discuss his written reports. He was quite thorough. Rarely was there anything to add in a private meeting that was not already included in his written reports. Krioni-na grimaced. He wasn't so ambitious that he had gone stupid. His contemplations gave him two troubling concerns.

The first was that he couldn't suppress the irksome thought that dripped into his mind like a persistent water leak. No matter what he included in his reports, the conversations always meandered around to what the Mighty Bashnar was doing. Now that Krioni-na thought about it, his conversations with the prince were more about the Mighty Bashnar than about Edwin, Jonathan, or the revival. His eyes narrowed.

He let himself think something now that hadn't made sense after one of his conversations with the prince a few months ago. *The prince had no interest in the Atlanta revival. He was only interested in the Mighty Bashnar.* The ambitious demon had been duped after all! This was why the prince had always hurried him through his reports about Edwin. He didn't care a thing in the world about Edwin. It was all about the Mighty Bashnar!

But why? Why such an obsession with this legendary warrior? His musings turned to terror when the distant dots connected. *Oh, my darkness. It's true! The prince wants to strip the Mighty Bashnar of his title!*

The second of Krioni-na's concerns suddenly became an immediate crisis that threatened more than his career. His very life was in danger.

This meeting among Edwin, Jonathan, and Sharon was certain to be one of significant strategic importance—the young girl's gift was growing, and it could make her even more of a pest.

Yet the Mighty Bashnar's volcanic red eyes were fixed on him. Not on Edwin. Not on Jonathan. Not on Sharon. On him. It was like he knew what he had been thinking. It had long been rumored that some great warriors could read minds. But it had never been determined that they could do so, and warrior spirits were famous for guarding their secrets. *Perhaps they were simply incredibly perceptive.*

For a moment Krioni-na's terror lessened to dread. But it was a brief moment. *Or maybe he can read minds.* He shuddered at the unnerving possibility and hoped his shaking wasn't noticeable. Everyone knew that the Mighty Bashnar despised any display of fear. Fear did something to warrior spirits—especially the one peering at him from the corner of the room.

The Mighty Bashnar hadn't moved one inch closer to the terrified demon. But this was irrelevant. Krioni-na looked at the large warrior's menacing eyes for the slightest trace of blackness. He swore by Satan that if he saw even a microscopic dot of murderous blackness in those eyes, he was out of there. Better to be a disgraced demon than a dead demon. The thought of being tortured to death by this sadistic warrior and then being confined to that hideous *Dark Prison* was unbearable.

The Mighty Bashnar glared at the prince's flunky in perfect stillness. His and Krioni-na's eyes bore into one another's, but for different reasons. One looking for weakness. The other looking for death. The great warrior saw not only weakness, but fear. It was all over this arrogant spy. He saw it in his stillness. He saw it in his micro trembling. (Only a warrior spirit would've seen it.)

Trembling. What a pathetic shell of a demon. He wasn't even worthy to be called a demon. The Mighty Bashnar's stillness was broken by a slight, but scarily noticeable half-scowl that formed as his nose moved when it sniffed the air.

Krioni-na knew what was happening. The warrior spirit had smelled his fear! *Oh, darkness!* This only made matters worse. Warrior spirits often went rabid at the sight or smell of fear. Even if for some reason—like hopefully having a powerful sponsor like Prince Krioni—they didn't immediately attack you, they would hate you forever and count you as a personal enemy.

The longer the Mighty Bashnar peered at the cowardly spy, the more he felt himself losing control of his rage. He had already crossed the line by killing Witchcraft. One could not touch such favorites of Satan without incurring his wrath. Although he had been suspected of the crime (It was no crime! How could it be a crime to destroy a spirit privileged with direct access to Satan who was so shamefully weak?), he had not been blamed for it because a formal investigation had found the probability of prayer residue in the area.

The evidence was inconclusive and the residue so scant that it couldn't be determined whether there had actually been any prayer in the general area of Witchcraft's death, or if there had been, whether it would've been enough to destroy such a powerful spirit. Nonetheless, based on experience, the investigators concluded that since even small amounts of prayer could sometimes cause disproportionate damage, it was wise to err on the side of the possibility that some pesky Christians had turned off their televisions and prayed instead. (Someone would pay for not keeping the Christians in the area distracted!)

He had been lucky that time. Great warriors were often lucky. But he was more than a great warrior, he mused. Great warriors were as the humans would say, a dime a dozen. He was also a great strategist. And great strategists used their minds more than their swords. He didn't see how he could kill this spy and get away with it—at least not yet. Not with him having such a powerful sponsor.

Nonetheless, his insides burned not only because this scum was trying to take his title, but also because of the putrid smell of fear that emanated from his enemy's pores. It was a rancid, pungent assault that violated his nostrils. True, it was a great weapon to be able to smell fear. But it was also true that the strong stench of fear literally agitated the lungs of warrior spirits. Some said that it wasn't the irritation of the lungs that could turn a calculating warrior spirit into a crazed, murderous animal, but the unacknowledged belief among such spirits that there was a danger that by breathing in fear, one could catch it, like a virus. That this was a myth, any warrior spirit would vehemently attest.

Yet, it was common knowledge that, though rare, there were documented cases of circumstantial evidence that supported the myth of warrior spirits catching the so-called fear virus. Those cursed warriors who had for whatever reasons been thought guilty of such shameful behavior were dealt with the way wolves treat one of their own that's caught in a snare. They were ripped to shreds by frenzied warrior spirits.

The Mighty Bashnar didn't know whether this myth was true or not. He couldn't care less. Virus or no virus, he was immune to fear. In fact, though the smell of fear was loathsome, its unforgivable scent also gave him fiendish delight.

There were few things as satisfying as causing fear by one's presence. No. What filled him with rage and threatened to push him to carelessness was the thought of this glorified nobody spying on him, and the thought that someone, be he a prince or otherwise, was trying to take his hard won title *Mighty* away from him.

*****

The angel, Enrid, was cloaked in temporary invisibility, compliments of prayer—it wasn't enough to last as long as he needed, but he couldn't let that stop him. He had been watching the whole thing. He was fascinated at his enemy's uncharacteristic behavior.

The Mighty Bashnar was known more for his intelligence than his fighting skills, though he was a most formidable fighter. Thus the title *Mighty.* Yet he appeared to be contemplating making a suicidal move against Prince Krioni's demon. Opportunities like this didn't happen often. His idea was dangerous. With so little prayer coverage, it could be considered by others as not worth the risk. But Enrid loved risk. High risk, high reward. The sons of the Father needed him to do it.

Now.

While the moment was right.

*****

Before the hapless demon knew what had happened, he was looking up into the death black eyes of the Mighty Bashnar. How had he gotten to him so quickly? He hadn't even blinked. As he stared into the mirror of his death, he wondered how many others who had died at this warrior's hands had been surprised by his speed.

"You want my title." Bashnar's words were slow, deliberate.

Krioni-na heard himself say in his mind, "The great Prince Krioni is my sponsor!" But the hot, horrid breath of the Mighty Bashnar pushed past his bared teeth, settling on the terrified demon's trembling face. Krioni-na looked first at one, then the other large fang, and thought it wiser to take a different approach. "You are the *Mighty* Bashnar. A title you earned a hundred times over. Your heroism and courage are known in both kingdoms." Krioni-na was amazed that he was still alive. "I was there at the ceremony," he said, trying to not sound as desperate as he was. Krioni-na heard a low growl deep in the Mighty Bashnar's thick neck. "When your brilliance and exploits were finally recognized. When you were awarded the *Mighty* title."

Flattery. The spy was using flattery to save his life. Now the Mighty Bashnar knew exactly why he was a favorite of Prince Krioni. This shadow of a demon fed his master's insatiable ego. Another reason to hate the prince. A true prince wouldn't surround himself with weak demons. Nonetheless, this weasel did speak the truth. Bashnar felt the pressure in his wide chest lessen. "You were at the ceremony."

"Yes, Mighty Bashnar."

"And yet you and your master have conspired to dishonor me."

"No. No. No. No. No. A thousand times no, Mighty Bashnar." Krioni-na needed to do something fast. "I can help you!"

"What could you possibly do for me?"

"Eyeeee..." *Cursed darkness! His only choice was certain death now or possible death later. If the prince ever found out—*

"Speak!"

Krioni-na spoke as fast as he could. "The prince didn't tell me this, but I think he wants your title. He sent me here to watch that weak worm of a man, Edwin. However, all he ever wants to talk about is you. 'What is Bashnar doing?' 'What did Bashnar say?' 'When did Bashnar arrive?' 'How did Bashnar respond?' I *may* have something else that could prove useful to you, *Mighty* Bashnar." The offer of a trade was clear.

The Mighty Bashnar peered at the spy/dupe. It didn't make any difference now which he was, he was compromised. You want to save your worthless life."

Krioni-na swallowed hard. "I would like very much to save my worthless life, *Mighty* Bashnar."

Oh, how you stink! "Very well," Bashnar answered. "Tell me something worthy of your life."

The bargaining demon searched desperately for something useful. "Uhhh...uhhh..."

"Uhhh?" Bashnar said with controlled fury. "Uuhhh is what you offer me?"

"The great prince is looking for a way to get you removed from the Atlanta revival." The words sped from his foul mouth. "He thinks a witchcraft spirit can do a better job. When Jonathan scorched you—" His mouth froze open. "Errr...*he* said when Jonathan scorched you, that was proof enough that you could not handle the..." The spirit dared not say the word.

"Dagger!" Bashnar finished the sentence.

"Uhhh...yes, *Mighty* Bashnar. Oh! He has two witches on the ready waiting for the slightest opening should it present itself." Krioni-na stared intently at the black eyes of his possible murderer. Elation grew as he watched fire red replace midnight black.

"If any of this is not true, I will hunt you down like the worthless dog you are."

"All true. Every...single...word—"

"Enough!" Bashnar looked at his targets in the order of priority. He scowled at Jonathan for a long, hate-filled moment. Then Sharon. Then Edwin. "First, a gangster warlock. Now two witches. What would the imbeciles think of next?" He would have to move against these three quicker than he had planned. His attack would have to be bold and overwhelming. "Job." The hated prophet's name slid out of his mouth before he could stop it. He remembered him with a mixture of delight and disgust. His attack on these three would have to be as devastating as that which Job suffered. He tore his eyes away from his prey and looked at the lap dog. "Perhaps you aren't as worthless as I thought you were."

Krioni-na answered with a nod.

"You will report to me anything of significance. Of this meeting, and of any you have with your master." *Master* was stated as contemptuously as possible.

"Yes, *Mighty* Bashnar."

Bashnar reflected. It would have been a terrible mistake, suicidal, to have killed this wretched flunky. Great warriors didn't depend on luck. But Bashnar admitted that he had been lucky. He was about to leave when he heard it.

What an idiot? The prince will have more than his bubble gum title when I tell him what happened!

The hand around Krioni-na's neck was as suffocatingly tight as it was surprising. The shocked demon looked up into two black holes of pure darkness and rage. Why was the Mighty Bashnar strangling him? He beat futilely on the backs of his attacker's powerful, hairy arms. It was like trying to move a building. His vision narrowed. He was passing out. The maniac was killing him. There was only one desperate and dangerous thing left that Krioni-na could do. But what was more dangerous than being strangled to death? He willed his leg up to where he could reach the dagger in his boot.

Three quick and deep thrusts of Krioni-na's blade into his muscled arm shocked the Mighty Bashnar. "RRRAAAAAAHHHHH!" He jumped back, while pulling out his own dagger. Yet he was back on Krioni-na so quickly that he appeared to have never jumped off of him.

Krioni-na dropped his dagger. What good would it do him? Crumpled on the floor, he asked, "Why? Why?" He coughed and spit on the floor. "I thought...we had...a deal."

Bashnar peered at the heap of demon, nearly dead. His black eyes narrowing. *Why? Why?* The demon's question slapped the enraged warrior. Bashnar, the warrior; Bashnar, the brilliant strategist; Bashnar, the *Mighty* remembered something in *The History of Exploits and Defeats.*

"NOOOOOOOOOO!" he screamed, when he realized what had happened. He pulled out his sword and swung it and his dagger several times with precision at the angel he knew was there.

The blades came at him fast and furious. So fast there was no time for offense. No time to pull out his own weapons. All he could do was move—fast! The shocked angel contorted, bent, ducked, hopped, and flipped out of the way of the lightning quick whizzes of blades coming at him from nearly every direction.

Enrid was a seasoned, Special Forces warrior, but he was thoroughly shocked by Bashnar's movements. The demon moved almost as though he could see him. *How could a demon fight this well against an unseen opponent?*

The demon crumpled on the floor was baffled to no end. His eyes, watery from his fresh strangling, bulged and danced in sockets that were too big for them. Had the Mighty Bashnar gone mad?

The great warrior spirit crouched low, sniffing the air. "Show yourself, angel," he demanded, insulted that he had been taken for a fool. *What angel would dare such a thing on the Mighty Bashnar?*

Krioni-na picked up his dagger and balled up against the wall, nearly paralyzed with fear. *Were they indeed under attack?*

Several tense seconds passed. The Mighty Bashnar was satisfied that the threat had passed. He stretched his hand. Long, razor sharp claws reported for duty. He put one on the tip of Krioni-na's pudgy, wet nose. "You tell no one of this incident."

"Of course, *Mighty Bashnar.*

*****

Enrid hovered over the Styles's home at a safe distance from Bashnar. It had been a dangerous longshot to get him to kill the prince's demon. And it had almost worked. That would've been a game-changer in the battle over Atlanta. But all was not lost. He had picked up some critical information about Prince Krioni's plans. Trouble rose in his heart. *They had barely made it past one warlock, and now the prince was planning on attacking with two witches.*

The angel's thoughts grew more somber. *To make matters worse, the Mighty Bashnar is going to try to do to Edwin what had been done to the prophet Job. He's going to try to overwhelm him! I have to tell Captain Rashti.*

*****

Edwin looked at a smirking Jonathan and wondered whether Sharon had shared her secret with him. He didn't know what the meeting was about, but her adopted uncle and his best friend certainly looked as though he knew more than he had let on. Characteristic Jonathan, he shrugged his shoulders and gave him his most *don't look at me* face. Edwin's expression told him that he knew better.

"Okay, Sharon," Edwin said, looking accusingly at her co-conspirator, "what's the topic of the super-duper top secret meeting? Is this where you tell me that my little girl loves me, and that she is going to prove it by going to her beloved father's alma mater and become a Georgia Bulldog?"

Sharon was a beautiful seventeen-year-old girl. Yet when she smiled at her father and slowly left her chair and walked toward his place on their sofa, something happened. It was like the protective father switch was flicked on. There were only two or three yards between them, but she seemed to walk a block in slow motion to get to him. Her little black dress suddenly appeared to be a microscopic little black dress. Where was the rest of the dress? Her legs were—well, that simply couldn't be the same dress she purchased with him. When had this happened? She wasn't a little girl any more. The beautiful *woman* approached him and sat on his lap.

"No, Dad. One, in case you haven't noticed, I'm not a little girl anymore."

Jonathan chimed in. "She's not a little girl anymore."

Edwin looked at him with mock irritation.

"I mean in case you haven't noticed," Jonathan said, smiling.

"Two, I haven't decided what university I'm going to."

"Don't do it," said Jonathan soberly. "I'm pretty sure there aren't any bulldogs in heaven."

"I'm pretty darn sure," Edwin said with a hard voice, "there aren't any beavers in heaven, either."

"Bulldogs are ugly," said Jonathan.

"Beavers are rodents," Edwin countered.

"I have a boyfriend," Sharon threw out.

"What!" Edwin and Jonathan gasped.

"I didn't say I was getting married, you two," Sharon answered playfully, enjoying the exaggerated shock of Jonathan and the true shock of her father. "Come on, Dad. You knew I wouldn't be a little girl forever." She kissed his forehead.

"Oh, why not?" her dumbfounded father asked.

She giggled. "Because it's not natural. That's why."

"Jonathan, how long have you known about this treachery?" Edwin asked.

Sharon kissed his forehead again. "It's not that bad, Dad."

"Not that long," Jonathan chuckled. "I just found out at the door when she let me in. Don't feel too bad. She bushwhacked me before I was even in the house."

"Doesn't this disturb you? You don't agree with this, do you?" Edwin asked, desperate for an ally.

"It'll be okay." Jonathan winked at a widely smiling and beaming young woman. "She's a good girl."

"I saw that, Jonathan! Don't encourage her. How can you do that to me? I thought you were my friend."

"Because she's my niece, not my daughter," Jonathan answered. "If she were my daughter, I'd kill the bum."

"Let's go get 'em," said Edwin.

"Right now? I know you don't want to be late for the dinner meeting."

"What's more important?" asked Edwin. "A dinner party, or getting rid of the threat?"

Jonathan rubbed his chin thoughtfully. "Yeah, you're right. Let's go get the bum."

Sharon stood up. She took Edwin by the hand and walked him to Jonathan and took his hand. "Come on. Stand up," she said, pretending to strain at pulling him up. This was only a slight pretense. He had gained a lot of weight in the past year. He exhaled deeply as he made his way up. Sharon looked at each of them intermittently as she spoke ever so softly. "Rob is not a bum, and neither of you are laying a hand on him. Is that clear?"

"I can't make any promises," Edwin answered.

"Is he tall?" Jonathan asked.

"Yes."

"Muscular?"

"Very."

"If he's tall and muscular, I promise not to lay a hand on him. But if he's really a runt, I'm gonna beat em' like he stole something." Jonathan kissed her on the forehead. "I love you, Sharon. I trust your judgment." Jonathan looked at Edwin.

"I trust her judgment. I just don't trust his," Edwin answered Jonathan's expression.

"You'll like him, Dad. He loves Jesus."

*****

The excited demon could hardly believe his ears. They had waited so long for this. He shot away from there rehearsing how he would present this good news to the Mighty Bashnar. Sharon the thorn was going down!

Chapter 2

Edwin smiled sympathetically at his wife, Barbara, who was in an animated conversation with Abbey Lockhart, a state senator whom he had had the displeasure of meeting, unfortunately, not once but twice. And if he counted this evening, that would be three unlucky interactions. She seemed to pop up everywhere. The Metro Atlanta Christian Leadership Association breakfast. The Georgia Alliance Against Human Trafficking luncheon. And now a dinner party in his honor hosted by Wallace and Marjorie Reynolds.

He thought about the irony of Wallace and Marjorie throwing him a party. Only a year ago they would have gladly thrown him out of the church. And now he was their hero. Edwin sipped his drink thoughtfully. *Guess it was as Jonathan said. You save someone's child's life, it's hard for them to stay mad at you.*

His thoughts hardened as he contemplated another bitter irony. Christopher was dead. No one had saved his son's life. *I pray for their son and God works a miracle in front of everyone. I pray for my sick son and he dies.*

Edwin looked across the Wallace's oversized living room onto the massive deck that overlooked the *Country Club of the South* 18-hole championship golf course. There were at least twelve or more people out there, and there was room for twelve more. Wallace was out there talking to some guy who no doubt was as loaded as he was. At least the guy had that look about him.

Marjorie walked across Edwin's view. He looked at her, then her husband. It wasn't revulsion for them that rose from his belly to his chest. He had no rational reason to dislike them. But he found it impossible to think about them or to be in their presence and not feel sick. *Why would God heal their son and let little Christopher die? I'm a pastor doing my best to serve God. Wallace and Marjorie are business people out to make a buck.*

It didn't make sense. It wasn't fair. Edwin needed to get away. To find some dark corner of this mansion where he could just sit and clear his head. He took a few steps down a long hallway, rubbing his eyes.

"Pastor Styles?"

Edwin heard a child's voice and turned around and momentarily froze before he could speak. "Hello there, Jason. How are you?" he asked, hoping that his own smile was genuine, and that the young man hadn't somehow heard his thoughts.

"Fine, uhh, I guess. I mean...." The boy squinched his face and shrugged his shoulders.

"Is everything okay?

"Well, no." The boy's answer was tentative, unsure.

"You wanna talk about it?" Edwin asked.

"Can I show you something?"

Edwin looked around at the people milling about, eating high-dollar hors d'oeuvres. He was hoping to make eye contact with Marjorie.

"I asked Mom already."

"You—oh, okay," he said, a little embarrassed. This kid was smart. He followed the boy up the winding stairs and down a long hall, passing several doors. He followed him into a bedroom that could've been a master bedroom had it not belonged to a twelve-year-old. A huge fan hung prominently from the trey ceiling. But besides this and its size, there was nothing in it that was unlike that of any boy his age. He had posters of who Edwin guessed were teenage celebrities.

But there was something unmistakably odd about his room. It was the *Atlanta Braves* baseball pennants hanging from little poles around the entire room near the top of the ceiling. Jason had every World Series pennant that the *Braves* had been in since 1914. *1914, 1948, 1957, 1958, 1991, 1992, 1995, 1996, 1999.* This was a baffling coincidence. But when Edwin focused on the wall to his left, the coincidence went from baffling to bizarre. His soul constricted.

Edwin took halting steps to the wall and lightly touched a picture of David Justice hitting the home run that won the *Braves* the 1995 World Series. "Who...who decorated your room? Did you," Edwin motioned around the room, "do this? I mean, well..." he looked at the David Justice poster with watery eyes, "I guess you would've." Edwin paused, trying to recover from what he was looking at. He continued, "It's just—
"

"I know," Jason interjected, "I wasn't around when they played those games. I wish I would've been alive when David Justice hit the home run."

Edwin remembered the moment. It was a good memory. He looked at Jason. He was hanging his head. Edwin realized that the young man's eyes had been sad since he had invited him to see his pennants.

"But I got to see it anyway," said Jason. "Even if I wasn't there. Did you go to the game?"

"No, I didn't go."

"Did you see it when it happened? When David Justice hit the home run?"

"I think everyone in Atlanta saw it when it happened." Edwin smiled through his pain. "Yeah. Yeah, I saw it."

"Me and Dad watched the whole game," Jason added.

Edwin felt the punch to his gut. He gasped and tried to cover it. The sick feeling that had subsided some was now at high tide. Edwin could feel it in his throat. He swallowed with much effort, trying to push it back down, and asked, "You and your dad watched the game together?"

"Yes," the boy answered, lowering his head as though he knew how sick he was making him. "Pastor Styles?"

Edwin looked at him. He would not try to speak now for fear of losing it. He looked down at the boy's sad blue eyes.

"I'm sorry," the boy said. He saw the question in the preacher's eyes. "I'm sorry for not dying."

Edwin's eyes bulged.

"Mom told me everything that happened. When I got sick...when those things hurt me, and you prayed for me...and you...you made them leave." Jason had to fight to not cry. "I know that you prayed for your son and he still died. I don't know why I lived and your son died. I just want you to know that I'm sorry, and I wish I could trade places with your son."

Edwin was stunned again. He took a few moments to recover. After he pushed out a long, therapeutic breath, he said to Jason, "Thank you, Jason. That's very kind of you. I bet your mom's wondering where you are. We better get back downstairs."

He knew he should have said more to the young man. He should have told him how wrong he was for saying something so awful. Christopher's death had nothing to do with him. But he couldn't say any of these *right* things, as much as he believed them. The aching pain in his heart wouldn't let him. It was an unreasonable pain that swallowed logic the way sinkholes in Florida swallowed homes. Edwin was ashamed of himself, but could do no better.

Just before they got to the stairs, Jason added, "Mom says you're a great man, and that you saved my life and showed her that Jesus is alive. She's sad that your son died." They reached the end of the hall. "Pastor Styles, can I pray for you?"

Edwin thought it was kind for the young man to offer to pray for him, but it really was unnecessary.

"You need help, Pastor Styles," Jason offered. He took the preacher's hand before he could object and prayed. "God, please help Pastor Styles. He's a good man, but he's confused. He saved my life, but he doesn't know why you didn't save his son. None of us know why. Uhhhh, I guess it's hard on him. Please help him do as Mom says. Help him to trust you even when he doesn't understand everything. Uhhhh...amen!"

Trust in the Lord with all your heart, and do not lean to your own understanding. Edwin didn't know where it was, but he knew this was a Scripture.

*****

Krioni-na looked at the familiar spirit who was assigned to Jason with mock sympathy. He knew exactly what the unlucky demon was thinking. "Yes, it's going in my report," he said to him.

"Of course, it is," the spirit said contemptuously. "We wouldn't want to be dishonest, now would we?" *Now I've got to include it in my report! You ugly bat! If I ever get a chance...*

Krioni-na ignored the slighted demon's crusty face and began to work on his two reports. One for his master, Prince Krioni. He would get his later. The other for that lunatic, the Mighty Bashnar. He would get his the moment this party was over.

*****

"Ohhh, Edwin," Marjorie waved, "there you are." The moment his feet came off the last stair, she slipped her arm over his and walked him to a large room that looked like another living room, but cozier. The carpet was so deep it practically begged to be lain on. Dim lamps reflected off the dark wood. Oversized floor plants were in two corners. A giant cuckoo clock was in another. "Here he is everybody. The man of the hour." Marjorie beamed; Edwin blushed. "You know most of these good folks, Edwin."

Sharon was on her father immediately, getting her hug in. "Hi, Dad."

"Heeyyy, you look like a little girl I once knew," said Edwin.

She narrowed her eyes and smiled scornfully and sat next to her mom.

Edwin walked over to his smiling wife. She closed her eyes and tilted her chin upwards, anticipating his hand. He cupped the side of her face in a full hand and kissed her gently on the cheek, eyelid, and forehead. She didn't immediately lower her head or open her eyes, but waited a couple of seconds, seemingly savoring the moment. The room's perfect silence hosted the moment several seconds after it was over.

Marjorie feverishly fanned herself with her hand. "My goodness," she laughed, "I don't know how much of that I can take." There were a few good natured add-on comments from others. "Let me introduce you to a few new faces while it's still intermission." She walked him around the room. "Edwin, this is Sheila Wilcox. She's one of two state senators we have here tonight."

The lady looked to be maybe thirty-five. She wore a dark, two-piece pants suit and gray pearls. She stood and gave what Edwin felt was a choreographed smile and shook his hand like she was trying to crack a walnut. "Hello, Reverend Styles."

"Hello," he said, shaking her hand. He pulled it away thinking, *Are you kidding me?*

Marjorie added, "She had a bruising campaign and election. Tough. Really tough. First, the primary. Then, the runoff. Then...oh, my goodness. Well, she won by less than sixty votes. Bless the Lord! Good job, Sheila." Marjorie crossed the room. "And this—"

"Abbey Lockhart. State senator, district six." Edwin smiled and held out his hand. "Hello, Senator."

"Whu? Oh. Well, oh my," Marjorie said, with a hearty chuckle. "We're already friends."

"Hello, Reverend Styles," said the attractive politician.

Marjorie placed her hand over her heart and bowed slightly to a distinguished looking gentleman. He wore a badge on his chest that said *Illegal Immigration* with a big red X over the words. "And this is Danny Green. He's the founder of Georgia Citizens for Legal

Immigration." She stretched her neck upward toward the tall man. "Hello, Danny."

He pecked her on the cheek. "Hello, Marjorie," he said, with a raspy voice.

"Well, finally I can sit down." She let out a happy breath. "We have a few minutes before we make our presentation to our wonderful pastor. A little birdie told me that you were having a fascinating conversation about illegal immigration."

Edwin's heart sank.

Sharon's heart sank.

Barbara lit up like a lighthouse at midnight. "Something *has* to be done," she said energetically. "We can't let our country be overrun by Mexicans. We're a nation of law and order."

That was enough blood to get the sharks going. It was also enough to get Sharon going. Edwin winced at the thought of his wife and daughter going at it in public.

Abbey's eyes caught fire. She rattled off several things the U.S. government needed to do immediately to protect the country and to bring it back to being a nation under God.

"And the church," Danny Green added, accentuating each word with a bouncing, pointing finger, "ought to be leading the fight."

*****

That was the statement that caused Myla to urgently request and get several angels to guard Sharon and Edwin. He knew he'd have to rush off to Captain Rashti as soon as the meeting was over. Regretfully, Myla wasn't able to provide Barbara with as much protection as he would've liked. Her heart was too divided to qualify her for the best protection. However, as the beloved Paul had told the Roman Christians in his blessed epistle, the unsanctified was often blessed because of the sanctified person. She was like Lot being blessed because of Abraham's intimacy with God and not his own.

Myla reflected. *But we've stretched that provision as far we can. Dear child of God...Barbara, sooner or later, and I think sooner, you're going to have to stand on your own two feet. You can't hide behind Edwin and Sharon much longer.* Nonetheless, unexpectedly angels also arrived for Barbara.

Grace! Oh, wonderful grace! the angel celebrated. *How marvelous are You in all your ways! Your mercy is beyond finding out! Your compassion of which there is not end! The depths—*

The grateful angel made himself stop praising his Creator, and carefully surveyed his surroundings as a good soldier must. There was a time for everything. At the moment, it was time for vigilance, focus, and perception. There was something pivotal about this meeting. He couldn't let anything slip by him.

*****

"Which fight? Whose fight?" Sharon challenged.

Her question momentarily muted the group. Danny Green's finger lost its bounce. Everyone looked at one another, waiting for someone to say something witty and wise to silence the teenager's ignorance.

"Sharon," Barbara said with a mother's gentle chide, "these are *big* and *important* matters, dear. We are being invaded by aliens. We can't afford to take care of everyone who sneaks in the country. They're bankrupting the nation. Someone has to do something."

"Isn't that what the Department of Homeland Defense is for?" Sharon retorted. "Isn't that what the government is for?"

Danny Green found his finger. "When the government doesn't do its job, it's our responsibility to make them do it."

Sharon heard something in his answer she didn't like. "And by *our* responsibility, you mean the church's responsibility."

Barbara spoke up. "It's the church's responsibility to get involved in what's going on in the world. If we don't get involved, we'll be irrelevant."

Edwin inched forward on his seat as though he wanted to say something, but didn't.

"Mom, we *are* involved. Last year this time we had eight hundred people in the church. And a bunch of them didn't even regularly attend. Now since Jonathan and Dad have been holding deliverance and healing meetings—" Sharon looked at her father. "How many members do we have now?"

Any time Sharon and Barbara get into it... "We have five thousand," he said, hoping this conversation ended soon without much more embarrassment.

"Jonathan and Dad are reaching thousands of people, Mom. People are being saved and delivered. Hundreds have been delivered from alcoholism, homosexuality, drugs...everything! How can you say we're not involved?" Sharon looked at her dad for support. "Dad?" she implored.

The spirit repeated itself to Edwin. *"Jonathan* and Edwin. *Jonathan* and Edwin. That's twice she said that. Your own daughter. She puts Jonathan before you. It's your church and he gets the credit. Remember at the house? She told him about her boyfriend before she told you."

Edwin looked at his daughter. She was looking at him waiting for him to say something.

"Oh," she huffed involuntarily, exasperated at her father's timidity. It was the one thing about her father that she didn't like. He had made such progress in this area since he had met Jonathan. But sometimes he had such lapses of courage that she found herself alternating between despising him and feeling sorry for him. Still, she was sorry that she had shown her frustration publicly.

"That brings us to a good point," said Senator Lockhart. "A church as vibrant as yours, Reverend Styles, could be a real force for good."

Sharon looked at her dad. There weren't any signs of a fight in him tonight. She looked at her mom. Her mom was pumped. Sharon got up. She couldn't sit through this. "Dad, I'm going to mill around and say hi to some more people."

Of course, darling," Marjorie said sincerely, trying to lessen the awkwardness of the moment.

Sharon went to her father on the way out and bent down to kiss him on the cheek. "Stay on track, Dad. You have to be strong. I love you."

He smiled and looked up. "I love you, too," he answered, louder than necessary as a cover for her whispering.

She left the room and so did Myla.

*****

Edwin rolled away down the long driveway, looking in his rearview mirror at Marjorie waving goodbye. He smiled. "That was some party, wasn't it?"

"Yeah," answered Barbara dryly.

"Uh, huh," said Sharon unconvincingly.

Oh, it's going to be a long ride home, thought Edwin. "You think Andrew is sorry he missed it?"

"He got to spend the night at Gary's," Sharon answered.

Pastor Edwin Styles was like every pastor. Several demons were assigned to him with specific agendas. But since he had been identified as a top threat in the region, a swarm of demons followed him. Edwin looked like he was inside a dark cloud of locusts. There was nothing in particular they were looking for. Any opening would do. One of these locust demons thought he saw something.

"He *got* to spend the night at Gary's? What does she mean by that?" the spirit said in a whispery voice.

"He *got* to spend the night at Gary's," Edwin asked playfully. "What do you mean by that?"

"Oh, Dad, I just mean I'm sure he's having fun with his friends."

"You don't think he would've had fun at my party."

"Dad, Andrew's fifteen," Sharon answered.

"You're seventeen," Edwin countered.

"Yeah, but I'm light years more mature than Andrew."

Edwin looked in the mirror. Sharon's face was soft with a little smile. The adult had won again. "He would disagree with you."

"That would be his immaturity speaking."

"Wait till I tell him what you said," Edwin said.

"I'll deny it."

"I have a witness," said Edwin.

"Mom is my witness," said Sharon. "Right, Mom?"

Barbara broke her silence. "That's right, baby. Girls have to stick together."

Sharon looked at her father looking back at her in the rearview mirror. She cocked her head sideways with raised eyebrows and a beautiful smile. "Girls got you outnumbered. I win."

A different spirit from the swarm spoke into Edwin's ear. "If Christopher were here, she wouldn't have you outnumbered."

The thought was like a heavy curtain pulled down, darkening the moment.

"The joy of the Lord is your strength," said an angel.

"Rejoice always," said another. He looked intently at Edwin. This angel looked back sadly at the others and said, "He's not listening. He's like a sponge, soaking up whatever these demons say." None of the angels said it, but they thought it—as angels wondered often—*Why were most saints passive? Why didn't they fight back?*

Another demon from the swarm saw that the man of God was focusing on his son's death. He needed to strike now. "Why did Jonathan have to leave early?" he said to Sharon. He waited. Nothing. He repeated himself and waited. Nothing. He did this repeatedly, waiting for the response that never came. The spirit fumed and asked that same question until it seemed he could ask no more. He hated this girl. She was so uncooperative. It always took an insane amount of energy to get her to do anything. Even the simplest things. He had hoped tonight would be different. He rejoined the swarm.

"Dad, why did Jonathan have to leave early?"

"Was that so hard?" a voice screamed from the swirling swarm of demons. Instantly, the demon rushed Edwin. "She sure is concerned about Jonathan. She hasn't made one comment about my special night. But, boy, she sure is concerned about Jonathan. She had her eyes on him all night. I bet she would never have told Jonathan to stay on track or to be strong. She adores Jonathan. She probably thinks he'd do a better job than me as pastor."

Edwin's face tightened as he watched the moving cars around them.

"Dad, why did Jonathan have to leave early?" Sharon asked again.

"Emergency," he nearly snapped. "Elizabeth's mother is in the hospital. Why don't you call him?"

"I will," she said, wondering if she had correctly detected an irritation in her father's voice. "It's not too late."

Edwin's passivity was like a stick hitting a bee hive. The dark swarm of frenzied demons swirled madly around their witless victim, their evil and troubling thoughts puncturing his mind and stealing his peace.

*****

Barbara was nestled into her husband, sound asleep. A leftover smile from their private moments refused to leave her face. Edwin pecked her on the cheek. Thank God, Jonathan got rid of *that* demon! he reminisced.

One of the swarming locust demons saw the opening and attacked.

The thought of being delivered from that tormenting spirit of impotence should have brought nothing but elation to Edwin. He was grateful. God, was he grateful! But the thing that ate at him now that he thought about it was he even owed his sex life to Jonathan. In a sense, his beautiful wife was lying next to him with a smile on her lovely face because of Jonathan. Edwin rolled over onto his back, as troubled and anxious as his wife was satisfied and relaxed. His mind wandered into dangerous places. He was like a man in a row boat flirting with perilous rapids filled with jagged boulders and unforgiving drops.

The swarm hissed in agitated, discordant unity when they saw the amber mist descend through the ceiling. It was an angel of peace. They knew they weren't in mortal danger. That is, as long as they didn't violate the rules of warfare. They could stick around Edwin as long as he allowed, as long as he entertained their thoughts. But if he ever believed the words of that cursed book, they'd have to go. They could persist for a while, but that's where it got dangerous.

The cursed enemy had made an unjust law that if any of His duped followers submitted themselves to Him and resisted them, they'd have to leave. Fortunately, they were usually able to stick around because the dummies never fulfilled the first part of that blasted law. They tried resisting them without submitting to Him. Submission required obedience, and some Christians played with it like it was a child's toy. When they grew bored of it, they put it back in the toy bin. This was a fool's paradise. And Edwin, his problem wasn't disobedience as much as it was ignorance. He didn't know the first thing about resisting them. So there was virtually no cause for concern.

The peace angel spoke many words to the troubled pastor that fell on deaf ears. He tried reminding him of promises in the Bible. Hopefully, that would provide a spark. If he could get him to think on the word of God, he could pull him out of this darkness. But the pastor was like a drowning man who fights his rescuer. He batted away each promise of God with a worry or accusation.

Finally, the peace angel left for a more opportune time. He hoped that would be soon.

Chapter 3

The Mighty Bashnar was immensely confident in his abilities. His confidence—which others saw as arrogance, he noted contemptuously—was one of the reasons he was the *Mighty* Bashnar, and not simply Bashnar, a warrior among warriors. He thought of the multitude of warrior spirits. The thought of being counted as one of a multitude of no-names was nauseating. Better to rot in the darkness of the *Dark Prison* than to languish in ordinariness. Worse, obscurity.

He closed book seven of the *History of Exploits and Defeats* and speared his heavy arms, elbows first, onto the desk. He interlocked his thick fingers between one another and stared ahead, thinking. There was always so much to think about. He looked down at the thick book. Within that book was some of his own great victories. Only the most outstanding victories were recorded in its revered pages. To be included in this book was to be immortalized.

He would have smiled were it not for the bitter fact that his monumental defeats were also recorded in its immortal pages—for everyone to see! Edict of the great evil one. Satan himself had named the book. Satan himself had ordered defeats to be listed in humiliating detail.

One of the things that ate at his gut like a bleeding ulcer was that he never knew when he entered a room whether he was stared at because of his victories or his failures. Were the warriors at the annual warriors' convention whispering to one another because of how he had destroyed that national ministry to homosexuals? Or was it because of how he had failed in Atlanta thus far?

Sometimes it seemed that he was going forward and backward simultaneously. His mind drifted into forbidden territory. *Sometimes it seems that we are on an evil roll that can't be stopped. And at other times it seems the whole movement is taking one step forward and three steps backward.*

Anger burned in his chest. *Not a single one of the defeats in that wretched book would have occurred had it not been for someone praying.* His simmering anger started to boil. He reluctantly thought about how unjust it was that the evil dog of heaven had given such power to the weak sons and daughters of Adam. *The whole movement is doo—*

*****

The familiar spirit stood outside the massive door that separated him from the Mighty Bashnar. He had no powerful sponsors or even contacts worthy of mentioning. So direct interactions with warrior spirits—especially one as murderous and volatile as this one—was not something to look forward to.

However, even though he didn't have a big-shot watching his back, he did have this report. He patted it on his hand and smiled. The Mighty Bashnar had been gunning for Sharon for a long time. He took courage and lifted his hand to knock on the door.

A thunderous roar erupted on the other side of the door just before he knocked.

The familiar spirit was sucked dry of his courage. His vile body trembled. He looked to the left and right as though speeding trains were angrily racing down on him from both directions. Administrative spirits were scattering in both directions, bumping into one another like bowling pins after a strike. The door swung open before the terrified spirit could join the other refugees.

"Familiar spirit," said Bashnar.

The undersized demon looked up at the Mighty Bashnar. Surprisingly, his greeting was void of menace. He had even acknowledged his function as a familiar spirit this time instead of his usual contemptuous nondescript greeting—whenever there was one—of "spirit." He was probably hoping he had good news. "The thorn...Sharon..."

"Go on," said Bashnar, with uncharacteristic patience, understanding the spirit's nervousness at being in his presence.

The spirit pushed down the wad of spit that was caught in his throat. "The thorn has a boyfriend." There was no way for the spirit to discern whether the expression now on the Mighty Bashnar's face was a smile. His face wasn't built to carry one. But there was something in it that showed dark satisfaction.

"Come in, familiar spirit." Bashnar sat down. He didn't offer him a seat. There wasn't one to offer. Only Bashnar sat down in his office. He reached for the folder.

The familiar spirit knew what to expect, and he wasn't wrong. After watching the Mighty Bashnar spend an hour reading a ten-minute report, he wondered silently, *Why doesn't he get some chairs? It doesn't make sense to make demons stand here while he takes his time.*

Finally, Bashnar looked up and eyed the spirit.

It was an eternity-filled few seconds. The demon felt as though he was the target on the other end of the Mighty Bashnar's rifle scope.

"Would you like a chair?" asked Bashnar.

"No." The spirit's reply was quick.

Bashnar's eyes narrowed. "Are you sure?"

"I am content to stand, Mighty Bashnar." He gulped.

Bashnar's hard face appeared to soften, as much as such a face could soften. "You have brought me good news. Very good news. On your way out—"

Out! Out! The spirit thought. *Thank the god of darkness!*

"—tell the clerk to send me in spirits of..." Bashnar thought about the team he'd need. "...compromise, seduction, lust, and fornication."

The familiar spirit had to make himself not run to the door.

"And tell him they *must* have significant resumes." Bashnar watched the demon eagerly leave. He didn't hate him for fearing him. He could expect nothing more from such a low-class demon. Besides, it was hard to be upset with the spirit that had just given him news that one of the Atlanta revival lead rats was about to get her pretty little neck snapped in his sex trap. *Rats love their cheese, and humans love their sex,* he thought.

Hours later, there was a knock on his door.

"Come in," Bashnar answered.

Compromise, Seduction, and Fornication entered one after the other. They stood side by side. Lust entered alone and walked toward the desk, looking around the room hungrily. The closer he got to the other spirits, the more they moved away from him.

Bashnar looked at the lust demon and thanked the darkness that fate had not made him a demon of lust. To be a demon of such influence, and yet be shunned by even the lowliest demons. But who could blame anyone for not wanting to get too close to such a spirit. They were so wet and sticky and they stained and ruined everything they touched. Once that sticky stuff got on you, you couldn't get it off without great effort. If too much got on you, you couldn't get it off without taking a steam bath that nearly burned you raw.

And darkness help the demon stupid enough to ignore dried lust juice on his skin. The stuff deadened the nerves and burned through the skin and entered the blood. It was one hundred percent fatal to any fool who let it progress this far.

Bashnar looked at the trail of droplets of sticky goo from the door to the feet of the huge-eyed demon that stood before him. He knew that by the time their short meeting was over, there'd be a mess at the lust demon's feet. It wasn't his problem, though. As soon as this meeting was over, he would meet Krioni-na at their secret rendezvous. By the time he returned, the mess would be cleaned up.

"You all are familiar with the thorn, Sharon."

"Yes," they each acknowledged.

"I've selected you four to destroy her influence." Bashnar waited. "None of you ask me how?"

"We know how, most Mighty Bashnar," answered Compromise. He took Bashnar's silence as an invitation to expound. "I assume the trouble-maker has a boyfriend," he said, with a self-assured smile. "I'll get her to compromise little by little. Nothing big at first. Just enough to slowly, but surely chip away at her sexual purity." Compromise anticipated Bashnar's concern. "Don't worry, most Mighty Bashnar. I won't scare her off. I'll use the same methods I used on the mighty King David."

"King David!" The Mighty Bashnar lost control of his emotions. "You are the spirit that took down King David?"

Compromise loved the prestige that singular feat had given him. Oh, there had been many other wonderful victories. But none as grand as this one. And none that had catapulted his career as had this one. He smiled inwardly. Even the great Mighty Bashnar was gushing over him. "It was a joint effort, most Mighty Bashnar. My friend here," he waved a gentleman's underhand to Lust, "and I worked together, along with our good friend, Adultery."

Bashnar looked at Lust. "You are *that* spirit of lust?"

Lust saw awe in the Mighty Bashnar's eyes. "I am *that* spirit."

Bashnar leaned forward in his chair, then sat back deeply into it. He looked at Lust in a different light. His grotesquely large eyes still danced annoyingly, as though he had no control over them. Grossly cock-eyed one moment, comically crossed-eyed the next. Looking, looking, looking. Giving the appearance of hungrily searching for what can never be found. And he was still disgustingly wet and sticky. But he was worth the mess he carried. "You and Compromise took down the great dagger, King David."

"Yes, and we will take down Sharon," Lust answered.

Compromise added, "I know you have read of our victory over King David in the *Histories of Exploits and Defeats.* But my friend and I would be honored to stay after our meeting to give you a firsthand detailed account of the battle." Bashnar nodded. Compromise continued. "Most Mighty Bashnar, King David was great. Much greater than Sharon could ever dream to be." Bashnar didn't necessarily agree, but there was no need to comment on this. "We humbled the great David by first attacking him indirectly. You recall most Mighty Bashnar that it was the time when the kings went out to battle that David fell."

He didn't have to say anything else. Bashnar's brilliant mind saw the entire strategy from beginning to end. "David should have been on the battle field fighting for his cursed lord. Instead he was at home. Idle. You got him to take a break from the enemy's battle when he should have been fighting. Compromise! He had no doubt seen Bathsheba bathing before from his balcony. But because he was so busy doing his lord's work, he didn't have time to follow the flesh. Probably just rebuked the thought. He would've had the power to do so at that point because his mind was occupied with his God."

Bashnar thought it through. "In fact, as the cursed book says, 'If you walk in the Spirit, you will not fulfill the lust of the flesh.' You got him to stop walking in the Spirit. David staying home from the battle was a symptom of the backslidings of his heart!"

"We do it with Christians and church all the time," Compromise said sneeringly, with a smile. "They stay home for the slightest reasons. I tell them they're free from legalism. Not to let it bother them. God is a good god, and he wouldn't want them to stress over going to church. They can have church at home or on the golf course."

Compromise slowly shrugged his shoulders and smiled like a pimp who could hardly believe his own success. "We make them think it's all about the individual. Not about the family of God. As much as the cursed book talks about their obligation to one another, we make them think they can opt out of God's family plan." He added philosophically, in a whisper, "That they can go solo."

Seduction chimed in with a creaky voice. "We get them to treat the commands of God like an insurance plan with outrageous premiums." He flicked his long, bony wrists dismissively. "We help them to opt out of the parts that are too expensive for their lifestyles." He smiled like a demon who had just impressed himself. "It's just a coincidence that the parts they opt out of are the very parts that would make them a threat to our kingdom."

"But," Compromise interjected, "we leave them with just enough form to make them think they have substance. That way they can still consider themselves Christians." Compromise shook his head. It was so easy at times that it was like being part of a sting operation, like they were being set up. But if this were a setup, it was a two-thousand-year setup. Their strategy and tactics had worked for that long. Longer if he counted pre-Christ. "These shell Christians are awesome! They do most of our work for us!"

"They give pastors hell." Seduction sounded almost sorry for his preacher enemies.

Compromise could see that the Mighty Bashnar was immensely pleased with their conversation. But he also saw that the great warrior was tiring of hearing of past exploits and of dupes who were no concern of his. He wanted Sharon. Compromise began to wind down. "If God's people gave themselves to Christ the way he gave himself to them, it would change everything."

"But they don't, and it won't," Bashnar declared. "They think only about themselves. He gets their leftovers."

"Fortunately," said Compromise, "this is true."

Seduction and Lust agreed.

Bashnar's attention turned to Fornication. "You have said nothing this entire meeting."

Fornication was not a great warrior, in the traditional sense. He knew this. But he was as great as the Mighty Bashnar in his own way. He had destroyed a hundred times more of the enemy than this great warrior would ever have the satisfaction of destroying. Great churches and ministries had been reduced to rubble by Fornication's tender strokes.

People who had been chosen by God and equipped with seedling spiritual gifts had been obliterated by his kisses and reduced to nothing by his passions. God's plans of shaking whole cities and even nations through servants who had cultivated His gifts by commitment, holiness, and use had never happened. Fornication didn't need a sword.

The Mighty Bashnar waited for an answer.

Fornication gave a half smile that carried the confidence of thousands of years of conquests. "Is that *r-e-a-l-l-y* necessary?"

Compromise, Seduction, and Lust were shocked at Fornication's brazenness. When they could finally tear their eyes away from the demon who had publicly disrespected this warrior, who was as famous for his butchery of demons as for anything else, they turned to Bashnar.

Fornication increased the three spirits' nervousness when he stepped forward and stood to the far left of Bashnar's desk. Far away enough from Lust, but close enough to Bashnar's personal space that it could've been considered disrespectful.

Bashnar stretched his thick fingers. Long thick claws that had ripped to shreds many who had been much less presumptuous came from under his rough hair. He danced his claws on the table as he looked at the pompous spirit. But he didn't rise.

"Mighty Bashnar," said Fornication, "you will have your Sharon."

A gurgling sound emitted through Bashnar's barely opened large mouth. His claws followed his emotions and went back to their covered home. It was then that Compromise, Seduction, and Lust perceived the connection that had just happened between the Mighty Bashnar and Fornication.

Now Bashnar stood.

Demons sometimes bowed slightly to one another to show respect or to admit inferiority. The three demons watching this theater were speechless, wondering whether one of these legends would bow to the other. It was a preposterous thought! Fornication bowing to the Mighty Bashnar? The Mighty Bashnar bowing to...anyone!

"Yes, Fornication," said Bashnar. "I believe I will have the thorn."

Fornication and the Mighty Bashnar stared into one another's eyes far longer than Compromise, Lust, and Seduction thought possible without the shedding of demon blood. They looked at both legends for the slightest evidence of a bow.

Finally, Fornication turned abruptly to his partners. "Let's go get her."

The three joined their friend. Once alone, they spoke energetically about the audacity of Fornication waiting for the Mighty Bashnar to bow to him. *Who else but Fornication would do such a thing?*

Fornication's only explanation to his friends' good-natured charge that perhaps he really was a spirit of suicide was, "I'm used to having my way."

Chapter 4

Krioni-na surveyed the desolate white landscape. He appreciated Bashnar's choice. This was truly a godforsaken place, and any place where God was not was the place to be. But he and the maniac, Bashnar, weren't meeting on a block of floating ice in the middle of the Arctic Ocean at the North Pole simply because of the absence of God. They were there also because of the absence of demons. No people, no angels. No people, no demons.

News traveled fast in the darkness. The last thing Krioni-na needed was to be seen consorting with Bashnar. Of course, he regularly saw the maniac in his own observations of the Atlanta revival culprits. But it would be impossible to have a meeting there without some nosey angel getting a whiff of what was going on. Here, they were surrounded by nothing, but thick floating sea ice. The nearest land mass was over four hundred miles away. So the chances of running into people with their angels and demons were remote.

"What do you have?" The demanding voice cut through the frigid air, surprising the contemplative demon.

Krioni-na whipped around.

Bashnar looked impatient.

Krioni-na was a master of adapting to circumstances. He rattled off his report in bullet points. "Wallace and Marjorie gave Edwin a party honoring his work as pastor. Jonathan was there, but had to leave early. His mother-in-law was sick. Sharon was there."

"Sharon," Bashnar slowly hissed.

Krioni-na looked up into Bashnar's angry face. *My goodness. He hates that girl. Almost as much as he hates Jonathan.* The demon saw in Bashnar's eyes that it was time to continue. "A lot of people were there. Most notably state Senator Abbey Lockhart, state Senator Sheila Wilcox, Dan—"

"The governor's sister-in-law," Bashnar interrupted.

"Yes. Yes, his sister-in-law." He paused, waiting for his cue. When he got none, he took that as his cue. "Danny Green, he's—"

"The immigration man. I know him. He works for us," said Bashnar.

"Huh, oh...yeah," said Krioni-na.

"What did they talk about?" demanded Bashnar. "Eternal consequence only."

Krioni-na was miffed, but he didn't show it. He didn't need to be told how to give a summary report. "A few developments. One, Jason, the young boy, prayed for Edwin. Two, Elizabeth talked to Senator Lockhart for a long time. They have a lot in common. Three, Sharon and the politicians got into it. The immigration guy, too."

"What's your take on this?" Bashnar asked. He didn't ask to gain new information, but to prove his thesis that Prince Krioni had selected an idiot with the brain capacity of a low wattage light bulb for such a critical intelligence task. He would be surprised if this lap dog could connect more than three dots without blowing up his stunted mind.

"You want to know what I think about this? An analysis, I mean?" Krioni-na asked, with surprise. "I typically provide only the facts."

Bashnar made himself answer without yelling. "Yes. I...want...your...a...na...ly...sis, if you don't mind."

"Well...well, I think that we should keep our eyes on Jason," the demon began. "He prayed for Edwin."

"About what?"

"His dead son, Christopher. He's having a hard time with his death. He wonders why God healed Jason, but let his son die? If we get Edwin to focus on his son's death more than on God's so-called faithfulness, we can turn his questions into bitterness. If we can get the worm to judge his creator, we'll have him!"

"Anything else?" Bashnar asked.

"Not of eternal consequence."

"What about Jason?" Bashnar pressed.

"I don't think his prayers helped Edwin the worm one bit."

You don't think his prayers helped Edwin one bit. "Anything else?"

Krioni-na hunched his shoulders, looking down at the block of ice with squinted eyes, as though he was searching for something else. "No," he said, shaking his head.

Totally underwhelming. He was more of an idiot than Bashnar could have imagined. There had been nothing to figure out. Everything was right there in front of him. A teenager was praying for his pastor instead of talking about him. Was this a thorn in the making? A dagger? Another blasted Sharon or Jonathan? And politicians had landed on Edwin's party like flies on garbage. They had their agenda. They always do. Could've been routine, but if it were, why had that wretched Sharon argued with them? What did she see that this imbecile didn't?

Bashnar shot into the sky and was gone.

Krioni-na was incensed. First, that this killer had forced him into this suicidal treachery against the great prince. He hadn't seen any angels or demons in the area, but one never knew. How long could such a conspiracy go on before something went wrong? Second, that he treated him with such contempt. He had left him standing there on a block of floating ice like a five-dollar whore. Who did he think he was? Third, and this was what infuriated him the most. He routinely insulted his intelligence.

True, Krioni-na had risen in the ranks by allowing others to think he was less intelligent than he was—stupid even. But by the time they found out differently, it was too late. Sometimes fatally.

How many who had thought themselves wiser or fiercer than himself had made their backs home to his dagger? Even the Mighty Bashnar had a back. A big one.

*****

Myla approached the gathering of angels from the east, Enrid from the west, almost simultaneously, but unaware of one another's presence. Both inquired of the guards what was going on and decided to wait for their beloved Captain Rashti to finish his introductions to the roughly one hundred front line battle leaders.

The backs of the angelic guards were to the captain and to the angels listening to him. Their eyes and senses scanned the horizon, focusing mostly on angels stationed on the far edges of the perimeter. Those angels out there would be the first to see anything amiss.

The angels being spoken to by the captain focused intensely on him. He was the Sword of the Lord. He was the hero of the Battle of the Resurrection, and of other monumental battles. He was the great champion of the sons of Adam. He was all that a great warrior was expected to be. But he was more. Captain Rashti was their mentor and friend, and for several he was literally their life-saver.

The leaders sat on the grass in no particular order. Perfectly silent one moment. Hushed conversations mixed with light laughter the next. Times were tough. They always were. But there was still room for laughter among those called to the honored task of working directly with and for the children of God. The joy of the Lord was not only the strength of the children of God. It was their strength, also. Besides, no matter how dark the moment, dark moments would inevitably give way to the light. Every angel knew this.

Yet every angel also knew that even though light would inevitably swallow all darkness, before that blessed moment came, many of God's sons and daughters would be themselves swallowed by darkness. Not because Satan was so strong; he wasn't. He had been thoroughly defeated by the cross and resurrection of the blessed Creator. But because saints so rarely lived up to their potential. They so rarely believed the word of God. They so rarely fasted. They so rarely prayed. At least not with a believing heart. Even among those who did pray, they rarely did so as those who had been given the responsibility and ability to move mountains.

And for these reasons, the forces of darkness enjoyed many victories by default. They won battles simply because God's team never showed up, or showed up unprepared. It was this sad and dark realization among the angelic hosts that kept them sober even when an occasion allowed a brief laugh.

Captain Rashti placed his hand on the shoulder of the last of the six angels. The faintest of a smile surfaced just beneath the angel's determined expression. "And, finally, this is Adaam-Mir."

"Adaam!" repeated several angels in low tones.

The great captain smiled slightly. "Yes, *Adaam*. Mir was honored with the blessed title for his great love of the children of God. Adaam-Mir," Captain Rashti declared to the rugged warriors.

The captain had explained common knowledge to them. True, none of the soldiers knew any of the six angels introduced to them, including this last one. But everyone knew that *Adaam* was a coveted honor given only to those who had demonstrated the highest levels of devotion to the children of God rendered in near or total obscurity for long periods of time. Smiles of admiration were on every face, including Enrid and Myla. No one would ever ask how long Mir had served in obscurity before being honored with *Adaam*. It was unnecessary. Plus, he probably wouldn't tell anyway.

"All of our brothers here will need to learn as much as they can as soon as they can," said Captain Rashti. "They have served admirably or they wouldn't be here. But they have supported the cause from afar." The captain's green eyes narrowed. The Sword of the Lord gripped his sword and held it to the sky. "Now they will be on the front lines where sword touches sword." He lowered his eyes and sword. There was Myla and Enrid. "Talk among yourselves," he told the leaders and new soldiers. He sheathed his sword and beckoned for Enrid and Myla. "Come."

"I have never met an *Adaam* before," said Myla.

"Neither have I," said Enrid.

"Great honor," said the captain.

"Is it true that *Adaam* is a derivative of Adam?" asked Enrid. "That the Lord Most High added an *a* to Adam because no angel could ever be considered worthy to share the name Adam?"

The captain started walking slowly toward another large tree, away from the other angels. Enrid and Myla followed. "We all have our place," the captain answered thoughtfully, like a sage who had access to hidden knowledge. "This present humiliation will soon pass, and then will be brought to past the words of our blessed Lord—"

"For the earnest expectation of the creation," interjected Myla, "eagerly waits for the revealing of the sons of God."

This made even the Sword of the Lord smile broadly. He placed both of his powerful hands on Myla's broad shoulders and squeezed tightly. A less powerfully built angel may have winced. "Yes! Yes, my brother! The *revealing* of the sons of God. The *sons...of...God!"* The captain looked intently into Myla's eyes. "Do you understand this?" He lowered his hands halfway and balled his fists until they trembled. He turned to Enrid. "Do you understand the coming glory?"

Both angels could have answered yes, but neither did. They knew there were different levels of knowledge and understanding. The blessed book was open for all to read. But reading it didn't mean one understood it. Even Satan and his followers read it. And how much of the blessed book did they understand? Its mysteries could only be unraveled with the help of the blessed Holy Spirit.

"Tell us, Captain...about the glory," asked Enrid, captivated by his leader's excitement.

"Yes! Yes! Tell us of the glory!" added Myla.

The captain lowered his hands. He paced back and forth in deep thought, looking at the ground beneath his feet.

Myla got on his knees and lowered his head and raised his hands. Enrid lay down prostrate. It was customary for angels to do this when being taught about the most holy things.

"The words of our Lord: 'For He has not put the world to come, of which we speak, in subjection to angels. But one testified in a certain place, saying: What is man that You are mindful of him, or the son of man that You take care of him? You have made him a little lower than the angels; You have crowned him with glory and honor, and set him over the works of Your hands. You have put all things in subjection under his feet."

The captain looked around. Rolling hills. Valley. Farm house. Long-eared dog running and nipping at a little girl who was laughing her heart out. The little girl had a fatal undiagnosed disease, but her parents didn't know it yet. He could see the spirits of infirmity and death that followed the little girl. She'd probably not make it very long.

"That which was ordained from the beginning," said the contemplative captain, "will soon come to past. Adam and Eve were created to rule God's creation." The captain's voice dropped. "They failed." He paused in thought. "But the gifts and callings of God are without repentance. His plan has never changed. The children of God were created to rule with our blessed Creator. They will do so. In a way that far surpasses anything we have ever imagined."

"Blessed be the name of the Lord," said both angels reverently and in unison, as though rehearsed, still in their positions of worshipful submission.

"It is hard to see now—the humiliation is so very great—but the children of the Most High will judge the world." Captain Rashti was awed as he spoke that which he had spoken thousands of times. The wonder of the blessed Lord's mercy was beyond...everything! It was impossible to get used to love unlimited. "They will judge angels."

Myla took a deep breath and exhaled slowly, saving the moment. He slowly and reluctantly opened his eyes. "Angels," he repeated with wonderment. He had heard this before. It was not a new revelation. But it was one that never got old no matter how many times he heard it. It always stretched his mind to hear of the things the Creator had planned for the children of Adam.

Captain Rashti looked at Myla, totally understanding the angel's awe and his unspoken questions. "To him who overcomes I will grant to sit with Me on My throne...heirs of God and joint heirs with Jesus Christ," he added.

Myla pondered these familiar words. His head slowly turned from side to side. "These words, my captain...they...they..."

Enrid made it to his knees. He, too, shook his head at the enormity of the implications of what these words meant if he and his fellow angels had interpreted them correctly. He made it to his feet. "They...are..." Enrid began, but his thoughts hit the same wall that had left Myla stupefied.

"I know," Captain Rashti answered their philosophical dilemma. "The blessed apostle Peter," he reminded them. "Things which—"

"Angels desire to look into," Myla and Enrid finished.

"Yes!" snapped the captain in uncharacteristic jubilance. "Yes, *in...deed!*" His mind wandered back to the great rebellion. "It was too much for Lucifer." His words were heavy with seriousness. "But it's not too much for *us*, the faithful of the Lord. Blessed be the name of the Lord. And blessed be the sons of Adam."

"Blessed be the name of the Lord," the angels repeated. "And blessed be the sons of Adam."

The captain looked again at the little girl playing with her dog. The angels followed his gaze. After several silent seconds, he turned his face back to them. "Now, our business."

Enrid motioned for Myla.

"You go, my brother," Myla deferred.

"Thank you." Enrid stepped forward. "Captain, the Mighty Bashnar and Prince Krioni have plans for Edwin."

"Prince Krioni?" asked the captain.

"Yes," said Enrid. "The Mighty Bashnar was going to kill Krioni-na. He offered this up to save his skin. The prince is going to attack with two witches."

"Two witches," said Captain Rashti, contemplating this new threat. He rubbed his chin with his index finger. "First, a murderous warlock. Now, two witches."

The captain knew Prince Krioni all too well. Bashnar was richly deserving of his infamous title. In his darkness, he was indeed a mighty enemy. His strength was primarily in his strategy. But he was as prideful as he was strategically brilliant. He would rather get hit by a train than to jump off the track if jumping off meant diminishing his great name. Pride went before destruction. It would be his undoing.

Unlike Bashnar, Prince Krioni was coolly calculating. He saw the big picture and didn't mind sacrificing a finger to save a hand. If he was now personally involved in trying to destroy Edwin, things were going to get worse than they had been with the warlock.

The captain looked at a small cluster of angels. "Adaam-Mir, come," he beckoned with his hand. "Join us."

The angels that spoke with Adaam-Mir hushed. The Sword of the Lord had called for the new angel. Adaam-Mir felt his breath quicken. He ordered himself to calm down. "Captain Rashti," the new angel addressed his leader, and nodded at the other two angels.

"This is Myla." The captain placed his large hand on Myla's shoulder. "There is no one more faithful." He placed his other hand on Enrid's shoulder. "And this is Enrid. There is no one more daring." He patted Enrid's shoulder and smiled. "He actually snuck into a meeting of the Council of Strategic Affairs and detonated a bomb. He took a bomb into the headquarters..."

The captain smiled, noting silently Adaam-Mir's polite, but blank expression. "Yes. Yes. Well, you'll soon learn of such things." The captain sat on the ground, facing the farmhouse in the valley below, noting the absence of mercy angels. The three angels sat, also. "What else did you find, Enrid?"

"The Mighty Bashnar let something slip," said Enrid.

"Slip?" the captain asked skeptically. "Bashnar doesn't slip."

"My captain," Enrid continued, "I do not think this is disinformation. The Mighty Bashnar was enraged at Krioni-ni. After he disclosed to him what the prince is planning, that's when Bashnar mentioned Job. There was no rational reason to mention Job. You know how the Mighty Bashnar hates the prince. I think he sees this as the prince—"

"Trying to steal his glory," the captain finished the sentence.

"Yes," answered Enrid.

"It makes sense, Captain," Myla added. "That's when he gets crazy. When you try to take his glory. That's what made him kill the witchcraft spirit that was going after our beloved Sharon."

"This demon you are speaking of, he killed a *witchcraft* spirit?" Adaam-Mir had never worked on the front lines of battle for the sons of Adam. But every angel of light knew the prominent position of witchcraft spirits in the kingdom of darkness. What kind of spirit must this Bashnar be that he could—or would—kill a witchcraft spirit?

"Yes, he did," answered Myla. "He did it because he is full of pride. He didn't want the witchcraft spirit to steal his glory. The odd thing is Witchcraft had been very effective against his target."

"Unfortunately for Witchcraft, fortunately for us, his target was also Bashnar's target." Myla saw Adaam-Mir processing this information.

"They fight against one another?" Adaam-Mir asked rhetorically. "But how can a kingdom stand that fights against itself?"

"It can't," came three simultaneous responses.

"And now this warrior spirit plans to attack Edwin," said Enrid. "He's the man chosen by the Most High to lead the Atlanta revival. But he doesn't just plan to attack him. He plans to do him the way Satan did the blessed prophet Job." Enrid stopped there. There was no need to explain further. Irrespective of position or assignment, every angel knew and revered the great prophet. He had remained true to God even through cruel sufferings at the hands of Satan.

"This is going to happen again?" asked Adaam-Mir.

"Not without permission from the Most High," said Captain Rashti. "Myla, what did you find?"

"Captain, I watched the party that Marjorie gave for Edwin," he answered.

"Yes," said the captain.

"There was an ominous undercurrent," Myla began. "There were politicians and social activists there. I think they're going to try to hijack the revival for their own purposes."

The captain looked at Adaam-Mir. "This isn't new. It happens with most powerful moves of God."

"Satan tries to subvert the light?" Adaam-Mir was new to front line warfare, but he wasn't new to the ways of the devil. "He corrupts it," he answered his own question.

Captain Rashti scanned the valley as he spoke. "Yes." The captain looked at Myla.

"Adaam-Mir," said Myla, "Satan first tries to stop you. If he can't stop you, he tries to corrupt you."

"Unfortunately," added the captain, "revivals can be corrupted without Satan. He gets a lot of undeserved credit. Revivals last as long as people want them to last."

"But the people of God *want* revival, do they not?" asked Adaam-Mir.

"There's a price to pay for true revival, Adaam-Mir," said Enrid. "Sometimes people get tired. Sometimes they get..." he was saddened to say, "they simply get busy."

"You'll learn, Adaam-Mir," said Captain Rashti, patting him on the knee. "Sharon," he said to Myla, "did Sharon pick up on it?"

"She's quite perceptive, Captain," Myla answered, almost smiling. It was hard to speak of his beloved Sharon without doing so, but the moment would not allow it. "She saw exactly what was going on. She challenged the usurpers. She even warned her father to be strong."

Captain Rashti pondered Edwin and remembered how Paul once had to publicly rebuke the beloved apostle Peter for his cowardice. Peter turned out well. Far beyond well. He had overcome his weakness, pride, and double-mindedness and became the rock that the blessed Lord had prophesied he'd become. *He hath chosen the weak things of the world to confound the things which are mighty.*

The captain thought of Sharon's courage and passion for the blessed Lord and suppressed his own smile. "She is perceptive, Myla." He looked intently into the guardian angel's eyes. "You love her."

"My captain," Myla answered, trying to control his enthusiasm, but his passion betrayed him, "she loves our blessed Lord with all of her heart. She...she..." he shook his head, "Sharon *loves* our Lord. I mean *really loves Him.* She loves righteousness. She prays. She fasts. And Edwin needs her. The revival needs her."

Myla's angelic mind soared without the crippling limitations of sin. And yet the angel was at a loss for the right word to describe this wonderful young warrior. For that was what she was. She wasn't simply a person who had repented of her sins and had believed the gospel. The gospel was more than, as the humans often said, fire insurance to her. She had actually entered into the passion of the Creator. She lived for His smile. "And, Captain, her prayers—you remember how our blessed Lord prayed in the garden on the night of His betrayal?"

The great captain looked keenly at his faithful friend.

Myla smiled. "Well, maybe I've gotten a bit excited."

"It's okay, my friend," said the captain. "It's hard not to get excited over a child of God who lives like a child of God."

"She reads Ephesians and Colossians," added Myla. "The three prayers—"

"Yes?" asked the captain.

"She prays them," said Myla. "She prays them every single day, Captain. Oh, how she cries out to God for revelation. She wants to know Him."

Adaam-Mir was fascinated with Myla. The way he spoke about this daughter of Adam. His passion for her. His front line experience. His war experience. *A guardian angel! And to guard someone as valuable as this Sharon!*

Adaam-Mir didn't envy Myla, or at least not the way a child of Adam or one of his fallen brothers would envy one another. But he had wanted to fight on the front lines for the sons of Adam since their fall from Eden. And now listening to this blessed warrior speak of Sharon—oh, how he hoped he would get to see her one day, or perhaps to even hear her pray!—his desire for front line service exploded within him. He literally felt his desire pushing against his chest. "Myla...brother, what is it like?"

"You and Myla will be able to discuss Sharon in detail. First, however, we need to go over some things." The captain gave him an approving nod and what appeared to Adaam-Mir as a hint of a smile.

"Yes. Of course, Captain," said Adaam-Mir.

Captain Rashti was the legendary *Sword of the Lord*. Myla was a guardian angel who was guarding one of the Lord's most devoted servants. Enrid was a fearless warrior who had won the Medal of Valor. This was why Adaam-Mir was shocked when they included him in this critical discussion. What did he know about warfare? And yet over and over they sought his opinion. Adaam-Mir *knew* he was not on their level. But he *knew* they accepted him as though he were.

"Adaam-Mir," said Captain Rashti, "if you were the enemy, what would your next move be?"

"Isolate Edwin," he answered, with more confidence than he had at the beginning of their session. "Drive a wedge somehow between him and Jonathan." He dug deeper into the possibilities. "Get him prideful." He paused. No one rushed to fill the silence. "Uhh, get him off track. Get him to focus on some project. It has to be a *good* one."

Captain Rashti, Myla, and Enrid shared feint smiles.

"Sharon has to be stopped!" Adaam-Mir swallowed with embarrassment. "I mean—"

"We know what you mean, Adaam-Mir. And you're absolutely right," said the captain. "The Mighty Bashnar hates her. I am sure that he sees her as more of a threat than he does Edwin. Sharon is strong. Edwin is weak—at least for now, he is. Bashnar only respects strength.

So we can safely assume that she will be attacked soon. This may be part of his Job plan."

"And Jonathan?" asked Enrid.

"Ah, yes, Jonathan," said the captain. "Jonathan is a hard target. It could cost Bashnar everything to go after Jonathan in a frontal assault. But Bashnar is proud."

"And fearless," added Myla.

"Yes," said the captain. "If this is truly a Job-like attack, he will attack Edwin on every side. He will strike everything and everyone close to him. That includes Jonathan."

"Would this Bashnar not have to attack with legions of demons? There are more of us than there are of them," said Adaam-Mir. "He could never win such a battle."

Enrid spoke up for the captain and Myla. "Sometimes less is more."

"I do not understand," Adaam-Mir answered.

"The Mighty Bashnar doesn't do frontal attacks. He's a strategist." Enrid tapped his head. "He's a sniper."

Adaam-Mir's question showed on his face.

"You remember King David?" asked Enrid.

This brought a wide smile to the angel's face. "Everyone knows David."

"You remember when the armies of Israel and the Philistines were encamped against one another? David and Goliath?" asked Enrid.

"Yes. I've read the history many times." Oh, how Adaam-Mir wished he had actually been there!

"When was the great battle of the opposing armies won?" Enrid asked.

Adaam-Mir didn't hesitate. "When David killed Goliath."

"Right!" exclaimed Enrid, glancing at the smiling faces of Captain Rashti and Myla. "David destroyed the entire Philistine army by killing one giant." He waited a few seconds to let this sink in. "That's what the Mighty Bashnar does. He doesn't normally attack armies. He goes after giants."

"He has killed many giants, Adaam-Mir," said Captain Rashti, deeply interested in the new angel's response to this information.

"This is why he is so full of pride," said Myla.

The new angel's face hardened. He looked at his three new friends with eyes that were not piercing until this moment. "Pride goes before destruction."

Chapter 5

"Just shut up and watch him! Don't *say* anything yet. Why do you think the turnover for this assignment is so high, you idiot!" The bossy demon wasn't all mouth. He spoke from experience. He was the veteran of the crew of harassing spirits that followed Jonathan. Two months on the case and he was the veteran.

"But, Harat—" an inquisitive demon began.

Harat's eyes bulged at the demon's insubordination. He flailed his long arms and swatted wildly at the air as though trying to fight off a swarm of bees. "Are you a spirit of deafness?" he shrilled.

"No," the little demon answered nervously.

"Aaaaarrrrrrrrrrr you a spirit of blindness?"

The little demon trembled, looking at the others for support he knew wouldn't come. They looked away. He swallowed hard. "No."

Harat's fist crashed against the demon's nose. Searing pain exploded inside the shocked demon's face and head. His nose felt like it had been dipped in a volcano.

"Then why didn't you see that coming?" Harat yelled half-way before abruptly freezing his movements and lowering his voice to a hush. He looked warily at Jonathan as though awaiting a punch to his own nose. A few seconds of nothing told him he wouldn't have to pay for his careless antics—this time. "Stop your squealing and listen up," Harat said through gritted teeth. "This is the one millionth and final time I'm going to say this. This man is a—" his face and crusty, curled lips rebelled against saying it—"*dagger*. You cannot treat him like an ordinary Christian. Do you understand?" They all nodded. Ten demons in all. "Good. Now, we were not given this assignment because we are lucky. We were given this assignment because we are *unlucky*. Let's try to stretch what little luck we have. Is that okay with all of you?"

More nods.

"Good," said Harat, in a hushed tone. "Now, let's get on with our mission. Speak just loud enough for him to hear the thought. But not too loudly, or he'll recognize the thought as coming from us. Oh! And don't forget to speak in the first voice." Harat looked at the demon whose nose he had broken. "We do know what the first person is...yes?"

The broke-nose demon didn't know what to do. Anything he did or didn't do may get him another punch in the nose. He hovered in petrified silence.

Harat was disgusted. "I didn't think so. The object is to make the target think our thoughts are his thoughts." He spoke in as condescendingly a tone as he could. "Do not say, You are getting fat. Say, I am getting fat. Eyeeeeee...eyeeeeee...eyeeeeee. Got it?"

Everyone nodded.

"Now get to work. Even daggers have their bad days," Harat encouraged. "Maybe this is one of them. Make him think our thoughts."

Broke-Nose and the other demons warily approached the idling car, while Harat stayed back at a safe distance. He said he could better supervise from across the street. Broke-Nose held his face and entered the car with the others.

Jonathan glanced at the red light, both hands resting lightly on the steering wheel. His fingers danced as his mind wandered. He watched an obese man and an equally obese woman cross the street. Each of their labored steps made his heart hurt for them. They looked so tired.

"That's you, chunky butt," said one of the demons to Jonathan.

"You're not...supposed to do that," said Broke-Nose, with much difficulty.

The demon looked at Broke-Nose with a scowl. "Not supposed to do what?"

The bullied demon held his throbbing nose. "You're supposed to talk in the first person. He's going to know it's you. You have to say, I'm a chunky butt."

The scowl didn't leave the chided demon's face. Who was this broke-nose runt to tell him how to plant thoughts? He needed to mind his own business. He turned back to Jonathan. But the runt was right—he'd never tell him that, of course. He had to be more subtle with this target.

The light turned green. Jonathan had to wait almost until the light turned red again before the hefty couple was out of his way. *Lord, bless those people,* he thought. Jonathan was sorry that he couldn't stay for Edwin's party. He smiled. Edwin had come a long way. He would've loved to have seen him honored. His mind abruptly switched to little Christopher's funeral. He worried about Edwin and Barbara. Neither of them had dealt adequately with their grief. Both of them had bounced back a little too soon.

Jonathan got off the highway and sped up to make the light, but didn't. A family of heavy people crossed the street. Two extremely overweight adults, presumably the parents, and three obese children. Jonathan thought about his own weight. He touched his large belly. His hand lightly cupped a handful of fat that hung over his belt. His fingers slid back and forth on the belt. *I'm getting bigger and bigger.*

He looked in the rearview mirror. His hair seemed to get thinner every time he looked in the mirror. "I'll have to stop looking in the mirror," he joked to himself. *Elizabeth is getting younger, and I'm getting older.* Jonathan broke his young promise and looked in the mirror again. He *was* getting older...and fatter...and balder. His full, wrinkle-free cheeks hid his grimace. *Elizabeth is in great shape. What does she see in me?* Jonathan knew the thought was silly, but there was a huge age difference between them.

The green light's appearance was like the cavalry in an old western movie rescuing him from the Indians. He took off a little too quickly and hurried down the street, as though he could outrun the troubling thoughts. He let out an exasperated breath when the light turned yellow as he approached. He came to a frustrated stop and looked to the right.

A woman who had to be at least two hundred pounds overweight sat at the bus stop. She looked him dead in his eyes. She had what appeared to be the largest drumstick Jonathan had ever seen in the world up to her mouth. There was no way that thing could've come from a chicken. Was she eating a turkey leg? She took a huge bite of it as she and he stared into one another's eyes.

For some reason, her exaggerated chewing reminded him of a cement truck, just turning and turning its load. He didn't try to imagine this. It just happened. He could almost see the grinding of meat, mixed with saliva, pushing against her jaws and the roof of her mouth. It was only with the greatest of effort that he could make himself stop looking at her. *I'm going to get as big as her. How much have I gained this past year?*

Jonathan tightened his jaws. "I am running into every overweight person in Atlanta." Finally, the light changed. He drove the last few miles trying his best to only see the pedestrians he had to see. He had to get the picture of that lady eating that drumstick out of his mind.

*****

Elizabeth looked with worried eyes at her mother in the hospital bed and buried her face in her soft hands. She opened her mouth and moved her tongue around in the hope that the dryness would leave. She couldn't cry any more even though she wanted to. It had been her only relief, and now even this shadow of relief was gone. *Jonathan, where are you?*

Jonathan walked unsteadily down the hall of the intensive care unit. He noticed the youthful appearance of most of the staff. Those who made eye contact with him smiled. He appreciated this, even though ICU staff smiles often seemed busy. Of course, they were busy, he chided himself. They were trying to keep dying people alive.

And what kind of smile could he offer if he were surrounded by death day and night? If he had to look in the faces of those whom he knew would soon lose their fathers, mothers, children, husbands or wives? *Lord, bless these wonderful servants of yours who do their best to save us from the consequences of life under the curse. Come quickly, Lord Jesus.*

Jonathan had visited ICUs around the world. India and England. Egypt and Switzerland. Nigeria and Canada. No matter where a person was, it was always bad to be in ICU. The threat of death was the same no matter where it was housed. But in some places, like Russia, its horror wasn't sanitized by a state of the art building, evidences of modern medical technology, or warm smiles from professionals.

Some hospitals, if they could even be called that, screamed *Death!* The dirt on the floors, the stifling heat or the chilling cold, or the overcrowding removed the façade that everything was under control. Every absence of what many in prosperous nations took for granted proclaimed boldly that ICU was the gateway to death. There was no dirt on this hospital floor and the temperature was comfortable, but this didn't change anything. It was the same gateway.

He neared the large window and looked in. His wife's head was bowed in her hands. He couldn't see her face. Her long, black hair covered it. But he knew the expression he'd find once she raised her head. She'd look exactly how she looked the last time they were here because of her mother's congenital heart problems.

He remembered with sadness how the grief of her mother's near-death experience had sucked the glow from his wife's beautiful face. He remembered the darkness of her countenance and the etched pain that wrestled away even the slightest memory of her infectious smile. She had come dangerously close to a nervous breakdown. But by God's grace, Ava returned to health and so finally did Elizabeth's glow and smile. He didn't want to see his wife in that condition again.

Jonathan slowly pushed the door open and entered. "Liz," he called softly.

The sound was as the voice of God. Elizabeth grimaced a smile and looked up into the face of her friend and protector. "Jonathan," she said, a tremendous weight rolling off of her, "you're here." She popped up from the chair and wrapped her arms around his waist, burying her head into his chest.

Jonathan hugged her tightly. He cupped the back of her head with one hand and massaged her neck. "I'm here, baby." He wished that he could take her pain and grief onto himself the way Jesus had taken the sins of the world onto Himself.

"She can barely get her arms around you, fat butt," said the demon.

"You're not supposed—"

The harassing demon jerked his neck around. "To say that!" he shouted to Broke-Nose. "I know! I know!" He glared at Broke-Nose, who still had his hand to his face. He slowly turned back to Jonathan. "She can barely get her arms around," the demon again glared at Broke-Nose, "me, me, me! Satisfied?"

"That's the way he told us to do it," Broke-Nose whined.

"That's the way he told us to do it," the demon mocked.

Jonathan held his wife and looked at Ava. The left half of her head was shaved. She had a lot of stitches in her head. *They've operated on her head,* he thought. He looked at the tube in her mouth. Then the machine that monitored her heart. He'd seen this before. She was in a coma. This blessed woman was in a coma. *She can barely get her arms around me.* He looked at Ava's head and was ashamed for thinking of his weight at a time like this. *Lord, forgive me.*

"I'm so glad you're here, Jonathan," said Elizabeth. She abruptly turned to her mother and touched her hand. "Mom, Jonathan's here. He's going to pray for you and get you out of here. Just like he did last time." Elizabeth wiped her face and eyes. She hugged her husband and stepped back and looked up to him with total trust. She formed a little smile. "Jonathan, pray for Mom and raise her up."

Jonathan looked at his wife. He was the luckiest—no, the most blessed—man alive. Who else but the Lord could bring together a feisty and fearless Argentine woman who rescued girls from sex slavery, an exploited and brutalized beautiful Somali teenager who was the *property* of a ruthless gang of pimps, and a fat black man? Elizabeth adored and trusted him. She believed he could do anything.

"Baby...Liz."

Her face was soft with comfort as she answered. "Yes, Jonathan?"

He searched for the right words. He didn't want to hurt her faith. "Baby, I heard from God that time."

The little smile was stubborn. "You can hear from God this time."

Jonathan lightly squeezed both of her shoulders. "Liz, I don't *tell* God when to speak to me. He's *God*. Do you understand what I'm saying, baby?"

The little smile disappeared. "Here's what I understand, Jonathan." Her voice was soft, but determined. "I wasn't human. I didn't have a soul until that woman," she pointed to Ava, "rescued me." She dropped her head. Jonathan imagined her difficulty at talking about this. She rarely did. She still had infrequent, but horrible nightmares about her time in bondage. "Mom risked her life to save a little girl from a sex-trafficking gang who employed people to adopt children for them."

"I know, Liz. Ava's a wonderful woman," said Jonathan.

"Jonathan," Elizabeth touched his face and slid her fingers slowly down, "you risked your life for me. There was only one day between me and General Lopez."

Jonathan was doing okay until this. During his time in Argentina, he had never met this infamous general. But he had heard a lot about him. He was more of a pimp than a general. He was well connected. And it was said that once a girl was purchased by the general, she'd never be seen again. It was rumored that he had brothels in rural areas that were like military fortresses. There was absolutely no way a girl could escape.

Unless God worked a miracle.

Jonathan's eyes got watery. He couldn't imagine his lovely wife being used as an object of some pig's lust until the day the general decided she was no longer worth the price of a bullet between her eyes. It was said that this was his choice of termination for disobedient girls or girls who were no longer exciting. As the general was reputed to have said, "Beautiful young girls are a commodity. So replacing one or two, here and there, is no big deal."

"God...spoke to me," Jonathan said, wiping his eyes.

"He'll speak to you again, Jonathan."

"Baby, this isn't magic. I'm not a psychic. I can't make God speak to me on demand."

Elizabeth lightly rubbed her mother's forehead. "Jonathan, you're right. I'm sorry. It's just that I love Mom." She began to cry.

"I love her, too," he said.

"I know you do," said Elizabeth. "God is bigger than an aneurysm, isn't He?" Tears rolled down her face. "Remember Derrick in Germany?"

Jonathan grinned at the memory. "Yes."

"He had a brain aneurysm, and God healed him," said Elizabeth. "Right there on the spot." She saw the event vividly in her mind. "You laid hands on him and rebuked the spirit of death." Her voice trailed off into the beauty and awe of the memory. One moment Derrick was good as dead. The next he was up and walking around as though he had never been sick.

"I remember," said Jonathan, sharing the several-year-old memory as though it had just happened yesterday. It had been a most dramatic healing. But as dramatic as it had been—especially because of the astounded medical staff—the thing Jonathan remembered most was how satisfying the healing had been. Derrick was a dear friend and incredible servant of the Lord. He owed so much to that dear brother, and it was nothing but the goodness of God that He had allowed him to be the instrument of his healing.

Elizabeth looked imploringly at her husband. Her friend and hero. "Pray for Mom?" she asked. Her request sounded like that of a little child.

The heart monitor and intravenous tube was on the bed's left. So he joined his wife on the right. "Baby, I wasn't saying that I wouldn't pray for Mom, or that God wouldn't work a miracle. I was just—"

Elizabeth placed two fingers on Jonathan's lips. "I know," she whispered. "Pray for Mom."

Jonathan placed his full hand on the side of his wife's face. She closed her eyes and let gravity pull her face into her husband's hand. It felt good to rest in the strength and warmth of his touch. Everything would be okay. Jonathan kissed her on the forehead. She opened her eyes and looked deeply into his.

"You ready?" he asked.

"I'm ready," she answered her hero.

Chapter 6

Jonathan shook Elizabeth on the shoulder. She could fall sound asleep in a couple of minutes, but it often took an invading army to wake her up. Jonathan was used to it after so many years of marriage. This time he wished he could let her sleep. She needed her rest. It had been a long night.

Her heavy eyes fought to open. Finally, her stubborn eyelids slightly parted. She looked through the slits with burning eyes. Her groggy brain hadn't yet caught up with her half-opened eyes. She slowly rose from her uncomfortable spot and sat up. She looked like a beautiful drunk about to fall over any moment.

Elizabeth's weary, unfocused gaze landed on the shaved head of the figure in the hospital bed. Adrenalin shot through her body. She leapt to her feet, wide awake. "Mom's not healed?" she asked with alarm. She lightly touched the back of her mother's hand. "Jonathan, Mom's not healed?"

"Not yet."

"Not *yet*?" she answered hopefully. "So she *is* going to be healed."

"Liz, I didn't mean it like that," said Jonathan.

"We prayed for hours, Jonathan. We spoke to the mountain." Her words were lightly laced with panic.

"Yes...we did, Liz."

"Then what *do* you mean, Jonathan? Please tell me. Is God going to heal my mother?" Elizabeth pressed. "Has God said nothing to you?"

Jonathan glanced at Ava and tenderly gripped Elizabeth's arm and pulled her to him. "Liz, Ava can hear everything we're saying," he whispered. "We shouldn't—*'Does Job fear God for nothing?'"*

"What?" asked Elizabeth.

Jonathan had a stunned look on his face. He closed his mouth and stood erect. He dropped his hand from Elizabeth's arm.

"What, Jonathan?" She looked at her husband with wife's eyes. She saw it. "You just heard from God, didn't you?"

Jonathan was shocked. He didn't know what to say. He knew exactly what this Scripture was saying—at least in the original context. Satan had approached God with the accusation that Job served God faithfully only because he was blessed. Job had gone through a long, terrifying trial to prove his unconditional love of God. But was that what God was saying *here*? *To them*? Were they about to go through a trial by fire?

Jonathan willed his heart to not break. His face to not betray his fear. He had to be strong for Liz. But he couldn't be strong if he jumped to the wrong conclusion. He reminded himself of the basics of prophetic ministry.

Revelation. Hear correctly. Speak only what you hear.

Interpretation. Interpret correctly. If you don't have the interpretation of the revelation, don't make up one.

Application. Advise correctly. Don't advise out of your flesh.

Secrecy. Keep thy big mouth shut. A biggie. The mistake of rookie prophets and the presumptuous. DON'T AUTOMATICALLY REVEAL EVERYTHING GOD GIVES YOU. God shares some things with His friends just because they're friends, and not because He wants them to spread His secrets.

"Didn't you, Jonathan?" Elizabeth had seen that look on her husband's face dozens of times when God had dropped thoughts into his mind. That's when some of his greatest miracles happened. They had talked multiplied hours about moments such as these.

"Eyeeee—" Another thought imposed itself on his mind as powerfully as did the first one. *Seal up the vision, for it refers to many days in the future.* "Oh, God," he said out loud, wishing immediately that he had better control of his tongue. But he had to say something. His *Oh, God* wasn't for Elizabeth. It was because this was God telling him he couldn't tell her what He had shared with him. In his estimation, this *Oh, God* was definitely justified. God had just gotten him into trouble with his wife.

"What did God say?" asked Elizabeth.

Jonathan's mouth was closed, but his mind was going *Uuuuuuuhhhhh.* "Not here," he said, buying some time. "Let's go to the hospital chapel."

They got there much too quickly for Jonathan.

"Now, Jonathan, what did God say to you? Did he tell you anything about Mom?"

"No."

Elizabeth just looked at him. Expectantly. He had never lied to her. She was sure he wasn't trying to be dishonest now. She'd let him gather his thoughts. And until he did, she'd stare at him.

"I mean, I'm not sure. I mean, I'm sure He spoke to me. I'm just not sure what it means."

"Let's make it easy, Jonathan," Elizabeth offered. "Tell me what He said and we can sort it out together."

That's not making it easy, Liz. He knew she was hurting. He knew she was desperate to hear from God. But He couldn't reveal God's secrets. "I believe God is telling us we have to trust Him." There. That wasn't the in-depth answer she wanted, but it was true, and he hadn't crossed the line with God.

Elizabeth's expression was *really* expressive. Her mother was at death's door. They had rebuked the effects of the aneurysm for hours. And God had spoken to a man with a miracle ministry comparable to what she saw in the books of Acts, and all He had said was to *trust* Him?

"Jonathan, is *that* all? Trust Him?"

"Liz...baby, what *else* is there besides trusting God?"

"There's healing. That's what else there is?" said Elizabeth. She shook her head, exasperated. This didn't make sense. "I don't—I'm not—I love God. I serve Him, Jonathan. You know I do. I've done everything He's asked." She didn't know whether to scream, cry, or fall to the floor in mute desperation.

Her last statement pierced Jonathan's heart. Not because of the deep sadness of her lyrical moan, but because it was true. It was absolutely true. As far as he knew, his precious wife had done everything asked of her by God. For certain, she had done everything he had asked and more.

There wasn't a place on earth she wouldn't work for God. (The only possible exception was Argentina.) There wasn't a comfort she wouldn't sacrifice for the gospel. But he knew that she knew he could provide more of an explanation. Yet despite this storm of testing, Liz was Liz. She wasn't Eve. She wouldn't put him in a position to betray God's confidence. She'd never hand him the forbidden fruit. She was the wife Adam never had. For this, he was eternally grateful.

Nonetheless, he was ashamed of himself. The woman who had sacrificed so much for him and others and for the sake of the gospel needed his help. She was drowning. But in the wisdom of God, he couldn't throw her too big a life preserver. The best he could do without interfering with God's work was to tell her to keep treading water. He couldn't even tell her to tread until help arrived. *He didn't know if help was going to arrive.* At least not the way they wanted it to come.

"Mom loves God," Elizabeth continued. She felt like she was presenting facts to the judge *after* the sentencing. What good was her pleading?

"She loves God very much. God knows she loves Him," said Jonathan.

"And yet she's dying," said Elizabeth. She looked around the chapel. It was nice and really thoughtful of hospitals to have chapels. Some of them tried a balancing act of political correctness and religious sensitivity. She was grateful that this one was not modest in its overtures to Christians.

There was a large cross centered on the wall directly opposite the front entrance. It was a cross with no Jesus on it. *Good. He is risen.* In front of the cross was a single golden lampstand with seven arms. There was a bowl affixed to the top, above where the flames would be had the lamps been lit. The lampstand no doubt represented the Holy Spirit. On either side of the lampstand was a replica of an olive tree.

Jonathan watched his wife's gaze. *Lord, may I?* He didn't sense a no. Still, he purposed to be careful with what he said. "Do you know what that is?" he asked her.

Elizabeth welcomed her husband's question. It reminded her of the hundreds of time he had asked her a question regarding God or the Scriptures only to answer the question. She knew there would be no satisfying answer to the one question she most needed answering. But she had often found comfort in these conversations with her husband. Perhaps he could share something with her that would take away this terrible fear that she would lose Mom. "The cross—"

"Oh, come on, Liz. The cross?" asked Jonathan, happy to see a semblance of his wife's silly self.

"Well, you asked," said Elizabeth.

Her voice wasn't playful, but it wasn't mournful either. That was good enough for Jonathan. "You can do better." He reached into his suit jacket pocket and pulled out a soft mint. He held it up and waved it. "There's a prize in it for you if you show me what you've got."

She looked at the damaged prize and said, "Where'd you get that candy?"

"Out of my pocket," he answered.

"Before that, Jonathan?"

Jonathan's eyes rolled.

Elizabeth shook her head. She knew from where that piece of candy had come. "When did you last wear that suit?"

Jonathan thought about it for a few seconds—a few seconds longer than necessary. He knew exactly when he had last worn that suit. "Uuhhh, couldn't have been that long ago."

"Jonathan, you wore it on our anniversary." She watched him go through his *Really? No way!* routine.

"Liz, that would be eight months."

"Yes, it would," said Elizabeth.

Jonathan tilted his head. "I know where you're going with this, Liz." She still wasn't smiling, and there was no energy whatsoever coming from her. But she was going along with his antics with the little strength she could muster.

"You're trying to give me a squishy, dried-up piece of candy that you've had in your pocket for eight months." If she had the energy, this is where she would've laughed, and Jonathan knew it.

"See, that's where you're wrong, Liz. Dead wrong." Jonathan smiled. "I had that piece of candy three months before I wore that suit."

Elizabeth shook her head and laughed despite her trouble. "Oh, Jonathan! What was God thinking when He created you?"

"He wasn't." Jonathan smiled. He jerked his hands up and looked at the ceiling. "No offense, Lord. Nooooo offense."

Elizabeth gave him a trouble-free smile and shook her head.

"What? Life is hard enough without ticking off a certain Somebody." He said this with his finger close to his chest and jabbing upward as though trying to keep this from God. "Thank you," he said.

"For what?" asked Elizabeth.

"That beautiful smile," said Jonathan. "It was worth the wait."

"You worked for it," she said.

"I worked hard." He saw the ponderings beneath the disappearing smile. "Now about that candy."

"It's the Holy Spirit," Elizabeth said. "The lampstand represents the Holy Spirit."

Jonathan smiled. "You're right. It does. You know, there's a place in Revelation that shows seven lampstands."

"Why seven?" asked Elizabeth. "Was God emphasizing the Holy Spirit? Or showing His completeness or something?"

"Well, not this time," said Jonathan. "This time the lampstands represented something else. They represented the church."

"This time it's the church." Elizabeth's voice was flat.

Jonathan pointed to the wall. "Now this lampstand is special—with the olive trees. That one comes from Zechariah 4. It's what he saw. It represents a beautiful message. God told him that the vision meant 'Not by might nor by power, but by My Spirit, says the Lord of Hosts.'" Jonathan was smiling. Elizabeth was not.

"How do we get 'Not by might nor by power, but by My Spirit' from that vision?" she asked.

"God told Zechariah that's what it meant," said Jonathan.

"And *how* do we get that message from a vision of a lampstand and two olive trees?" Elizabeth's voice was a little louder than before and had a noticeable edge.

Jonathan was bewildered. First at the question, and then at his wife's tone. She so rarely displayed a bad disposition, even when he thought she had a legitimate reason to do so. "An angel told him the meaning of the vision."

"An angel?" said Elizabeth.

There was no mistaking this time. She was irritated. "Yes, an angel." Jonathan looked at her wondering. And waiting. This was so unlike her.

"Zechariah sees a lampstand and an angel tells him it means 'not by might nor by power, but by My Spirit.' John sees seven lampstands and God tells him—"she looked to Jonathan for confirmation. He nodded. "The lampstands represent the church," she continued.

"That's right," said Jonathan, wondering what in the world was going on with his wife.

"And what does this mean, 'They shall lay hands on the sick and they shall recover'? And this, 'The prayer of faith shall save the sick, and the Lord shall raise him up'? Or this one, Jonathan, 'Whosoever shall say unto this mountain, Be removed, and be cast into the sea, and shall not doubt in his heart, but shall believe that those things which he says shall come to pass, he shall have whatsoever he says'?"

Jonathan slowly shook his head. "Liz?"

Elizabeth stood up. She wasn't a shouter. In the rare event that she was really upset, one had to focus on the tremor in her voice rather than its volume. She spoke softly, but Jonathan heard a loud tremor. "Jonathan, my mother is upstairs dying. I have done all I know to do to get her healed. We have seen people healed all over the world. I'm not trying to be mean or self-righteous. I'm just telling the truth. The truth that you know yourself. Many of those people were not even Christians. You remember the hooker?"

Jonathan shook his head and shrugged his shoulders.

"Vegas. The lesbian—alcoholic—hooker," said Elizabeth.

"Oohhh...oh, that one," he said. How could he ever forget *her?* She was one of the most morally and sexually depraved, and angry persons he had ever ministered to.

"Yeah, *that* one." The tears flowed down Elizabeth's pained face. She looked at the ceiling. Her eyes saw nothing but ceiling and lights, but by faith her spirit stood before the throne of Almighty God. "God, You healed a lesbian hooker. A lesbian hooker of cirrhosis and liver cancer."

Elizabeth's breath quickened. She battled the emotions that were trying to overcome her. "A lady who cursed us—" Her face twisted in torment, her lips and tongue rebelling against her will, fighting her words. She pressed forward. She needed to talk to God. She needed Him to talk to her, like He did to the prophets. "A lady who spit on us before and after she was healed. A lady who told You to stick your healing up—"

Elizabeth broke and crumpled to the floor on her knees before rolling over on her side. Her head hit hard against the wooden pew. Blood poured from a gash just above her eye.

The sound of his wife's head crashing against the pew sounded like a clap of thunder to Jonathan. "Oh, my God!" he said. He rushed to her side and put his hand under her head. He lifted it. That's when he saw the stream of blood. "Liz, oh, my God, Liz. Hold on." He looked frantically around the room.

"I'm sorry, Lord," Elizabeth cried, the pain in her heart more searing than the throbbing of her face.

A box of tissues on a table.

Jonathan sat his beloved wife up on the floor and pressed the tips of her fingers against the gash. "Liz—"

"Lord, You have to speak to us," she cried inconsolably. "What do your promises of healing really mean? What's the real meaning? Do you have one more angel? Just one more? Please..."

"Liz...Liz, hold your fingers against the cut," he pleaded.

She put her hand absentmindedly to her face. No part of her hand touched the opening over her eye. Blood poured scarily into her eye and over her hand. Jonathan jumped up and ran to the table and snatched the box of tissue. He jerked out several, balled them up, and pressed them to her face.

"Jonathan, God healed an alcoholic lesbian—a prostitute." She heaved between words. "Will—He—heal her—and let—my mother die? Will He, Jonathan?"

Jonathan pulled back the tissues to see how bad the cut was. Good thing they were in a hospital. He'd have someone look at her.

"What part of the Bible can I believe, Jonathan?" She looked at him desperately.

It was the same look she had when she was being brutalized by that gang of pimps in Argentina. The same look she wore even after he had told her he had a friend who could help rescue her. She had looked at him with the most pathetic expression of hopelessness and despair he had ever seen. It broke his heart then. It was breaking his heart now.

His chest exploded in emotion. Tears gushed from his eyes. He had told her that he would love her forever and protect her always. His love was forever, but he feared that this time he might not be able to protect her. How could he protect her from God? Who could've protected Job?

He sat next to her and hugged her tightly, pressing fresh tissue to her face. His tears were as strong as hers. Neither could speak without difficulty. "Believe it all, Liz. Believe it all."

"You have to help me, baby," she begged. "I—want—to believe God, but—I can't. My heart hurts."

Chapter 7

The first perimeter demons watched with disgust and fear as Sharon walked groggily from the bathroom and got on her knees beside her bed. This was a horrible way for their day to start. This sickening prayer of hers was going to attract angels. Weren't there enough angels hanging around this wretched daughter of Adam already?

Their fear far exceeded their disgust when they saw the unusually high number of angels enter the room. The appearance of Enrid stirred their nervous imaginations. What was *that* hideous angel doing here?

Adaam-Mir's open mouth mirrored his fascination. What blessed providence that his first observation of this esteemed servant of the Creator would begin with prayer! He looked at Myla, Enrid, and the other angels with a look of wonderment. They were used to this. He was not. He was about to see a daughter of God talk to the Creator. Maybe she would help Him rule the world this morning—in front of him!

Sharon smiled and lifted her face toward heaven. She breathed in deeply. Her chest expanded with delight. She exhaled.

Myla nudged Adaam-Mir. "Watch this."

His nudge was unnecessary. Adaam-Mir's eyes were stretched as wide as they could get.

Sharon lifted her arms over her head. "Lord…Father," she paused, savoring her Father's love, "I love you. I love you. I love you." Each declaration was stronger than the one before.

Adaam-Mir struggled to maintain his composure. As long as demons were present, one had to be vigilant. He wasn't a front line soldier, but he knew this much. Nonetheless, he couldn't stop his heart from warming or his eyes from releasing tears. "Myla, it has been several minutes and she hasn't asked the Creator for anything."

"Yes," answered Myla.

"Will she?" asked Adaam-Mir.

"Most likely," said Myla. "She must. It is her duty and privilege as a priest of the Most High."

"But she continues to worship Him." Adaam-Mir wanted to move nearer, but the moment was sacred. He didn't want to violate protocol. He had much to learn.

Enrid looked at the new angel. "You can get closer if you'd like," he said with a smile.

Adaam-Mir was surprised. "I can?"

Myla and Enrid both answered, "Yes."

"The more the sons and daughters of God pray, the closer we can get," added Myla.

Makes sense; *I guess*, thought Adaam-Mir. He took three tentative steps toward Sharon and looked back at Myla and Enrid. He saw looks of encouragement and understanding on the faces of the other angels. "You may sit with her," said an angel from the crowd.

Adaam-Mir's eyes jumped back to Myla. He received a nod. Adaam-Mir slowly sat down. He was less than a foot in human measurement from a daughter of God. He didn't know whether the rapturous revelation of light had burst within him or had come upon him. But something wonderful had happened when he sat down.

Daughter of God.

Suddenly, a torrent of thoughts washed over him like relentless waves. They swept him up and carried him where his mind had never been able to take him before.

Sharon is My daughter.

I live inside of her.

She will rule and reign with Me forever.

She rules with Me now in prayer.

Everything you see belongs to her and her brothers and sisters in Me.

She is in Me and I am in her.

I and the sons and daughters of Adam are one.

On and on the thoughts came, one after the other. Adaam-Mir had no time to recover and no desire to recover. He was overwhelmed with his new understanding of heaven's old knowledge. The Almighty had sovereignly pulled away the veil from his eyes. He shook his head. He was glad he was sitting. It would have taken a monumental effort to not fall to his knees had he been standing.

"Look!" screeched a demon, pointing at what was descending. Bulging, terrified eyes of every demonic sort followed their motivated feet as far away from the Styles' home as possible. The pointing demon looked around and saw that he was the last demon there. He quickly joined the others.

Adaam-Mir looked up.

"Adaam-Mir," Enrid called, "come."

The angel looked into the approaching brilliant light. His strength was gone. He faintly heard Enrid call, but he couldn't move. His body wouldn't respond to his conflicted mind. Something instinctive told him it was proper for him to move away from Sharon now. But there was something else instinctive that craved the approaching light. He wanted to enter it and be lost forever in its brilliance.

Enrid hurried to the nearly limp angel and put him across his shoulder and carried him away. Adaam-Mir's head and arms dangled as Enrid and every other angel moved several feet away. The angels had not moved away for fear, but out of respect. The light had come for Sharon.

"Use me for your glory," was the last thing Sharon said before the light she did not see engulfed her.

*****

Edwin sipped his coffee and looked at his phone on the table. He had left two messages for Jonathan. There wouldn't be a third.

Barbara finished chewing her food and swallowed, studying her husband. Her veggie omelet this morning was good, but her midnight snack had been absolutely wonderful. The sexy smile she wore had nothing to do with eggs. "Expecting a call?" she asked.

"No. No, I—"

"You can call him, you know," said Barbara.

"Call who?" said Edwin.

She tilted her head with a pretty little smile. "Edwin Styles, you know perfectly well who."

Edwin rolled his eyes and blew out air.

Barbara smiled and whispered, "You're acting like a child." He lifted his eyes and met hers. "But we both *know* you're a man."

Her smile and the way she emphasized her words made it perfectly clear what she was talking about. Edwin smiled. Actually, he blushed. But he wouldn't let her see him blush this time.

"You're blushing," she said.

Barbara was glowing, her skin radiant and alive. This didn't surprise him. She always glowed afterwards. She was like a plush garden after a good rain. The leaves greener. The grass taller. The flowers fuller. Everything more alive. "Yes," he confessed warily, anticipating his wife's customary high school banter that would've shocked her little girl.

"You've nothing to be ashamed of Edwin Styles," she whispered across the small circular table, wagging her head at him with a smile and twinkling eyes. "If you're blessed, you're blessed."

Edwin fought hard to keep a semi-straight face. This lady was something else.

"Would you like some more coffee, dear?" she asked.

"Yes," came his quick answer.

This made Barbara chuckle.

Sharon walked into the kitchen. Barbara didn't see her.

"Oh, Sharon," said Edwin, "your mother was just telling me how blessed I am." He looked at Barbara with his own twinkle. He was safe again.

I wonder if she told Larry he was blessed. The thought came hard, landing on Edwin like a missile finding its target. The memory of his wife committing adultery a year ago with his best friend exploded in his mind.

Barbara poured Edwin a little more coffee. She smiled at him as she pulled her hand away. He offered a tight smile in return.

"Good morning, Sharon," said Barbara.

Sharon was wide-eyed. She sat down and stared out the window into the big, wooded backyard.

"Honey," Barbara said to Edwin, "are you going to call Jonathan?" An inexplicable, faint flash of anger hit Edwin in the belly and lodged in his chest. "We haven't heard from him since he left the party to check on Elizabeth's mom. I bet he'd really appreciate you checking on him." She sat with Edwin and Sharon. "Oh, I almost forgot. That guy from *Charisma Today* magazine called again."

"*Charisma Today*? Again? They've already done one story on me," said Edwin. "Why would they want to do another?"

"They want to do a story on Jonathan," said Elizabeth. "The guy, Anthony Winonzo or Winatza or something—"

"Winzinski," said Edwin, suddenly finding the name distasteful in his mouth.

"Yeah, that's it," Barbara cheered. "Anyway, they want to write about how Jonathan has changed your ministry. He said something about showing the before and after."

"Sort of a power behind the throne story," said Edwin.

Barbara smiled and thought about it. "Yeah," she smiled, putting some omelet in her mouth and chewing as she looked at Sharon. "Are you okay? Did you have a bad dream? You look like you've seen a ghost."

"It wasn't a ghost," she answered.

"Ohhh," said Barbara sympathetically, "let me get you something to eat." She hopped up and went to the large island. "What was your dream about?"

Sharon struggled.

"You haven't had a nightmare in quite some time," said Edwin.

"It wasn't a nightmare," said Sharon. "I wasn't asleep."

"Oh?" said Barbara.

"Yeah, Mom," Sharon's eyes were glazed, "I was praying. I think I went into a trance."

Barbara looked at Edwin. "A trance, dear? We don't know anything about trances. Do we, Edwin? Should we get Jonathan in on this?"

"What did you see?" asked Edwin.

"Well, I was praying. Then I felt something come over me, like a...a blanket or something. Then, Dad, I don't know how to say this, but it was like my pores opened and something gushed in. I mean all over me, inside of me. But it wasn't my skin. It was like I had a body inside of my body. The stuff went into that body. Then this voice said, 'Seeing, you shall see, and hearing, you shall hear.' Then the voice said, 'Look. What do you see?' So I turned and saw a bunch of elephants and donkeys running directly at us. You, me, Mom, everybody...the whole church."

Barbara looked at Edwin with raised eyebrows, then at Sharon. How was a parent to answer a nightmare of stampeding elephants and donkeys? "Well, you're okay now. What do you want in your omelet? Your usual?"

"Mom."

"Tomatoes and peppers?" asked Barbara.

"There's more."

Barbara looked at Edwin and saw the request. She sat down with them. "What else did you see?" asked Barbara.

"It's not good," Sharon answered.

"It's okay," said Barbara, rubbing her daughter's forearm. "It's just a dream. Go on."

"I wasn't sleeping, Mom," said Sharon.

"What else did you see, Sharon?" asked Edwin.

"There were a lot of owls with the other animals," she said.

"With the elephants and donkeys," stated Edwin.

"The elephants and donkeys charged us, but a lot of the people didn't run. Mom," said Sharon, "you didn't run away from the animals. You ran toward them. They ran over you." Sharon vigorously shook her head. "Mom," she moaned, "you wouldn't listen to anyone. Jonathan tried to save you. I tried to save you. But you ran into the running animals and were trampled."

"I was killed by the animals?" asked Barbara, moved more by her daughter's emotion than the dream itself.

Sharon wiped a tear from her eye. "I don't know if you died. I don't know how you could have survived it, though. They were all over you."

Something told Edwin he was not going to like the answer to this question. "And what was I doing?"

"Nothing," she answered.

Edwin felt like he had just been indicted by the grand jury. Not guilty, but not really presumed innocent either.

Sharon saw it in her father's face. "I mean not *nothing*. You were standing there scratching your head, trying to figure out what to do."

The little fireball of anger in Edwin's chest was now roasting his lungs. "My wife is about to be trampled to death by animals. Jonathan rushes in to help while I scratch my head." His words were heavy with resentment.

"It's a good thing Jonathan was in her dream, wasn't it, Edwin?" said Barbara, trying to lighten the moment. "He wouldn't let anything happen to me. Jonathan's a good guy. Remember how I used to feel about him?"

Sharon smiled at her mom. She was proud of how she had grown in that area. "Dad, what do you think about it? I've never had a trance before. What do you think the voice meant by 'seeing, you shall see, and hearing, you shall hear'?"

Edwin could have screamed. He didn't. "I don't know," he answered like an adult.

"What about the animals?" asked Sharon.

Edwin could have screamed louder. He paused before his emotions got the better of him. "I don't know," he answered, with as little emotion as possible.

"Dad!" Sharon beamed. "Remember the trance?"

Edwin looked baffled.

"The trance...the trance, Dad," Sharon said excitedly. "The one Jonathan had. He told us about it on the camping trip."

The memory arrived like a rambunctious door-to-door salesman at midnight. *Of course. How could I have forgotten Jonathan's angel guided tour of Satan's kingdom?* "Yeah, I remember."

"Mom, we can ask Jonathan," said Sharon. She closed her eyes. "Oh, we thank You, Lord, for Jonathan. He's such a gift." She opened her eyes and hugged her father. "What would we do without Jonathan?"

Chapter 8

Enrid tried to be calm, but he was excited. The captain had dropped bits and pieces here and there about a critical and exceedingly dangerous mission that would help the Atlanta revival. He was not at liberty to share all the details with Enrid, but that didn't bother him. Enrid was Special Operations, not strategy. He did what he was told.

Captain Rashti knew the answer before he asked the question. "Do you accept this assignment?"

"Yes," Enrid answered without hesitation.

"Do you see any way it can be done?" the hero of the Battle of the Resurrection asked.

"None."

"Good," answered the captain. "Then neither will the darkness. Their invincibility will make them vulnerable where they least expect it. Pride goes before destruction."

Enrid left wondering how the completion of this assignment could possibly help the Atlanta revival.

*****

The Mighty Bashnar stood outside the door of the Council of Strategic Affairs (CSA). He was incensed at several things.

First, he was the Mighty Bashnar. Why should he have to go through this demeaning process of asking permission to increase his attacks on the worm, Edwin Styles?

Second, that despicable Prince Krioni was still chairman of the board. He would have to present his case to him. That scum would try to make him grovel. This was reason enough to burst a blood vessel, if he had one to burst.

Third, he had Crucifix, but he didn't have his other trump cards, Destruction and Chaos, in his pocket. There was no way he could have given them what they wanted in so short a time. All part of their plan, no doubt. They didn't have the backbone to tell him pointedly to his face to go to light when he asked for their votes.

And, last, he'd knock on the door and they'd make him wait—the way he made others wait—like a beggar waiting for someone to drop a coin in his hat. The Mighty Bashnar was no one's beggar!

The Mighty Bashnar gritted his sharp teeth and knocked. He waited and waited and waited. He could see in his mind the panel talking among themselves as though the Mighty Bashnar was not waiting to be heard by their pathetic bureaucracy.

Finally, the chief bureaucrat spoke. "You may enter," the gruff voice of Prince Krioni bellowed.

The Mighty Bashnar reminded himself of the humiliating protocol and entered with his head bowed. He looked at the floor, careful to not look up unless given permission. He waited to be addressed before speaking. This, too, was another way to humiliate whoever was unfortunate enough to stand before them.

All five members of the board looked at their supplicant as though he were a slave on the block, waiting to be purchased. Even his friend, Crucifix, sneered at him. For friendship among demons was purely commercial and self-serving. The value of the friendship was only as great as what each demon could get out of the other. When favors stopped, so did the friendship.

"Your sponsor, Crucifix, has prevailed upon us to grant you an audience." The chairman was as condescending as Bashnar had anticipated. "We will hear our next proposal in ten minutes. So waste no time with our graciousness."

The Mighty Bashnar seethed, but said nothing.

"State your business." The chairman's words dripped with contempt. He knew this warrior despised him. He studied him for the slightest trace of insubordination.

"Great Prince Krioni—" Bashnar began before being interrupted.

The salutation caught the prince by surprise. This warrior spirit was smarter than he had thought. "You may look upon us." He wanted to see this proud, defiant supplicant's face as he paid him homage.

The Mighty Bashnar slowly lifted his head and looked at each of the ruling spirits. Each face was as hideous as his own, and each monstrous expression conveyed nothing but the purest of wickedness and ill intent.

Nonetheless, his warrior instincts told him that despite the ferocity of their appearances, with the exception of the prince and Hades, there was a definite absence of malice. Crucifix, yes. They traded favors. But Destruction and Chaos? Why was he sensing their cooperation? He had not been able to carry out the assassinations they had demanded for their votes. *Most interesting.*

"State your case," ordered the prince.

The Mighty Bashnar smiled inside his dark soul. "Great and illustrious prince, Chairman of the Council of Strategic Affairs, and ruling spirit of the Georgia region, I salute you."

The prince peered at the warrior spirit. Was this foot soldier mocking him? In front of his peers? How dare he! He would most certainly pay for his insubordination. But the outraged prince's thoughts hit a wall. The warrior spirit had slyly hidden his contempt. The prince trembled with hidden rage. His revenge would have to be fully satisfied another time. So be it. But this warrior spirit's arrogance had just earned him a summary judgment of no. It didn't make a difference what he was asking for.

The Mighty Bashnar saluted each of the board members with the same honor. There were nods of approval. "Your time is valuable. I will not waste it. The Atlanta revival is growing. It must be stopped. I have put a plan into motion that will crush it once and for all."

"We have heard this from you before," said the prince.

The Mighty Bashnar smiled again inside. The idiot prince was like so many other fools who had underestimated him. "Most honorable prince, I was the executioner of other spirits' plans."

The prince's anger flared. This warrior spirit was indirectly calling his strategy a failure.

"Plans that I am on record as opposing from the beginning. What I propose is an all-out blitz against the Atlanta revival on all fronts," said the Mighty Bashnar.

"All fronts?" the prince asked with a raised voice.

"Honorable prince," said Hades, "may I?"

The prince flicked his hand and huffed his permission.

"Exactly what do you mean, all fronts?" asked Hades.

"Chairman?" said Crucifix.

"The floor is opened," said a thinly veiled disgusted chairman.

The questions from the board were rapid, comprehensive, and blunt. Some even disrespectful. But this was to be expected. The chairman's ten-minute limit was blasted by more than two hours. The Mighty Bashnar displayed presentation and political skills that shocked the prince. This was no ordinary foot soldier. The prince wouldn't let his hatred cloud his judgment. He would treat this enemy with the respect due a worthy foe.

"You will destroy Sharon?" asked Crucifix.

"Yes," said Bashnar resolutely.

"You will destroy that wretched Jonathan?" Chaos asked, hopefully, but determined to not get too emotionally invested in this improbability.

"Yes," Bashnar said, with an involuntary sneer of hatred for the servant of the Lord who had scorched him. He would never forget how he had burnt his glorious mane.

"And the anointed one?" asked Destruction.

"The anointed one?" asked Bashnar.

The prince perked up and had to quickly hide his giddiness. "Yes," he said, "the anointed one." Prince Krioni smiled inside at this so-called legendary warrior's amazing blind spot. "Edwin Styles."

"Edwin Styles is a worm. He is a weak worm of the dust. He will be destroyed along with the others. He is already in my hands."

"You are aware that the enemy has surrounded this worm of yours with a host of warrior angels who may disagree with your assessment." The prince had regained his footing.

The Mighty Bashnar lifted a balled fist that trembled with determination. "Grant me the authority to overrun him with the same ferocity that our father, Satan, unleashed against the prophet, Job."

"Do you have any idea what that would require?" the prince scolded.

The Mighty Bashnar glanced at his unexplained allies.

Destruction spoke up. "From time to time such humiliations are worth it. Besides, I'm getting tired of explaining why this Atlanta revival hasn't been destroyed yet."

The prince's eyes bore into the warrior spirit. Ordinarily such things were not discussed with demons of such low rank. But this one had gotten under his hard skin. "No. You do not have any idea what you are asking. For your request to be granted, we have to request permission from heaven."

The warrior spirit's expression said it all. He didn't understand.

"God!" screamed the prince. "Maybe you've heard of Him. It is not our authority to grant. Our father, Satan, had to ask God for permission for that kind of authority. He had to go back to Him for each escalation. We can't just do whatever we want to do. Or haven't you heard? The evil dog of heaven has rules and protocol and boundaries and..."

The prince stopped flailing his arms and calmed down. He had said far too much. Spirits of his stature rarely admitted to themselves the oppressive and unjust rules they had to operate under. And they even more rarely spoke openly of these humiliations.

But now that this arrogant warrior spirit had pushed him to such undisciplined speech, he couldn't stop himself from thinking the same troubling thoughts that had tormented him since the Great Rebellion.

We are losing. We have lost. It's just a matter of time before God casts us all into the lake of fire and these wretched sons and daughters of Adam inherit what was rightfully ours. We have been played for fools. The Lord has used our rebellion to separate the true from the false among His people. He is behind the scenes, orchestrating and making fools of us all. Satan has led us into a war that was impossible to win. Why did we ever follow that liar?

"Great prince. Great prince," he heard someone call.

The prince snapped out of his embarrassing daydreams. This wretched warrior spirit had driven him into thoughts that had gotten others thrown into the *Dark Prison*. "Leave the room," he abruptly ordered the warrior spirit.

The Mighty Bashnar left the room with malice and murder in his heart.

The board of the Council of Strategic Affairs voted on whether or not they should make a formal request of heaven that the warrior spirit be allowed unusual access to Edwin Styles.

The prince was stunned when Chaos and Destruction joined Crucifix in support of the warrior spirit. Their treachery enraged him. However, it would not stop him from proceeding with his own witchcraft plan against the Atlanta revival. The way he saw it, the odds were in his favor. Either his plan would work and Bashnar would be humiliated, or Bashnar's pride and ignorance would do him in. *How can such a legendary warrior not know that God takes pleasure in using weak people to humiliate the kingdom of darkness? What fascinating ignorance!*

The prince and Hades left out the back door. Crucifix, Chaos, and Destruction left out the main door and approached their friend, The Mighty Bashnar. They shared the news. The great warrior spirit celebrated his success behind his hard face. He wondered as he watched his three friends walk away. Why were there three friends and not only one? Before he got to the end of the long hall, someone called his name. He turned. It was Chaos hurrying toward him.

Chaos was a formidable mass of hardened muscle and battle scars. He was a few inches taller than the Mighty Bashnar and just as wide. He stepped closely to him and said in a low voice, "I do not know how you did it. Nor do I care." Chaos pushed his face toward a grimaced smile. "We are even?"

Bashnar said nothing at first. He simply looked at Chaos, wondering.

"We are even?" Chaos repeated.

"Yes, we are even," said Bashnar.

Chaos turned and walked away.

The Mighty Bashnar watched Chaos walk away until he saw him walk past Destruction, who was coming toward him. Destruction walked up to him and stepped closely.

He spoke in a low voice. "We are even?"

"Yes," answered the Mighty Bashnar without hesitation, "we are even."

The Mighty Bashnar left the Castle with a light heart. He didn't know how things had worked so magnificently in his favor, but sometimes odd and unexplainable things happened in war.

*****

Enrid had watched the enemies of Chaos and Destruction with perfect stillness. If he had been discovered even a fraction of a second before his perfect moment of attack, he would've been overwhelmed by the formidable defenses of this dark assembly. Actually, even if everything went as planned, it was a plan that could've easily qualified as a death wish.

Stealth. Skill. Discipline. Fearlessness. They all played a role in enabling him to assassinate these ruling spirits so the Mighty Bashnar would get credit for their kills and be assured a favorable outcome when he stood before the Council of Strategic Affairs. *Manipulating the darkness was a fundamental strategy of the light.*

Enrid rolled violently down the side of the mountain. He landed hard against the ground. He crawled desperately to the edge of the river's rapids and rolled himself in. Hopefully, the fast- moving currents would carry him away before the demons could catch up to him. He hit the cold Colorado water. His eyes fluttered between consciousness and unconsciousness. His last thought before passing out was, *For the glory of God and the sons of Adam.*

Chapter 9

Sharon was buoyed by the thought of talking to Jonathan about her trance. She fidgeted in her seat as she chewed quickly on her omelet. She hurriedly swallowed and gulped the rest of her orange juice. She swiped her mouth with a paper napkin. "Okay," she said, hopping up. "I'm gonna call Jonathan."

Before anyone could say anything to her, she was gone. Barbara smiled and shook her head. "Your little girl is crazy about Jonathan."

Edwin said nothing.

Barbara narrowed her eyes and tilted her head. "How do you feel about that?"

"Lovely," he said, unconvincingly.

Barbara made a pouty face and flicked his bottom lip with her finger. "Don't be jealous, Daddy. She's still your little girl. Always will be."

Edwin gave her the expected smile. If he didn't, this could turn into a conversation he didn't want.

"Thatta boy," said Barbara. She began to clear the table and clean a little. "We should be grateful for Jonathan. God knows she talks to him about stuff that neither of us can help her with. It's a good thing God has sent a man like that into our lives. Don't you agree?" she said, as she put the last dish into the dishwasher. "He'll be able to help her with her dream."

Krioni-na watched and listened to this conversation intently. He knew that brute, the Mighty Bashnar, would find something of value in the worm's growing envy and insecurity. Something moved at the corner of his eye. He turned his head a little, then snatched it all the way around. His body followed.

The Mighty Bashnar stood there not ten feet from him, hands poised on his sides, with his red eyes glaring at the worm. Sheeesh! He never knew when that maniac would pop up. Krioni-na looked at the Mighty Bashnar. The maniac didn't even look at him. He just glared at the worm. Krioni-na wondered what had he done to deserve such bad luck as getting mixed up in this mess between Prince Krioni and a psychopath without the psychopath's usual phony charm. Even a little phoniness would make this a bit more bearable. He looked at his tormentor for a long while until he was certain he was not there for him. He turned back to continue his surveillance of the worm.

Krioni-na's vile body jerked involuntarily when he saw the three warrior angels standing around the worm with swords in one hand and daggers in the other. He immediately kicked out of his mind the impulse to get the dagger in his boot. That would've been plain stupid. His only hope was the maniac. He flung his head around as though his neck was made of rubber. The maniac was gone. He was on his own.

Gulp.

Edwin's lukewarm coffee mixed with the fire in his chest. "I'm sure he can," he answered, genuinely believing this. But this didn't diminish the fire. He was sick of hearing about how great Jonathan was.

God has sent a man like that into our lives.

God has sent a man like that into our lives.

God has sent a man like that into our lives.

The last time he had checked, *he* was a man. Just a little while ago his wife was practically purring about how much of a *man* he was. Now God had sent a *man* into their lives. Jonathan was Barbara's *man.* He was Sharon's *man*. It was only a miracle that he wasn't Andrew's *man*. But who knew? There was still time for Andrew to dump his father for Jonathan. Before Edwin could stop his runaway mind, he thought, *The only thing keeping little Christopher from choosing Jonathan over me is a six-foot-hole.*

The thought was like a spiked boomerang. Its callousness hit him hard, cracking the shell of his already damaged ego. What kind of father would dump on his dead son? He needed to get out of the house. He scooted his chair back and started to get up. "Barbara—"

"Honey, I want to talk to you about something," said Barbara.

Edwin released a disguised deep breath. "What's up?"

Barbara dried her hands on a towel, tossed it on the counter, and sat down. Her eyes were full of excitement. "Last night I had a good conversation with Abbey Lockhart. The senator."

"I know her," said an underwhelmed Edwin.

"She has some good ideas about where we should be going as a church."

Krioni-na glanced to his right. In a flash, the demon was gone. *Who was that?* He had only caught a glimpse of the spirit, but he knew he had seen him before. *But where?*

*****

Edwin walked up his stairs. Abbey Lockhart. The nerve of that woman. It wasn't enough that his wife and daughter had practically voted him out and Jonathan in. Now this obnoxious politician was trying to run his church. That was a conversation that should never have taken place. *What possessed Barbara to give this lady reason to believe I'd let her use our church as a political platform.* And why was his wife setting up meetings between him and this woman?

But as troubling a development as this was, he knew the more pressing question was, Why didn't he simply tell his wife that there would be no meeting tonight? He told himself that he'd do better at speaking up.

Edwin paused and took a deep breath. He put a trembling hand on the doorknob to little Christopher's bedroom and opened the door. He stepped inside and closed the door behind him. He leaned hard against it and looked almost disbelievingly around the room.

Edwin's face matched his hurting heart and confused mind. This made only the third time he had been inside the room since his death a year ago. The grief that was always just beneath the surface, like the hidden hands of menacing underwater currents awaiting an unwary swimmer, pulled at him. He looked at the Atlanta Braves World Series pennants that hung from the walls. He and Christopher had them all. They even had the World Series pennants that the Braves had been in and lost.

His scrambled thoughts took him to the iconic David Justice poster that showed him swinging at the pitch that he launched for a home run, winning his team the 1995 World Series. He thought of Wallace and Marjorie Reynold's son, Jason. His room. What were the odds of someone else collecting all of the World Series pennants that the Atlanta Braves had been in, and of hanging them around the room just as he and Christopher had done? And what of the David Justice poster? *What's going on? What kind of coincidence is this?*

Was God trying to talk to him? If so, what was He trying to say? And if He was trying to talk to him, why didn't He just do so, like everyone else, instead of speaking in riddles? Edwin dropped this senseless line of reasoning. He was only flattering himself. Why would God talk to him?

"It's not like I'm Jonathan," said a harassing spirit.

Without hesitation, Edwin cynically said, "It's not like I'm Jonathan."

*****

Edwin walked from the parking lot toward the third baseline bleachers. There weren't too many people seated there. Actually, only three. This wasn't unusual. There wasn't the same interest in Saturday morning practice that there was in an actual game. He sat near the three spread out fathers. He recognized one of them. He was a regular. The others weren't.

The coach hit the ball hard to Andrew several times in a row. Some right at him. Some at his feet. Some a couple of feet above his head. Some on the ground, seemingly out of reach. Andrew made every catch and fired the ball accurately to first base or he helped turn the double-play.

Edwin's chest expanded with each catch. He grinned toward the other fathers, especially the one whose son Andrew had beat out for the shortstop position. Danny's father had all but assured Edwin that Andrew was wasting his time competing with his son.

Edwin knew gloating was inappropriate, but he wasn't gloating. He was merely smiling—with exceedingly deep and euphoric satisfaction—in the direction of a man with a mouth as big as the Hoover Dam. It wasn't prideful to acknowledge the obvious. Andrew was gifted. He was quick as a cat. He could stretch like he was six-six. And he had a laser-guided cannon for an arm. There was no reason for him to feel guilty that his son was going to be a major league star shortstop and Hall of Famer.

Krioni-na watched with intrigue the interactions between the angels around Edwin and the approaching three demons. *What is that they're carrying?* he wondered. He saw one of the demons show an angel a document. The angel took the document from the demon's hand, read it, and stood nose to nose—Krioni-na was sure their noses must have touched—and said something to him that didn't go over too well.

The demon huffed and went to the other two demons. The angel who read the document said something to another angel. That angel shot toward the east like a flash of lightning. And like a flash of lightning, he was back in a moment. The first angel beckoned the head demon and apparently gave him some instructions.

Krioni-na didn't know the details, but he knew what was going on. *How did that angel confirm the authorization so fast? Why is their communication so much better than ours? And why are we always the ones asking for permission?* He grimaced in disgust. He wouldn't let himself think along these lines. Each time he did, it only upset him.

The coach hit a blazing line drive several feet to Andrew's left that hugged the ground like a cruise missile. Automatic base hit.

Not so fast.

Andrew.

Future major league shortstop and Hall of Famer.

Edwin watched his son get the jump on the ball as though he had been tipped off. He dove head-first with a long outstretched arm.

Thump! The ball slammed into the glove's pocket. Andrew leapt from his belly to his feet like he had been helped by angels and shot the ball to first base.

Edwin jumped up. "Yeah! Go Andrew!" he yelled.

"Gimme a break," said Danny's father.

Edwin didn't hear the comment. He looked at his son. Andrew dusted off his jersey and got back in his stance. Edwin sat down. That was odd. Andrew acted like he didn't hear him. He didn't even glance at him. *Maybe he didn't hear me,* thought Edwin against his better judgment.

On the next play Edwin stood up. "That a boy, Andrew! Nice catch," he yelled.

Andrew didn't acknowledge him.

"Hate to see how he treats you once he gets that fat contract," said a harassing spirit to Danny's father.

Danny's father chuckled at the thought. "Hey, Mr. Styles?"

Edwin looked down the bleacher to a man wearing a huge t-shirt. If the shirt's size was a strategy to hide the man's swollen belly, it was a failed strategy. *Why does this man call me Mr. Styles?* "Yes, Mr. Kremins?"

The guy's meaty face pushed up into a full smile. "Preachers oughtta be able to hide their hatred better."

"I don't hate you, Mr. Kremins," Edwin answered with a tired voice that conveyed *I don't hate you. I simply find you disgusting.*

"Yeah...yeah...of course not," he answered with amusement. "I was just going to say I'd hate to see how he treats you once he gets that fat contract."

"Fortunately for you, that's a problem you'll never have," said Edwin. He knew this was mean when it was in his mind. It sounded even meaner now that it had left his mouth. He'd apologize to the Lord, but he was *not* apologizing to this man. He stood up. "Have a good day, Mr. Kremins."

The man gave an open-mouth smile. "You, too, preacher."

Edwin wanted to yell across the field, "See ya later, Andrew," but if for some crazy reason he didn't answer him, he'd hear from the Hoover Dam again. Wasn't worth it. He walked across the parking lot covered in a dark, frenzied swarm of locust spirits so thick he couldn't be seen.

His next stop was the cemetery to visit Christopher.

*****

"Then three demons came, "said Krioni-na. "Two of them carried a large curtain. They held it between the worm and his son. I lost sight of Andrew until they lifted the curtain. That wasn't until the worm was driving off. I don't think Andrew could see his father when the curtain was there."

"What *incredible* powers of observation you have," mocked the Mighty Bashnar. "Of course, Andrew couldn't see his worthless father. That was the whole idea."

Krioni-na's deplorable face used wrinkles to convey the question.

"It was my curtain, lap dog," said the Mighty Bashnar.

*****

Edwin headed for home. The cemetery had been crueler to him than the baseball field.

Chapter 10

Jonathan stared at the large, beautiful home God had given them with detachment. Things were temporary. They came. They went. You could only get into trouble by getting too attached to anything you were destined to lose.

A few Scriptures broke through the rich soil of his well-tended heart. *Set your affection on things above, not on things on the earth...Seeing then that all these things shall be destroyed by fire, what manner of persons should you be in holy conduct and godliness...? Thou fool, this night shall your soul be required of thee. Then whose shall these things be which you have stored up...?*

These admonitions weren't rules he tried to live by. They were words spoken by God that were as much a part of him as the blood that flowed through his body. He could live without neither. So he welcomed the spontaneous wisdom. But he recognized that the admonitions were due more to Ava's condition than to any possible attraction to stuff.

The hard fact was that Ava had rescued a terrified little girl whose body had been ravaged by strangers and whose soul had been stomped by every lustful man with enough pesos to satisfy her pimps. And she had not only rescued her; she had adopted her. She became her mother.

It had taken Ava years to love away the empty, zombie-look off of Elizabeth's beautiful face, and even more to free her from the debilitating panic attacks and tormenting nightmares—although there were still infrequent episodes of both. Jonathan knew his wife. If Ava died like this, she'd never consciously accuse God. She loved God too much. She'd fight to keep her heart pure. She'd fight to not grow bitter.

But Jonathan's fear wasn't that she would accuse God or become bitter. His fear was that her faith would be damaged. When he had first met her, she was a tender, but soiled dove whose wings had been broken and mangled seemingly beyond repair. But God's love and power flowing through Ava, and later through him, had helped to heal her. Her recovery had been slow, painful, tedious, but remarkably thorough. It was not a stretch to say *miraculous.*

The little dove with the mangled wings had transformed into a soaring eagle. But if Ava died like this, Jonathan's gut told him that he would never see the eagle again. And he feared (he prayed he was wrong) he may only see a shadow of what the dove used to be. Of course, he was only human. Elizabeth was resilient. He could be wrong.

But he could be right, too.

He drove up the long driveway and parked the car outside the garage. He knew what prayer battles awaited him once he entered the house. Mountains were stubborn things. So he would savor the last few seconds of warm sunshine on his body. He opened the front door, stepped inside and disarmed the alarm, and dropped his Bible on the sofa before joining it. He closed his eyes and exhaled deeply. He opened his eyes. There was no time to spare. He had to begin now. Ava could die any moment. Strongholds required strong responses. Strong, tenacious, desperate responses.

*****

The Mighty Bashnar's direct gaze was on Jonathan, but he sensed someone to his right, about twenty yards away. This wasn't an angel. He didn't see any angels. Those cowards often hid themselves in invisibility. For all he knew, there could be five, ten, twenty in the room this very moment. Who knew? He twisted his face. The coward angels could only hide because of this wretched dagger's prayers and close walk with the enemy.

The warrior spirit's face twisted more when a Scripture came to his mind—how he hated that cursed book! But one had to be familiar with one's enemy. So he read it. And he read it. And he read it some more. Much of what was in the book of the sons of Adam remained a mystery no matter how much he studied it. But the hideous Scripture that scoffed at his darkness was all too understandable.

He shall cover you with His feathers.

Psalm 91. What a detestable Psalm. And what a detestable and formidable weapon of the enemy. At times He hid His servants with this stealth technology. He wanted the darkness to think this power had something to do with prayer. But lord Satan had long ago exposed that this wasn't the power of prayer as much as it was the enemy's use of an unknown technology on behalf of the sons of Adam when they prayed.

The Mighty Bashnar watched the dagger drink a bottle of water before going into the garage. He knew what that meant. A low growl bubbled up from his throat and escaped through the spaces in his bared teeth. The dagger was getting ready to go into the presence of the enemy. Who knew what havoc he would unleash with his deplorable prayers?

The Mighty Bashnar whipped his head to the right. He saw him. The demon who had intruded. It was only a flash of a moment that he saw him before he was gone. But it was long enough for him to determine that he had seen that face before. But where?

*****

Elizabeth clutched the pillow and watched the thin parade of doctors and nurses coming and going. She stretched her back. It ached in at least twenty places. Surely, someone had beaten her while she slept. Her ears perked up at the new hushed discussion of the three people huddled to the side of Ava.

The doctors and nurses hadn't been talking in whispers until now. Actually, Elizabeth felt they had been talking too loud and too freely around Ava. It was inexcusable for them to talk as though she were already dead. Ava could possibly hear everything they were saying, and it wouldn't help her faith to hear people speaking death over her. And that was exactly what she had told them. *Don't speak death over my mother!* Elizabeth connected the dots. *Maybe this is why they're whispering.*

She approached the team. "Dr. Mullins, is there something I should know?" Her request was low, polite, and tired. She had been praying non-stop whenever she hadn't dozed off—which she had been fighting desperately to not do.

The doctor's lips tightened before he gave her the news.

Elizabeth listened as bravely as she could until the doctor began to explain that they thought Ava had suffered a stroke and that her brain was swelling. They weren't sure how much more her body could take. That's when Elizabeth's legs went wobbly and things got dark.

*****

Prince Krioni and his co-conspirator walked down the long dark hall with slow steps. Apparently, they were the only ones in this part of the mammoth labyrinth of basement corridors. They were in no hurry to get to any particular place. Their only hurry was that arrogant Bashnar. They had to stop the Atlanta revival before he did. He had failed so far, but this was no consolation.

As arrogant and as insubordinate as that son of an angel was, he did learn from his mistakes. It was only a matter of time before his adjustments found the winning combination. Prince Krioni gurgled.

Perhaps his Job strategy is the winning combination. A troubling thought, indeed.

"Great Prince," whispered Controllus, "we cannot let that son of an angel achieve such a notable victory. He's already out of control. What would he do if this achievement were added to the great book?" The witchcraft spirit's words were low and filled with contempt and conspiratorial possibilities. "He has already killed a witchcraft spirit. We have no proof, but we know he did it. What next? A ruler spirit? A council member?"

Prince Krioni was amused. Control was the crack cocaine of witchcraft spirits. They were always either passing the pipe or putting it to their own mouths. "Let's not waste time playing manipulative games, Controllus." The prince's tone wasn't confrontational. "We both hate Bashnar for our own reasons. I don't need another reason to hate him."

Controllus saw that the prince had seen through him. He smiled slyly. "Forgive me, great prince. I did not mean to control you."

"Of course, you did," retorted the prince. The witchcraft spirit opened his mouth to defend his motives. Prince Krioni waved him off. "Take this control of yours and put it to use on fools too stupid to know what you're doing."

Everything in the witchcraft spirit yearned to push the argument. His nature wouldn't allow him to let it drop. But his common sense would. Even though he was a witchcraft spirit, it was bad business to antagonize a ruler spirit, especially if he happened to be the chairman of the Council of Strategic Affairs.

"Here are the reports from my observer spirits," said the prince. "They've been watching that whole band of rebels."

The witchcraft spirit took the documents and began to read them, line by line.

Prince Krioni's patience with the witchcraft spirit was wearing thin. "Are you going to read them all in their entirety here? In the basement?"

"What? Huh?" answered Controllus, looking up.

"Go—do—what—you—do." The words sounded more as though spoken by the chairman of the Council of Strategic Affairs than by a ruler spirit trying hard to not sound condescending to a witchcraft spirit.

Controllus held his expression in check. "I will—"

The chairman abruptly turned and walked away. He disappeared into the darkness, leaving the witchcraft's spirit's words hanging from his lip.

Controllus glared in the direction of the chairman. He cursed under his breath until he could no longer see the chairman's wide back or hear the sound of his boots hitting heavily against the damp floor.

*****

The angel maintained his invisibility as he approached the hospital. He hated hospitals. Scores of people stricken down by dreadful diseases and horrific accidents and crimes. It was like entering Satan's trophy room. As his habit was, he reminded himself that as terrible as the present condition was, it was temporary. The Creator had appointed a day when—he remembered the phrase from the blessed book—*And God will wipe away every tear from their eyes; there shall be no more death, nor sorrow, nor crying. There shall be no more pain, for the former things have passed away.*

"Hold on, children of Adam," he whispered. "Just a little while longer. Your day of redemption draws near." He steeled his emotions. This was not a time for sadness, but vigilance. He stepped out of the cover of Jonathan's prayers of protection for his wife and approached the guardian angels.

"Aenean," said one of the guardians, clasping his friend's forearm.

"Victor, my brother," said Aenean. "Good to see you." He handed him a sealed scroll. Aenean's face asked the questions he held in his heart.

Victor looked at the seal on the scroll. He slowly lifted his head and looked Aenean in the eyes. "This is the Lord's seal."

"Yes," the courier angel said softly.

"The Lord's seal?" said a couple of guardians.

The commanding angel turned away and took a few steps. He turned toward the others and broke the seal of the Most High and read.

One of the guardians saw Victor's concern. "What is it, brother?"

Victor gathered his thoughts. "We must leave."

The angels all looked at one another with questioning eyes.

"The gold must be tried by fire," Victor said with a low-key authority.

"When do we leave?" a guardian asked.

"Now," answered the commander.

*****

Controllus approached the hospital cafeteria with a half-dozen of Prince Krioni's own elite council guards. It was doubtful that any one of them was a match for Bashnar. But it was certain that Bashnar was no match for any three of them together. There were six. And he made seven. And the document in his hand made it ten thousand a hundred times over. Let the so-called Mighty Bashnar get in his way.

The witchcraft spirit saw his prey. No angels. His eyes widened with excitement. Just as quickly, however, they narrowed. He halted his detachment. Why were there no angels? Were there really no angels? Or were they lurking in the dagger's prayers, waiting to ambush them?

"You and you," Controllus pointed, "approach the woman."

The demons glared at their temporary boss.

"You have a problem with my order?" said Controllus.

The larger of the two spoke up. "No. I have a problem with your cowardice." He turned to the others, but he kept the witchcraft spirit in his view. "All of you, come with me."

The other four soldiers joined the two that Controllus had so casually sacrificed. The defiant castle guard stepped up nose to nose with the witchcraft spirit. He whispered in his ear. "You can lead me and my comrades into this ambush. Maybe we'll live. Maybe we'll die. Or you can watch us go into the lion's den. If we get wiped out, you can make up some convincing story of how bravely you fought as me and my friends died in battle. How...ever," the word scraped the demon's throat and mouth on the way out, "if me and my friends survive the ambush, or worse for *you*, if there is no ambush, me and my five friends will cut your worthless darkness into six pieces. One for each of us."

"You dare—" began witchcraft.

"No one will ever know what happened," continued the demon. "We will explain how bravely you fought in the battle. Now," the word catapulted from the furious demon, "what is your future?"

Controllus could hardly believe his ears. No one threatened witchcraft spirits. They were favorites of the lord of darkness. But the dark father wasn't here and these six renegades were. It was his word versus theirs. Yet his immediate problem wasn't winning an argument later. It was staying alive now.

Controllus was in a predicament, but showing weakness would only make matters worse. "My future is quite secure," Controllus spat back.

The offended demon took a step backward. Controllus walked determinedly to the front of the elite castle guards. He pulled out his sword and dagger. He looked at them all. "Well?"

"One of the other castle guards said, "Well, well, well. A witchcraft spirit who's not afraid to get his hands dirty."

Controllus swallowed hard and approached the woman. The other demons followed closely in disciplined formation. Two faced the woman. Two walked backwards, covering the flank. One watched the left. One watched the right. They may be overwhelmed, but they would not be surprised. The closer they got to the woman, the slower they walked. Their steps were more deliberate. They acted as though they were walking through a minefield. One errant step and boom!

The seven demons heard it—*them?*—before they saw anything. The sound of a roaring fire all around them. But there was nothing. There was no heat. Just a sound like fire. Then they heard the piercing sound of a trumpet and what sounded like the unsheathing of a hundred swords.

With the exception of Controllus, the demons were battle-hardened front line soldiers. They had faced the might of God and had lived to tell the story. That's why they had been chosen above legions of others for their choice assignment. They were *elite.*

Nonetheless, there was something about walking into an ambush and being surrounded by the fire of God and a host of invisible warrior angels that dampened the mood of carrying the *elite* badge. Still, the enemy would pay a terrible price before the last of them were destroyed. They crouched low, searching nervously for the first wave of attacking angels.

Then something happened that left them bewildered. The piercing trumpet abruptly stopped. The sound of the fire died down and stopped. Out of the invisible dimension a voice commanded, "Retreat! Retreat! Retreat!"

The demons kept their defensive posture for several minutes of tension-filled vigilance until they were sure the threat had passed. They stood up straight and looked at one another. "We live another day," said one.

"What do you think scared them off?" asked another.

"Doesn't matter," answered the head demon. "Just good to know the prince has our back."

Controllus tried to look as though he faced this sort of thing all the time. "Let's get her before they come back."

Elite castle soldiers or not, this was a good idea. The demons and Controllus approached the woman sitting at the table.

Controllus sat next to her and draped his arm around her neck and shoulder. "Elizabeth, I'm Controllus. I'm a witchcraft spirit, and I'm here to help."

Chapter 11

Prince Krioni was enraged, but his hardened face didn't show it. He was still embarrassed that he had allowed Bashnar's arrogance get the better of him the last time he was here. There would be no repeat of that mistake. But—it—was—nearly—impossible—to not blow up! How had the request been approved? He had personally made sure that the request to overrun Edwin with the Job strategy was filled with language that would guarantee rejection.

The Mighty Bashnar stood before the council. His head was bowed by the protocol of ruler spirit ego. The chairman let him stand like this for several minutes. This warrior spirit needed constant reminding of his lesser rank.

The Mighty Bashnar's face carried something that faintly resembled a fraction of a smile. If the request had been denied, the wretched prince would have wasted no time in shouting it from the roof. His request had been approved. He'd stand there all day just to see the look on the great chairman's face.

"Lift up your head," the chairman finally ordered.

The Mighty Bashnar looked into the ruler spirit's eyes. But the prince looked instead at the open document in his hands and read without looking up. He was loathe to read it, but there was no way protocol would allow him to delegate.

"Your request—" A wonderful thought came to the chairman's mind. He *would* look at the arrogant bag of feces that stood so boldly before his presence. "The council has a strategy to destroy the Atlanta revival. We call it our Job strategy. I assign you the task of fulfilling our desire. It is not a complicated strategy; so you should be able to comprehend it."

The prince noted the effect of his words on the great and illustrious warrior spirit. *Wonderful.* "Do you follow me, *Mighty* Bashnar?" The prince peered into the warrior spirit's eyes, as did the rest of the council.

The Mighty Bashnar's eyes strained towards blackness. Black eyes would assure his death. He willed them to stay red.

The prince waited a couple of moments. "It's okay," he answered Bashnar's silence, "I know it's a lot for you to process. We have written it out for you so you don't forget what we want done." The prince looked at the council members on his left side and said, "For the record." He looked at the members on the right and said the same thing and continued, "Torment, scandalize, destroy," said the prince. "Do whatever it takes to get rid of this cursed revival. Leave nothing. We have taken care of the wretched forces of light. The only thing you can't do is kill Edwin. Clerk," called the prince, "give this document to the warrior spirit."

The Mighty Bashnar took the document from the timid clerk.

The prince enjoyed the expressionless look on Bashnar's face. He knew what was behind his thin curtain self-control. He lifted his hand and shooed him away as though he were a fly. "Go."

The Mighty Bashnar turned and took a couple of steps.

"Oh, and warrior spirit," said the prince, "for the record, you will notice that the document in your hand also gives full authority and access to Controllus—he's a witchcraft spirit—to work simultaneously to destroy this revival."

That's where I saw that demon, thought Bashnar. *He was spying for the prince.*

"Unfortunately, the last witchcraft spirit assigned to the Atlanta revival was killed. Some feel he was *murdered*." The prince looked to his left and right. "For the record," he said to both sides, before turning back to Bashnar, "should Controllus meet a mysterious death or come up missing, it will be assumed that he was murdered—by you."

The Mighty Bashnar was glad that he had not turned around when the prince called him. Blackness erupted and swallowed his red eyes. He lowered his head and marched out the door as quickly as possible. The sounds of laughter behind him made him walk faster.

*****

The Mighty Bashnar wasted no time. He channeled his rage and humiliation toward the worm. The first thing he did was test the perimeter around Edwin. He wasn't fond of ambushes. He ordered a detachment of ten soldiers to rush the worm with their swords drawn. This would be clearly seen as an attack to destroy and not routine temptation. His order was for them to get as close as they could to Edwin and to speed by him.

The warrior spirit watched execution of his tactic with a feeling of dark euphoria. No angels. He took a deep breath and exhaled slowly. This was *nice*. He turned and looked at his vast army.

"Set up the perimeter," he bellowed. "We will destroy the worm. We will destroy Sharon. We will destroy Jonathan. We will destroy everything and everybody that is remotely linked to any of the rebels. We will destroy the Atlanta revival and take back what is rightfully ours."

The Mighty Bashnar turned to his right and walked toward a small group of demons distinguished for their abilities to destroy ministries and churches. These were all personally chosen by Bashnar and all had worked with him before. They would act as his highest ranking officers. "Let's get to work."

*****

Edwin sat in his car brooding. Everything was a mess. The more he thought, the more he circled the toilet. Powerless against the flush of depression that was sucking him into a hole.

The Mighty Bashnar walked toward the worm. His sword in one hand. His dagger in the other. He was ready for any surprises. Beside him were two demons. One on each side.

One was an obscenely muscular demon of unforgiveness who dragged a heavy ball and chain with each hand. Demons of unforgiveness were stocky, barrel-shaped spirits of hard muscle. They fed off of bitterness, anger, self-righteousness, and most of all, memories.

The other was a tiny, harassing spirit of guilt. He would replace the one that had sat on Edwin's neck for thirty-five years before he had been fried on the spot by a lightning bolt from heaven when Jonathan rebuked him a year ago.

"Have a seat," Bashnar told the spirit. The worm's response to this first attack would confirm what he knew. Edwin was weak. Despicable. Unworthy of the attention of a warrior spirit of his stature. At least Sharon and Jonathan were real warriors. They believed and obeyed the cursed book. They weren't pretenders like this worm.

The harassing spirit knew what had happened to the previous demon, but what could he do? Tell the Mighty Bashnar no? He climbed up Edwin and sat on his neck with both legs dangling over his chest.

The Mighty Bashnar stepped back a couple of yards. "Begin," he ordered.

The little spirit's three eyes looked first to the heavens. Would he be fried like the spirit before him? He lifted his suction-filled paws and smashed hard on Edwin's head. He waited for the zap! There was no zap! He looked at Bashnar and smiled. He closed his eyes and furiously massaged.

Edwin's mind was suddenly flooded with filthy images. But they weren't random images. They were sharp, clear movies of him and his uncle. The memories with all of their hurt and shame and guilt hit him with all of their original force. But how could this be? He had lived free of this torment for a year. Jonathan had set him free. How could the demon have returned?

He felt something like slime ooze down his head to his torso and finally down below his belt. It stopped at his lower belly then lodged in his groin and buttocks. "Oh, God," he moaned. "What's wrong with me?"

The Mighty Bashnar stepped back further. The longer he looked, the more disgusted he became. He stepped forward and spit in the man of God's face. "What's wrong with you is you're a worm. You're not a man. You have degrees in the cursed book, but you believe little of it, and you obey even less. What's wrong with you, Edwin *Worm* Styles is you live off of others' spiritual handouts. You have degrees in the Bible! Degrees! Degrees! And you believe nothing. How long did you think you could pretend?"

"Why, God? Oh, why?" Edwin whined as he held his head and cried.

The more Edwin cried, the more agitated he made Bashnar.

"What kind of a pastor are you?" seethed Bashnar. "What kind of a husband and father are you? What kind of a friend are you?" He shook his head. "For the life of me, what does Jonathan see in you?"

Bashnar trembled with rage as he glared at the worm. He could curse and berate this imposter forever, but there weren't words suitable for such a waste of human flesh. Weakness! He was the personification of weakness. There was no fight in him. "Your God is no longer with you. So I will answer your question. The book. The cursed book you claim to believe. It says in Luke 11 that when the unclean spirit goes out of a man, he goes through dry places seeking rest and finding none. He then returns to his house—that would be *you* Edwin—and finds it empty, swept, and garnished. Then the spirit—that would be the one on your neck, Edwin—returns with seven spirits more wicked then himself, and the state of that man is worse than before.

"We don't have a lot of demons to spare. So you don't get seven more, and you don't deserve seven more. More would be a waste on a worm like you. I don't know why I can't kill you now. You're no good to heaven. You're no good to hell. You're worthless. Oh," Bashnar flicked his hand in disgust, "I wish you were hot or cold."

The Mighty Bashnar remembered something that Prince Krioni had said. He looked at Edwin with a frown. "The *anointed* one. The idiot thinks you're anointed of God. But I'll tell you what you are, Edwin. You're cursed of God. That's why I'm standing here and your guardian angels are—well, where are they? That's why there's a demon on your neck. And do you know why all of this has happened?"

Edwin cradled his face in his hands. Tears chased one another down the backs of his hands. "He hurt me so badly." Edwin's low, whimpering voice sounded like a little child telling mommy what happened. "Help me, God."

The Mighty Bashnar flinched at the explosions and crouched, simultaneously snatching out his sword and dagger. He circled, looking for the ambush. The warrior angels that must've been hiding in someone's prayers. He was baffled that no one appeared alarmed until they saw him crouching with his weapons. What was wrong with these idiots? Were they all deaf?

He heard the booming sounds again. But this time the explosions sounded like four messages.

One of three choices. Follow the document. Depart. Be destroyed.

The Mighty Bashnar was still crouched.

Instincts. *Assess the situation.*

He looked at everyone looking at him. He thought on the words he had heard and slowly got up. This was most confusing. It didn't make sense.

Edwin was a worm.

There were no angels.

He had authorization.

He pulled the document out of his breast pocket and scanned it hurriedly. *There!* The enemy was interpreting a vague phrase in such a way that the Mighty Bashnar was forced to speak truth to the worm, or defy this stipulation and eat a lightning bolt.

He stuffed the paper into his pocket. "Back away!" he yelled. The demons began meandering away from him and Edwin. "Back away, you fools! God has claims on the worm!"

Demons scurried away, looking toward the sky as though boulders were about to be dropped upon them. The demon on Edwin's neck made like he was going to join the others.

"Sit!" ordered Bashnar. He looked at Edwin. "It seems that they've run out of toilet paper in heaven and could use your services. I don't have much time." He shot a glance toward the sky. "Worm, the demon has returned because you did not draw closer to God once you were delivered." Bashnar looked nervously at the sky again. "You didn't close the door."

Bashnar couldn't believe he was in such a demeaning and awkward position. *He was counseling the worm.* And if the worm corrected himself, much of the Job plan was doomed. "You have only two choices. One, forgive your uncle completely, and believe and obey all of the curs—errr, Bible. Answer the call of God without reservation. Or, two, go your own way." Bashnar looked at the sky and did not take his eyes off of it as he kept talking. He saw something odd. Like a sliding back of blue. "Choose this day, life in the Spirit or life in the flesh," he said hurriedly.

Edwin pulled his hands back from his face. He recoiled at the strong thoughts that had just displaced the images of nudity and perversion. *Forgive my uncle? Forgive that old, perverted bas—?* The thought of forgiving his uncle was so repugnant that the curse word in his mouth was consumed by the flame of hatred in his heart. He would *never* forgive him. Never.

"I will *never* forgive that man," Edwin said.

The Mighty Bashnar's facial muscles struggled to make a smile as he looked in the direction of the God behind the sky. No forgiveness meant no threat. God was absolutely stubborn on this point, and would not forgive anyone who withheld forgiveness from another. So who cared whether the worm found a backbone and tried to walk in the power of God? The Mighty Bashnar had become a legend by destroying powerful, but unsanctified ministers. It was always just a matter of time before their disobedience led them to disaster.

He motioned to the demon with the balls and chains. The spirit of unforgiveness clamped a shackle with its short, thick chain and large, heavy ball onto each of Edwin's legs. The Mighty Bashnar patted Edwin on the shoulder. "You hold on to that bitterness and unforgiveness, Reverend Edwin Worm Styles. This serves me well."

Chapter 12

Sharon placed her phone lightly on the table and sat up on the edge of the sofa. Her knees pressed against one another under her dress. She was worried. Neither Jonathan nor Elizabeth was answering their phone. She had left several messages. This wasn't like them. Something was wrong. *Ava must not be doing well,* she thought.

Sharon looked at Mom and Dad. Mom was humming, happy about something as she prepared dinner. *Must be some dinner. She's starting early.* She thought Mom may have said something to Dad in the morning about him checking on Jonathan.

"Mom," said Sharon, "I haven't been able to reach Jonathan or Elizabeth all day. They're not answering their phones. Have you or Dad heard from them?"

Barbara stopped chopping the vegetables. "Hhmmm. You know, you're right. I think your father called twice and didn't get an answer." She went back to chopping. "Check with your father."

Sharon hesitated. "Mom, Jonathan looked really worried when he got the call. I think it's serious."

Barbara frowned. The tomato was squishy. She needed firm tomatoes. "Oh," she smiled, "it's serious. It's too soft."

"Mom," said Sharon, "I mean Jonathan."

Barbara looked up, smiling. "I'm sorry. I wasn't listening, was I?"

"Mom, Jonathan didn't look like himself when he got the call. He got really tense. He looked like—"

"Calm down, darling," said Barbara. "I get the picture. When it comes to Jonathan—"

"He looked worried, Mom," said Sharon. "You *know* he doesn't worry."

"But *you* do," answered Barbara, sitting down and motioning Sharon to join her. She did. "Now let's not forget who you're worrying about," Barbara reminded. "Have you ever seen anyone do the things this man does? I think Jean's asthma is really gone. It was chronic, you know." An afterthought trailed. "Thirty years of smoking couldn't have helped any."

"Mom, just because a man has a miracle ministry doesn't mean he doesn't need friends. We have to make sure everything's okay," Sharon pressed.

Barbara smiled. "You're right, honey," she gave in. "Your father was going to take a nap, but I think he's in his study. Maybe you and he can go see Jonathan before dinner. If you're going to go, the sooner the better. We're having company."

"You're right." Sharon stood. "Thanks, Mom. I'll talk to Dad." She took a few steps and turned around. "Who's coming?"

"Some people from the church," she answered.

Sharon waited for details. Barbara stuck her head in the refrigerator for what seemed to Sharon a ridiculously long time. Some people? This didn't sound good. *Oh, brother, I hope it's not the Tea Party people?* she thought. There wasn't time to get into it with Mom. "Oh," Sharon said, hesitantly, "okay."

Sharon went to Edwin's home office and knocked on the door. "Dad, are you there?"

Edwin was reading the *Charisma Today* magazine article about him when Sharon knocked on the door. The article's praise was glowing. *Reverend Styles is pastor of one of the fastest growing churches in America...blah, blah, blah...Reverend Styles is leading a spiritual revolution...blah, blah, blah...Reverend Styles is*—"a farce, a fake," Edwin interjected.

His face was on the cover of the magazine. He ripped it off and balled it up and threw it in the waste basket. He ripped out the pages of the article and tossed them too. He was tired of being a fraud. He heard a knock. "Yeah, come in, Sharon."

She did.

"What's up?" He tried to sound normal. He even managed a smile.

"It's Jonathan, Dad," Sharon began.

Edwin had seen a movie years ago named *Man in the Iron Mask*. In the movie, the protagonist had been condemned to wear an iron mask and thrown into prison. For some reason, Edwin thought of this movie when he heard his beloved daughter bring up the name of the man whose goodness and strength and perfection were tormenting him. Edwin was the protagonist and the iron mask he wore was hypocrisy. His prison was his weakness.

He wanted to be free of the suffocating and humiliating mask. He wanted to be free of the prison. But the mask wasn't all bad. It was, after all, made of *iron*. So as harsh and uncomfortable as it was, it protected him. And as debilitating and embarrassing as his prison was, he was like many prisoners. More at home in prison than out of prison.

Prison was hard, but predictable. It required nothing of you, but your dignity. Don't think. Don't take initiative. Don't do anything, but obey the rules. And above all else, don't stand out. Standing out made you vulnerable.

But how much longer could he—he was going to think *live like this?* But he wasn't *living*, he was *existing*. And the deeper they got into this revival thing, he was really only *surviving*. Would he ever be able to take off the mask? Would he ever be freed from his prison? How was one supposed to live on the other side of the wall of weakness? How could a genuinely weak man become genuinely strong?

Sharon looked at her dad's distracted eyes. He was looking directly at her, but she knew he didn't see her. She knew he was in his troubled world. "Dad, you wanna talk about it?" Her voice was soothing, loving.

Edwin often wondered where his teenage daughter got her insight. This was one of those times. She had laser perceptivity. He knew that she knew he was weak, and it killed him. A man should be his daughter's super hero. But there was no such thing as a weak super hero. Yet there was something reassuring about being truly *known* by his daughter. He embarrassed and let her down time after time with his weak ways—her eyes were sad at times like these—but she loved him anyway. Her love was unconditional.

He looked into her eyes. *Your mother's eyes, but God's heart*, he thought, then was quickly ashamed at the implications of that thought. He wasn't trying to say that his wife was heartless. "Jonathan?" he said.

Dad didn't want to talk about it. Whatever *it* was. She hadn't really expected him to. *Okay.* "I'm worried about him. Well, really about Elizabeth and Ava," said Sharon. "They're not answering their phones. I think something's wrong. Remember last time? When Ava was sick? Elizabeth didn't do too well."

"But Jonathan came to the rescue," said Edwin.

Sharon didn't catch her father's bitterness. "Yeah, but something's wrong, Dad. I think we need to go over there."

"Go over where?"

Sharon didn't physically hunch her shoulders, but now that she thought about it, Dad was right. Go where? "The hospital?" she answered weakly.

"Which hospital?" asked Edwin.

"I don't know, Dad. Northside, maybe?"

"Maybe?" said Edwin.

"Or Kennestone," said Sharon. "She could be at Kennestone."

"Or maybe Saint Michael's," said Edwin.

"Saint Michael's?" said Sharon.

"Or one of Emory's, or Piedmont."

"Emory or Piedmont?" said Sharon rhetorically.

"Maybe even Grady," said Edwin.

Sharon frowned. "Grady Hospital? That's downtown Atlanta. And I'm sure she has insurance, Dad."

"She may have been near Grady when the emergency occurred." Edwin continued without any apparent emotion, energy, or interest. "I'm sure she does have insurance. Jonathan would see to that, wouldn't he? I hear Grady has a great trauma department."

"So are we going to Grady?" Sharon asked.

Edwin looked into the eyes of the one person who loved him the most, and the one person who constantly paid the price for doing something so stupid. He didn't know why, but her question caught him flatfooted, like a boxer's punch that should have caused little damage, but instead had knocked him on his back.

Sharon looked at her dad and listened to his inexplicable silence in disbelief. "You don't want to go."

Edwin was still groggy from the phantom punch. He dropped his eyes and looked at the bottom of a bookshelf.

Sharon slowly shook her head. "I love you, Dad, but sometimes..."

Edwin closed his eyes and held back the tears. *I know,* he thought. *I don't know what's wrong with me, Sharon.*

Sharon struggled with her thoughts. She didn't want to hurt Dad, but the pressure in her chest had to be relieved. And the only way to do that was to say something. "Sometimes..." she was going to say it.

An angel of mercy whispered into Sharon's ear. *Love is patient. Who are you to judge another's servant? God is able to make him stand.*

The Scriptures that bubbled up inside of Sharon made the pressure in her chest lessen. It didn't go away altogether—she was angry and disappointed—but it lost its power to push her to say something she would later regret.

"Dad, you are my dad and I love you. No one can take your place. But Jonathan has done a lot for you, for this family," she continued. "God sent him here to help us, and he has. He'd give his life for you. I don't know what's going on—I know something's bothering you—but this isn't right. We can't wait until everything is going right in our life before we help someone. We'd never help anyone if we did that." Sharon took a deliberate breath and let it exit slowly, letting the rising calmness of her spirit overcome the agitation of her emotions. "Dad."

Edwin continued looking at his Matthew Henry commentary set on the bottom shelf.

"Dad, please look at me," asked Sharon.

Edwin looked up and focused on her nose. He found it difficult to look her in the eyes. However, the little demon that sat on Edwin's neck found it impossible to not look directly into her eyes. There was something strange about them.

"I'm going to find Jonathan and Elizabeth. I need the keys," she said softly.

He pulled them out and handed them to her with his head hanging. "I'm sorry, Sharon."

She let out a troubled breath. "I know you are, Dad. I'll be back in time for the dinner meeting. I won't let you face that bunch alone," she tried to joke. "I love you."

Edwin sat in the solitude of his office for several minutes trying to shake the thoughts from his mind. He knew it didn't make sense. He should be focusing on his daughter saying she loved him. Instead all he could hear was her saying, "Dad, you're my Dad, but Jonathan."

But Jonathan!

Sometimes it seemed as though there were demons all around him. Feeding him thoughts the way babies were fed food. He wouldn't be surprised if there was one sitting on his neck. Isn't that what Jonathan had said a year ago before he had freed him from that spirit of torment? And now he was tormented again. *Guess I should've purchased the extended warranty.*

Edwin shook his head. *I don't understand all of this deliverance and healing and prophecy and revival stuff. I'm about sick of it.*

The demon on his neck dangled his legs playfully as he massaged Edwin's head. "That makes two of us," he said. "I'm about sick of it myself."

Chapter 13

Sharon tossed the tablet onto the passenger seat, got into the car, and closed the door. She began making phone calls.

Seduction looked at his comrades, Compromise, Lust, and Fornication, with a sly grin. He knew that his friend, Compromise, knew what he was going to say before he said it. "Time to catch a couple of little fisheys, gentlemen." He was feeling good and his tone said so. "Our little thorn here should be getting a call right about...." He lifted his hand. Sharon ended her call. "Now," he said, dropping his hand.

Seduction and Compromise smiled at one another and looked at the others.

"Rob, hey, how are you?" said Sharon.

"Didn't know she could grin that widely," said Lust.

"She'll do more than grin when I get a hold of her," said Fornication.

"They always do," snickered Lust.

"Listen and learn, my friends," said Seduction, with a comfort level normally not seen among demon teams who spent as much time conspiring against and fighting among themselves as against the people they were trying to destroy. "Fornication among committed Christians doesn't just happen. We have to build a context. Give them the right atmosphere. We have to build trust. We have to build a comfort level and familiarity among the victims that will help them take liberties with one another."

Lust and Fornication got fidgety at this.

Compromise and Seduction laughed, and Compromise spoke up. "Calm down my friends. That will come soon enough. First, comes the friendship."

"Then the need," said Seduction.

"The need," said Lust and Fornication, nodding their heads.

"Not that need," said Seduction. "The need that leads to the need."

Compromise looked at Seduction with admiration. "That's good."

"Yes, it is, isn't it?" answered Seduction. "Thank you, my friend." He looked at Lust and Fornication with devious, red eyes. "The first need is emotion." Seduction stuck his long finger in his mouth and sucked as he thought. He slowly pulled it out, as though he were savoring the last taste of something delicious. "Sharon is passionate about the enemy. She will only commit fornication with someone who is passionate about God."

"Yeesssss," said Fornication, with a long s-sound. "I've seen this oddity over and over again." He looked at Sharon, smiled appreciatively, and turned his smile to the others. "Lovers of Christ one moment. Lovers of flesh the next." He snapped his fingers. "In a *moment*."

"We're after that moment," said Seduction.

"But that moment will only come with the right context," said Compromise. "Rob has to fill Sharon's emotional needs before we can get them into bed."

Fornication spoke up. "But this Sharon's emotional needs are so wrapped up in the Christ that—" He stopped. His narrow face brightened, as much as it could. He laughed inside. Then he laughed outside.

"You see it, my friend," said Lust.

"I most certainly do," Fornication answered with resolve. "It is in their own cursed book. '*But each one is tempted when he is drawn away by his own desires and enticed. Then, when desire has conceived, it gives birth to sin.'* Her own desires."

"Exactly," snapped Compromise. "They don't have to be evil desires. Impure desires. Rebellious desires. Just so long as they are *her* desires."

"Yes! Yes! Yes!" Lust screeched, with his hand over his mouth, as though trying to keep a secret that might attract a gold rush of demonic competition. "It's the little things! The little things!"

"Even the largest, thickest door is unsecured if no one locks it," added Lust.

"It's why the cursed book says, 'If you hearken diligently...if you listen carefully.'" Compromise added, "We just need to get our girl off track a little. If we play our cards right and stay patient, we can maneuver her and her mysterious boyfriend into that moment."

"What about him?" asked Lust. "There are gaps in the report. Actually, there's not much said about him at all. Who is he really? What's his background? What kind of prayer cover does he have? What are his weaknesses? How do we—"

Fornication held up his hand and Lust stopped talking. "It doesn't matter. Who was King David?"

Every demon smiled.

"Sharon is a beautiful girl, and unless this young man is blind or his parts don't work..." said Fornication confidently.

"He's not blind," said Seduction.

"And I'll find out if his parts work," said Lust, with an evil chuckle.

"Good," said Fornication. "Then shortly he'll be using his parts for us."

Sharon was giddy. "You will?" she asked Rob. "But what about the game?"

"You're more important than a game," Rob answered. "I want to be there for you. I'll meet you."

"Oh, thank you, Rob," said Sharon. "I need someone right now."

Fornication looked at his friends. "She has *needs*. Let's satisfy them."

*****

Controllus stuck his finger into Elizabeth's eye. It nearly shocked him that he had been able to do so. It was most unusual to have this kind of access to Christians who didn't dabble in some kind of witchcraft. *Hhmmm,* he thought, *is there something about you my dear that I don't know? Horoscopes? Psychics? Ouija Board? Oh well, we don't need details just yet. We'll be getting much more acquainted with another in the days ahead.*

Elizabeth sat with her elbows on the table and her face in her hands. She was tired. So very tired. Her eyes were closed, but this didn't stop the burning, especially her right eye. It felt as though something was in it. She squinted several times, trying to coax the offending object from her eye.

"Excuse me," someone standing over her said. "May I sit here?"

Elizabeth looked through squinted, blinking eyes, one of which was watering and starting to burn to the point of being painful. An attractive white female with fabulous hair, maybe forty years old, stood over her. She was carrying a sleeping baby. "Yes...yes, of course."

The lady sat. "You have something in your eye."

Elizabeth smiled bravely, still squinting, and rubbing her eye, which had suddenly begun to throb with a growing pain. "Yeah, I think—well, I haven't gotten much sleep. But it does feel like something is in it."

"Let me see," offered the lady. She looked into Elizabeth's eye. "My goodness, have you gotten *any* sleep? Your eye is almost all red. I don't think I've looked that bad on my worst drinking binges."

Elizabeth's brave face left. The pain was now horrible.

"Would you like for me to pray for you," asked the lady. "I'm a healer."

Controllus's eyes widened in anticipation of the Christ-lover's answer. *Oh, taste and see that the darkness is good,* he said to himself.

"You believe in God?" Elizabeth asked through the pain. The pain had spread to the whole right side of her face. She pressed her hand hard against her face and grimaced.

"Of course," answered the lady, "how else would I heal you?" The lady's answer was polite and sympathetic.

A thought so faint it was nearly impossible to hear echoed from a mile deep in Elizabeth's heart. *For such are false apostles, deceitful workers, transforming themselves into apostles of Christ.* Elizabeth felt a chill descend on her soul.

The lady sensed Elizabeth's hesitance. "You don't believe in prayer? You don't believe in miracles?"

"You're a Christian?" asked Elizabeth.

The lady smiled widely. "What would I do without the Christ spirit? It is everything to me," she answered passionately.

Elizabeth felt something was wrong.

The lady smiled and rubbed Elizabeth's arm. "Oh, you poor thing. You don't believe in God's power. You should. I've seen many wonderful healings. Once I laid hands on a woman—"

"You lay hands on the sick?" asked Elizabeth.

Controllus flailed his arms. "Get on with it! Get on with it! This isn't a job interview!"

"What is wrong with her?" asked one of the demons with Controllus.

Controllus sneered at her. He gritted his teeth and pointed at her, then waved his hand in disgust. "Some of them are like this," he spat. "They're always testing, testing, testing. Probing, probing, probing. Comparing everything they hear with that blasted book. You can hardly get this kind of Christ-lover to do anything. I *hate* this kind of Christian."

"Is she or isn't she going to take the bait?" the impatient demon demanded. "We don't have all day. The enemy could return any moment."

The witchcraft spirit looked at Elizabeth with all the scorn his ugly face could carry. "It depends," he said with a heavy voice.

"On what?" demanded the leader of the six council demons.

Controllus found a way to put more scorn on his face. "On whether or not she ignores that irritating, still, small voice I know is there telling her something is wrong."

"Yes," answered the lady. "That's how I heal the sick—laying on of hands. I received my anointing through laying on of hands. Laying on of hands is in the Bible."

Laying on of hands. Christian. Christ. The Bible. Why did Elizabeth still feel that something wasn't right? *I'm just being silly,* she thought. *What harm could it do to let a Christian pray for me?* "I'm sorry, I just, well you can't be too careful."

"Of course," the lady heartily agreed, wasting no time in laying her hand on the side of Elizabeth's face. "Not all energy is good. There's bad energy, too."

Energy? thought Elizabeth. *Energy? What is this lady talking about?* Then it clicked. *Christ spirit.* But it was too late.

"Receive the energy of the life force," said the Reiki healer. "Be healed."

Elizabeth was incensed. She opened her eyes. "What do you think you're doing?" she demanded. "I would not have let you lay hands on me if—" She stopped. She put her hand to her face and was dumbfounded.

The lady was beaming. "You're healed, aren't you?"

Elizabeth shook her head to test the supposed healing. There was absolutely no pain. This lady had healed her. "How did you do that?"

"You were here," the lady answered with a smile. "I'm a Reiki healer. I did it by laying my hands on your face and releasing the life force of God. Your energy was low."

"Reiki? The life force?" snapped Elizabeth. "Low energy?" she said, wiping her face to get the occult mess off. "The *only* energy I have is the energy of the Holy Spirit, and it never runs low."

"Oh, my God, I'm so sorry," the lady apologized. "I shouldn't have imposed on you like this. I was just trying to help." She started to get up.

"Wait," said Elizabeth. She didn't mean to be mean to the lady. After all, the lady was only trying to help her. And she had given the lady permission to pray for her.

Controllus turned and looked at Prince Krioni's six demons in triumph.

"What are you so happy about?" asked one. "She knows what you're doing. She knows that it's witchcraft. She has rejected you."

Witchcraft looked at the six muscle-bound idiots. This was the reason they could only dream about having the access to Satan that witchcraft spirits enjoyed. "It doesn't work that way," Controllus answered smugly. "It doesn't make a difference how much she resents the draft. The door is open."

*****

Compromise, Seduction, and Fornication followed Sharon's car from a distance. Lust trailed closely behind them. Sure, they were authorized closer access to the girl. Bashnar had worked out a deal. But what did that mean, really? That they wouldn't be attacked? They were sure there was nothing in that piece of paper that said the thorn couldn't fight back.

There didn't appear to be any angels around. But that was part of the problem. There didn't *appear* to be angels around. That didn't mean they weren't around. For all they knew, there could be warrior angels lurking in the girl's prayers. Better safe than sorry. They would move in closer only when the thorn and her righteous boyfriend gave them permission with their thoughts or behavior.

"Wait a *minute*," Seduction exclaimed. "This is the dagger's house."

"So that's why everybody's scurrying around like they're about to be attacked." This was Compromise.

"But we have a piece of paper to protect us, don't we?" jeered Seduction.

"Let's hope we don't run into any angels who can't read," said Fornication, his words fully expressing how much he disliked working under such conditions.

Sharon rang the doorbell. She and Rob waited several minutes as Sharon intermittently rang the bell as they waited. Sharon let out a discouraged breath. "We've checked everywhere."

"We'll find them, Sharon," said Rob.

"I hope so," she answered. She looked out onto the street. From their elevation, they could see over a large portion of the neighborhood. Things were quiet. Peaceful. Perfect lawns. It almost looked like a movie set. "Rob!" Sharon turned and took him by the hand. "Come on."

He followed her to the garage. She looked in. "There he is," she squealed. "He's in there. Jonathan's in there."

Rob cupped his hands to the garage and looked into the dark. He didn't see anyone. "I don't see him."

"Look in the corner," she said. "He's under that blanket."

Rob pulled back from the window. "Under the blanket?" He put his face back to the window. Yep, the blanket moved.

Sharon knocked on the window.

Jonathan stopped praying and opened his eyes under the blanket.

Sharon knocked again and the blanket came off. She waved.

Jonathan looked at the garage door window and waited for his eyes to adjust. Two people were looking in his garage. One of them was Sharon. He opened the door.

Sharon could hardly wait for it to lift before she was hugging him. "Oh, Jonathan, we've been everywhere looking for you and Elizabeth and Ava."

Jonathan smiled over her shoulder at the young man who was with her. "Well, you've found me. Let's go into the house so we can talk. Who might this be?"

"This might be Rob, Jonathan," said Sharon.

"Hello, Rob," said Jonathan.

They went into the house and Sharon led Rob and Jonathan into the living room. "Jonathan, do you want something to drink?"

"No."

"You, Rob? What do you have, Jonathan?" asked Sharon.

"No, I'm good," Rob answered, smiling. "Make yourself at home, Sharon," he joked.

"I will and I have," she answered her boyfriend playfully. "We're family. Right Jonathan?"

"That's right, Sharon," he answered. "Family forever." He looked at them both with a light smile. It looked like a *polite* smile to Sharon.

"I'm sorry we disturbed your prayers," she said.

"Ava's dying and I have to save her," he said.

"Ava's dying?" Sharon was shaken. Her mouth dropped open. She looked at Jonathan. "Oh, I'm so sorry. What's wrong?"

"She had an aneurysm in her brain. She's having complications. Me and Liz prayed for her throughout the night. Liz is not taking it well." Jonathan stood up. "Anyway, that's why I was in the garage praying."

Sharon and Rob stood.

"I'm sorry," said Jonathan. "I don't mean to be rude, but every moment is critical."

"Oh, yeah. Yeah. Of course, Jonathan. I understand," said Sharon. She started walking toward the door.

"Sharon, can I talk to you for a minute before you leave," asked Jonathan.

"Yeah. Sure. Rob—"

"I'll wait in the car," said Rob. He stretched forth his hand to Jonathan. "Nice to meet you, sir."

They shook hands. Rob pulled his hand away, but Jonathan held it and looked deeply into the young man. "Nice to meet you, too, Rob. Be strong in the late hours. You can move any mountain out of your life that you don't enjoy. Go with God."

Rob looked at Jonathan with a smile and a question mark. He lowered his hand and furtively shared a look with Sharon on the way out.

Jonathan and Sharon watched Rob until he closed the door behind him. "The trance," said Jonathan.

"Did you talk to Mom or Dad?" she asked.

"Haven't spoken to either of them since I left the party last night," he answered.

"Then how did you—?" She smiled knowingly, but disbelievingly. "God told you about my trance?"

"Yes," he answered. "And he told me about the prophetic anointing you received in the trance."

Chapter 14

Sharon and Rob sat in the car in one of the parking lots of *Perimeter Mall*, where she had picked him up to help her look for Elizabeth and Jonathan. The mall appeared to be as crowded with people as Sharon's mind was crowded with one big thought. Rob hadn't said one word since they had left Jonathan's, and she couldn't tell, but his hands appeared to be trembling. He seemed to be deep in thought.

"Rob," she said, "when Jonathan said, 'Be strong in the late hours,' what did he mean? And what did he mean about moving mountains you don't enjoy?"

Rob shrugged his shoulders and opened his hands, shaking his head. "I don't know. I was wondering what that was about, too. You know him; I don't. Does he always talk like that?"

"Like what?" asked Sharon.

"I mean, like...in riddles. 'Be strong in the late hours.' What does that mean?" Rob asked.

"You don't have *any* idea what he could be referring to?" asked Sharon.

Rob didn't say anything. He just shook his head and said with his eyes that he didn't know.

The spirits in Rob trembled at Sharon's question. First, that man at the house with the glowing eyes peering at them. Now this interrogation. They moved deeper into the darkness of their home.

"He's a prophet, Rob," said Sharon. "He can be weird sometimes."

"Yeah," he agreed, "that was out there."

Without thinking, Sharon rested her hand lightly on Rob's thigh.

The fornication team of spirits fidgeted with excitement, especially Fornication himself.

"But he's godly weird," said Sharon. "Like Jesus was weird." Rob gave her a puzzled look. "You know, talking to trees. Talking to dead people. At funerals," she answered his eyes. "Putting spit in people's eyes to heal them. Weird stuff like that."

"Okay," said Rob questioningly.

"What I'm getting at, Rob, is he must've sensed or saw something or he wouldn't have said something like that."

"Don't move an inch," ordered the head demon in Rob. "Don't say one word." He knew where this discussion could lead.

"Something like what?" said Rob.

"I don't know," answered Sharon. "Are you battling anything? You can tell me if you are. The Bible says that we should confess our faults one to another that we may be healed."

"You mean am I being tempted by something?" he asked. "Yeah, I guess. Aren't we all?"

One of the demons in Rob said in a panic, "We have to do something!"

"No!" snapped the head demon. "He's not going to tell. He's covering. He's going to play off his bondage as a regular sin. Just wait," he ordered, with a frown that said his order better be obeyed.

"I mean I have the same struggles as everybody else," said Rob.

"Any particular struggle?" Sharon asked. "Any sin or habit that you can't get rid of no matter how hard you try or how hard you pray? That's something that Jonathan asks people all the time whenever he speaks at our church. It's a sign they may need deliverance from demons."

"He asks them that?" said Rob. "Wow...that's...bold. That could be embarrassing."

"It's more than bold, Rob," said Sharon. "It's truth. It's the truth that sets us free. I'd rather be embarrassed publicly now than to be embarrassed publicly on Judgment Day. We shouldn't let our pride keep us from freedom."

Rob looked intently into Sharon's eyes. His face needed no help to be attractive, but his half-smile and the curly black lock that hung over his right eye piled it on. He placed his hand atop her hand that was on his thigh and wrapped his fingers around hers. "I'm okay, really. I'd tell you if I needed help. I'll remember what your friend said just in case. Okay?"

Sharon broke out into a wide smile. "Promise?"

"Promise," he said.

The fornication team watched Rob and Sharon hug before he got out of the car.

Lust spoke up first. "I—like—Rob."

"So—do—I," said Fornication.

"He lies effortlessly," said Seduction admiringly.

"I don't know," added Compromise. "For a moment it looked like he was going to tell the truth."

Lust laughed a couple of sticky droplets onto the ground. "Be at ease, my friend. Righteous Rob doesn't know what the truth is. He's conflicted. Part of him fears he's a slave." Lust looked Compromise in his eyes. "Part of him believes he's free."

"True enough," said Seduction. "But he *did* lie about the extent of his struggle." Seduction appreciated a good lie, and a good liar even more.

"Most Christians in bondage do lie about their struggles," said Lust.

*****

Sharon waited for the garage door to close behind her. She dropped her hands from the steering wheel and leaned her head back with her eyes closed. She hoped Rob was telling the truth. He probably was. He was a good guy and he loved God. She had met him at one of their church conferences. She tried to remember which one. *Oh, yeah, the Holy Spirit and Supernatural Ministry* conference. Plus, his dad was pastor of Grace Community Church. And his family and church were heavily involved in fighting sex trafficking. His two sisters were awesome.

Sharon reminded herself of the Scripture. *Love thinks no evil. Love believes all things.* "Lord, I'm not going to lay a judgment on Rob. It's just that I know Jonathan would not have said that unless something was wrong."

A thought entered Sharon's mind that made her heart glad. "Or Lord, if you were *warning* him of something. He doesn't actually have to be doing something wrong now. You could've been warning him about the future. I don't know, Lord. Whatever's going on, I ask that you help Rob. If he's battling a secret sin, I ask you to help him confess his faults. If the devil's planning something, I ask you to expose the enemy and help Rob say no to the devil's temptations. In Jesus's name. I love you, Lord. Amen. Oh, Lord, if my feelings for Rob are drowning out your voice or blinding me to your leadings, I ask you to overrule my mistakes. I ask you to protect me beyond my knowledge. Please be strong where I am weak."

Sharon's prayer made her feel light. She smiled and opened her eyes and immediately felt the heaviness of that night's upcoming dinner. Her mom had invited some people over. And for some reason, Sharon had a bad feeling that it would be those people from the night before, or some version of those people. "Lord, help my dad to not let those people run over him."

She entered the house. Mom was still in the kitchen. Still humming. *How does she do it?* "Mom, you *luuuuuuuv* cooking."

Barbara spun around with a large, fresh smile and eyes full of energy. "I do love cooking, Sharon." She walked toward her with a bounce. "And I especially *love* cooking for my wonderful son, my wonderful husband," Barbara kissed Sharon on the forehead, "and my wonderful daughter."

Sharon grinned. "I think I'd love it if I were any good at it."

Barbara puckered. "Oh, you're getting better."

Sharon's grin remained. "Better than what, Mom?"

Barbara stumbled for words.

Sharon slowly nodded her head backward, then deeply forward. "Exactly."

"Oh, honey, don't be hard on yourself," said Barbara. "It takes time."

"I'm running out of time, Mom," said Sharon. "I need to know how to cook before I get married. I need to know how to cook *if* I am to get married."

"What is all of this talk about getting married?" asked Barbara. "We are speaking rhetorically here, aren't we?"

Sharon dropped her head to the side. "Yes, we're speaking rhetorically, Mom. You'll be the first to know when I'm to get married."

"Well," Barbara's smile returned, "now that we've settled that. Did you find Jonathan and Elizabeth? Did you see Ava?"

"We found Jonathan," she answered. "He was at home. But we didn't find Ava. We called everywhere, and everyone said they didn't have an Ava Santos. The odd thing is she's at Northside, and Northside is the first place I called."

"How's Elizabeth's mom?" asked Barbara.

"She's dying."

"Dying?" asked Barbara incredulously. "How could she be dying? Didn't Jonathan pray for her?"

Sharon didn't want to sound condescending. "Mom, it doesn't work like that."

Barbara stood more erect. "We see it work like that every week. Every time that man has a healing service at our church, we see it work like that."

"But Mom a lot of those people don't get healed the first time they're prayed for," said Sharon. "And some of them have been prayed for several times and they're still ill. What about Ms. Lyons? She's still sick. And she's been prayed for by everybody."

"Maybe it's her faith," said Barbara.

"Mom, you sound like your sister, Jessica," said Sharon. "Healing's not a formula."

At the sound of her sister's name, and especially at hearing her daughter compare her to her insane sister, she evicted her smile. "How could you compare me to Jessica?"

Sharon knew she had made a big mistake. "Mom, that's not what I mean."

Barbara jabbed her finger at Sharon. "That woman humiliated us and dishonored our son. How could she do something like that?"

Sharon felt as though she had been driving in a huge parking lot with no other cars there, but the one she was driving, and yet she had found a way to run into a pole. How could she have made such a dumb mistake? She knew how crazy Mom and Dad got when Jessica's name was mentioned. "Mom, I take back what I said about you being like Jessica. I was just trying to make a point and I messed it up. Okay, Mom? Can we forget I said it?"

"Sharon, I am not my sister," said Barbara. "My sister attended our three-year-old son's funeral and pulled his body out of the casket in front of everyone and tried to raise him from the dead. Does that sound like something I would do?"

"No, Mom, it doesn't," Sharon answered humbly.

"My sister dropped my son's dead body on the floor," said Barbara, her voice trembling and threatening to fail. "Does that sound like something I would do?"

Sharon's eyes were watery. "No, Mom, you wouldn't do that?"

"Then don't ever compare me to that woman again. Okay, Sharon?" said Barbara.

"Okay, Mom. I'll never make that mistake again." Sharon wiped a tear from her own cheek. She hugged her mom. "I'm sorry, Mom. I'm really sorry. I didn't mean to ruin the evening for you." She let go of her mom and stepped back. "I'm going to go to my room."

Barbara spoke softly, sniffling. "Ok, Sharon."

Sharon started walking away.

"Sharon," said Barbara.

Sharon turned.

"I'm sorry," said Barbara. "I overreacted."

Sharon rushed to her mom and hugged her tightly. "It's okay, Mom. I should've been more sensitive."

Barbara broke. Her shoulders heaved up and down as pent-up, bitter emotions rushed from her eyes and throat. "I miss him, Sharon. I miss my Christopher. He was only three."

Sharon pulled her mother into her bosom and tried to absorb the pain. Maybe if she held her tighter, some of her pain would go away. "It's okay, Mom. Chris is with the Lord. We're going to see him again." Sharon stroked her mother's head and hair as she comforted her. She missed Chris, too. But there was no one to hold her and help her through the pain.

So she leaned totally on the Lord.

*****

Sharon was lying on her bed thinking. In an odd way, she felt exhausted and energized. So much had happened in just one year. She had always known in her heart that the Bible wasn't supposed to be read like a history book. It was God's word. It was His instructions on how people were to live. Once she had seen the truth, she had no problem obeying what God had said about holiness and morality. (Well, except for her brief, but disastrous period of backsliding with her girlfriend, Toni.) That was the least she could do for her wonderful savior.

It was the other stuff in the Bible that had given her problems. The stuff about miracles and prayer and demons. And the promises! Why would God say stuff like, 'Truly, truly, I say unto you, he who believes on me shall do the works that I do, and greater works than these shall he do'? Why would He say, 'All things are possible to him who believes,' if He didn't mean it? Why would He tell the church to heal the sick, cast out demons, and work miracles if they weren't supposed to do those kinds of things? That kind of thinking never made sense to her.

Then came Jonathan. Strange Jonathan. Sharon smiled without knowing she was smiling. She would absolutely never forget anything about that night Jonathan first spoke at their church. The power. The revelation. It was as though—it was as though God was actually alive. Like He had stepped off of the pages of the Bible. And Jonathan. Jonathan was like someone from the book of Acts—like the apostles. She had seen so much in such a short period of time. That was the reason for the enthusiasm. She knew there would be more.

But she was as exhausted as she was excited, and she didn't really know why. All she knew was that she felt heavy inside. It was hard for her to process how she felt. She remembered the first time Jonathan took her for a ride in his friend's airplane.

Pure exhilaration. Sitting in one of the two front seats. Only inches separating her from the controls and the huge Garmin 1000 GPS. It was a feeling she had never felt before. Like she could go anywhere and could see anything. And that's where the exhilaration and strange heaviness she had been feeling strangely merged.

The higher Jonathan had taken her in his friend's *Mirage*, the more she could see. And the more she saw, the more she wanted to see, and the lighter she felt. Similarly, the higher he took her into God's power and revelation, the more she saw. And the more she saw, the more she wanted to see. But the strange thing was, the more she saw, the heavier she felt. Wasn't this odd? Shouldn't she feel better at this higher spiritual altitude?

The Holy Spirit inside of Sharon continued to speak to her.

Then the light shone in the darkness. She felt something happen to her heart. It was like the flower of her spirit was being fed some kind of *Miracle-Gro™* for revelation. She literally felt herself grow the more she thought on this mystery.

She saw it now. The higher the altitude, the better the sight. And that's where the heaviness came in. There was so much misery, pain, and suffering in the world. So many sick and desperate and grief-stricken people, and many of them children of God. And yet they suffered. And often it appeared that they suffered with the same randomness, severity, and sudden brutality as those who didn't serve God.

Sharon thought of the many people whom she had seen healed at their church. Since Jonathan had begun helping Dad, there wasn't a service where there weren't several people claiming to have been healed. And many of the healings were so spectacular they could only be defined as miracles. That's why the media were always around, obviously or secretly. Some radio guy, or journalist, or news person cornering one of them for an interview. Even out-of-state, and more recently, out-of-country preachers were visiting the church to see how to start their own revivals.

The Holy Spirit blew in and on Sharon.

The angels and demons present in the room all saw the wind. The wind appeared to blow from her and upon her. It was impossible to tell exactly the direction of the mysterious wind or its origin or destination. It was simply *there*.

Sharon was certain she felt a breeze. Strangely, though, the breeze wasn't simply touching her skin—and there was nowhere a breeze could come from!—it was blowing *inside* of her. She didn't know how, but she could even feel it in her bones. Whatever this wind was, it was soothing and beautiful and infinite.

An image interrupted Sharon's beautiful moment. It was of a little girl in a wheelchair who had been rolled up to the altar for prayer. It had happened only a week ago, so the memory was fresh. The little girl had muscular dystrophy. Sharon recoiled at how horribly twisted the little girl was. But as shockingly horrible as that little girl's condition was, the more horrible thing was that she wasn't healed. Her parents had driven from Dallas, Texas to get their little girl healed because they had heard that Jesus was healing people in Atlanta.

Sharon looked at the memory as though she were watching a murder. Why wasn't this little girl healed? How could God let that poor family drive so far to have their hearts broken? And how many times had those parents driven to other places trying to find someone who could help their daughter?

Another memory shoved Sharon against the wall. The very next person to be prayed for in that prayer line was an old woman with crippling arthritis. She was healed. What sense did that make? A little crippled girl, who is facing an entire life of sitting in a wheelchair with twisted and dangling limbs, is prayed for and not healed. But an old woman with arthritis, who has lived nearly her entire life, is prayed for and healed. That little girl needed to be healed more than the old woman. Why would God do this?

Sharon continued to look down from the soaring heights into the troubled valley below. It hurt to do so, but she wouldn't turn away. The truth was there were far more people who were not healed than were healed. She and her parents and others left each meeting excitedly talking about the miracles and healings, conveniently not mentioning those who had not received. But then she remembered something.

Jonathan often looked and acted sad after each meeting. He'd always try to play it off with his jokes and stuff, but now she understood. And now she knew why she had seen him crying alone so bitterly in prayer sometimes after those meetings. He felt what she felt. *He was heavy, too.*

Sharon's tender heart ripped inside of her. The tear was heard throughout heaven.

Chapter 15

The attacks were to be devastating. The equivalent of tactical nuclear weapons. Small bombs that obliterated everything in their unbelievably wide range, leaving nothing but the rubble of Jonathan's, Sharon's, and Edwin's faith, and the smoldering ruins of this embarrassing revival. It had made a mockery of him long enough.

Nothing could be left to chance.

The Mighty Bashnar looked out across the vast auditorium of demons. He had commanded the attendance not only of high-ranking spirits in the region, but even of second- and third-tier demons. There would be no miscommunications.

He fixed his attention on the demons on the front couple of rows. He knew the politics involved in getting front row seats. He knew the ravenous ambition of these demons. In this sense, he was like them. He was driven by it like a train without brakes. He couldn't stop himself, and he had not yet run into the wall that could stop him. Grand achievement was his fate. His manifest destiny.

He wondered as he looked at the front row faces. Some he recognized. Some he didn't. *Which of you are truly worthy of this honor? And which of you are seated so closely before me because of your gift of sucking up?* He admitted to himself that the sons of Adam did have useful terminology.

"I *know* that each of you have carefully read the *Job Strategy* document." Characteristic Bashnar. No niceties. Start the meeting with intimidation. "The plan is basic. Destruction 101. Set-up and execution. The principal targets are Jonathan, Sharon, and Edwin. In that order. Here is how we will destroy them. First, Jonathan is everything. We destroy him and the revival is over."

The Mighty Bashnar anticipated there would be murmuring at the mention of the dagger's name, but it irritated him, nonetheless. "How do we destroy such a man? you are asking yourselves. Section One discusses the separation phase. This has already begun with great progress. The worm is eaten up with envy of Jonathan. We must sever this relationship permanently. That will leave the worm alone."

The Mighty Bashnar knew what they were thinking, but were too afraid to ask. "If Plan A were to fail, then we would commence Plan B. You have read Plan B. Sharon owns his heart. At the appropriate time, we'll use her to get rid of him once and for all." Bashnar sneered and cleared his nostrils of dark mucous with a strong huff of air. "We'll let love put the blade in his Christ-loving heart. 'Love never fails,'" he said, mocking the cursed book.

"What is the timeline?" someone in the darkness of the middle of the room asked.

"Who said that?" asked the Mighty Bashnar.

No one answered.

"Who said that?" he ordered.

Still no answer.

He knew he wouldn't get an answer. The malcontent was hiding in the darkness. He'd only make a fool of himself giving orders no one would obey. "Soon," he answered gruffly. "Sharon's set-up is progressing perfectly. She will destroy herself and Jonathan." Bashnar turned back toward the first pages of the *Job Strategy.* "Set-up is critical. Tonight our people will have their second meeting with the worm. With Barbara's help, we'll divide the church into factions. We'll get the church's focus off of the supernatural. These signs, miracles, and wonders have been drawing too much attention to the risen

Christ. We have to put him back into the grave, and we can only do that if the church forgets his power. The dagger will not be there, so our only opposition will come from Sharon."

The Mighty Bashnar folded his hands behind his back and stepped in front of the lectern and paced the edge of the stage. He looked at the floor as he spoke. "Would anyone care to ask why we're expecting the worm's wife to help us?"

No answer.

"Hmmm. The spirit of curiosity has left the room," he said. "The worm's wife will help us for two reasons. One, the worm has a demon on his neck that is offensive to his wife's lust for sex. The woman is too hot for her own good. Two, she will work for us for the same reason other so-called Christ-lovers work for us. She's pregnant with our seed. We expect her to give birth tonight during dinner with our people."

*****

Sharon looked at the people to the left and right and those across the table. She looked at Dad. This was worse than she had imagined it would be. Not only had Mom invited the politicians and the self-appointed immigration sheriff, she had invited a lady who wanted Dad to get rid of poverty, political corruption, police brutality, and sex trafficking. She had also invited a guy who felt it was Dad's responsibility to fix all the wrongs that were done to the Native Americans.

Sharon sipped her water and reminded herself to not embarrass her father. "So, Mr. Henry, how would that look?" she asked.

Edwin and Barbara looked at their daughter. Sharon saw them look at her from the corner of her eye. She knew that the more she spoke, the more nervous they were getting.

Mr. Henry was all of five-feet and two inches, but his dreams were ten-feet tall. He was slim, but not skinny. His chin was long and had a cleft. The mustache over his lip helped to cover a set of big teeth. He dabbed his mouth with a cloth napkin. "How would it look?" he repeated Sharon's words as though he had been asked this a thousand times.

The Republican side of the table appeared to ready themselves to hear Mr. Henry present his proof that the world was flat. Danny Green, the founder of Georgia Citizens for Legal Immigration was wearing his badge with the big red X over the words *Illegal Immigration*. He rubbed it with a smug smile. Senators Sheila Wilcox appeared as amused, but less smug than the immigration sheriff. Senator Abbey Lockhart looked as though she were on a televised debate. Controlled cynicism was the word for her.

They listened to Mr. Henry.

Then they listened to Amanda Billory talk about the horrors of sex trafficking and give impassioned pleas for social justice. The Republican side of the table initially responded to the woman like they were kings behind impregnable walls of a castle and she were pounding on them with her fist. But there was something about the lady's eloquence, energy, and formidable education that wore them down and caused them to start pouring hot tar on her from the top of the castle walls.

Sharon knew that Dad couldn't do everything. They had to stay focused on the revival. But she was captivated by the lady's pleas for victims of sex traffickers. Her stories of the girls gripped Sharon's heart. It reminded her of Jonathan's wife. Plus, Jonathan had helped this lady rescue some girls.

"Have you ever personally been the victim of a crime, Ms. Billory?" asked Senator Lockhart.

"It's Mrs. Billory," the lady with the lethal tongue answered with a polished smile. "But you may call me Amanda. And, yes, I've tasted crime. Violent crime. Unfortunately, more than once. Compliments of helping to shut down *The Mansion*."

"And did you call the police to help you get that taste out of your mouth?" asked the senator.

"I called on the Lord to get the taste out of my mouth. I called on the police to report the crime," the lady answered.

Sharon was impressed with three things. First, that Mrs. Billory had called on the Lord when she was in trouble. And, second, that she was so passionate about helping people who couldn't help themselves. And, third, that she could debate these people with such love. She sounded the way the apostle Paul must've sounded when he had debated the Jews about the resurrection of her Lord.

"And do you not see a conflict in denigrating the police force one moment and calling them the next when you're in trouble?" The senator's face held an expression of trained nothingness. She did absolutely nothing that would've revealed that behind that pretty face of innocence she was giving herself a high-five.

"I see no more conflict in calling on an imperfect police force to report a crime than I see a conflict in calling on an imperfect politician to report my desire for lower taxes. There has always been and will continue to be corrupt police and corrupt politicians. But until there's a viable Plan B..." She smiled.

"Necessary evils?" countered the senator.

"Necessary humans," said Mrs. Billory.

Sharon had to make her jaws not drop. This lady was something else. The only person she had ever seen talk like that was Jonathan. She had to talk to this lady again, alone.

The senator's façade was cracked. She appeared embarrassed.

Barbara looked at her and came to the rescue. "Senator Lockhart, you have some good ideas for the church. Would you care to share them?"

Edwin's look of shock came out before he could conceal it for the sake of marital privacy.

"It's not that bad, Reverend," kidded the senator. "Just some ways the church can become a more viable community force through strategic partnerships."

Sharon was more successful at not revealing her shock. She released it in her heavy breathing and rapid finger-tapping on her thighs. She had promised herself that she wouldn't embarrass her parents. So she sat...and she sat...and she sat. Everyone had a plan for their church. Everyone, but her father, the pastor.

Everything in her ached to do either one of two things. Jump up and scream, "Get out, in the name of Jesus!" Or to get up and run, not walk, to her room. But since she could do neither, she asked God to help her honor her parents by keeping her mouth shut, and by silently supporting them in prayer.

Finally, everyone moved to the great room. And it was a great room—in size anyway. This house was much larger than their old house. Sharon hoped that somehow the change in rooms would change the topic. It didn't. She watched her parents. They were exact opposites. At least as far as this meeting was concerned.

Dad looked as though he were trying to smile and be polite while he was being crucified. Mom looked ecstatic to be the one to supply the hammer and nails. What was going on with her? And when would Dad stand up to—she was going to say *Mom*. But the truth was he rarely stood up to anyone or for anything. Why was Dad so weak?

Mercifully, mercifully, it appeared that the marathon crucifixion—or was it more appropriate to say *coup*—was coming to an end. "Okay," said Sharon, standing up and stretching and yawning.

Edwin stood also and let out a deep breath.

Everyone else stood. Everyone except Barbara, Senator Lockhart, Senator Wilcox, and the immigration sheriff.

The Mighty Bashnar wanted this moment of triumph to be seen by several of his top officers. They were there with him to witness the material progress of their plan to dilute the revival. Krioni-na was there, too.

And under the cover of prayer, the Sword of the Lord was there with Trin, Myla, Adaam-Mir, and a host of warrior angels. There were strict stipulations to the agreement that was awarded the Mighty Bashnar. Sharon was God's friend. If this demon proved as reckless as he was arrogant, and took one fraction of an unauthorized step against the young girl, Captain Rashti would cut out the thick tongue that had railed against the blessed Creator, and would make the Mighty Bashnar eat his sword.

Barbara looked at Edwin and Sharon with lively eyes. She went to Edwin first and took him by the hand. Then she took Sharon by her right hand.

Sharon looked at Edwin and shrugged. Edwin smiled.

"Senator Wilcox...Senator Lockhart...Danny," she took a deep, happy breath. "Here goes," she said, with a sunburst smile.

They smiled at her knowingly.

"I'm going into politics," said Barbara.

"What?" exclaimed Edwin, jerking his head hard enough to get whiplash.

"Politics?" said Sharon, sharing the same whiplash. Sharon looked at Edwin. "Dad, did you know about this?"

"No, I didn't. This is the first I've heard of this," he said.

The senators and immigration sheriff congratulated her profusely. Mrs. Billory and Mr. Henry couldn't believe they were witnessing something like this.

"Barbara, what do you mean, you're going into politics?" asked Edwin.

Barbara looked at Senator Lockhart with a smile. "There's a state senate seat that's ours for the grabbing. It's right here, Edwin, where most of our people live. I gave the church mailing list to Abbey and she had the demographics analyzed. Surely, we can get our own people to vote for me."

Edwin felt conflicting emotions. He almost couldn't believe what he was hearing. He was flabbergasted and humiliated, but he was more angry. "Have you lost your mind?" he yelled.

Yeah, Dad! thought Sharon. *Stand up! Do something! Don't let these people run over you!*

"No, I haven't," she answered indignantly. "The governor needs that seat to go to someone who will support him, and he asked Abbey and Sheila to ask me if I'd run."

Edwin turned abruptly to the senators. "Are you telling me that the governor has personally asked you two to recruit my wife to run for the senate?"

Three big smiles answered him. Senator Lockhart stepped forward. "It's not unprecedented, Reverend. The governor has an uncanny ability to pick winners."

"The governor didn't pick my wife, senator. You did." Edwin turned to Barbara. "You'd do this without talking to your family first?" Edwin shook his head. "And wait a minute. When did you become interested in politics?"

"Edwin, you know I have always been concerned about where our country is going," she answered.

"Well, I'm concerned about where my wife is going," he answered angrily. "And I'm concerned that she has planned a long, expensive, life-changing trip without talking it over with her husband."

"The governor really—" began Senator Wilcox.

"I don't give a—" Edwin looked at his wide-eyed daughter. He pointed his finger at Senator Wilcox, then at Senator Lockhart. "If the governor needs someone's wife to run for office, he has one living with him. I suggest he try her and leave mine alone."

Barbara looked at her husband with a glare he hadn't seen since Christopher's funeral when crazy Jessica yanked their son's body out of his casket. "Edwin, I have walked around with a gaping hole in my heart for one year. I have let you chase this revival thing for that long. This is not doing it for me. I need more. I'm running for office."

Edwin was stunned. He said nothing when she huddled with her new friends.

Sharon was crushed again. It had looked like Dad was going to stand up. But again he whimpered. She turned and went to her room.

The Mighty Bashnar watched a few minutes with deep satisfaction. No need to hurry away the moment. He turned to his officers. "Another critical piece of the puzzle falls into place." He saw their admiration. *This is why I am the Mighty Bashnar.* "Next we will—" He stopped when Sharon reentered the room. Her eyes looked strange.

She stopped in the doorway. "Mom," she said in a voice loud enough to cut through the clutter. Everyone turned. "The Lord just spoke to me. He said to tell you and Dad and everyone else here that He is the Governor, and beside him there is no other."

This caused some awkward expressions.

"Did she say what I think she said?" asked the guy who was trying to get the Native Americans their land back.

"Yep," said the guy trying to save America from the Mexicans.

"Sharon?" said Barbara, with a puzzled look.

Sharon stood there clearly struggling about what to do next.

"Is there something *else*?" Edwin asked, more out of shock than wanting to encourage her to say anything else.

"Yes," she summoned the courage, "I had a trance and saw elephants and donkeys trampling my mother. Dad, I told you and Mom about this." Sharon looked directly at the visitors. "You are the elephants and donkeys."

Sharon had basically just told their guests that she was mentally ill. Of the dinner guests, only Mrs. Billory didn't look at Sharon pathetically. There were murmurs of, "We better go," and "It was a wonderful dinner."

Once the last guest had left, Sharon's warring parents were united in their shock at their daughter's behavior. They walked like zombies from the front door to the great room. Sharon was seated on a sofa with her shoes off and feet balled up under her bottom. She had a pillow hugged to her chest.

"What was that?" asked Barbara.

Edwin forgot how angry he was at Barbara and sat next to her. "Yes, let's start there. What was that?"

Sharon rocked back and forth. Big tears rolled out of her eyes. "I have something to tell you."

They waited.

The Mighty Bashnar and his officers waited.

Captain Rashti and his angels waited.

She looked up. Her lips trembled. "I'm a prophetess."

Chapter 16

Edwin tried to focus on his sermon, but it was impossible. His thoughts were scrambled. He had Moses killing Goliath and King David parting the Red Sea. How could his wife and daughter both go crazy on the same night? Not a politician *or* a prophetess. He had a politician *and* a prophetess. What were the odds of that?

I'm a lucky man, Edwin thought cynically. *The governor wants my wife and God wants my daughter.* He rubbed his forehead and looked at what he had written. He had been up since five. He hated doing things at the last minute, but Barbara's dinner had eaten up much more time than he had planned. He glanced at the wall clock. A gift from Jonathan. *What country did he get that from? Focus, Edwin. You've got two hours and you still don't know what you're going to say.*

Edwin huffed. This wasn't going to work. He had to talk to Sharon. He had talked to Barbara last night after Sharon's proclamation. But there were a lot of hushed, heated words and accusations, but no communication. Their conversation had started at *bad*, went to *worse*, and ended with *How did we get here?*

Edwin went to Sharon's door and knocked lightly. "Sharon," he said.

"Dad?" In a few moments the door opened. He didn't look good behind the pastor's smile. "Give me a few and I'll come to your office."

"Okay," he said, feeling better already. What was it about that girl? She was definitely his flesh and blood, but she and he were not of the same spirit. *This must've been how Mary felt with Jesus,* he thought. *He was her son, but He was so much more.* He went back to his office and sat on the sofa. He laughed lightly. Now he had a large study. Big desk. Sofa. New house. *How times have changed?* He wondered whether his new fortunes were compliments of a high-interest loan from the devil. *Is there any loan from the devil that's not high interest?*

Sharon entered and closed the door.

Edwin had purposefully sat on the sofa for two, and was glad when she sat on it instead of one of the chairs. "Last night was quite the night," he said.

Sharon looked at her father and loved him. "You had a hard night, Dad."

"Yes, I did." His pain was sharp, but his senses were dulled. He wondered what to say next. "There's a lot on the table."

Sharon moved closer. She posted a grimaced smile. "I didn't mean to pile it on. I just...well...Dad, I tried to not say anything. It's hard for me to not say anything when I see people treat you like that. I did good most of the night. I'm sorry if I embarrassed you and Mom by calling those people donkeys and elephants."

"But you do believe they're donkeys and elephants?" he said. "That they're what you saw," he made himself say it, "in the vision?"

"Yes," she answered softly.

"Then don't be sorry, Sharon," said Edwin. "Don't be like me. You believe what you believe, and you stand up for what you believe. That's a good thing to have." He paused. "I don't agree with your mother. But," he said, shaking his head, "*she* stands up for what she believes." Edwin looked into his daughter's eyes and immediately fixed his attention on her nose. "I don't know about your vision, Sharon, but I'm not going to say those people aren't donkeys and elephants."

"Jonathan said that sometimes God's hardest visions are hard because we overlook the obvious," said Sharon. "He told me that I should try interpreting the vision by asking myself what donkeys and elephants represent."

"Jonathan," said Edwin.

"Yeah. Yesterday when me and Rob went to his house—"

"Jonathan met Rob," said Edwin.

"Yeah," Sharon smiled. "I think he gave him a prophecy. Or something. I don't know."

"Jonathan's school of prophecy," he said under his breath.

"What?" she asked.

"Nothing. Please continue," he said.

"So I asked myself what donkeys and elephants represent," said Sharon. "Democrats are donkeys and Republicans are elephants!" Sharon's eyes sparkled. "Right, Dad?"

Edwin cocked his head with raised eyebrows. He saw how she could get that.

"Makes sense, doesn't it? It happened just as I saw it. Look what they've done to Mom. They trampled her. And they're trying to take over the church."

He thought on it. "While I scratch my head."

Sharon was silent.

"I'm sorry, Sharon," said Edwin.

"What are you going to do about Mom?" asked Sharon.

He could not say to his daughter, *I don't know.* "We're going to talk," he answered.

"You talked last night?" she asked.

"Yes."

"And you're going to talk again?" She winced at how that sounded.

"Yeah. Hopefully, I can—"

"Dad, Mom is out of control. You have to *do* something." Sharon looked at her father, eagerly, desperately awaiting the take-charge answer she knew wouldn't come.

"What can...?" His voice faded, not strong enough to carry the thought of action.

Sharon felt the pressure of her father's cares. She had never been a fearful or indecisive person. So it was difficult to deal with her father's behavior. But her heart was tender. She didn't have to like his behavior or understand him to love him. He was her father.

Be a man! is what she screamed in her mind. But with her mouth, she softly said, "Dad, why don't *you* stand up for what you believe?" It had come out as respectfully as she intended. Sharon sighed in relief.

Edwin looked at his daughter. It was a simple enough question. He wondered if she understood that she had reached inside of him and put her finger on the now exposed nerve of his shame.

Sharon looked at her father's eyes and wondered if she saw pain.

There was a long silence. Finally, Edwin turned the final corner in this bewildering maze of emotion and self-discovery. "I think I don't stand up for what I believe," he rolled his lips, "because I don't believe in anything."

The truck hit Sharon and parked on top of her. She tried unsuccessfully to not let her shock show on her face. "Nothing?"

"You. I believe in you, Sharon." Edwin saw the absolute dread in her eyes. He squeezed her hand and smiled. "Breathe, Sharon. I do believe in God."

Sharon burst out in tears.

Edwin pulled her to him and held her until she stopped shaking.

"I thought you were going to say you didn't believe in God." Sharon wiped her eyes more than once. She was still trembling.

"Oh, Sharon," he coaxed, cradling her head in his large palm, "I believe in God. I just don't believe in me."

Sharon pulled back. Tears had joined the pain in her father's eyes. Her dad was crying. But what could she say?

"I'll be okay, honey," he said. "Now tell me why you think you're a prophetess. Did Jonathan tell you that you're a prophetess?"

They really needed to keep talking about him, not Jonathan, thought Sharon. How could a pastor function like this? It did answer a lot of things. Why he let Mom and everyone run over him. He was hollow inside. Something had gutted her dad. "No, it wasn't Jonathan. It was God," she answered.

"When did this happen? Last night?" asked Edwin.

"It started in the trance," she said, "when that stuff went inside of me."

"What stuff?"

"It was like something was poured into me," she said.

As odd as this sounded, Edwin was relieved. She obviously felt something happen to her. He didn't have an explanation of what happened. But this feeling could be interpreted as a lot of things other than becoming a modern Joan of Arc. The 15th century wasn't kind to its prophetess, and neither would the 21st century be kind to his. *Oh, Sharon. Why a prophetess?* "Okay, so you felt something. That could mean—"

"And I heard His voice," she said.

Edwin's words got stuck in his constricted throat. When he could finally speak, he asked, "What did the voice say?"

"He said, 'Do not say, "I am just a teen-ager," for you shall go to all whom I send you, and whatever I command you, you shall speak. Do not be afraid of their faces, for I am with you to deliver you, says the Lord.'"

"You heard a voice tell you this? I mean a *clear* voice?" She nodded yes. How was he going to handle this? He knew his daughter. She wasn't big on theory. If she believed something, it would definitely show up in her behavior. She already made things quite interesting. How much more interesting would things get? "What do you think the voice wants you to do?" Edwin braced himself.

"Dad, I know what God wants me to do?"

"You do?" asked Edwin, nervously.

"Last night when I left all of you and went to my room," said Sharon.

"Yes?"

"I saw a hand come down from heaven. It touched my mouth. It felt like my mouth was on fire." Sharon was so lost in reliving the glory of the moment that she didn't see her father's glazed look. "Then that same voice said, 'Behold, I have put My words in your mouth. See, I have set you over the city and over its evil kingdoms, to root out and to pull down, to destroy and to throw down, to build and to plant.'"

"You heard all of that last night?" asked Edwin.

"Yes," she answered. "And I heard the words again in a dream last night. And when I woke up this morning, I heard someone say them again. Only this time it wasn't as loud."

Edwin gave his best fatherly look of support. This sounded a lot like Joan of Arc.

*****

Sunday mornings were tense and always violent. Angels vigilantly watched for the soft blue mist of the Holy Spirit. If the mist hovered over a home or person, they knew that God was actively appealing to someone to either respond to the gospel, or to go to a church service. Not surprisingly, demons watched this activity with great interest, ready to pounce upon anyone who showed interest in the enemy.

It had been a long, profitable Saturday night at *Man Land. Man Land* was at the top of the strip club chain. Its owner was no common thug. Michael Bogarti had an MBA from Cornell and took great pride in using sound business principles in expanding his empire of flesh.

Proper branding was critical. His brand and trademarked logo, *Sophisticated Sin*, had become so popular that he had negotiated lucrative license agreements.

Horizontal integration was critical. Successful strip clubs and adult novelty stores had seen the light and had eagerly agreed to sell him their businesses at a discount. Those who did found that, coincidentally, their luck immediately changed for the good. Their animals stopped being killed. Their friends stopped having horrific and suspicious accidents. Their family members stopped being singled out for random violent beatings, rapes, kidnappings, and even murders.

And those who hadn't yet seen the value of selling their businesses to him? Well, to date there was only one.

Negligee's was a successful restaurant that had a theme of serving food in a bedroom setting. Of course, the servers were beautiful women in negligees. The owners, two women, Jeri and Tamira, originally felt his offer was ludicrously low. Unfortunately, Jeri committed suicide shortly after she laughed at him. Tamira was understandably shaken by the out-of-the-blue suicide of her happy, full-of-life, childhood friend. She surprised him by disappearing. But he was certain she'd turn up and sign the papers.

The next business principle that he had used with great success was strategic alliances. He had cultivated mutually beneficial relationships with politicians, judges, and police. He even had a friend in the Atlanta division of the FBI, and he had friends who had friends. Some of these friends were friends because they shared mutual interests. Others were reluctant friends.

Their reluctance was due to the fact that he had masterful proficiency in using technology to make people become his friends. For instance, Judge Harper was a superior court judge who had a penchant for young girls. Really young girls. And through Mr. Bogarti's other business principle of diversity, he was able to provide him with all the young love he wanted.

It wasn't until later that the judge found out that every one of his deviant acts had been recorded in clear audio and high definition video. The judge was assured that suicide was unnecessary. His secrets were secret as long as they remained friends.

Diversity. The mantra of savvy investors and shrewd businessmen, of which he was both. Girls dancing on poles was a legal money machine that was so profitable, he didn't know why everyone wasn't doing it. Well, yes he did. The cost of entry could be formidable. Even deadly. But as profitable as the strip club business was, there was another that was even more profitable. That was sex slavery. And this is where the owner of *Man Land* used one of the most sacred principles of business. Ruthlessness.

Vivian Bogarti didn't know everything about her husband's business, but she knew a lot. She would know a lot. For she was more than the wife of a connected criminal. She was in many ways his chief operating officer. The girls at the clubs dealt with her, not her husband. *She knew everything about the girls.*

She had a master's degree in accounting and did the books, and a graduate certificate in cyber security. She made sure that her husband wouldn't go down like Al Capone. If the government ever did get him, they would have to work for it. It wouldn't be for his taxes. *She knew everything about his money.*

Yes, Vivian knew a lot. But she didn't know that a soft blue mist had enveloped her large home. Nor did she know that an army of demons had fought a desperate, but losing battle this morning to protect her from the light.

Chapter 17

Controllus and his six council guards were stage left. The Mighty Bashnar and several of his officers were stage right. They looked at one another like rival gangs who had just discovered the other on its turf. The turf was the packed-to-capacity sanctuary of Edwin's church.

Controllus spoke to the demon next to him, but looked at the humiliated warrior spirit as he spoke. He spoke loudly enough for Bashnar to hear him. "Deveeous, have you heard that there is a new prophetess in the city?"

Deveeous looked contemptibly at Bashnar. "Yes," he said loudly, "I have heard. Who is she?"

"She is Sharon the thorn," said Controllus.

"The daughter of Edwin and friend of Jonathan, am I right?" he said.

"You are right," answered Controllus with glee.

"How can this be?" the spirit asked. "The great and mighty Bashnar was given authority to destroy this revival a year ago."

Controllus relished his next words. "He has failed in his task. That is why the great Prince Krioni has given authority to me to destroy this revival."

The Mighty Bashnar peered at the good as dead demon. The council guards and Controllus studied his eyes. Controllus eyes widened when Bashnar started walking toward them. The Mighty Bashnar stopped in front of Controllus and put his face next to his.

"At the time and place of my choosing, I will kill you," said the Mighty Bashnar. He turned and put his hands on his sword and dagger and went back to his side of the stage.

The six council guards looked at Controllus with disgust. How could he let this warrior spirit talk to him like this? He shrugged it off. "Never mind this loser. We have work to do. Hinduism will be here shortly," he said with a snap. "This is a grand opportunity for witchcraft to enter the church."

Edwin was in his church office still sorting out what he was going to say. Sharon and Andrew were in their usual seats. But Barbara had chosen this time to sit onstage. Sharon wondered with concern what that was about. She would soon find out. Barbara was giving the announcements instead of Maggie.

Controllus waited impatiently for the big announcement.

Adaam-Mir wondered about the large gathering of witchcraft spirits gathered around the church building.

Myla answered his thoughts. "They are waiting for the invitation from leadership. I will explain later."

"Why is Mom giving announcements?" Andrew asked Sharon. "She never gives the announcements."

Sharon had a sense of foreboding. "I don't know, Andrew."

Barbara looked out at the vast audience and smiled. She'd have to get used to this. Taking a more active and public role in the church would help her. "Good morning everyone," she said. "I have a few announcements to share with you."

Sharon and not a few others suffered through her mom's exaggerated enthusiasm over Senators' Lockhart's and Wilcox's itineraries. She sounded like a cheerleader who had been given one last chance to win a spot on the squad. Sharon shared her grimace with her lap. She was not going to lift her head until Mom sat down. *Please sit down, Mom.*

"I have one last announcement," said Barbara.

"Thank you, Jesus," said Sharon.

"Starting this week..." Barbara looked at a piece of paper and used her finger to scan a few paragraphs. "Oh, here it is. Starting this week, we will begin having morning kundalina yoga classes. It's taught by a certified instructor who studied many years in India. Oh, goodie. I can't wait. You can get more info on our website. Or—"

That was all Sharon heard. *Yoga?* She didn't know a lot about yoga. But she did know that when Mom said the church was going to start having yoga classes, she suddenly had a strong urge to throw up. She stood up and hurried to the restroom.

Adaam-Mir watched the invasion of witchcraft spirits. They had swarmed on the church building the moment Barbara said they would start having yoga classes. Obviously there was a connection, but what? Controllus had mentioned that he was waiting on Hinduism to arrive, but instead there were these hundreds of witchcraft spirits.

"Adaam-Mir," said Myla, "come with me. I'll explain to you what has happened."

Adaam-Mir noticed the retreat of many angels. "Where are they going?" he asked.

"Come with me, Adaam-Mir."

Myla flew away and Adaam-Mir reluctantly followed. Adaam-Mir was relieved that they did not go so far away that they could not quickly return. He sat and waited eagerly to learn of this mystery.

"Adaam-Mir, you have just witnessed a great tragedy," said Myla.

"Those witchcraft spirits," said the inexperienced angel, "they're so many of them. How can they invade as they did? Why didn't we stop them?"

"Adaam-Mir, our Lord has given great power to the church. Whatever it binds on earth, is bound in heaven. Whatever it looses on earth, is loosed in heaven. Unless the Creator commands differently, we cannot go beyond what the church desires."

Adaam-Mir thought on these words. Surely his mentor would clarify his statement. The powers of angels were strictly limited. How could the church have nearly unlimited powers?

"The witchcraft spirits overran the church because they were invited in. Barbara loosed witchcraft," said Myla.

"But how? She's not the leader of their church. And she didn't say anything about witchcraft. And what about Controllus? He said they were waiting on Hinduism. Where is he?"

Myla looked intently into Adaam-Mir's inquisitive eyes. "Hinduism is yoga, and yoga is witchcraft."

Adaam-Mir shook his head. "I'm sorry. I do not understand."

"It's understandable, Adaam-Mir," said Myla. "Your previous position would not have exposed you to this. There are some things you can only learn on the front lines. In battle." Myla looked to his left. The witchcraft spirits looked like a frenzied school of piranha. The sight was pathetic. He turned back to Adaam-Mir. "Yoga is the child of Hinduism. They are different, but are of the same spirit."

Adaam-Mir waited for more.

"Controllus spoke of Hinduism because yoga is his son. He has legitimate claims on people who practice yoga. Yoga is a door that leads to him." Myla waited for the question he saw on the angel's face.

"How is this so, my brother?" he asked.

"Adaam-Mir, there are many kinds of yoga," said Myla. "The kind of yoga most acceptable to this land is that presented as exercise and deliberate relaxation. Breathing...meditating...stretching."

"But there is more?" asked Adaam-Mir.

"Much more. There is always *much* more with Satan," said Myla. "With Adam and Eve, it was a piece of fruit. But it wasn't the fruit that destroyed them. It was the desire for what they could attain by eating the fruit."

Adaam-Mir's expression was thoughtful.

"The fruit was the door." Myla paused.

"The breathing and meditating and stretching, this is the door?" asked Adaam-Mir.

"Yes." Myla's answer was punctuated with energy.

"The door to what?" Adaam-Mir asked. "Adam and Eve were prohibited from eating of the tree. The sons and daughters of Adam, they are not prohibited from exercising and meditating and stretching. Is this not correct, my brother?" Adaam-Mir was a student of the blessed book and of history, but there was so much he didn't know. He could not take it for granted that he understood even the most elementary facts and concepts.

"That is correct, my brother," Myla answered. "The door to fellowship with demons. Intimacy with Satan."

True, Adaam-Mir was inexperienced. There was much he did not know. But this concept of fellowshipping with demons and of being intimate with Satan was too much. It was repugnant. He raised his arms up and down and paced, shaking his head. "No, my brother. Such a thing—" The magnitude of such wickedness could not be put into words. "I do not challenge your words. I know you speak only truth." Adaam-Mir grasped both of Myla's thick biceps. "But how can such a thing be? Satan is evil!"

Myla heard the passion in his voice. He saw the fire in his eyes. This was why the Lord had chosen him for front line duty. And it was why the Sword of the Lord had put him on a fast-track to be trained as soon as possible. "He doesn't announce who he is or what he's doing. He transforms himself into an angel of light. And he is careful to present himself in a package acceptable to the people whom he deceives."

Adaam-Mir understood this. He nodded his head.

"Reincarnation," said Myla. "In India you live and die and come back as a cow, a bullfrog, or maybe a son of Adam. In America you live and die and come back as a human. American culture is too materialistic to embrace the possibility of life as a lizard or hog. So Satan presents multiple lifetimes as a son or daughter of Adam."

"And this yoga?" asked Adaam-Mir.

"As it is with reincarnation, so it is with yoga," said Myla. "There are many kinds. Some too intense and too obviously demonic for the typical American. So the great traitor gives them a watered down version. One they can accept."

"But the danger...?" Adaam-Mir began.

"Yes," answered Myla, "it remains."

Adaam-Mir resumed his pacing, with his hands folded behind his back. "Ingenious. Same lie, different package. He gives...whatever they will receive," his voice fading.

Myla continued. "Because yoga is the child of Hinduism, it has its blood running through its veins. It has its DNA. The deceiver has masterfully camouflaged this by presenting it in a nonreligious package. He tells people it isn't religious."

Adaam-Mir waited for more. More wasn't given. "This is it?"

"This is it," said Myla.

"And they believe him?" asked Adaam-Mir.

"They want to believe him. They want to believe they can get what they want without going to God. So they try another way. For some, it's yoga."

"But a thing is not true simply because you believe it to be true," said Adaam-Mir. "And a thing is not safe just because one believes it to be safe." The angel ran his hand through his long hair. "This is difficult truth, my brother. Tell me, how shall Controllus use this? Will we be able to stop him?"

"The essence of yoga is supernatural phenomenon. The people who participate seek for supernatural experiences, despite what terms they call them. Some will receive them; some will not. But all will open themselves to the influence of witchcraft."

"Through exercises," muttered Adaam-Mir.

"Much more than exercises," said Myla. "It's the spiritual roots and direction of yoga that is dangerous. It's the antichrist perspective that is nurtured. Adaam-Mir, there are occult practices that teach out-of-body experiences."

"I have heard of this," said Adaam-Mir. "The angels that I was with on my first day—when captain Rashti introduced me to all of you—two of them were discussing this. Astral projection."

"Astral projection. That's right. It's at the core of yoga. The evil one encourages his victims to seek a higher consciousness through meditation. Once they reach a high enough level, their astral body leaves their physical body."

"For what purpose," Adaam-Mir asked, not understanding why a son of Adam would want to leave his physical body if it were not to be with the Lord. "And what is an astral body?"

"Satan's counterfeit of the spirit," said Myla. "Adaam-Mir, he counterfeits everything. In yoga there are so-called chakras in the body, spiritual energy centers. Each of these centers has an association with a Hindu god. It is through one of these chakras that the person in yoga exits to go into the higher spiritual realm."

Adaam-Mir's eyes were absent their earlier fire. Now in place of fire was a dull sadness. He seemed to be holding up his head with great difficulty as he asked, "The sons and daughter of Adam actually believe they can experience greater spiritual awareness by going through mystical energy centers in their bodies that are linked to demons?"

Myla had only known this angel for a few days, but he was as connected to him as though he had known him since his own creation. It would be impossible to not love an angel who so loved God's sons and daughters, and one who spoke the truth as did he. "Most do not think that deeply, my brother." Myla wondered how he would take the next thing he had to share with him. "My brother, they also believe there is a snake at the base of their spine that can be awakened through deep meditation. When the snake is awakened, it rises through their spine and passes through the chakras. This has to happen for them to achieve God consciousness."

It was understood that angels often passed out in the presence of the Lord. Totally overwhelmed by the intensity of His glory, power, and goodness. It was even expected. But what was not expected was for an angel to fall out for any reason other than being overwhelmed by the Creator. Adaam-Mir didn't think he was on the verge of passing out. He was in total command of his faculties. But this concept made him feel odd. He sat down on the side of a curb.

"A snake in their spine?" asked Adaam-Mir. "But Satan is the serpent. They *know* that Satan is the serpent. How can the sons of Adam believe such a thing? How can they believe they can get closer to God by having fellowship with demons? My brother, the blessed book, their own blessed book says, 'I do not want you to have fellowship with demons. You cannot drink the cup of the Lord and the cup of demons; you cannot partake of the Lord's table and of the table of demons.' How do they do such things? The blessed book is there for all to read. Why would they sell their souls to Satan in an effort to get what is so freely given by the Lord? Please, my brother, tell me the answer to this great mystery."

Myla could have answered. He knew the truth. Every angel who had been on the front lines for as long as he had been knew the truth. *The sons and daughters of Adam loved sin and hated God.*

But Adaam-Mir's question was coming from a broken heart. No amount of truth would remove the pain. Actually, he knew that an angel such as this one, one who loved God's creation as he did, and had proven it by faithfully working for them behind the scenes for thousands of years, would only hurt more if he went into detail now. He would save that conversation for another time. "Adaam-Mir," said Myla.

The angel who had been promoted by the Lord because of his intense love of the sons and daughters of Adam looked hopefully at the angel who was mentoring him. "Yes."

"The snake in their spines is called *kundalini*.

Adaam-Mir's face was blank. *What was kundalini?*

Myla looked grimly at him. He saw when it happened.

Adaam-Mir's mouth widened. Trouble filled his face and eyes. "The woman...Barbara...she said *kundalini.* She said they're going to teach kundalini yoga."

Myla squeezed his shoulder. "That is so."

Adaam-Mir screamed a long scream that filled the area, then collapsed, overcome with grief.

*****

Somehow Edwin had made it through another sermon. It was a masterpiece of preaching about a victory he didn't understand nor have. He looked at the packed auditorium. So many eyes looking to him. He felt as though he were a mega bestselling author of books on how to lose weight. The problem was he weighed four-hundred pounds. Couldn't they see that he was fat? That he was a farce?

So many eyes.

The only thing worse than talking about a god he didn't really know—he didn't let himself think it, but deep down he meant he didn't know Him *like Jonathan knew Him*—was being expected to make Him real to others through signs, miracles, and wonders. *That magazine guy is right. This thing really is all about Jonathan.* This couldn't go on much longer. He couldn't live in Jonathan's shadow forever. It wasn't right. He was going to have to do something about this.

The ushers had dutifully lined up the first wave of people across the front of the sanctuary. There was a lot of room up front, so it could handle the people as they fell out. Another thought tempered this one. *Jonathan's not here. You don't have to worry about anyone falling out when you pray for them.*

Edwin shuddered. People didn't fall out when he prayed for them. But he reminded himself that many people had been healed when he had prayed for them. *But Jonathan was always here when that happened.*

"Pastor Styles," said the usher, "this man has persistent stomach pains."

Huh? Edwin smiled with an assurance he didn't feel. He put one hand on the man's shoulder. *Now what?* He closed his eyes.

"Praise God!" the man screamed as loud as his powerful lungs would allow.

Edwin jumped back, startled, and thoroughly embarrassed at his exaggerated reaction to the man's sudden scream. Had he really left his feet when the man screamed? He recalled Jonathan's words. *'There's a reason the Bible says, watch and pray.'* He immediately resented that he was leaning on Jonathan again. *Get out of my head, Jonathan!*

"I felt something," the man gushed. He pressed on his belly. "My Gaaaaawd. My God. I felt something."

The usher, Josh Kleunder, was a Josh Brolin look-alike, as in Hollywood Josh Brolin. This was one of the reasons Jonathan had fondly nicknamed him Hollywood Josh. And Josh apparently liked this comparison to a Hollywood hunk because the name had slipped out of his own mouth more than once.

Josh put the hand-held microphone to the excited man's mouth and looked at the crowd as though he were a game show host. He smiled. His eyes twinkled when he asked with a radio announcer's voice, "And what did you feel?"

The man laughed and pressed hard on his belly. "Something inside of my stomach popped. It just popped. Poof! Just like that."

Hollywood Josh looked at the audience with a handsome smile and held it for effect. "Poof?"

"That's right—poof!" said the man.

Still smiling at the audience, Hollywood Josh said, "Just like that?"

"Just—like—that! Yessiree! Pain's gone. I'm healed. Glory to God."

The man turned to go back to his seat.

Edwin was stunned. Jonathan wasn't here and this man was healed—even before he prayed for him. He had simply touched him and he was healed. "Sir," Edwin called to him. He had to call him a few times before the man could hear over the crowd praising God. The man turned. "What was wrong with your stomach?" asked Edwin.

"Shot in a robbery two years ago. Pain's been terrible ever since. Not a day goes by that I don't feel it." The man's hands shot up. "But I don't feel it now!" He started jumping up and down and praising God.

The place went pandemonium wild. Edwin just stared at the man, wondering. This was the kind of thing that happened when Jonathan was there, and Jonathan wasn't there. Finally, the man and the audience calmed down. "Look, Reverend, I'll show you the bullet hole." Before Edwin could object, the man's shirt was up. The man looked around his belly as though he had lost something. "It's gone! My God, the bullet hole is gone!"

Back to jumping he went, and back to pandemonium wild went the church. Edwin looked around. It looked to him like everyone was throwing a fit. Even Hollywood Josh was into it. But then that was no surprise. He and the healed man were twirling, arm in arm, and saying something in tongues.

How did this happen? How did I become pastor of a church like this? Edwin stood at the front of the church, pacing back and forth in front of the line of people awaiting his touch. His head was lowered in what everyone thought was prayer. But Edwin was wondering how in the world he had become pastor of a church like this. When he reached the end of the line and turned to return, he saw Sharon waiting on him. He walked toward her cautiously. She had a *Joan of Arc* kind of look on her face. *Oh, Sharon, what have you seen? What have you heard?*

"Dad," she said.

"Yes, Sharon," he answered, with hesitance.

"I saw something," she said.

Of course, you did. "What did you see, Sharon?"

"There's a lady in the back of the church with a blue mist all over her." Sharon sounded as reluctant to give him the message as he was to receive it.

"What do you think this means?" he asked.

"I think we're supposed to pray for her," she answered. "I think God is dealing with her soul."

No Sharon, let's not pray for her? How far would that go with his daughter? Why fight this battle? "Go get her, Sharon," he said, with little energy.

Sharon lowered her head and walked slowly, but determinedly, down the center aisle like a two-legged possum. She didn't lift her head until she got to the lady. She was sitting on the end, the first seat. Sharon stood by her. The lady looked up. Sharon said nothing. She turned and walked back toward the front.

The lady said nothing. She clutched her $28,000 *Fendi Baguette* bag and followed the young girl down the aisle. Immediately, the somber man sitting next to her rose and followed the boss's wife. Another man, whose face had never smiled, was sitting two rows directly behind her. He stood and followed the boss's wife. A third man sitting across the aisle called someone on his phone. In a moment, he and another man stood in the lobby by each of the two doors leading into the sanctuary.

The lady had no idea why she was in church today—and in such a strange church. She knew even less of why she had followed this young lady to the front of the church.

Edwin looked at the woman with interest. The guys with her looked and acted like bodyguards. He looked at Sharon. *You do keep things interesting,* he thought.

Vivian Bogarti wondered what she was doing here.

Chapter 18

Andrew was the first to see it as they drove up the driveway. "Dad, why is there a gay flag hanging on a pole over our house?"

"What?" exclaimed Barbara, bending her head to see it. "There is a flag hanging from our house, Edwin."

"What the—?" Edwin didn't park the car in the garage. He got out and walked underneath the flag pole. Someone had removed Barbara's American flag and had replaced it with a rainbow flag. "Who would do something like this?" he said.

"I'll tell you who would do something like this?" said Barbara.

"Who?" asked Andrew, Sharon, and Edwin.

"Liberals," she said.

Edwin looked at the flag and started looking down the streets, as though the culprits were still there.

"Liberals, Mom?" Sharon shook her head and left her parents in the front yard.

Andrew entered the house before her. He looked around in shock. "Whoooaaa, did liberals do this, too?"

Sharon followed close behind with a wide open mouth. Someone had trashed their house. Everything was broken and thrown all over the place. "What?" was all she could get past her shock. She walked slowly from room to room. Each room was worse than the one before, like the people got angrier as they entered different rooms.

Barbara entered the house and screamed, "Edwin! Edwin!"

Edwin came running. He hit an invisible wall when he saw the mess. It was like a tornado had gone through their home. *Why would someone do this?* he thought. He walked through the first floor, sharing everyone's shock. His eyes widened. He took off up the stairs and went into Christopher's room. He let out a moan and leaned against the wall before sliding down it. "I'm sorry, Christopher. I'm sorry, son," he said. "I don't know why they did this. I'll get you some more pennants." By now his voice was cracking.

He felt the depression descending. It wasn't depression because of what happened to the house. The house could be fixed. It was depression because of what had happened to his son a year ago. That could not be fixed.

Suddenly, something clicked inside of him. He couldn't be weak now. His family needed him. *God, help me to be strong.*

*****

Adaam-Mir looked at Myla with excited, hopeful eyes. "My brother, the son of Adam, he has asked for help. Will we attack? Will the Lord answer this prayer?"

Captain Rashti didn't hear Adaam-Mir's words, but he saw his eyes. He answered from several yards away. "Yes, Adaam-Mir, the Lord will answer this prayer—and more."

Finally, we do something! Finally, we attack! thought Adaam-Mir.

"Pull back to the third line," bellowed the captain.

Myla didn't hesitate.

Adaam-Mir followed, but with his hand on Myla's arm. "Where are we going? Why are we pulling back? The son of Adam asked for strength."

The captain and Myla shared looks. Myla didn't understand the order, but he trusted who gave the order.

"The sun will rise at its appointed time, Adaam-Mir," said the captain before he went away to another near location.

"What does this mean? I do not understand?" Adaam-Mir said to Myla.

Myla looked at his friend. "Now you begin to understand the creation you serve. The sons and daughters of God live in a world of uncertainty and unanswered questions. They love a God they do not see and must remain true to Him even when it appears that He is not being true to them."

Adaam-Mir's response was quick and vigorous. "But the Lord is faithful! He is faithful, my brother! They must know He is faithful!"

Myla stopped and turned. "Why must they *know* He is faithful?"

Adaam-Mir inhaled deeply, ready to answer the obvious with a long list of unassailable reasons.

Myla put up his palm. "Adaam-Mir, you asked me why the captain ordered us to the third line. You said you do not understand."

"I do not understand," Adaam-Mir answered. "The son of God prayed for help, and instead of helping him, we pull back farther."

Myla looked intently into the inexperienced angel's eyes. "You have seen the Creator. You have seen the glorified Christ. You have seen the Holy Spirit. You have seen the angels of the Lord. These realities are ever before your eyes. Are they not?"

"They are, my brother," said Adaam-Mir.

"Captain Rashti is the Sword of the Lord," said Myla. "Is he not?"

"Yes."

"And he does only the will of the Lord. Do you believe this to be true?" asked Myla.

"Of course, I do. He is the blessed champion of the Battle of the Resurrection. He has vanquished the enemy in Rome, in Babylon, in Ephesus. Yes! Yes! He is faithful to the Creator!"

Myla smiled. "So passionate. And yet you have questions."

Adaam-Mir knew he was missing something. But he wasn't going to ask again about the order to pull back. He knew that he was presently being taught even if he didn't understand the lesson.

"My friend, it is permissible to ask questions," said Myla. "It is not when we ask questions that we get into trouble. It is when we provide our own answers to our questions."

"Why did the captain order us to fall back?" asked Adaam-Mir.

"Good. Good. Humility asks. Pride answers," said Myla.

Adaam-Mir waited. Myla appeared to have forgotten the conversation. "The order, my brother."

"It is awkward, is it not, to ask a question of someone whom you know has the answer and to get no answer?" asked Myla.

"Yes," answered Adaam-Mir, pondering Myla's words.

"But you have asked a question and have received an answer, and yet you have not heard it."

Adaam-Mir thought of their conversation. He didn't see it. "I am sorry, my brother."

"You asked why we pulled back. The captain answered, 'The sun will rise in its appointed time,'' said Myla.

"But what does that *mean*?" asked Adaam-Mir.

"You are frustrated. Good," said Myla. "You are an angel. You have seen the Creator and His Christ. You have seen the Holy Spirit and the holy angels. And yet you have questions. Think on this, Adaam-Mir. The captain of the Lord's army answered your question face to face and you didn't even know it."

"I do not mean to be disrespectful, my brother. But I asked a question and he answered in a riddle."

"You are an *angel,* Adaam-Mir. Why was the captain's answer not satisfactory?" asked Myla.

"Because it does not answer my question," said Adaam-Mir.

"Excellent. Now you will understand," said Myla. "Captain Rashti answered your question, but it's in a riddle. Feel your frustration, Adaam-Mir. Now imagine the frustration of the sons and daughters of Adam. They are not angels. They do not see God. They do not see the Christ. They do not see the blessed Holy Spirit. They do not see the holy angels. They see *nothing*. Nothing, Adaam-Mir. They pray, and do you know what they get?"

"Riddles?" asked Adaam-Mir.

"Sometimes they get a clear word from the Lord. But mostly it's riddles or silence." The teacher saw the question in the pupil's eyes. "You may ask the obvious, Adaam-Mir."

"Thank you, my brother. Why?" he asked. "Why doesn't the Lord speak plainly to His people? It would be easier for them to obey—to please Him. Is this not so?" Adaam-Mir was certain there could be no other explanation. But if there were no other explanation....

"There are many answers to the question you asked, and to those you did not ask," said Myla. "God is a spirit. The words He speak are spirit and truth. Whether He speaks in plain speech or in a riddle, he who hears must hear through the filters of spirit and truth. The blessed apostle Paul tried to teach the Corinthian saints the knowledge and ways of the Lord, but in his own words, 'And I, brethren, could not speak to you as to spiritual people but as to carnal, as to babes in Christ. I fed you with milk and not with solid food; for until now you were not able to receive it, and even now you are still not able.'

"Do you see, Adaam-Mir? That was a son of Adam speaking to sons and daughters of Adam. Yet Paul could not communicate with them as he desired because they were not able to hear him."

Adaam-Mir added, "And they could not hear because they were carnal, earthly-minded."

"Yes," said Myla. "Flesh and blood does not inherit the kingdom of God. A son or daughter of Adam must be changed. If they are earthly-minded, they will corrupt God's words no matter how clearly He speaks to them."

Adaam-Mir felt light entering his spirit. "I think I see, my brother."

"My friend, look at the blessed book. The Creator has given the world such a gift, and yet they do not understand," said Myla.

"I also love the blessed book, my brother," said Adaam-Mir. "But it is true that much of it is difficult to understand. And some of its truths are hidden. If it is difficult for angels..."

"It is difficult for angels because it was not written for angels." Perhaps Myla could build upon this statement. "It was written for the sons and daughters of Adam. But only those with ears to hear may understand. Those who desire its truth will receive its truth."

Adaam-Mir looked in the direction of Edwin. "But what of Edwin? What about day-to-day living, when the sons and daughters of Adam are living their lives and trying to be led of the Spirit?"

"Specific guidance? Specific words?" Myla asked.

"Yes, specific, clear words," said Adaam-Mir.

"Adaam-Mir, listen closely. The Lord never stops speaking to his sons and daughters. If there is any shortage of communication between the Lord and His children, it is not because He has stopped speaking. It is because they have stopped listening."

"But some of them, like Edwin, seek to hear from the Lord and hear nothing," said Adaam-Mir. He had heard some of this man's prayers.

"Adaam-Mir, you ask good questions. Reasonable questions. The answers are in the blessed book. It is written, 'Now we have received, not the spirit of the world, but the Spirit who is from God, that we might know the things that are freely given to us by God. These things we also speak, not in words which man's wisdom teaches but which the Holy Spirit teaches, comparing spiritual things with spiritual. But the natural man does not receive the things of the Spirit of God, for they are foolishness to him; nor can he know them, because they are spiritually discerned.' Do you understand? Adaam-Mir?"

"It is what you said earlier," he answered. "There are some things that are difficult for the children of Adam to understand."

"That is true, Adaam-Mir, but it is more than difficulty in understanding *some* words of God. It is the process of hearing *any* word of God. No one understands another unless he understands that person's language." Myla looked into the angel's face. He tried to will understanding into him through the intensity of his gaze. "No matter how clear the language, it is not clear to the one who does not know the language."

Adaam-Mir smiled and nodded his head. "Yes. Yes. Yes. I see. You must know the language. Otherwise, it's all a riddle. Everything's a riddle to the one who doesn't know the Creator's language."

Myla stepped back and let out a long sigh of satisfaction. "Yes. Comparing spiritual things to spiritual. When Edwin asks God a question, he almost always compares spirit with flesh instead of spirit with spirit."

"Comparing spirit with spirit," said an animated Adaam-Mir. "This means what?"

"Adaam-Mir, this is surprisingly simple, yet exceedingly difficult. Listen closely. It means the sons and daughters of God must see as God sees. They must value as He values. They must believe as He believes. In essence, they must continue as they began."

"They must continue as they began?" said Adaam-Mir. He wanted to figure this out before Myla explained it. He thought as hard as he could. He tried to connect the dots, but some appeared to be missing.

"My friend, how is a sinner rescued from the wrath to come? He finally sees as God sees. He finally aligns his values and beliefs with God—at least enough to produce a new birth. The sinner forsakes his worldview and wisdom for God's worldview and wisdom. This new birth into the family of God begins in faith and dependence on God. Sons and daughters of Adam routinely enter the life of faith only to forsake faith shortly thereafter."

Adaam-Mir's face went through a quick series of alternating expressions that showed his surprise, shock, outrage, and sadness. "Apostasy, my brother? This is the rule? *Most* of them leave the Lord?" The angel took a few steps, running both hands back and forth through his hair. The sons and daughters of Adam were a great irony. It would take forever to figure them out.

"I am not speaking of apostasy, my friend," said Myla.

The troubled angel quickly lifted his head. "Then of what do you speak?"

"I am speaking of trying to live for God without continually hearing His voice," said Myla, with a sad note.

"I do not see how they can live in such a dangerous environment in such a weakened condition and successfully live for God without hearing His voice," said Adaam-Mir. "How is this done, Myla?"

Myla pointed toward Edwin. "Like that. They accept some of what the Creator says, and reject or explain away anything He says that isn't acceptable. Of course, this makes it impossible for them to fully function as sons and daughters of the Almighty. But they have an inexplicable ability and predisposition to accept mediocrity and to live infinitely beneath their high callings."

"But the young thorn, Sharon? And the dagger, Jonathan? What of them?" asked Adaam-Mir. "Why are they different?"

Myla's answer was quick and forceful. "They choose to be."

They both looked toward Edwin. "And this son of Adam," said Adaam-Mir, "what will become of him?" Adaam-Mir had been assured that questions were welcomed. But what he had to say was more than a question. "He is so appallingly weak. How can the Lord use such a man?"

"The Lord chooses the weak to confound the mighty," said Myla.

Adaam-Mir was convinced of the Lord's ability, even if he didn't understand His choice of instruments. This showed on his face.

Myla stepped forward and spoke resolutely. "The son of Adam, Edwin, he will conquer his weaknesses and fulfill his calling, or he will die a miserable failure."

Adaam-Mir looked at Myla. He was surprised at the frankness of his words.

"There are no gray areas with the Lord, Adaam-Mir. That is a seed of Satan that grows in the soil of the rebellious heart. Grow or die. *That* is the way of the Lord."

"He asked for help, my brother," said Adaam-Mir.

"The Lord has answered. He will grow or die," said Myla.

*****

The police had advised them to leave everything as it was until they came to investigate. Now they had come and gone. Somehow the mess looked worse now than before the police had come. The family moved robotically in disheartened silence. It took too much energy to speak.

The Mighty Bashnar and his crew walked among the rubble. He lifted up his *Job Strategy* authorization to twelve demons. "Make this piece of paper mean something. It won't last forever," he barked to his crew and left.

Andrew left his room and went to the top of the stairs. The spirit waited for him with dancing claws. Andrew carried a box in both hands. He lifted his leg. It was just about on the first step when Andrew felt something tear into his left hamstring. He screamed and dropped the box and tumbled down the stairs. The last part of his body to stop moving was his head as it slammed onto the hardwood floor at the bottom of the stairs.

Sharon wasn't sure of the bouncing sound she heard on the stairs. But the loud thud she heard at the base of the stairs scared her. She hurried toward the sound. Andrew was motionless on his back. Sharon gasped and ran toward him. Three spirits with long arms waited for her. One wrapped its arms around her arms, pinning them to her body. Another demon wrapped his arms around both of her legs. The momentum of her body threw her forward. The third demon turned her falling body and guided the back of her head to the last hardwood stair.

Edwin was in Christopher's room. His handsome features were draped with sadness. He looked around his son's room wondering when the pain would end. Would it ever end? The poster of David Justice hitting the home run was crumpled on the floor. He reached down and picked it up. He unfurled it and grimaced. He could replace the picture, but he couldn't replace the memory of his little boy selecting this exact picture. He balled the picture up and tossed it back on the floor.

"Edwin!" he heard Barbara scream his name.

"Oh, my God," he said, when he saw both of his children laid out at the bottom of the stairs. He hopped down the stairs two at a time. "What happened?"

"I don't know. I don't know." Barbara was frantic. She went to lift Sharon's head.

"No," said Edwin. "There could be damage to her neck. Sharon, baby," he said, gently tapping her cheek. He looked at Andrew. "Son. Son." He tapped his cheek. Nothing. "Barbara, we gotta call the ambulance. We don't want to make it worse by moving them."

Barbara hurried away to find her phone. She looked everywhere for it. The phone was in her purse. The purse was on the kitchen counter. And a demon sat on the counter, covering her purse. "I can't find my purse," she said, hurrying from room to room, her panic growing. She came back to Edwin. "I can't find my purse," she said, with flailing arms.

"Get mine. I think it's in the car," he said.

Barbara came back. "It's not there." She was beside herself. "Edwin, we have to get them to the hospital."

Edwin looked at Andrew and Sharon. It was dangerous to move an injured person. He didn't want to hurt his children. But he couldn't waste time searching for phones either. His mind felt like a rubber band pulled to its maximum just before snapping. He made himself calm down. *Lord, help me,* he thought, *without thinking*.

Sharon was first. Edwin cradled the back of her neck as he moved her to the SUV. He did the same with Andrew and raced away.

Chapter 19

Jonathan had been praying and fasting for two days. He was on his stronghold schedule. According to Jonathan, strongholds were those impossible situations that laughed at regular prayers. They even laughed at praying and fasting *if they weren't done long enough or with enough intensity.*

How did one know what was long enough and intense enough? As far as Jonathan was concerned, there were only two fail-proof ways of knowing when one had dealt with a stronghold properly. One, pray and fast until you get a clear word from God that it is time to stop. Two, the mountain moves.

He had not heard God tell him it was time to stop. And the mountain was still there. Ava was at death's door. That meant his life's agenda and schedule was simple: pray, fast, sleep only as long as necessary to have adequate strength to pray and fast, drink enough water to be strong enough to pray and fast, and go to the restroom. To do anything other than this would be tantamount to letting Ava die.

Since Elizabeth had passed out in Ava's room, the hospital had not allowed her to return without him. This had posed a problem. She, understandably, wanted to be there with her mother. He wanted to be somewhere where he could cry out to God. Hospital rooms weren't the best place for this. Neither were hospital chapels. Hospital staffs often had problems with people moaning and groaning and screaming and crying desperately in their little chapels.

Fortunately, Elizabeth hadn't pressed him today to go to the hospital. He hoped she wouldn't. But the strongman inside of Ava had put out a desperate plea for assistance. He was offered more demons to fortify the stronghold. This only incited the strongman's rage. His answer was, "There aren't enough demons to stop this madman. What good are more demons who will only be cast out? What I want is for someone to stop this man from praying and fasting!"

The usual task force for such a prayer stoppage included spirits of doubt, carnality, distraction, self-rejection, self-hatred, unbelief, and tiredness. However, after Jonathan's case was reviewed, it was determined that his understanding of his sonship in God was so strong that self-rejection and self-hatred were to be replaced with spirits that would at least have half a chance. So spirits of doubt and distraction took their place.

Jonathan was in the garage. Both vehicles were parked outside. So he had all the room he needed. He liked to walk as he prayed, especially when he was on a long fast. Walking did at least two things for this dagger.

First, it was a natural outlet for the emotional duress he felt. Prayers of this sort were physically, emotionally, and spiritually draining. They required everything of him. Most people didn't understand his praying style because they didn't understand spiritual warfare, and they didn't believe their prayers could and would affect what they were praying for anyway. It was only natural for people who didn't understand or believe in prayer to not put as much energy into it as he did.

Second, walking as he prayed kept him from falling asleep. A successful prayer warrior had to be as practical as he was spiritual. He had only been fasting two days, but the body responded differently to fasts. Sometimes a three-day fast seemed like it would kill him. Sometimes a ten-day fast was relatively easy. He had only been on three forty-day fasts. And each of those had been different. These longer fasts had their cycles of heaven and hell days.

The one common thread of all his fasts, however, was that his body had a way of telling him it didn't appreciate going without food. One of those ways was physical weakness. With physical weakness came the increased probability that when he kneeled to pray, he'd wake up mad later.

Jonathan walked slowly in a square, close to the garage walls. His body dragged. Each step felt as though he were taking the last step of a vigorous mountain hike. "I rebuke you, in the name of Jesus." His voice was stronger than his body felt.

A jolt shook the dagger's body. He didn't feel it, but the three pudgy demons did. The fattest of the three had his arms wrapped around Jonathan's torso from the back. He gripped one of his own wrists tighter. His legs were too short to wrap around the dagger. So he tried to secure his position by stepping on the heads of the two demons who had each wrapped themselves around Jonathan's legs.

Jonathan's eyes burned. He continued to walk. "I rebuke you, spirit of death, in Jesus's name. Come out of her!"

A tremor came over the dagger's body, slight at first, but its intensity grew. The three demons had to work harder to hold on, especially the one wrapped around his torso. He was literally stomping the heads of the other two demons trying to stay on.

It came suddenly.

A jolt hit the dagger's body that sent the three demons spiraling. They hit the walls and fell to the floor in a collective stupor. *What was that?* But their questioning was but a brief moment. Something instinctive compelled them back to their prey. The demon who had been wrapped around Jonathan's torso tried to take one of the legs. The demon already there beat him back. He tried the other leg and was beat back again. He immediately climbed up the dagger and wrapped his arms around him as though he had fully expected his attempts to get a leg would fail.

This cycle of the demons of tiredness jumping on the dagger and being thrown against the wall continued, but in no particular order. Sometimes the demons were hurled against the wall at or near the time the dagger rebuked the devil. Sometimes the jolt came with no sign whatsoever. But always the pig-looking demons recovered and immediately returned.

*****

The strongman would not fail. *He would not fail!* Death inspected the walls of his stronghold himself. As demons often did, he resorted to the imagery of the world of the sons of Adam. His walls looked as though they had taken direct hits from army tanks and artillery. Christians all over the world were praying for this Ava woman.

Fortunately, however, these were mostly *prayers in passing*, as demons were fond of calling them. Passing prayers were those offered with little emotion, fervor, or tenacity. But even these kinds of prayers were often troublesome. If enough of them piled on, they could eventually reach a tipping point that would unleash an avalanche of power.

Plus, sometimes the enemy treated a short prayer as though it were one of those loathsome, dagger-like prayers. He called it grace. But call it what He may, it was another proof of His unjust and arbitrary rule.

To make matters worse, there was Elizabeth with her constant, repulsive pleas and cries to God, and the thorn, Sharon, being a constant pain in his darkest area. Then there was that disgusting hemorrhoid of a dagger, Jonathan. His pounding of their position was relentless.

Death thought cynically of the precarious position he was in. *This dagger must be stopped or I'll be humiliated.*

Death was pure darkness. The blackest of black. The core of his body was solid, but a never-still, wavy mist emanated a few feet from his core. Hidden in the mist were clawed hands that periodically reached out and swiped, like a beast hunting for unwary prey.

Death tapped the toe of his large boot on the ground. Something had to give. Angels were snatching demons from their posts before his very eyes. His stronghold was slowly, but inevitably becoming a stronghold in name only. He'd have to use every weapon at his disposal to fight off this ferocious attack. The rest would be luck. He'd have to hope that this dagger would grow tired and quit. Or maybe the dagger would have a lapse of faith and focus on the apparent power of the stronghold instead of the real power of his hideous God.

But Death couldn't accept betting his life on winning a spiritual lottery. The *Dark Prison* was full of demons who had purchased losing tickets (although spirits of death weren't ever punished by Satan in this way). No, if he was going to rely on luck, he'd have to help luck look his way. Somehow he would get more distracting demons assigned to that dagger.

*****

The Mighty Bashnar had to weigh Death's request carefully. On one hand, Jonathan was focused on Ava, and as long as he was focused on Ava, he was *not* available to help the worm and the Atlanta revival. On the other hand, if Jonathan stayed focused on Ava, the chances were good that the stronghold would eventually fall. This would release another terrorist dagger. Plus, when strongholds fell, the calamitous effect was often more far-reaching than anyone ever anticipated.

The Mighty Bashnar's dark mind recalled many such so-called no-win scenarios, and he was still here to reminisce. *Death by blade or bullet* was all the menu offered. Blades could be just as lethal as bullets, but they were slower. He chose the blade. This would give him a little more time. The warrior spirit's face carried a heavy scowl. He was a master strategist. *A little extra time in the hands of the Mighty Bashnar is all I need*, he thought.

He would send Death hundreds of demons, even thousands if necessary, to reinforce his stronghold. This would keep the dagger busy and unavailable for the worm. But he would not send more distracting spirits to the dagger. They probably would fail anyway at getting this man of God to stop praying, but what if they did succeed? The last thing he needed was a dagger with a lot of time on his hands.

The Atlanta revival was priority number one. Death's predicament was his own pot of stew. The Mighty Bashnar would do all he could to let it simmer as long as necessary.

*****

News travelled fast in the dark kingdom. Everyone had heard of the siege of Ava's stronghold. Controllus explained the situation to Prince Krioni and was granted access to as many distracting spirits as he needed to break it.

*****

Jonathan had been praying for several hours. He hadn't expected an easy time in prayer. But he hadn't expected such resistance this early in the prayer. He was only closing in on three days. This felt like a ten-day battle already. He unfolded a chair and sat down. This felt soooooo good.

Get the iron. Get two bungee cords. Go to the den. Stand beside the bookshelf.

Jonathan's eyes popped open. This was not a still, small voice. It was loud and distinct. The words made no sense, but that was irrelevant. Many of God's words didn't make sense—until they did make sense. It didn't make sense when the Holy Spirit had told Jesus to put mud in a man's eyes for his healing either. He grabbed two bungee cords and quickly left the garage. He went upstairs to get the iron. He saw Elizabeth taking a nap.

Jonathan stood by the big bookcase. He carried their iron in one hand and the bungee cords in the other. He stood there for, oh, he didn't know. It had to be forty-five minutes or so. He often didn't wear a watch when he was on his stronghold schedule. Watches were just distractions when dealing with strongholds.

He let out a tired breath and rubbed his eyes with the hand that carried the bungee cords. *How long are you going to stand here?* he heard the thought. *Until God tells me not to,* he thought. He stretched his neck and peeked around the bookcase. Someone was tapping at the window. Who could that be? Sharon? No, that didn't make sense.

The glass broke.

Jonathan's body tensed. Someone was breaking into their home. Jonathan pressed his body against the wall and glanced around the room with wide eyes. He saw a gloved hand reach through the broken window and turn the latch.

The iron!

Jonathan gripped the iron tightly. What better way to welcome a burglar into his home than by breaking his hand? He was about to come from behind the bookcase when he thought about the bungee cords. Why had God told him to carry two bungee cords? *Yes. That's it!*

Jonathan pressed his back against the wall again. He tried to control his rapid breaths. He couldn't do anything if he passed out first.

The burglar lifted the window and stuck his head in. Jonathan waited until the man was half-way in. He slammed the flat part of the heavy iron on the intruder's head. The man's body went scarily limp. Jonathan hoped that the man wasn't dead. He stood there for a moment just looking at him. First time for everything.

He grabbed the man under both arms and pulled the rest of him into the house. He put the man's hands behind his back and wrapped the bungee cords as tight as he could. *Too bad, buddy, if it's too tight.* He did the same with his feet.

What if he's not alone? he thought. His momentary humor was replaced with alarm. How many times could the iron trick work? He crept to the side of the window. He reminded himself that God probably had other plans for him today than being killed by burglars. Otherwise, why would He have told him about this fellow? He pushed out a breath and pulled back the curtain.

No one.

Jonathan let out a really long and grateful breath. But was there someone waiting on the street? He stuck his head out of the window. He couldn't see around the house. He looked at the knocked-out burglar. "You wait right there," he said to him. Jonathan went to the front door and looked out the peephole. No one. "Liz," he yelled upstairs a couple of times before he got a response. "A guy broke into the house. He's tied up in my den."

She ran to the bannister and looked down. "What? Somebody broke in?"

"Yeah. It's okay. He's tied up in my den. The Lord told me he was coming. Call 911 and go into our room and lock the door. Don't come out until you hear me say, 'The Lord is good, and His mercy endures forever,'" he said. "Things get interesting, you know what to do, Liz."

Elizabeth ran into the room and locked the door.

Jonathan cracked open the front door and pulled it slowly. There was a car parked on the street at his mailbox. He put his hand behind him and took a few steps forward. He knew the guy in the car couldn't see that his hand was empty. "Your friend's inside. Come on up," said Jonathan, motioning with his arm. "The cops are on the way, but we can have a little chat before they get here."

The man in the car looked at the man walking toward him. He couldn't see what he had behind him, but he didn't have to see it to know what he had. The car's tires squealed, leaving a trail of black rubber burned into the street.

"Thank...you...Jesus!" said Jonathan. He hurried back up the hill and into the house. He went into the den. "Good," said Jonathan, to the back of the man's head. "You're still here. At least you're not rude. Hold up for a second. I have to get my wife. I'll be right back."

Jonathan stood beneath the upstairs bannister "Liz, come on down and meet our guest. The Lord is good, and His mercy endures forever." Jonathan walked back to the den. He turned the burglar over onto his back.

The man was young. Late twenties. Early thirties maybe. But they were hard years.

"Meth?" asked Jonathan.

The man glared at Jonathan in silence.

"Figured," said Jonathan. "It'll do that to you."

Elizabeth walked into the room sideways, like a ninja warrior. In her hand was a large pistol.

"Liz, is that really necessary? I told you he was tied up," said Jonathan. He looked at the burglar. Fear had replaced the glare. "What's your name?" he asked him.

"T," he answered.

"T? Just T?" asked Jonathan. "Well, T, we have ourselves a situation here. You have broken into our home. My wife, the one with the Glock 32 in her hand... For the life of me, I don't know why she chose that one. Why a .357? She has a real problem with ex-cons breaking into her home."

The man wouldn't take his eyes off of Elizabeth. It could've been because she had come into the room like she was the FBI. It could've been because she looked very calm with a gun in her hands—it was the calm ones you had to worry about. They had some killer in them. Or it most likely was because she had pointed that pistol at him since she had entered the room.

"Elizabeth loves the Lord," said Jonathan, "but she still has some fleshly ways about her. I've tried to talk to her about guns and all, but she has some things in her past that, well, I'll just say that I'm a Psalm 91 guy and she's a Glock 32 girl."

"How'd you know I'm an ex-con?" the burglar asked without taking his eyes off of Elizabeth. She looked like she was thinking crazy.

"Your tattoo. Your cute little tear drop by your eye," said Jonathan. "Where you do your time?"

The man laughed and said, “Which time?” He looked at Elizabeth. His laughter went on mute.

“Never mind,” said Jonathan. “It’s irrelevant. Liz, what do you think we should do with him?”

“Whadda’ya mean?” the man asked nervously.

“T, I was speaking to my wife. Liz, what—wait a minute.” Jonathan turned the man over on his belly and lifted up his jacket. He looked at the gun and smiled, but a chill went over him. He turned the man back over on his back. “T, you have a gun. You are an ex-con with a gun committing a crime. That’s bad news. But that’s your business. What I want to know is why did you come here to kill me and my wife?”

“What?” said Elizabeth.

The burglar looked at Elizabeth with wide eyes. “Wait. Wait. Wait, man.” He took a breath. “Just wait a minute. I didn’t come here to kill nobody. I came—”

“Shut up,” said Jonathan. “You came to kill us, and I want to know why.” The man opened his mouth, but Jonathan put his finger to his lips. “Liz, this man didn’t come here to steal from us. He came to kill us. Now I’m sure you’ll agree that the best way to deal with this kind of sinner is to kill him. We can do that. I can set him up and you can pump two bullets into his chest.”

“Wait a minute!” said the burglar.

“I thought I told you to shut up,” said Jonathan.

“Just call the police, man. You don’t have to do this,” the man begged.

“Jonathan, are you serious?” asked Elizabeth.

“Are you people serious?” the man yelled. “You’re a preacher. You can’t go around killing people like this.”

Jonathan turned his head one way and then the other. He looked at his wife, then at the would-be killer. “So this wasn’t random, T? How’d you know that I’m a preacher? Who wants me dead?”

“Man, if I tell you, they’ll kill me,” he answered.

“Liz,” said Jonathan, “we heard something, got the gun, came into the den—”

"Okay. Okay." The man shook his head. "They gonna kill me for telling you this." The man looked at Elizabeth. The crazy broad was still pointing that freakin' gun at him. "All I know is you made somebody real mad when you and those people got the feds to raid that mansion."

"The Mansion?" said Elizabeth. "The girls."

"Yeah, the girls," said the man.

"The name. Give me the name," said Jonathan.

"I didn't talk to the man, you know face-to-face." The man wasn't trying to be funny, especially with Elizabeth pointing the gun at him, but he chuckled. "I mean the man don't talk to you face-to-face. He don't—"

"Can't you think of better things to do today than to get yourself shot? Give me the name, T," said Jonathan.

"Michael Bogarti," the man said. "Now will you call the police?"

"They're already on the way. They should be here any minute," said Jonathan.

"What? Man, you played me. You played me. I don't believe this. You wasn't gonna kill me," said the man.

"Liz, lower the gun, baby, and go get this gentleman a bottle of water."

She left and Jonathan got on one knee next to the man. "T, I'm a servant of the Lord. I don't tie up intruders and shoot them. I'd at least take the bungee cords off you first. If they're too tight, we can take them off when my wife comes back." Jonathan smiled at his frightened visitor. "Don't be so serious. I'm just kidding."

The intruder let out a nervous breath.

Jonathan's smile left. "T, the Lord Jesus saved your life. You could've just as easily have met Mrs. Glock instead of Mr. Iron. You understand what I'm saying?"

"Yeah," the man answered. *What is taking those freakin' cops so long to get here?*

Elizabeth returned with her Glock 32 and a bottle of water.

Chapter 20

The Mighty Bashnar and his officers watched Edwin and his family get into their car and leave the hospital parking deck. “You’ll never make it home, worm,” he said.

*****

Barbara was not convinced that Andrew getting a concussion, and Sharon knocking herself out on the stairs was good news. “How can this possibly be considered good news, Edwin?” she asked.

Edwin turned on his left signal and looked both ways and pulled out. “Not good news, honey. Just not as bad as it could’ve been. Andrew has a mild concussion, no broken bones. And Sharon got a strained neck, but didn’t get a concussion. And no broken bones.”

“We should praise the Lord, Mom,” said Sharon, closing her eyes. “Thank you, Jesus, for protecting us. We love you.”

Barbara rolled her eyes and exhaled sharply. “Really, Sharon. Now we’re thanking God for accidents.”

“No, Mom, we’re thanking God despite the accidents,” said Sharon. “We’re supposed to give thanks to God in everything.”

“That’s easy for you to say,” said Andrew, offering a straight-faced joke.

Sharon looked at his neck brace. "I think it makes you look cute. It'll probably help your posture."

"Ha, ha," said Andrew. "Very funny. You get to use yours like it's make-up. I've got to wear this thing forever."

"Oh, stop whining, will you?" laughed Sharon. "You can use my make-up any time you want?"

"Don't even play like that, Sharon. This country's in bad enough shape already," said Barbara.

Sharon and Andrew looked at one another and stifled their laughs.

The blocking spirit hovered at the intersection.

Edwin smiled at the banter and looked ahead as he approached the intersection. He drove past the edge of the block.

"Edwin, watch out!" screamed Barbara.

Edwin whipped his neck in the direction of his wife's terror. He slammed his foot on the brake pedal. The Rover slid forward, carrying them into the middle of the intersection. A fast approaching car from the right swerved to its right and barely missed them. They heard a horrifying screeching sound to their left. Everyone in the car turned to see the wheeled missile sliding toward them. It seemed to screech forever before stopping only inches from their vehicle.

They sat there in the middle of the intersection at a red light, while everyone around looked at them. The guy whose car almost slid into them glared into their car.

Edwin lowered his window. He lifted his hand. "I'm sorry."

"I agree, you idiot. How could you not see that red light?" asked the man.

Edwin grimaced in embarrassment and drove away. No one said anything until Edwin almost drove through another red light at the very next corner. The car skidded to an abrupt stop, well past the end of the corner. Everyone sat in frozen silence, staring at Edwin like he was insane.

"Edwin, what is wrong with you?" demanded Barbara. "Are you trying to kill us?"

"Dad, you alright?" asked Andrew.

"Dad, let me drive," said Sharon, opening the door and stepping outside.

Edwin was shaken. He didn't know what was happening to him. Was he sick? Had he had a stroke?

Sharon opened Edwin's door. "Come on, Dad. I'll get us home." She touched his arm and smiled. He got out and they switched seats.

The Mighty Bashnar looked around in a complete circle. He didn't see any angels. He didn't sense any angels. But twice this worm had been spared. He yanked the *Job Strategy* authorization paper from his pocket and thrust it into the air over his head. "Is this how you honor your word, oh, Lord Most High? I have authority to destroy this worm!" He turned to the demons who were with him. "Follow me."

*****

The blue mist was large enough to cover a person. It moved slowly down the dark, narrow streets of English Avenue. The crime-filled neighborhood was one of Atlanta's worst. There were nearly as many vacant homes as there were homes with people living in them. But many of the vacant houses were only sporadically vacant. For some of them were favorites of the homeless or drug addicts or prostitutes and their clients.

Ironically, this desert of poverty, crime, and despair attracted a constant stream of suburbanites who wanted to alter their state of consciousness with something other than alcohol. Day and night, they brazenly descended from all over Atlanta in their nice cars upon this economically depressed and business forsaken community of dilapidated homes to buy heroin.

Oh, there had been well-intentioned efforts here and there over the decades to do something about the blight and crime and heroin trafficking. But the demons that drove this area outlasted the momentum of politicians' speeches and infrequent local news stories.

This was the community known as *The Bluff*.

Octavius "Prince" Monroe opened the door and stepped onto the porch of a house that appeared so feeble he might've fallen through its floor to join the rodents below. He pulled the sweatshirt hood onto his head, covering his pride and joy dreadlocks. One hand was deep into his pants pocket. The pocket with the gun it. The other hand held his pants up. He looked out into the darkness and rocked his head. "Yeah," he said to himself. "Nigga, gone be paid tonight."

He ran down the crooked stairs and crossed the street and walked across the gravel lot that was next to a house that had almost burned to the ground before the fire department stopped the blaze. Lil' Rick had died in that fire. The house ruins sat as a testament to the community. What had been lost in the fire was gone forever; what had escaped the fire was not only worthless, it was ugly.

The Mighty Bashnar loved this community. It was a good community. Death was everywhere. Not just the many death spirits that lingered over the area, or those that hung around homes where junkies had overdosed. It was not the spirit of death, but the essence of death in a community such as this that was so invigorating.

The Mighty Bashnar took a deep, satisfying breath. Once the last of this breath had joined the stillness of the night, he looked at the blue mist slowly making its way down the street. His gaze followed the path of the mist across the gravel lot. The same path that Octavius had taken.

"What is that thing doing here?" asked one of the demons with Bashnar.

The Mighty Bashnar didn't answer.

They all followed the mist that was following their man. They saw him and another guy get into their stolen black Toyota RAV4 and drive off to go, as they called it, *shopping*. They watched with enraged intrigue as the blue mist descended upon the vehicle.

*****

Sharon pulled into the Kroger's parking lot and drove slowly past a Toyota RAV4 that was parked at the base of the hill. She didn't see the car or the people in it, but they saw her and the 2014 Range Rover Sport.

"You see that white girl?" said Ant, short for Antoine.

Prince rocked his head back and forth, showing teeth that hosted two gold ones on the top, and holding himself between his legs and squeezing. "Yeah. Yeah. I saw it, Dog. But I *wanna* see it. You feel me? You see that Rover?"

"Time to go shopping," said Ant. He posted a big smile that looked more like a snarl.

"Be right back." Edwin hopped out and went inside the store.

A black vehicle turned into the parking space next to where Sharon was parked. The driver put his left hand up to his face and turned to the right. The passenger slipped on a ski mask large enough to handle his dreadlocks and pulled his sweatshirt hood over the mask. He put his head down and walked up to Barbara's window and tapped.

"What does he—?" She saw the gun and froze.

Sharon's mouth gaped. She saw the ski mask. She saw the angry eyes. But most of all she saw the gun pointing at her mother. The robber twirled his hand, motioning her to roll down the window. She pushed the button and nothing happened. The robber aimed the barrel right at her mother's face. Sharon didn't know what to do. She saw the robber's mouth moving and heard sounds coming from his mouth, but her fear didn't let her understand what he was saying.

"You deaf?" barked Prince. "You want me to cap you, girl?"

Sharon trembled her head no.

"Turn the key," ordered Prince.

Sharon pushed the ignition button.

"Now open the door," he ordered.

She unlocked it.

He yanked open Barbara's door. "Get out and get in the back seat."

Barbara hurried and obeyed. Andrew scooted to the far left as his mom got in next to him.

Prince got in where Barbara had been sitting and slammed the door. “Who wants to get shot?” He looked at Andrew and pointed the gun in his direction. “You?”

“No,” Andrew answered quickly.

“Well don’t yo’ crippled butt try to be no hero, and maybe you won’t get shot tonight,” said Prince.

“What do you want?” asked Barbara.

The robber’s face twisted. He looked at Barbara as though she were crazy. “What do you think I want? I’m in yo’ car with a gun in my hand. I want some money.”

Barbara started to open her purse.

He snatched the purse out of her hand. “You trying to get shot. How do I know you don’t have a gun in here?” he said, rummaging through her purse, throwing stuff on the floor.

“I don’t have a gun. I don’t believe in guns,” said Barbara.

The robber smiled. “I like that. Leave the guns to people like me.”

“You’ve got my mom’s purse,” said Sharon. “Just take the money and leave. You can have our phones, too. And take Mom’s watch and just go.”

Barbara nearly scratched herself to death trying to get the watch off. “Here. Take it.” She tossed it onto his lap.

“What?” the robber snapped. “Did I ask you for your phone?”

Sharon sighed heavily. “No,” she said in a whisper.

“What kind of phone you got?” he asked.

“Galaxy 6s,” she answered.

“That the one with the little pen thing?” he asked, as Sharon handed him her phone.

“No. That’s the Galaxy Note. Mom’s got a Galaxy Note,” said Sharon.

He looked at the phone he pulled out of Barbara’s purse and smiled. “Yeah. Yeah,” he said, rocking his head. “This tight. I been wantin’ one of these little pen things.”

"Now you've got one," said Sharon. "Will you leave us alone now? You've got our phones, our money, and Mom's credit cards. Can you just—"

"You talk a lot," he said.

Sharon stopped talking and started praying.

"We gone sit right here until Daddy comes back," he said.

This triggered something in Sharon. Before she knew what she was doing, she reached for the door.

"Girl, what the—?" He slammed the side of the gun against her head twice. Sharon screamed and grabbed her head. Barbara and Andrew started to lunge forward to help Sharon. The robber pointed the gun at Andrew. He reached back and pushed Barbara in the face. "Y'all, better sit the hell down! You think this is a joke? You think I'm a joke?"

Sharon was doubled over. She held her head in her hands with her eyes closed. Her head was throbbing. Her neck felt like a knife was hanging out of it. She had never felt pain like this before. She started crying. "I'm sorry," she sobbed. "I don't think you're a joke. I think you were created in God's image and you don't know it yet. It's just that I love my dad and I don't want you to hurt him. Ohhhhh, Mom, my neck."

Prince twisted his nose like something stank. "Whu? Girl, you one crazy sumpmem." He looked at the blood coursing down her face.

Barbara listened to her daughter's groans. She wanted with all of her heart to help her, but couldn't. The feeling of helplessness and shame overwhelmed her. She burst out in tears.

Prince shook his head. "Momma, what's your name?" he asked without turning around.

"Barbara," she whimpered between sobs.

"Barbara, if you don't shut up, I'm going to crack her upside her head again."

Barbara gulped down her tears and quickly wiped her face. "Okay," she said.

Prince looked out Sharon's window. "Here comes Daddy. I swear to God, if he doesn't get in this car, I'm going to shoot all of y'all.

Edwin walked toward the car with a couple of plastic bags in one hand and a large broom in the other. He daydreamed as he walked. He had almost killed his family twice in one day. *Run a red light twice within a minute?* He walked to the back of the vehicle and opened the back and put the bags and broom inside. Just before the door shut, he saw what appeared to be someone sitting in the driver's seat. It wasn't Sharon. He walked up to the door and it opened.

"Get in the back or I'll cap you right now," said Prince.

Edwin didn't move. He looked at the eyes behind the mask. He looked at the gun pointed at his belly. He looked inside the open back door. His family was terrified. Edwin glanced around the parking lot. Two-hundred people in the store and almost no one in the parking lot. And those few people weren't paying them any attention. He looked back inside the car. Sharon was bleeding.

"Nigga, I ain't got all day. Get in the car," ordered the robber.

Barbara scooted over. Edwin sat down and shut the door.

"Drive," ordered the robber.

"Where to?" asked Sharon.

"Just drive, girl," he snapped. "I'll tell you what to do."

Edwin reached across Andrew and pulled his wife's head to his cheek. "Are you okay?" he asked.

"Yes," she answered weakly. "I'm okay. He hit Sharon."

"I'm okay, Dad," she said. "The Lord will protect us."

"She's okay, Dad. The Lord's got her back." Prince looked at Sharon. He showed those two gold teeth. "Yeah," he said, with a rocking head, "I bet you got some back, too."

Edwin's eyes got dark. "You filthy—"

The gun barrel pointed at his forehead froze him in mid-lunge. "Do you care about your family?"

Edwin glared into the robber's eyes before answering. "Yes."

"Then sit down," he ordered.

Edwin sat back in his seat.

"Thank you, Dad," said Sharon.

Edwin and the robber looked at Sharon, wondering.

The robber directed them to a bank ATM.

"Hero," he said to Edwin, "what's your daily ATM limit?"

"A thousand," said Edwin.

The robber smiled. "What about your credit cards?"

"I don't know," he answered.

"You better hope it's enough," said the robber.

Edwin got out of the car and looked at the SUV that had parked several spaces away. He was following them. They were working together. Edwin came back to the car with a handful of money. "Enough?" asked Edwin.

The robber bared his golden smile and rocked his head. "Yeah. Yeah. Nigga gettin' paid." He looked at Sharon. "Nig-ga getting paid," he said again. "What?" he asked, in response to her frown.

"Why do you call yourself that?" she asked.

"What?" he asked.

"*That*. You know. The N-word," she said.

He found this quite funny. "Oh, Lawd" he said, when he finished laughing. "The *N*-word," he teased. "Now it's the N-word. You crackers sumpmem else. You serious? Y'all created the word. Now you gone tell me it's wrong." He shook his head and enjoyed intermittent chuckles. "Go to 400 South," he said. "It's right when you say it's right," he muttered under his breath, "and wrong when you say it's wrong. Y'all can go to hell."

"Why'd you call my father the N-word?"

"What?" Prince looked at Sharon. He couldn't believe this girl. "Do you ever shut up?"

"Sharon," said Edwin.

"Sharon, listen to your dad," said Prince.

They drove in silence for about a minute.

"Why'd you call my dad the N-word?" asked Sharon again.

"What...the...hell?" said the exasperated robber. "Snow White, I call everybody nigga. You, me, him, yo momma, yo broke-neck brother, everybody. Okay?"

"You're not a nigger," said Sharon.

Edwin, Barbara, and Andrew sat as though someone had just shoved ice sickles up their spines.

Prince shook his head. "Dad, can you do something with your daughter?"

"He did do something with me. He brought me up in the fear of the Lord," she said.

"Fear of the Lord? The only thing you need to fear is me," he said. His tone was serious.

"I don't fear you," said Sharon.

"Oh, God," whispered Barbara. "Edwin, make your daughter be quiet."

"You don't, huh?" The robber answered as though he was more than willing to give her a reason to fear him.

"Do you want to know why?" she asked.

Andrew shook his head in disbelief for everyone in the back.

"The only way to shut you up is to shoot you, isn't it," said the robber. Prince shook his head in defeat. "Why?"

"Because God sent you to us," said Sharon.

"Oh, Sharon, please!" begged Barbara.

"God sent me to you?" He chuckled. "Momma, did God send me to you?"

Barbara cut nervous eyes at him without actually making eye contact.

"Better listen to yo momma, girl. God didn't send me to you. Satan did."

Sharon looked at him a long time.

"Sharon, keep your eyes on the road," said Prince.

"Oh, so now I'm Sharon." A little smile formed on her face.

Barbara was aghast. "Edwin," she whispered, "is she flirting with him?"

Edwin wasn't going to waste the effort it would take to answer his wife. He took a deep breath and went back to praying.

"Don't try to play me, girl," he said.

"I'm not trying to play you," said Sharon. "It's just that I was right about you."

He looked at her.

"Under that mask is a person. Not a robber. Not a killer. And not a nigger."

"Nigger?" he said.

"Oh, I'm sorry. I pronounced it wrong. I meant to say nigga," said Sharon. "You're none of those things. You're someone valuable to God. Someone special."

The man in the mask stared at her for a few moments and turned and looked straight ahead. "Keep your eyes on the road, Sharon."

"Who's praying for you?" said Sharon.

Oh, my God, this white girl is crazy. "Nobody," he said.

"That's not true. Who's praying for you?" He didn't answer. "You don't have to be afraid. You're the one with the gun."

"That's enough, Sharon," said Barbara.

"Yeah. Will you *pleeeez* be quiet?" said Andrew.

"Mother? Grandmother?" asked Sharon.

They drove in silence for a couple of minutes.

"Mother," said the robber.

"I knew it!" Sharon exclaimed. "That's why God sent you to us. Your mother's prayers sent you here because God knew we'd tell you about His love." Sharon bounced with glee as she spoke. "I don't know why, but I think God wants me to tell you something."

The robber waited. What else could he do?

"I'm a prophetess," she said.

"Edwin, are you going to do something?" This time Barbara didn't whisper.

"Snap, girl. My momma's a prophetess. She got like fifty or sixty people in her church. She the pastor." The robber said this with pride.

"You see—" Sharon stopped when she was about to say his name. She didn't know his name. "I know you can't give me your name, but can you just make up one I can use for now?"

"Yeah. Call me Prince," he said.

"You can be more than a prince," said Sharon. "God is calling you to be a king."

"King? Girl, you trippin'."

Sharon's mouth fell open. She looked at Prince. She looked at Dad."

"Look where you going," said Prince, his old robber's voice returning.

"Dad, God spoke to me," she said.

Oh, God. Oh, God. Oh, God, thought Edwin.

"Octavius," she said.

The robber jumped in his seat. "What the hell?" he yelled.

"Octavius Monroe," she said. "Your name is Octavius Monroe. They call you Prince."

The robber frantically looked to the right and left out all windows. He even looked up at the sky as though SWAT was going to repel from a helicopter onto the car.

"Octavius—" Sharon began.

"Shut up!" Octavius yelled. "Keep driving." He pulled out his phone and called the guy following him. "This cracker know my name! What? I don't know, man."

Sharon and her family sat in silence as the robber said nothing for a long while to the person on the phone. The robber hung up. "Get off at the next exit," he ordered.

"What are you going to do, Octavius?" asked Sharon.

"Stop saying my name! How the—?" He shook his head. This couldn't be happening. That judge had told him that if he saw him in his courtroom for any reason, even if he was there as a witness for someone else, he was going to send him away for at least twenty-five years. He had three white people in the car. Three kidnapped white people. Three counts of kidnapping. Three counts of armed robbery.

Assault with a deadly weapon. *Who knows what else that fat cracker will come up with? Man, that's life! I'm not going to prison for life.*

"Look at me, Octavius," Sharon pleaded. "Don't panic. God told me your name so you'd know He's real."

Octavius was going to put the gun up to Sharon, but she was just crazy enough to not care. He turned around and pointed the gun at her father. "Get off at the next exit or I'll shoot him first, then her, then your brother."

"Do what he says," Barbara begged.

"Sharon," Andrew also begged.

Edwin exhaled as slowly as the situation would allow. "Honey, follow your heart."

Sharon almost couldn't believe it. Her face didn't smile, but her heart did. She stomped on the gas pedal. The powerful engine propelled them forward.

"What are doing?" screamed the robber. "Stop this car!"

"Calm down, Octavius!" screamed Sharon. "You don't have to be afraid. You're not going to jail!"

"Sharon, stop the car!" he yelled. He looked forward and behind. He didn't see any cars. "Don't make me kill y'all."

"That's what you're planning to do anyway, Octavius. I know that's what you're planning. That's what that guy told you on the phone." They were doing one hundred miles per hour. "Octavius, there's some cars up there. I'm not slowing down."

Octavius thought about it. If he shot them fast enough, he could grab the steering before—

"Don't try it, Octavius," said Sharon. She could see his fear under the mask, in his eyes. "Lower the window and throw the gun out. I'll let you out."

"What the hell you take me for?" he asked.

"Octavius, you believe in God. I know you do. You know where you're going if we all die. You're going to hell, Octavius. Is that what you want?"

Octavius looked around like a cat surrounded by wild dogs. He had no answers. "Sharon, please, I don't want to go back to prison."

"Throw the gun out the window."

He did.

"Now take off that stupid mask," said Sharon.

He shook his head in disbelief and pulled it off.

Sharon took her shaking foot off the gas pedal and pulled over on the side of the highway. She got out and ran a few yards away from the back of the car. She doubled over and threw up. She spit and looked up, holding her belly. She saw her mom throwing up. After a few minutes, all that was going to come up had come up.

Sharon walked over to her mom and dad. "I'm sorry, Mom."

Barbara couldn't talk. She patted Sharon on the shoulder and nodded.

Edwin pulled out his phone.

Sharon covered his hand. "What are you doing, Dad?"

"I'm calling the police," he answered.

"Please don't," she asked.

"Sharon, look at your head. Look at your mother. He was going to kill all of us," said Edwin. "You want to let him go so he can do this to someone else? The next person may not be so lucky."

Sharon covered Edwin's phone with both hands. "Dad, we weren't lucky. You know that. You know God sent him to us. How do you think I knew who he was? Do you think God sent him to us so we can send him to prison or so that we can save him from prison?"

Edwin's face was hard. He didn't answer. He gently touched his daughter's head. "I'm so proud of you."

Sharon started crying. She smiled through her tears. "And I'm so proud of you." She took his hand. "Dad, I told Octavius that he wouldn't go to jail. But you're my father. I'll accept whatever you decide."

Octavius sat half in and half out of the car, one foot on the ground, one foot in the car. When Edwin and Sharon walked up to him, he didn't even lift his head. He had the look of a condemned man. *Twenty-five years. Maybe more.*

"Octavius," said Sharon.

He looked up. His face full of shame.

"You have beautiful hair," she said.

Tears came out of his eyes. His voice cracked as he spoke. "You crazy, Sharon." He looked at the ground and grimaced. His life was over. He was going to prison forever. He thought about his mother. Her heart was going to be broken. She had prophesied over him that he was going to make it out of *The Bluff.* She had said that God told her he was going to be a great man of God, and that he would go all over the world preaching the gospel and saving many. *Saving many,* he thought cynically. *Guess Momma was wrong.* "Police coming?" he asked Sharon.

Sharon looked at her father. "Dad, are the police coming?"

He turned away and clamped his jaws tight. He closed his eyes. "God help me to be like Sharon," he said under his breath. He turned back around. "No, Octavius. Prison is no place for a king."

Sharon screeched like a child. "Thank you, Lord! Octavius, you're going to be a great man of God. Don't be surprised if God sends you all over the world preaching the gospel. He's got plans for you."

*****

Krioni-na looked at this spectacle with a mixture of disdain and delight. This worthless thug had repented of his sins and had become a child of God. It was almost as if the enemy had used the Mighty Bashnar to orchestrate this whole thing. He could not wait to report this to Prince Krioni.

And there was no way the Mighty Bashnar could stop him, even though he was but mere yards away watching this himself. Because they were not alone. Not too far in the distance was Controllus and the prince's six guards.

"Another flaming example of your brilliance and infinite wisdom," taunted Controllus before flying off.

The Mighty Bashnar was not stunned. He had seen remarkable conversions before. But he was immensely intrigued at the timing of this conversion.

Chapter 21

Michael had never been fascinated with the female body. At least not in the usual way men are fascinated with female anatomy. Nature had created women to give men babies and orgasms. He appreciated their ability to provide babies because of his father's heart. He loved children. He appreciated their ability to provide orgasms because of his MBA. He loved money. Fatherhood and pimping were in his blood.

Pimping.

It had gotten a bad rap. Everybody did it, but only a relatively few owned up to it. And those who did were persecuted. But what was pimping anyway? It was easy for most people to limit it to people being made to sell their bodies so others could profit. Girls on the corner with provocative clothing, with a pimp driving by keeping an eye on his merchandise. Girls kidnapped and holed up in a basement by brutes who make them do things demons wouldn't do. That was the comfortable definition. But what about the truth?

The truth was that American society had no problem with some kinds of pimping. Did it have a problem with pornography? Maybe some religious people. But most of the people who criticized it publicly, participated in it privately, even the religious folks. Their preachers had proven that point.

And it wasn't just dirty magazines and porn sites. What about those romance novels? They were filled with porn, and women couldn't get enough of those books. That was why romance had been, and probably always would be, the most popular book genre. And what about movie stars and singers? They weren't showing so much skin because it was a hundred and twenty degrees. *They were selling sex and everyone knew it.*

If pimping was using physical or psychological force to get someone to sell their bodies so others could profit, how was it not pimping for the entertainment industry to use its monopoly power to get people to take their clothes off on camera or stage to sell more tickets or magazines or movies or whatever?

Were the "artists" who did this any less whores than the girls on the corner? The only difference between the two was the amount of money they were paid and the level of respect they were given or not given.

What about the "managers" of these "artists?" How were they any different from traditional pimps who managed the careers of traditional whores? Sure these "managers" had contracts with their "artists," but traditional pimps also had contracts with their prostitutes. Of course, due to the prejudices of society, the contract relationship between pimps and prostitutes were verbal, but this didn't diminish their working relationship. They understood one another well.

Michael Bogarti both understood and scorned society's double standard. His kind may have been judged as criminals, but he was merely a persecuted businessman. Persecuted for doing exactly what others were celebrated for doing—making money off of sexual lust. As far as he was concerned, he was an honest businessman. A broker who brought together demand and supply.

There was one other hypocrisy about pimping that ticked off Michael. *The government's double standard.* He owned thriving clubs that employed hundreds of girls who made a killing selling sex. Oh, government regulations for Sexually Oriented Businesses (SOBs) prevented his girls from having sex on the premises, or contracting on the premises to provide paid sex off the premises. But his girls could slap their naked butts on a man's lap and gyrate until the poor fool exploded in his pants. That was all legal, and he had the licenses and paid the taxes to prove it.

The government and society, however, had a real problem with him diversifying into the sex slave business. He was apparently taking advantage of the weak and innocent. He admitted without hesitation (at least to himself) that there was some truth to this.

He exploited the weak at every opportunity. But if it was anyone's fault that the weak were exploited, it wasn't his. It was God's fault for making lions and lambs and putting them in the same neighborhood.

As for the accusation that his kind were ruthless exploiters of the innocent, who were the innocent? What made a woman innocent? Her age? What was that magic number? Fourteen- and fifteen-year-old girls had sex all the time. The first time he had sex, he was thirteen. She was twelve. Was she innocent?

The truth was there was no such thing as human innocence. A baby was only a sinner who hadn't yet learned to purposefully hurt people, and hadn't yet become strong enough to carry out those natural urges. Which one of his *permanent* girls who worked in any one of his many unregulated businesses under different circumstances wouldn't have shaken her butt in one of his clubs for a thousand dollars a night? So much for innocence.

Everyone wasn't honest about it, but everyone was on the take. And at the top of the food chain of hypocrites on the take were those who for obvious reasons used the services of his permanent workers. Michael had no philosophical problem with the fat cats who appreciated the services of his permanent workers. A successful businessman should be able to enjoy the fruit of his labors.

No, rather it was the politicians, judges, district attorneys, and law enforcement people whom he despised. But since it was extremely beneficial to do business with such people, he made sure he was their broker of choice.

Michael Bogarti downed the rest of his drink and put the glass down on the table hard. He looked across the table into the faces of two men who had been with him a long time. They were loyal. Smart. Ruthless. The only way anyone would get to his wife was over their two dead muscled bodies. That's why he had chosen them to guard his wife. That's why he had taken a drink after they told him what happened at the church.

Naked and nearly naked women were all around the three men. Some doing their things with the poles. Others selling souvenirs to men willing to pay ridiculous prices for items from beautiful girls wearing nearly nothing. Lust. Alcohol. Music. This finely tuned orchestration of commercial hypnotism and debauchery was there, but not there to Michael and the bodyguards. Even the best champagne lost its allure after drinking a bath tub full of it.

"A preacher pushed my wife down," said Michael, in a no-nonsense tone.

"He didn't push her, Mike. I was right there. He asked her if he could put his hands on her forehead to pray for her. She said yeah. He put—it was just the tips of his fingers. Bam! She hits the floor." This was Rick Marcello.

Rick was a straight shooter. Michael knew that if Rick said it happened like that, it happened like that. "And she came up saying *what?*" he asked.

Rick looked at the other bodyguard that had been there with him. The other bodyguard wasn't volunteering to answer. "We don't know?" said Rick.

"What do you mean, you don't know? She got up talking, right?" asked Michael.

"She was still on the floor," said Rick.

"Okay," said Michael, impatiently, "she's on the floor. She's talking. What did she say?"

"I don't know."

Michael gave him a look that said he didn't appreciate the answer.

"Look, Mike, Vivian fell out. The preacher didn't push her. She wiggled around on the floor like a snake or something and started talking funny." Rick looked at the other bodyguard. His expression told the other guy that he needed to say something.

"Vivian. My wife. The mother of my three children goes to a—what kind of church did you say?" said Michael.

Rick looked at the other bodyguard.

"Charismatic," said Lenny, the reluctant bodyguard.

Michael frowned and waved his hand. "A charismatic church, whatever that is, falls down at the front of the church and," he looked at Rick and Lenny and did his hand side to side, "wiggles like a snake and talks funny. Rick, Lenny, are we going to get to the part where one of you tell me what my wife said when she was rolling around on the floor?"

"Before she started talking funny," said Rick, "she said, 'Thank you, Jesus. Thank you, Jesus. I'm sorry. I'm going to make it right.'"

"So this is not the talking funny part?" said Michael. "There's another talking funny part?"

"Yeah, Mike," said Lenny. He cleared his throat. "She started saying some stuff, man. It was like she was really talking, you know. I mean like a language."

"I think she was talking in tongues," said Rick. There, it was out.

Michael's face didn't move. It held the cocked position it had when that last word came out of his trusted friend's mouth. A few more seconds of Michael sitting like a statue passed. When the initial shock wore off, he sat back in his chair.

No one knew what to say. So they said nothing for a couple of minutes.

Rick broke the silence. "Sounded like Japanese."

"Japanese?" said Michael.

"I don't think it was Japanese, Mike." This was Lenny. "My little girl's taking Japanese and it didn't sound like Japanese."

"Karen's taking Japanese?" asked Rick. "Hmph. They start 'em young, don't they?"

"I think it was Chinese," said Lenny.

Michael held his palms up, stopping them. "All this time, you're a linguist and you're just now telling us. Listen, I don't care if it was Japanese, Chinese, or Korean. What I *do* care about is what Vivian meant by 'I'm gonna make it right.'"

"Mike, there's something else," said Rick.

Mike shook his head with a cynical chuckle. "Of course, there is. What is it? It's not enough that Vivian's rolling around on the floor with the Pentecostals."

The two bodyguards looked at one another.

Lenny spoke up. "It's that church."

"That church," said Michael inquiringly.

Lenny saw when the darkness settled on the boss's face. Their eyes met. "Yeah, that one," he said.

The bodyguards knew what would come next. The boss's carefulness bordered somewhere between brilliant and paranoid, but that was fine with them. His skittishness had proven both ridiculously profitable and safe. Neither of the bodyguards saw the excitement in being the richest guy in prison. So they both went into what they called the zone. The zone was where everyone spoke as though they were being recorded by the FBI.

The zone was more than Michael Bogarti's *Never Go To Jail* card. It was also the organization's way of finding and eliminating informants. People with loose lips, people who spoke plainly, and people who asked questions were either stupid or working for the feds. These people were eliminated.

"Ironic, isn't it?" said Michael. "A thousand churches in Atlanta, and which one does Vivian choose to roll around on the floor in? Can you believe this? It's like a bad movie."

"There's something else, Mike," said Rick.

Mike looked at him with an *Are you kidding me?* expression.

Rick gave him a zone look. "That black rooster is still crowing."

Had an onlooker been asked to comment on Michael Bogarti's response to being told that Jonathan Banks was still alive, she would have said, He didn't respond. But Rick and Lenny saw the subtle anger. They also knew that this anger wouldn't go away until Jonathan Banks was dead. His anger was their orders.

"Gentlemen," Mike poured drinks for them all, "I'm sorry that you had to see this. Vivian doing something like this."

"It's okay, Mike," said Lenny.

"Yeah," added Rick, "women, they get emotional."

"It's humiliating," said Mike. "A woman of her stature shouldn't be on anyone's floor. My children's mother should not be on anyone's floor. It's humiliating."

There was silence.

"I'll talk to Vivian," said Mike. "She's a smart woman. She'll see that this isn't good for us." The men waited for their orders. "Churches like that...they're an embarrassment. *Sacred Heart* wouldn't do something like this. Do you see Father Russo pushing people down? That church humiliated me. That preacher—what's his name?"

"Edwin Styles," said Lenny.

"That Pentecostal preacher, Edwin Styles, he humiliated me and my children," said Michael.

Orders given. Orders received. Both men got up from the table and left.

*****

Michael sat with his leg crossed at the little table for two in their master bedroom. It sat next to an oversized window that overlooked the golf course. Their master bedroom was a *master* bedroom by any stretch of the imagination. Opulent and spacious. Michael thought of moving their discussion to the balcony, but his wife coming out of her deep, walk-in closet derailed that thought. He slowly put down his drink.

Vivian was a forty-year-old Italian beauty whose voluptuous body and exotically beautiful face had defiantly refused to age or to show evidence of having carried three children. Her long, dark hair draped freely over her shoulders as she lightly guided her long legs toward him. She had never needed make-up—her natural beauty was ravishing—but he saw that she wore eye make-up the way he liked it. A bit exaggerated. Really, the way she and he knew made it impossible for him to stop looking at them. *Vivian, what are you doing?*

She seemed to take forever to get to him. He was desperately intrigued by what she wore. Actually, by what she wasn't wearing. Their sex life had been like a rocket that had run out of fuel. Powerful, gravity-defying lift-off. Mellow, heavenly orbit. Sudden, unexpected crash. But the wreckage had not been totally unexpected.

The woman standing before him in a black negligee and matching panties and bra had told him months ago with tears in her eyes that he should not ask a question if he couldn't handle the answer. He had gotten the idea from the pain in her voice and the ice in her eyes that her answer would take them to a destination of no return. He remembered how she had dealt with her sister. *Vivian didn't have the capacity to forgive.*

He had a scary idea of why this amazing beauty, the one woman in the world whom he actually respected and admired, had quietly but firmly left him with nothing to hold, except the heat of his own memories. But some ideas were better left unexplored.

Vivian sat in her chair and crossed her long bare leg. "We need this talk."

Mike said nothing.

"I guess Lenny and Rick told you what happened," she said.

He nodded.

She smiled. "Hard to keep something like that a secret." She furrowed her eyebrows and thought about the day at the church.

Michael was lost in her eyes. Every time she batted her eyes, he felt like he was a fish on a hook being tugged in by an angler who wouldn't let go. An angler in a black negligee.

"Honestly, Mike, I don't know what happened. This morning I suddenly got a strong urge to go to church," she said.

"Not our church? Not *Sacred Heart*?" he asked.

"No," she said, thinking deeply.

Those eyes.

"I got this picture in my mind of the church I went to. I had never been there before. Don't know anyone who goes there," she said.

"You wouldn't," said Mike. "They're not Catholic."

"I know. That's what was so odd. Why would I go to a church like that?" she asked rhetorically.

That's what I want to know, thought Michael.

"Michael, I don't know why I went to that church. I don't know everything that happened to me. I'm still trying to figure that out. I can't believe—" She stopped herself from revealing that Lenny had shown her video on his phone of what she was doing on the floor. He wouldn't like that at all. She looked at him with a look he had *never* seen on her face. It was peace. "Here's what I do know that happened to me." A beautiful, soft smile rose on her peaceful face. "I felt something come inside of me that pushed out all of my anger."

This got Michael's attention. He shifted and put his elbow on the table and rested his chin in his hand.

"I forgive my sister for stealing my fiancé," she said in a dreamy whisper.

Michael stared at her intently. This time not because of her beauty. She *hated* her sister. A time or two she had even seemed but a step away from asking him to have her killed. He wondered how falling out on the floor in some weird church could cause such an unbelievable change in his wife. *Vivian didn't forgive anyone.* He trembled coolly as he contemplated how far she was going to take this forgiveness thing. How far she *could* take it.

"Amy is my big sister," said Vivian. "She was always my hero. I wanted to be like her in every way." Vivian looked at her husband with teary eyes. "Every way, Mike." She grimaced and the tears that had so suddenly appeared rolled down her face. She took a deep breath and regained her composure. "Until she broke my heart. Until she betrayed me."

Michael tensed.

"I almost asked you to help me with that problem," she said. "More than once."

Michael admired his wife freshly. This was just one of the reasons this woman had set herself apart from the gender he considered capital. She wasn't only smart. She wasn't only passionate. She wasn't only the mother of his children. She was deadly. She understood business. And she understood respect. "I know you did," he answered.

"I have something else I need to say, Michael," she said.

Michael Bogarti was a sex trafficker on an industrial scale.

Michael Bogarti was a violent extortionist.

Michael Bogarti was a killer and a friend of killers.

Michael Bogarti was terrified.

He went to lift his drink, but a soft, manicured hand with black nails touched his wrist. He put the glass down.

Vivian got out of her chair and kneeled before her husband. She looked up at him. "Michael, I knew there was no way you couldn't ask me to marry you after I let you taste what could become your regular diet."

Michael's eye twitched. Was she making a joke? Or was he simply hoping so? Where was she going with this?

"But I was honored when you asked me to become Mrs. Vivian Bogarti." She smiled and seemed to look into the past. "I promised myself that I would take care of you. I told myself that I would be everything you ever needed or desired." She looked at him with swift eyes. "Have I been, Michael?"

He swallowed. "Yes."

"I agree. I've been everything any man could ever hope for in a woman." She grinned without the accompanying emotion. "Am I beautiful, Michael?"

"Yes," he answered.

"As beautiful as our girls?" She spoke of the women who worked at their strip clubs.

"More beautiful." His answer was genuine. Inside, he was shaking his head. He had hoped for the impossible. This car was headed for a cliff.

Vivian took one of her hands off of Michael's legs and lightly stroked his cheek. "I am more beautiful than our girls, and yet you go to bed with our girls."

Michael closed his eyes and pushed the breath out through his nose. This was the cliff.

"Open your eyes, Michael," she asked softly.

He did.

"I forgive you," she said.

Michael didn't answer because he physically could not. He needed time to process what he had just heard.

"God has forgiven me, and I have forgiven you," she said. Vivian added to the shock when she got off of her knees and straddled her husband's leg and draped her arms around his neck. Her lips were close to his. "But Michael, even though I forgive you, it is important for you to know that I have been bleeding ever since the day I found out that my husband is a whore who feels I am less than a whore." She put her face next to his and felt the warmth of his skin touching hers. "I wanted to hurt you. I wanted to destroy you. Instead I said nothing." Vivian pulled back and looked resolutely into her husband's bewildered eyes. "Do you have a problem with firing every girl who you've bedded?"

Michael's throat was parched dry. "No."

"Do you have a problem with starting over?" she asked.

"No," he answered truthfully.

"Michael, a young lady at the church said that God told her to tell me that I needed to forgive my sister and my husband. I don't know how she knew about you and Amy. The only thing I can come up with is it was God."

The eyes that looked at Vivian weren't those of a ruthless sex trafficker or of a greedy extortionist. They were the eyes of a man whose head was spinning. In a moment he had gone from a dangerous divorce to a strange reconciliation.

"I'm going to do my best to show God and you that I forgive you with all of my heart. But first I need to tell you something else," she said. "If I ever hear of you going to bed with anyone other than me, only God will be able to help you. I've taken precautions, Michael. Do you understand?"

"Yes."

Vivian took her husband's face and pressed her open mouth lightly against his and managed his passive lips. She pulled back. "Do you have a problem with making love to your wife?" she asked.

"No."

He made love to her as though everything he had built depended upon what he could do to his wife's body in one evening. If it had been done at any time in any way in any society, he had desperately done it tonight. There was simply nothing left to do that could be done. Finally, he was spent. Depleted physically, but most of all emotionally.

Michael wasn't asleep, but his eyes were closed. It was after three in the morning when Vivian hit him in the head with a hammer. It wasn't a real hammer, not a tool of metal used to build things. This was a hammer of words whose blow had knocked him silly and had put him squarely right back where he was before this marathon of love-making began.

What did she mean she wanted to get more involved in that church? How did the chief operating officer of *Sophisticated Sin, Inc.*, an enterprise of strip clubs and adult novelty shops and sex-themed restaurants, get more involved in a Pentecostal church?

That statement alone was worth the alarm that shrilled through his business mind and MBA soul. But it was what she said next that made him wonder whether the dull pain in his chest was the beginning of a heart attack.

"I've never felt so alive as when I visited that church. I believe I met God there...and felt His love. There's something about those people and that place that's special. What do you think of this, Michael?" asked Vivian.

Michael was hundreds of feet up in the air on a tightrope. He held a long pole to balance himself. There was no net, and the ground below would eat his flesh should he take one careless step. "I'm Catholic. We're Catholic. Our families are Catholic. This church, it's not Catholic, but they helped us. How much do you want to give?"

"They saved us, Michael. They saved our marriage, our family. I want to give more than money," she said.

"Vivian, how is this going to work? We're in the sex business. Father Russo is a good man. He understands our business. These people, these Pentecostals, I'm sure they're not like that. How can you get involved with people who think we're the devil?"

After a short, but seemingly long period of silence, Vivian spoke. "I know you're right, Michael," she said in a whisper. She was on her side with her back to Michael. He couldn't see the tears that rolled down her face. "It's absurd. Too much to ask. Too much to expect. Just the ramblings of a formerly blind girl who is trying to figure out how to live in the light. Let's get some sleep. We have a lot of business to take care of at the new club."

He kissed her on the cheek. "Good night, Vivian." He rolled over onto his back and stared at the ceiling. He was at a crossroad. Husband thoughts one moment. Killer thoughts the next. For now, it appeared that all roads led back to that church.

It had gone from being a church to a dangerous competitor that was trying to bust up his business. It had to be destroyed.

*****

The Mighty Bashnar looked at the officers who were with him. He saw it in their faces. They saw the brilliance of the plan. He didn't have to say anything. But he did. "Any fool can fight. Any fool can try to knock down a wall by slamming his head against it. Strategy. That's what wins great battles." He pointed at Vivian. "Darkness, the enemy has marked this traitor for salvation. Fine. We will use his own light to destroy that wretched church."

Chapter 22

Barbara was still in mild shock. She had hardly spoken since Sharon had talked that thug into letting them go. *How did she do that?* So much had happened in one day. Their home had been vandalized—thoroughly trashed. Their children had both fallen and lost consciousness. They could've been killed. Edwin, bless his heart, had almost gotten them all killed twice in less than two minutes. And they had been carjacked. *Them.* A good Christian family. The liberals had made such a mess of things.

Thinking of messes, their house was still such a mess. They had barely gotten started cleaning up when Andrew and Sharon had to be rushed to the hospital. It had been an absolutely terrifying and draining day. The last thing on Barbara's mind to do when she returned home was cleaning up. She just didn't have the energy. It would have to wait until tomorrow. What she needed now was her husband.

Two things were at work here. First, the carjacker was gone, but in Barbara's mind his gun was still pointed at her. She was still shaking from the ordeal. Edwin could fix this. Second, it had been two days since she and Edwin had been intimate. Barbara's sexual DNA required relief at least every forty-eight hours. She didn't do well after that. She knew it, and Edwin knew it. But that was a moot point. She wasn't single. So she didn't have to carry that impossible cross.

Barbara released a long and slow breath. She opened her eyes and got out of the large tub. She reached for a towel, but smiled and decided against drying herself. She walked into the bedroom with the towel in her hand.

Edwin had disrobed down to his underclothes and was sitting with his back against the headboard. He wasn't usually an early adopter. And when it came to getting a laptop with a touch screen, he had had his doubts. But this wasn't bad at all. He flicked the screen with his finger and smiled. He looked up and smiled more.

"I was hoping you'd dry me off. That you'd help me cool down," said Barbara. Her try at feigned innocence failed to the nth degree. Instead her expression came across as that elusive look of dangerous sexiness chased by professional models and their celebrated photographers. It enflamed her target.

"I have no intentions on helping you cool down," he said, getting up and walking toward her.

"Reverend Styles," she said playfully.

"He left the moment I looked up," said Edwin. He placed his large hands gently on the sides of her face and kissed her. He took his time. He pulled back and looked at her. She didn't open her eyes for a few seconds, as though she were relishing every moment. Edwin joined his wife's attire. He moved her backwards toward the bed.

The demon's little legs and heels bounced excitedly against Edwin's hard chest. He gyrated and screeched in anticipation of the pleasure he would feel when the tiny suctions on his hands touched Edwin's head. He stretched his hands above his own head and came down hard on the man of God. He massaged furiously until the green slime that oozed from the openings from the suctions covered Edwin's head and face.

Barbara stepped backward with closed eyes. Her breaths were short and accelerated. Hallelujah, the forty-eight-hour fix was on the way. She backed up again. Her mouth parted to let the rapid breaths escape. She felt the distance between them grow. *Something was wrong.* She opened her eyes. She hadn't seen that look in a year.

Edwin stood there with his eyes partly open, but blinking, as though there was a struggle in them staying open. His mouth was open. His face was pained. She looked down at his hands. His hands were repeatedly opening and closing into tight, trembling fists. She saw Edwin, but she didn't see the horror movie, nor hear the tormenting voices that had exploded into her husband's mind.

His uncle took him by the hand and walked him into the room. Edwin looked at the little boy being led into the room. He felt everything now as if he were there again. He saw the little boy look up at Uncle Ted. He felt again the little boy's trust, his innocence.

Uncle Ted closed the door and told him they were going to play a secret game. Edwin trembled heavily now, but he hadn't trembled when it happened. That's why he was trembling now. Why hadn't he known something was wrong with this "game"? How could he have not known something was wrong with it? There was only one explanation. He had known something was wrong, but did it anyway.

Edwin looked in silent, agonizing horror as the vivid movie encircled him. The movie was everywhere.

Barbara twisted her face and backed away. This was exactly the strange way he had acted before when he had driven her to take matters into her own hands.

Edwin looked at the graphic movie of the little boy being used as a woman by his uncle. He flinched again and again and again at the pain. *"Do you know why I do this to you, Edwin?"* Edwin saw the little boy wipe away his tears. *"Do you remember when I asked you and your brother who was the strongest?"* Edwin saw Uncle Ted chuckle. *"You jumped forward like a little frog and said, 'I am. I'm the strongest boy in the whole wide world.' That's what you said—the strongest boy in the whole wide world. We get to play this game because you're strong."*

The visions and voices faded, but they didn't go entirely away. They were there, in the back of his mind, like a screen with a curtain over it and like a speaker buried under a pillow. He looked around the room and shook his head. He had to get his bearings. *He was an adult. He was a father and husband. He was—*

Oh, no! he thought. *It's back. Barbara? Where's Barbara?* He went into the bathroom. Barbara was sitting on the vanity with a dazed look. She didn't acknowledge him. For a minute or so, he didn't say anything.

"I know what this means," said Barbara. There was an ache in her voice.

"We can get past this, Barbara," he said.

"Are you going to talk to me?" she asked, turning her head to him.

Edwin got a sick, panicky look on his face.

"I'm going to bed, Edwin." Barbara sounded tired and dejected. "Excuse me."

Edwin didn't move at first, then he did.

She brushed past him and went to bed. He didn't follow.

*****

Lust was on one side of Sharon's bed. Fornication was on the other.

"She is a lovely creature, isn't she?" said Lust.

Fornication's eyes feasted on the dangerous, young beauty. He got fidgety. "Oh, to touch her," he said.

Lust jumped back from the bed in terror. His eyes searched in every direction. His sword and dagger ready. Fornication had done the same.

There! They heard it again. The sound of another sword being unsheathed. Their heads pivoted in every direction at the sounds of swords all around them.

"What is this? What is this?" asked Fornication.

"Angels! It must be angels!" Lust answered. "We have authority—"

Lust and Fornication came out of their crouch and lowered their weapons when they saw him.

Myla descended onto the floor with an extra-long sword in each hand, at least two-feet longer than either of the swords carried by the demons. It was on fire. The demons were unsure of how close the angel could get without them being burned. Yet both felt that any movement, even backwards, would trigger an immediate attack. Mercifully, the angel stopped just far enough away that they didn't catch fire.

Fornication watched the long sword rise in the hands of the angel. Its point stopped menacingly close to his face. He felt the heat, but dared not move for fear of provoking an attack.

"You do not touch the young woman without her permission. Do you understand?" said the angel.

"Yes," Fornication answered immediately.

The angel lifted from the ground without taking his stare off of Fornication. He kept his sword pointed in his direction. The demons watched him until he disappeared into the night. They turned to one another. "Where did they come from?" asked Fornication.

"Where did they come from?" Lust eyed Fornication with a look of disgust, but his feeling wasn't directed at him. His disgust was aimed at the unfairness of their predicament. "*Come* from? I'm beginning to think they don't *come* from anywhere. I think they're always with people like this Sharon." His face twisted. "Those who serve the enemy as fanatically and as stupidly as she does."

Fornication found this problematic. If this outlandish statement were true… "You think the lie may be true? That the angel of the Lord actually *encamps* around those who fear the Lord?"

Lust looked at his comrade. "What were you thinking?"

"The young girl? Touching her? Yes, that was a mistake," said Fornication.

"That mistake almost got us butchered and sent to the *Dark Prison*," said Lust.

Fornication nodded his head. "Agreed. It shall not happen again." The demon looked hungrily at the young woman. "My good friend, Incubus, he has such success with Christian women." He closed his eyes and shook his head and wiggled his body. "Oh, the tales he tell. They actually welcome him into their beds and tell themselves it is the Lord meeting their needs."

Lust reared his head back. "That is even too much for a demon to believe. But I know it to be true." He looked at Sharon. "We have work to do."

They both went back to the sides of her bed.

*****

Be strong in the late hours...You can move any mountain you don't enjoy, the man had said to him. He had played this off with Sharon as an odd statement that he didn't understand. But he had been painfully aware of what that guy was talking about. Rob sat in front of his computer looking into the window of hell. He knew it was wrong. He knew it was shameful. He knew it could destroy him—if there were anything left to destroy. He knew all of this.

But he couldn't stop. He was a slave.

He had struck his chains of bondage with everything he could think of, but all of his efforts had failed to even dent one of the chain's links. He had prayed and fasted. He had cried out to God for hours at a time. He had read every book that could possibly help him. He had memorized Scripture.

He had looked at the videos of a televangelist hundreds of times who had gotten caught twice in sexual sins. He saw how these revelations forever destroyed this man's reputation and ministry. He saw how this preacher's sins had given the world an occasion to blaspheme God and to celebrate another moral failure of a Christian leader. He saw how even after the preacher had apparently repented in genuine remorse, the world and some portions of the church had not let him forget sins committed and repented of over two decades ago. It was King David all over again. Sins whose debts were never satisfied.

Rob didn't want to be like the televangelist. He didn't want to be like King David. Even as his hand energetically moved the mouse and rolled the wheel and clicked on one unfulfilling image and video after the other, he thought desperately how he didn't want to be like

Samson either. That was another man of God who had never found victory over his sexual urges. Where did it get him? Rob thought fearfully. *Captured. Blinded. Imprisoned. Mocked. Buried under tons of rock.*

Rob stopped rolling his finger. He looked at his right hand. He could just lift his hand from the mouse and stop. He didn't do it. He kept his hand on the mouse and with his left hand he frantically turned the pages of his Bible. He found it. The Scriptures hadn't helped him before, but maybe they would now.

He read Proverbs 7. Shame-filled tears raced one after the other from his eyes. This was describing him. He was the dumb ox willingly going to the slaughterhouse in verse twenty-two. He was the one shot in the liver with an arrow. Hard cries followed his thoughts. *No one hears an arrow coming. Who can live with an arrow hanging out of his liver?* He kept reading the Scriptures even though they only added to his misery. He had no choice.

He had broken his arm twice. Each time he was faced with the options of saving himself more immediate pain by not setting the arm properly and just letting it grow back crooked. Or he could suck it up and let the doctor fix his arm even though the process would hurt badly. With his arm, he had chosen to fix it. But what was he going to do with his broken spirit?

There was no choice but to read the Scriptures even though all he got from them was condemnation for his behavior. Maybe, just maybe a miracle would happen and he'd be set free from this cycle of sinning and repenting for the same filthy behavior. The last few verses he read twisted the arrow in his liver.

> *Do not let your heart turn aside to her ways. Do not stray into her paths. For she has cast down many wounded, and all who were slain by her were strong men. Her house is the way to hell, descending to the chambers of death.*

Rob had lost count of how many times he had read these Scriptures. But he was freshly terrified, nonetheless. Pornography was a destroyer of *strong* men. Strong men, not only weak men. He recalled how he had read several Christian articles that reported that anonymous surveys of Christian pastors had revealed that nearly seven out of ten struggled with pornography. *Seven out of ten!*

"Lord, I don't want to be one of them," he muttered pitiably. But his finger kept rolling and clicking.

The disorderly crowd of sexual, vulture demons around Rob stopped pushing and shoving one another. All eyes were riveted on the pure, white light from the sky that had pierced their thick darkness and was now shining directly on them.

An angel came forth from the light and descended through the roof. His hands carried no weapons. This fact momentarily stupefied the demons. Their first instinct was to protect their property. Their second instinct, and the one they went with, was to take a few defensive steps backward to assess the new situation.

The angel landed next to Rob. A brilliant, but not overpowering, white light emanated from his body. He looked at the hungry crowd of vulture demons with not the least concern that he had interrupted their meal. When he lifted both his hands and spoke, it became apparent why he was unconcerned. His weapon was in his mouth.

"The Lord rebuke you." He didn't shout. The declaration was given with as much emphasis as a man saying, "It looks like it's going to rain." Yet when he spoke, every demon felt himself being pushed away as though they were standing before a slow-moving wall.

The angel turned to Rob while the demons were still being pushed away. The wall stopped. There was now a perfect circle around the angel and Rob. The vultures were crowded upon one another at a distance of twenty feet.

Rob scrolled the endless menu of naked flesh. He didn't know what to click on next. The hunger in him was so great that if it were possible, he would have clicked everything at once.

"Rob, go back to the Scriptures. Read verse twenty-five," said the angel.

"He's pointing him to the word," said one of the demons.

"So what?" snapped another. "The word only helps them when they obey it. You think he's going to choose self-denial over what we give him?"

Rob didn't hear the angel. *Lord, help me,* he prayed as he clicked picture after picture.

"Go back to verse twenty-five," repeated the angel.

Go back to verse twenty-five, Rob heard the fleeting thought that was being drowned out by the noise of his lust. Rob's finger rolled and clicked for hours. The angel was there the entire time repeating the same message. Finally, Rob had exhausted himself and was weary under the weight of his filth. He went back to verse twenty-five.

Do not let your heart turn aside to her ways.

Rob looked at the words. He shook his head. This was what was so tormenting about the Bible. It made it seem like he *could* turn aside from his lust. But he had tried over and over to stop giving in. He couldn't stop!

How...how, Lord, can I stop? I've tried everything, he prayed.

The angel was released to say more since the man of God had now departed from unbelief. Unbelief was such a powerfully blinding force that heaven was often silent until the sons and daughters of Adam acted upon what had already been given.

If your eye offend you, pluck it out, said the angel.

How do I pluck out my eye? thought Rob. *How do I do it?*

You do it, said the angel and ascended into the night's sky.

The wall remained. The demons pushed angrily on it. Some howled and made animal noises. One got an idea. He'd go over the wall. He flew atop the wall, but it curved over their meal and formed a dome. They were locked out. Finally, they stopped their futile frenzy and simply watched like a bunch of jackals waiting for powerful lions to leave the scraps of their prey.

The more Rob thought on plucking out his eye, the more it made sense. Jesus wasn't saying it was easy to conquer lust. He actually was saying it might take extreme measures. He was saying that a person had to be willing to do *anything* to be holy. He was using this example to say that Rob had the power to get rid of his lust problem. No one else could pluck out his offending eye. It had to be him. And once he plucked it out, he had to cast it from him. Otherwise, there would be occasion to pick it up and stuff it back into the socket.

Revelation poured into his soul. He thought of the Scriptures in James. He was being drawn away of his own lust. His *own* lust. He had always looked at this as an attack of the devil, or a weakness of the flesh. But it was more than that. It was him desiring to satisfy sexual urges outside of God's plan. It was him willingly giving in to temptation—and he was jolted by this admission—because he enjoyed it. *He enjoyed this sin*. That's why it was so hard to stop it. Deep in his heart, he didn't want to stop it. Why hadn't he seen this before?

Rob took his hand off the mouse and sat back. Plucking out his eye meant taking radical steps to be holy. It meant taking authority over his computer and any other device that made it easy to fall into sexual temptation. He may even have to get rid of them.

It meant he had to stop looking at this sin as something he was falling into. He wasn't falling into sin. He was jumping into it. He thought of Romans 13. He was making provision for the flesh. Planning to sin and then acting surprised and heartbroken when it inevitably happened. He'd have to examine his life and be brutally honest with himself about the things he was doing or not doing that made it easy for him to do this nasty stuff.

"What is he doing?" asked one of the spirits of pornography.

"I think he's thinking about what that angel told him," answered a demon.

"Don't worry," said another. "Let him think about it all he wants. When he sees that bloody cross, it'll be time to eat."

Rob thought about what the Scriptures said about Satan walking around like a roaring lion seeking someone to devour. Why was he seeking someone to devour and not simply grabbing anyone he desired? It must be because some folks are easier victims. Why are some easier to get to? Why had he been so easy? *That's it!* he thought excitedly. *Be sober, be vigilant. Because your adversary, the devil, walks around seeking someone to devour. He can't devour the people who are watching for him.*

A thought followed that one. *Watch and pray.* That's what "watch and pray" meant! This was a literal battle plan. He had to live his life as though he was in a real war with Satan and with his own flesh. He had to awaken every day with a militant attitude, determined to live righteously. *That's what Peter meant when he said to gird up the loins of your mind.*

The circling demons saw the glow around their food.

Rob looked down the long, dark tunnel and saw a faint light. There was a way out of his bondage. He felt a strange sensation. The more he thought on the Scriptures and let himself be honest with himself and God, the more he felt like weight was being lifted off of him.

He smiled.

But then he thought of the energy it would take to live holy and his smiled dimmed. He thought of how he'd have to change his lifestyle and his smile dimmed more. He thought of how he would have to deny himself and take up the cross and follow Christ and the smile disappeared altogether.

Rob put his hand on the mouse and moved the cursor...and clicked.

The wall holding back the vulture demons lifted.

Time to eat.

Chapter 23

Jonathan had been in fervent prayer and fasting for three days now. Elizabeth knew that he was doing everything he could to help her mother. He loved her as much as she did.

But he doesn't need her as much as you need her, Controllus impressed upon her mind.

That was right. He didn't need her the way she did, but what did that have to do with anything? She dismissed this thought as silly. She thought of going into the garage to talk to Jonathan. But what was there to say? Jonathan was praying as hard as he could. She had been praying as hard as she could. Her mother was dying. Talking about it wouldn't help anything. They had to keep praying.

Call the Reiki healer, said the witchcraft spirit.

Elizabeth shuddered at the thought of calling some so-called healer to help her mother. She shuddered more that she would even get such a thought. She was a Christian. She loved the Lord. She'd never go to Satan for help.

Controllus reminded Elizabeth of how she had been healed by the Reiki healer. He and the six demons with him were interrupted by a bright light from heaven that shone on Elizabeth like a spotlight. The demons saw a figure descending in the light. They pulled out their weapons and got into defensive postures. Their nervous eyes looked in every direction for the other angels they knew were there.

He stepped out of the light and was surrounded by seven armed demons.

Controllus and the others saw the definite calm in his face. They were right. There were other angels. Why else would he be so calm? Hey, what kind of trap was this? He was unarmed.

They were wrong. His weapon was in his mouth.

The angel looked at Controllus and lifted his hands. "The Lord rebuke you," he said, with a calm that bordered on being dismissive.

Controllus and the six demons felt themselves being pushed backward by something like a slow-moving wall. It stopped about twenty feet from Elizabeth in all directions. They walked around the invisible wall, pushing and probing and wondering.

The angel put his hand on Elizabeth's shoulder. "Remember King Saul," he said softly.

She did. Fully. Powerfully.

She remembered the story as though she were actually there when it occurred. King Saul had outlawed witchcraft in Israel and had made any violation of his decree punishable by death. But then he had gotten into a bad situation where he had needed to hear from God, and God had refused to answer him.

In a panic, he went against his own law and consulted with a witch. Surprisingly, God interrupted King Saul's sin and used the prophet Samuel, who had died earlier, to appear to him. But it was a bad meeting. The prophet sternly rebuked the king and told him that it was wrong for him to seek answers from others when God had chosen to not speak to him.

The angel bent his head down and spoke directly into Elizabeth's ear. "The Lord destroyed King Saul for his unfaithfulness, and for consulting a witch. The blessed book records this tragedy. Do not follow Saul's example. God is no respecter of persons."

Elizabeth's frightened, big eyes rolled as she contemplated the strong thoughts. What scared her was that she knew she was hearing from God. But why would He warn her so severely to not consult with a witch? Was it because of what had happened at the hospital? She hadn't known that woman was a witch. She reminded herself that her Father was gracious and kind and forgiving, and most of all that He knew her heart.

Ironically, it was this last thought that birthed a trembling in her spiritual bones. Why did the thought of God knowing her heart make her feel like she was in a row boat getting close to the point of no return at *Niagara Falls*? Why did she feel such dread?

"Search your heart," said the angel.

Elizabeth looked inward. Was there some darkness in her heart she was unaware of? She recounted her interaction with the Reiki lady. No, she hadn't done anything wrong. She had rejected the lady the moment she knew what she stood for. *Then what was it?*

"What about the healing?" asked the angel.

What about the healing? She hadn't known the lady was involved in demonic power until after she had been healed. Elizabeth was stumped.

"The *healing,*" said the angel.

The healing? thought Elizabeth. *What about the healing?* She genuinely didn't know what God was talking about. What could she do about the healing? She didn't even know it was coming. And she certainly didn't know it was going to come from the devil. She couldn't give it back to him.

Something clicked.

Give the devil back his healing? What does this mean? How do I give the devil back his healing?

The daughter of Adam's genuine desire for the truth, and her tender heart toward God, gave the angel permission to speak to her more clearly. "Remember Moses, the servant of the Lord. 'You shall burn the carved images of their gods with fire; you shall not covet the silver or gold that is on them, nor take it for yourselves, lest you be snared by it, for it is an abomination to the Lord your God. Nor shall you bring an abomination into your house, lest you be doomed to destruction like it. You shall utterly detest it and utterly abhor it, for it is an accursed thing.'"

The angel entered the light and ascended into the sky.

Seven demons watched in humiliation. The enemy's technology had routinely made open fools of the darkness. How was he able to do the things he did? Sentiment among the darkness about this was swayed one way, then the other, depending upon what was going on at the moment.

One moment, He was inherently Almighty God, and they were all doomed. *Fighting was futile.* The next, he was inherently Almighty God, but he had waxed himself into a corner by creating man, and by basing the legitimacy of his kingdom on his righteousness. *Prove God's righteousness a lie, his right to rule is exposed to be a farce.* Or next, he was Almighty simply because he had harnessed the use of a mysterious power. *Get access to this power and fight fire with fire.*

But these were arguments for another day. Presently, all that mattered was that a single unarmed angel had treated seven high-ranking demons like ladybugs. Just popped out of the sky. Flicked them out of the way by the power of his words. Talked to their woman. And floated back to wherever he had come from.

Elizabeth pondered the Scriptures. She was familiar with them. Jonathan used them all the time when he ministered to people who had been involved in witchcraft. She thought of how severe her husband sounded when he preached to Christians about the dangers of witchcraft. He had often told them that many of them would never be freed from Satan's power because they wanted to be free from the curse that came from witchcraft, but didn't want to let go of the silver and gold that were on the idols.

She knew what this meant. The Israelites were God's people. But He had solemnly warned them that when they went into the Promised Land, they were not to fall into idolatry. They were not to participate in witchcraft *in any of its forms.*

The command was comprehensive. God wasn't just prohibiting offensive behavior. He was prohibiting offensive thoughts and desires. He wanted his people to hate idolatry and witchcraft so thoroughly that they would despise even the silver and gold that were on the idols.

The way Jonathan explained it was that people could only be totally freed from the power of witchcraft and its built-in curse by radically severing all ties to the forbidden practice and casting out the spirits of witchcraft. The severance of ties included not only behavior, but anything of value provided by witchcraft.

Elizabeth wondered how this applied to her. She didn't value witchcraft. So why did she feel like a fly standing on flypaper. This thought that she was holding on to something wouldn't let go. She had been healed by the Reiki lady, but—

"Oh!" Elizabeth gasped. She saw it. The healing. She never would have allowed the Reiki lady to pray for her if she had known about her power source. But she had to admit that since she had been healed by her, she had let thoughts about that lady praying for her mom stick around in her mind. She also had to admit, as bad as this sounded to her, that since the healing, she felt less antagonistic toward occult healing. *Oh, God, I'm so ashamed,* she prayed. *I'm just being honest with You.*

"Liz," she heard Jonathan call. He went into the living room. "Can I talk to you for a few minutes?"

"Sure," she said. She got some water and sat next to him. She smiled, but he didn't. He seemed anxious.

"Liz, God wants me to talk to you," he said.

"*That's* nice to know," she said, with a smile.

"This is serious, Liz," he said.

Now she was scared. "What's wrong?" She felt tears immediately fighting for an exit. She held them back.

"We've seen God work miracles all over the world," he said.

"Yes," said Elizabeth weakly.

"Astounding miracles."

She shook her head and softly grunted her agreement.

"We've left more people sick than we've left well," he said.

Now the tears came. Elizabeth shook her head.

"Jesus was God in the flesh, and He left more people in need of miracles than people who received them," said Jonathan.

"Jonathan, what are you saying? Is Ava going to die?" Elizabeth asked sadly.

Jonathan scooted closer. He tenderly wiped away her tears and cupped her face with one hand. She leaned into it. "I don't know if Ava's going to die," he said. "But I promise that I'll stand in the gap for her in prayer and fasting until the end, whatever that end is."

Whatever that end is.

This was not a new concept to Elizabeth. Jonathan never guaranteed outcomes unless he heard from God. Obviously, he hadn't heard. That was what she *knew*. But that didn't help how she felt. How she felt was that it was a lot easier accepting *whatever that end is* with someone else's mom rather than your own.

"What I need to know—really what God needs to know, is what would you do if she did die?" said Jonathan.

Elizabeth felt Jonathan's words put their large, powerful, cold hands around her throat and squeeze. She couldn't breathe. Her mouth opened. She tightened her eyes as tightly as she could over and over as though she could make the choking stop by squeezing her eyes. She waited to feel Jonathan's assuring squeeze of her shoulder. A supportive word. Something.

There was nothing.

Jonathan watched his wife with a broken heart. But according to the word of the Lord, he did nothing but watch until his beloved wife appeared to have found a little relief. "What would you do if Ava died?"

Elizabeth looked bewildered. "After all this prayer...and fasting?"

Jonathan got right in his wife's face. "Yes," he said. "After all this prayer and fasting, what would you do if Ava died?" He stroked her face, but it didn't remove her look of dazed confusion. "You don't have to answer me." He didn't smile, but he did soften his face. "The one who loves you, He wants to know." He kissed her on the forehead and went back to the garage and began deep moanings in prayer.

It was as though a bomb had exploded next to Elizabeth. It wasn't just the ringing in her ears or the numbness of trauma that cascaded over her body that disoriented her. It was the violent moving of and then the disappearance of her spiritual floor that sent her hurtling into the blackness of nothingness below. When her spiraling body finally crashed into the reality that her mother was going to die, she made a fateful decision.

*****

The buzz throughout the Georgia region was electrifying. Prince Krioni was on stage about to address an assembly of spiritual wickedness in high places. A jubilant spirit handed him a note and watched him keenly as he read it. The prince's face carried several expressions. Shock. Inquisitiveness. Pleasure. Resolve.

I must see this for myself, he thought. When he shared the news with the general secretary of the assembly of princes, he was granted immediate leave.

"You do not object if I send an observer?" said the spirit.

"Of course not. Of course not," Prince Krioni answered hurriedly. "Send as many observers as you'd like. If this is true...if this is true..." He turned to the general secretary. "Why don't you come?"

The general secretary grimaced a smile. "I think I will."

*****

Elizabeth walked quickly toward her mom's hospital room. She knew that it would have made more sense to walk slowly, hesitantly, even haltingly. But she couldn't do that. That would give her too much time to think. To listen. To hear.

She shut down her mind and passed the last room before she got to Ava's room. She didn't stand outside the door and wring her hands with last-minute questions and doubts. There was nothing to question. There was nothing to doubt. She was wrong. What she was about to do was wrong. But she was going to do it anyway.

She was going to do what so many other Christians had done. She was going to deliberately reject the command of her God and take matters into her own hands. She was going to do this and then she would ask for mercy after she had gotten what she wanted. This was as bad as it sounded, she knew. But Elizabeth had no intentions of going any further into darkness than just enough to help her mother.

Then she was out.

Forever.

She had never done anything like this before. And this would be her first and last time she'd ever deliberately sin against God. She only hoped that she wouldn't bring a curse upon herself for getting her mother healed through the Reiki lady.

Elizabeth was an antelope.

She knew there was a hungry lion in the cave.

But she was going to willingly enter the cave and hope that somehow everything would turn out well in the end.

Elizabeth entered the cave. She loved on her mom for several minutes, praying for her and kissing her face with tears flowing from her own. She spoke Scriptures over her until the nurse entered. Shortly after the nurse left, Elizabeth looked up into the beaming face of her Reiki savior.

The lady looked at her tenderly and cocked her head. "Aawwhh," she said, with open arms and walking toward her. "You need some positive energy." They hugged and the lady rocked with her from side to side while rubbing her back in rapid circles. "I just want everything I have to enter you." She looked at her supportively.

Elizabeth winced. *Lord, please don't let that happen. Please...don't...let...that...happen.*

They separated and the lady held Elizabeth's shoulders. "I'm sorry I was late. I didn't mean to be so long at the psychiatrist's office. We're having a bit of a problem getting me the right meds. Depression is a terrible thing. I tried to kill myself three months ago. Dr. Harris has become such a good friend." Still holding Elizabeth's shoulders, she looked at Ava. "This is your mom."

Kill yourself? "Yes. This is Mom," said Elizabeth.

The lady dropped her hands and went to the side of the bed. "Oh, your mom looks a lot like my AA sponsor."

AA? Alcoholics Anonymous? thought Elizabeth.

Where is her baby? came the thought.

"Where is that beautiful baby?" asked Elizabeth.

"Tamara's with my wife." Without touching Ava, the lady jabbed her hands toward her a couple of times like someone checking to see if the water was cold or hot. "Ooooo, lots of positive energy. *Lots* of positive energy. That's really surprising. But it's good," she added with excitement. "Are you ready?"

Your wife? thought a shocked Elizabeth. This was like signing a contract and then discovering terrible things in the fine print. But she had not signed the contract. She could still walk away. The churning in her abdomen and spirit told her to run away. Elizabeth looked at Ava.

"Ready, Elizabeth?" asked the lady. "You were a bit unsure when I healed you." The lady smiled as though she had just seen a glimpse of heaven. "I have strong psychic abilities. I see you crossing a line and your eyes being opened, and you entering a new world of power. I think your mom's healing is that line. Are you ready to cross it, Elizabeth?"

The room was filled with demonic dignitaries not only from the Georgia region, but from regions all around the world. Jonathan and Elizabeth had ministered together on every continent, and in over thirty countries. Jonathan had been to even more countries alone. And without exception, these two people had earned the fear and hatred of the demonic rulers of those areas.

Elizabeth wasn't Jonathan. But then Eve wasn't Adam, either. Sometimes the best way to stop the head was to break the foot.

*****

The scene outside the hospital in the spiritual dimension was a mixture of jubilation and tension. Thousands of demons had surrounded the grounds. They were armed, but they didn't behave as an attacking army. They were lighthearted, happy even. Like a raucous rock and roll crowd waiting excitedly for the main attraction.

Elizabeth was the main attraction. All they needed her to do was to cross the final line. She had already crossed many—and this had compromised her and Jonathan greatly—but this final one was the killer. For once she crossed it, she was theirs.

Hordes of witchcraft spirits, under every name of the occult, were closest to the building, in bunches waiting hungrily for their property. Others who shared first rights on people who opened the witchcraft door were demons of confusion, darkness, depression, nervousness, sickness, disease, insomnia, fear, insanity, and antichrist.

Fierce demons representing every curse listed in Deuteronomy 28 were also there in great numbers. Poverty, plague, inflammation, fever, itching, tumors, scabs, calamity, accidents, and others.

Surrounding the demons was Captain Rashti and at least three times the number of angels as there were demons. He and his army were on the outer periphery according to the rules of engagement.

Elizabeth had already sinned against the Lord in her heart. This allowed the forces of darkness to claim the close ground. However, even in situations like this where servants of the Lord had put themselves in horrible predicaments, warrior and mercy angels were often positioned to enforce the mercy of the Lord should the situation allow.

Such engagements and rescues of offending servants of God were always followed by accusations from the darkness that God had violated the law of sin and death. Heaven's response was always the same. Mercy rejoices over judgment.

The Sword of the Lord had a long sword in one hand, a dagger in the other, awaiting heaven's command.

*****

Lord, forgive me, prayed Elizabeth. "Yes," she answered the Reiki healer.

The healer smiled and furrowed her brows. "I don't know why," she said, "but something is telling me that you need to say you are crossing the line."

Lucifer. Eve. Esau. Samson. King Saul. Judas. Elizabeth heard each name announced in her mind just as clearly as she heard the healer. She knew the tragic narratives of each. She looked at the tubes coming out of the woman who had rescued her from a miserable life of sex slavery and had become her mother.

Lord, please don't hold this against Jonathan. "I cross the line," she answered.

The Reiki lady tightened her mouth into a cute grin and nodded approvingly. "Goodie! Oh, I felt such release when you said that. Did you feel it?"

"I felt something," said Elizabeth, certain that she and the healer had felt vastly different things.

"Come stand next to me," said the healer.

Elizabeth did.

The lady put forth her hand to touch Ava's forehead and sneezed. "Oh, excuse me." She sneezed again. "Excuse me again," she said, taking her forearm down from her face. Again she sneezed. Again and again and again. The lady couldn't stop sneezing. The sneezes grew in rapidity and intensity. The lady doubled over and sneezed twenty or thirty times. Elizabeth didn't know how many times. The lady dropped to one knee, still sneezing. Then she was on her hands and knees, sneezing as though she were about to go into a seizure.

Elizabeth ran out of the room to get help. She returned with two nurses. She trembled as she watched the hospital staff help the sneezing woman out of the room and down the hall.

Controllus assigned spirits of guilt, shame, and unworthiness to Elizabeth. This was standard operating procedure. Tempt the person to sin. Condemn them for sinning. Make them so ashamed of committing the sin that they feel too unworthy for forgiveness and too embarrassed to seek help.

I've crossed the line, said the guilt spirit repeatedly to Elizabeth. *God can never forgive me for this. I knew what I was doing. How could I do this to my Lord? I'm cursed.*

"I've opened the door," Elizabeth said softly.

"Yes, you have," said Controllus.

"He tried to stop me," she said.

"Yes, he did," answered Controllus.

"I'm cursed," Elizabeth muttered.

"Yes, you are," said Controllus, for the amusement of those watching. "And God is not mocked. Whatever a woman sows, that shall she also reap. You have sown a wonderful seed of rebellion. Now it's time to reap your crop." Controllus smiled and looked at the spirits around him. "That's in your cursed book, daughter of Adam."

Chapter 24

The Mansion had been an unbelievably ambitious sex slavery business run in Alpharetta, Georgia, an affluent northern suburb of Atlanta. It was only a thirty-minute drive from Atlanta city hall to Alpharetta on Highway 400, and fifty to sixty minutes from the Hartsfield-Jackson Atlanta International Airport to the building known underground as *The Mansion*. But this was a moot point.

All clients were blindfolded and wore earmuffs before being driven around in a circuitous route of neighborhoods and highways before landing at *The Mansion.* This precaution was compliments of Michael Bogarti's paranoia.

The precaution was extreme, but due to the overwhelming consensus among customers that secrecy was worth the drive, the drive was viewed more as a long trip to the candy store than as an inconvenience. And the anticipation of the wide variety of *The Mansion's* tantalizing and exotic candy acted as a buffer to any aggravation.

Nonetheless, Michael Bogarti's many precautions weren't enough to hide and protect his money factory. *The Mansion's* guise of being an exclusive, high-class country club in the woods was revealed to be a literal underground brothel. Its overt physical presentation and its below ground structure was ingenious. Yet *The Mansion's* irresistible lure was Bogarti's creativity. He was an industrial pimp with the mind of a *Walt Disney* or *Steve Jobs.* It was all about imagination, product, and service.

Unfortunately, the FBI didn't appreciate Bogarti's brilliance. At 2:00 a.m. on a Saturday morning, a little army of FBI agents were making final preparations to raid *The Mansion*. They were twenty minutes away when the accelerant was lit and the several buildings went up in flames. The girls had been secretly removed hours earlier and transported to other locations. It was good to have friends in high places.

Friends were invaluable. But nothing took the place of precaution. It was precaution that had made Michael arrange for this property to be purchased through an elaborate arrangement that could never be traced back to him. Yet precaution had prompted him to place a contingent contract on the one person with a one percent chance of pointing the feds in his direction. It was amazing how far five thousand dollars could go in some countries.

But his network of friends and his practice of caution had not been enough to stop one preacher and one woman from shutting down one of his most lucrative houses and costing him millions of dollars in lost revenue, leverage, and favors. And now his own wife had become a fan of the church of this big-mouth preacher.

Michael Bogarti weighed his options. Vivian wasn't the kind of woman who could be ordered to not go back to that church. So he'd have to work behind the scene to convince her to not go back. He had fun toying with the idea in his mind of how he'd do this.

He chuckled. He had a little something up his thousand dollar sleeve. He had people digging up stuff on the Styles, and he had someone watching them. This digging had produced something useful. Something about the reverend that he would use tonight.

*****

Sharon was lying on her back staring at her bedroom ceiling. She had been spending a lot of time in prayer to help Jonathan and

Elizabeth with Ava. She had even fasted all day. This was not the first time she had fasted, but it felt like it was. It had been *hard*. She really could've used the sleep. But it was after eleven and she couldn't go to sleep. Well, she could've, but she was afraid to.

Lately, she had been having an unexplainable problem with lust. It had started the night before, on Sunday of all nights. The day their house had been vandalized, and the day they had been carjacked. That night she had had the eerie feeling that something was in her room looking at her as she rested. Whatever it was wanted to get in bed with her. She thought that maybe she had been dreaming—and maybe she had been—but she felt this same presence even when she wasn't asleep.

That was disturbing enough, but then there were the dreams. She had had several graphic sexual dreams that were so real that she had awakened throbbing and fully aroused. She had asked God in tears to forgive her for what she might have done to herself while sleeping.

Sharon got out of bed and kneeled beside it. "Lord," she prayed, "what's going on? I don't know what's happening to me. Where are these dreams coming from? You know I love you. I don't want these images in my mind. Today at school I could feel the guys looking at me, but it wasn't like it was before. Today it was like I—" Sharon started crying softly. "It was like I enjoyed their lustful stares. But I *really* didn't. It was like another part of me was being satisfied by what I imagined they were thinking. I'm so sorry, Lord. I don't know what's happening, but my eyes are on You."

Sharon got back in bed and lay there for a few minutes before going downstairs. She got a cup and pushed it against the lever on the refrigerator. She heard a cough. She went to her father's study and looked in.

"You're up," she said.

"You're up, said Edwin.

"Couldn't sleep," said Sharon.

"Me either," said Edwin.

Edwin patted the sofa. Sharon sat down and cuddled up next to her father.

"I was thinking about that adventurous ride you took us on yesterday," he said with a grin.

"Uh, excuse me. You mean the one with the guy pointing a gun at my father?" she said.

"Yeah. That would be the one," he said. "Your friend the robber said something I have to agree with."

"Oh, what's that, Dad?" asked Sharon.

"You crazy," said Edwin, trying to mimic the robber's voice. "Yeah. Yeah. Snow White, you craaaazy."

They had a good laugh.

"Nice that you can laugh about it, Dad," said Sharon.

"Well, I'm laughing now. I was crying earlier." He kissed her on the head. "I don't know what I'd do if anything happened to you."

"You'd grieve, Dad. Like we grieve Chris. But you'd keep serving God. Like you're doing now."

Sharon couldn't see her father's invisible smirk. *Like I'm doing now*, he thought.

"Dad, promise me that no matter what happens to me, you'll keep serving God," said Sharon.

A light moment had suddenly turned heavy. Edwin took a little too long to respond for Sharon. "We are all gifts to one another, Dad. We can't ever place the value of the gift above the giver of the gift. Promise, Dad, that you'll never value me above our heavenly Father."

"I promise," Edwin said promptly. But this was a promise made under the duress of his little girl's gaze. He couldn't imagine a recovery from such a loss. He pushed the troubling thought out of his mind.

"Now make me a promise," said Edwin.

Sharon smiled. "Okay."

"Promise me that you'll live to be at least ninety," he said.

"I can do better than that," she said. "I promise to live forever."

He shook his head. "I'm talking about in *this* life, young lady."

"I'll do my best, Dad. That's all I can give you," she laughed her response.

"Okay, I guess I'll have to settle for eighty-nine," said Edwin.

"Change of subject," she said.

"Okay," said Edwin.

"This prophetess thing—Dad, I want to do it. I want to do whatever God wants me to do," she said.

Edwin waited.

"It's just, Dad, I get these pictures and movies and stuff..." Sharon shook her head. "And I hear things. Sometimes I feel like I'm going crazy."

Edwin pulled his daughter to himself and held her. "Sharon, honestly, when you first declared that you were a prophetess, I didn't know what to think." He shook his head and raised his eyebrows. "A prophetess? It's 2017."

"Daddy, God never changes," said Sharon. "He's the same yesterday, today, and forever."

Edwin made a couple of faces and rubbed his chin. "I can't argue with you, Sharon. Not after yesterday."

"Octavius?" said Sharon.

"Yes. Octavius, and the elephants and donkeys," said Edwin.

Sharon smiled.

"And you," he said.

She narrowed her eyes, wondering what he meant.

"You're Sharon," said Edwin. "You love God like no one I know. You serve Him like no one I know. You believe Him like no one I know. I shouldn't be surprised that He talks to you. Even if they didn't cover this in seminary." He smiled. "There's a lot they don't cover in seminary."

"So I hear voices and I'm *not* going crazy?" said Sharon.

"Sharon, God's not in the business of driving people crazy," he said.

"Unless you're Nebuchadnezzar," she joked.

"You're not Nebuchadnezzar," said Edwin. "Remember the Scripture that says 'if you ask for a fish, he won't give you a scorpion?' I think it's safe to say that the Lord hasn't given you a scorpion."

"But, Dad, I didn't ask for this," she offered.

Edwin smiled knowingly. "Have you ever asked God to talk to you?" He saw the light of understanding rise in her face. It wasn't often that he was able to give her something spiritually that she didn't already have. She had outgrown his faith and understanding of God within a year of committing her life to Him. So he was deeply satisfied to be able to help her understand her calling. "You asked for a nickel. He's giving you a million bucks. I guess we'll have to get used to having a prophetess in the family." He waited a few seconds. "You know those things I said about the lottery? Maybe I was wrong."

"*Daaaaad*," she said.

"Just kidding. Just kidding," he said. "I wouldn't dare ask you to prostitute your gift—even if the Powerball is up to three-hundred and seventy-five million dollars."

Sharon stood up. "When my dad starts to be silly, it's time to go to bed. Good night, Dad."

"Good night, Sharon," he said.

She turned back around. "Dad, I didn't tell you before because I didn't want you to think I was crazy. But now I can tell you."

"Okay," said Edwin.

"Saturday I saw you in a vision talking to a little boy who had his room made up like Chris's. You know, with all that *Atlanta Braves* stuff. I kind of got the feeling when I saw it that the little boy represented Chris, and that God was saying Chris loves you, and that you and he would decorate a room together again in heaven." She shrugged her shoulders. "You're already on record as saying I'm not crazy. Night," she said, as she left with a smile.

Edwin didn't move. He couldn't.

"If you run into a little boy with a room made up like Chris', remember what I said," said Sharon's fading voice.

The phone rang.

Who would be calling this late? Sharon rushed to the phone so no one would be awakened. "Hello," she said.

"This must be Sharon," said the man's voice.

"Yes, it is," said Sharon. The man didn't sound nice at all. "May I help you?"

"I'm sure you can, but that's another conversation. There's a message for your father taped to the door," said the man. "Tell him we said to mind his own business and leave ours alone."

"What—?"

Click.

Sharon put down the phone and went to her father's study. "Dad, that was some man who said to tell you to mind your own business and to leave theirs alone."

"What?" said Edwin.

"They said there's a message taped to the door," said Sharon.

Edwin walked toward the front door.

Sharon grabbed him by the wrist. "Dad, maybe we should call the police."

"And tell them to check our front door?" he said.

"Well, be careful. Maybe it's the people who broke in," she said.

That was sobering. But it didn't stop him from going to the door with a tight scowl. He looked outside first. Nothing. He opened the door. A piece of paper with a picture on it was taped to the door.

Edwin looked at the picture. At first his mind wouldn't let him process the obvious. But then shock gave way to clarity. He backed up in horror, his bottom lip trembling. "No," he said, shaking his head in denial. It couldn't be.

Sharon's innocent mind was even slower than Edwin's to grasp the horror of the picture. She read the engraving. It couldn't be true. No one was that evil.

"Put some clothes on, Sharon," said Edwin. "I'll meet you at the car."

Sharon ran upstairs. She put on some jeans and a top and ran downstairs. *I left my brace. Leave it.* She hopped in the car, and she her father disappeared into the night.

But the car that followed them had no problem staying on their tail.

*****

Edwin turned the car into *Eternal Light Memorial Park*. He drove past the wide open gate, looking at it suspiciously. It was after hours. Surely, it was supposed to be locked. He drove down a long winding road. He started looking to the right. "Do you see anything?" he asked Sharon.

Sharon strained to see in the dark. Everything looked exactly alike. "No," she said. She was surprised that she wasn't creeped out being in a graveyard at midnight.

"I think it's up this hill." Edwin turned to the right. What he saw seized his chest. His lungs felt like iron.

Sharon saw the mound of dirt and jumped out of the car while it was still rolling. "Christopher! Christopher!" she screamed, running toward the hill of dirt. She looked at the dirt. She looked at the hole. The open casket. Her eyes snatched away from the violated grave and looked around.

Edwin ran around the car and looked in the hole. "Where...where..." he gasped. It was almost impossible for him to breathe. "Oh, my God! My God! My God! My Gooooooooooood!" he screamed.

"Daddy!" Sharon screamed. "How could they?"

"What?" He ran to her side and froze.

There he was. Little Christopher's three-year-old corpse was lying on the ground with a stake above his head with a sign on it. The sign said, "Don't' f--- with us!"

Sharon turned to her father. Her eyes carried the horror that he felt in his soul. She screamed into the still night with a tortured cry. Her cry seemed to go on forever, carried first by the wind, then by the laughter of hell.

Finally, Sharon's lungs could expel her pain no longer as the last of her cry stopped its piercing. She cried and wailed as though she were releasing all the pains of the world since the beginning of time. Her knees buckled and she was on the ground, on her knees at first, then on her face. She was oblivious of the dirt.

Edwin knew what was going on with his daughter. Her torture was only a few feet away. He needed to help her. And he would. As soon as he could get control of himself. As soon as he could free himself from the weight that had just dropped on him. He felt the energy of grief's gravitational pull yanking him to his knees. It was impossible to stand.

He fell. He was on his hands and knees. He wanted to die. He wanted to cease to exist. Why would someone do something like this? *I have to help Sharon.* Edwin crawled to his daughter and sat flat with his legs spread apart around his daughter. He pulled her to himself and held her as tightly as he could. "It's okay, Sharon," he made himself say to his inconsolable daughter. He tried to say more. He needed to say more.

"Daddy, why'd they do this to Christopher?" she cried. "He's just a little boy. He's only three," she whined.

"Remember the vision, baby? Remember the vision?" he said, rocking her and letting his own tears run freely.

She didn't answer. She couldn't answer what she couldn't hear. Her cries gushed from an unstoppable source.

"God showed you a vision of me and Christopher," Edwin pushed through his anguish. "He showed me and Christopher in heaven decorating his room with *Atlanta Braves* stuff. Remember, baby? I don't know why they did this, Sharon, but they can't take that from us. Christopher is in heaven. They can't hurt your little brother. They're trying to hurt me."

"But why?" she wailed. "You didn't do anything, Daddy."

"I must've done something, Sharon. I must've done something right." He held onto his daughter and wondered at his words, and the trace of strength he felt when he heard the unexpected words come out of his mouth. "You made me give you a promise. Remember?"

"Yes," she moaned.

"You made me promise that no matter what happens to you, I'll keep serving God. You told me to not value you above our heavenly Father. You remember that, baby?"

"Yes, Daddy," Sharon whimpered.

Edwin put his chin atop his daughter's head. She was this strange gift from God. A thousand-year-old sage. But she was just a little girl. A little girl. She didn't deserve to see this. "Promise me that no matter what happens to me, you'll always serve God."

Sharon's crying stopped immediately. "Daddy, I don't want anything to happen to you."

"But if anything does happen to me—take care of your mother and Andrew. Help your mom see God," he said.

Sharon didn't answer.

"Okay?" said Edwin.

"Okay," said Sharon.

Edwin positioned himself before his daughter. He looked at her with a resolve Sharon wasn't used to seeing in her father. "Sharon, the people who did this are animals. They did this because they know people like you and I and your mom and Andrew have hearts. They need to know that no matter what they have done, and no matter what they do in the future, no matter how they may hurt us, we won't be intimidated. We won't stop serving God. They *need* to know this, Sharon."

"What do you want me to do?" she asked.

"I want you to trust me," he said.

"I trust you, Daddy," she said.

"I think we're being watched," said Edwin.

Sharon's eyes got big.

"Where is Christopher?" he asked.

"In heaven," she answered.

"*Where* is Christopher?" he asked again.

"In heaven," she answered.

"Trust me, Sharon," he said.

"I do," answered Sharon.

Edwin took off his jacket and laid it on the ground. He looked at his daughter, asking with his eyes for her to help him. He started putting his son's bones onto the jacket. Sharon was hesitant at first, but she joined in. They put Christopher's old clothes onto the jacket also. Edwin rolled the jacket and put it in the back seat of the car.

Edwin and Sharon got in the car. They sat a minute, saying nothing before Edwin said, "My son is in heaven."

Sharon said, "My brother is in heaven."

They understood one another.

Edwin steered the SUV slowly down the path. He stopped at the gate that led back out onto the main street. He looked at the cars across the street and those parked along the streets to the left and right of them. Whoever was following them could be in any of those cars.

Edwin got out and picked up the jacket with the bones. He looked at Sharon. Her face and eyes were puffy. There was no expression, but Edwin saw the agreement. He walked toward the street and looked slowly around in every direction. He tossed the bones and clothes onto the sidewalk with one determined motion and got back into the car.

"Dad, even though this doesn't look right," Sharon said with trembling lip, "it's the right thing to do. Now whoever they are, they know they don't have anything on us. They know we count all thing loss that we might gain Christ." Sharon continued with tears. "They can't take what we've already given to Christ."

"Thank you for understanding, Sharon," said Edwin. Edwin knew his daughter was proud of him. The heavy darkness of cold despair in his heart was joined by the warm light of winning Sharon's respect.

A black car with tinted windows sat across the street in the parking lot of a fast food restaurant. Two men sat inside. “Do you believe this crap? He threw his son’s bones on the street,” said Lenny.

“That’s one sick SOB,” said Rick.

“Guy’s a lunatic,” said Lenny.

Chapter 25

The Mighty Bashnar stood in Edwin's driveway. His hands were posted on his waist. As much as he despised this worm, he admitted to himself that that was no worm move last night. That was a man's move. His face twisted. It was the kind of thing he would have expected from Jonathan. But this...this *worm?*

He had thought the sight of dear little Christopher's grave violated and his bones setting atop the ground would've broken the worm. Instead, he and that hideous daughter of his talked about counting all things loss that they may gain Christ. This was a bad omen that would most likely prove a passing cloud—at least as far as the worm was concerned. Sharon, however—yuck!—that little pain in the darkness seemed to get worse every day.

"So you count all things loss?" said the Mighty Bashnar. "Good. Then you won't miss what you're about to lose." He turned to the small band of spirits of infirmity. "They count all things loss that they may gain Christ. Let's help them gain Christ. We'll find out if Christ really is enough."

The Mighty Bashnar's bitterness rose into his thick neck. "I'll tell you what we'll find." He peered at the demons. "Once we touch their bodies, they'll ask questions. Then they'll go from asking questions of the God they love to demanding answers from the God they resent.

"When they see that their service to the dog of heaven has gotten them nothing but troubles, they'll forget everything He's ever done for them. They'll forget the great promises of the world to come, and of ruling and reigning with the great imposter. They'll curse him." The Mighty Bashnar pumped his fist to the heavens. "They will curse you to your face!" He looked at his demons. "Go...make...them...curse...God!"

*****

Forty people were gathered for the yoga session. Thirty-five women. Five men. Four of the men were in the back. The other was behind Barbara, who was in the front row. She stretched her side by poking out her hip and bouncing it a few times. First, the left. Then, the right. Next, she had to stretch her abdomen. She placed her hands on her narrow waist and arched her chest forward while pushing out her buttocks.

Out. In. Out. In. Out. In.

A little faster to get the kinks out.

The guy directly behind Barbara greatly appreciated her stretch routine.

Out. In. Out. In. Out. In.

"Eeuuww!" she yelped. "Isn't this exciting?" she said to the lady on her immediate right.

The lady's wide eyes danced with excitement. "It is," she sang. "Yogi Abayomi Singh is wonderful. I follow him wherever he teaches. He's so transcendent."

"Oh?" said Barbara.

"You'll see," said the lady. "He has a real gift. He'll have you spiritually awakened before you know it."

"Spiritually awakened?" said Barbara.

The lady smiled. "My name's Jennifer."

"I'm Barbara."

"Barbara, you don't know too much about kundalini yoga, do you?" said Jennifer.

"Nothing, really." Barbara chuckled. "Except that it's exercises and breathing techniques."

Jennifer smiled. "It's much more." The lady's eyes followed a man who entered the room. "That's him. Yogi Singh."

"Good morning," said the man, as he walked toward the front of the room. "Are you ready for a journey into your true, awakened self?"

*****

Adaam-Mir's eyes were wide. This was only his fifth day on the front lines with Myla, but already he had learned so much. Much of what he had learned was jolting and inexpressibly depressing. He watched the beginnings of the kundalini yoga session with rising concern. Witchcraft spirits were everywhere! Oddly, many of them appeared as coiled snakes.

Myla saw the concern and questions in Adaam-Mir's eyes. "The snakes are the kundalini. They enter those who seek spiritual awakening."

"Spiritual awakening? But this comes only from the Lord God," said Adaam-Mir.

"*True* spiritual awakening comes from the Lord God," said Myla. "These people do not seek to be awakened to God. They seek mystical experiences in the place of God."

"But why seek mystical experiences? If the sons of Adam seek to be awakened, why not be *awakened*? Why seek light in a dark cave?" Adaam-Mir's passion was on full display.

"Adaam-Mir, why did Adam and Eve eat the forbidden fruit?" asked Myla.

Adaam-Mir's expression showed that he knew the answer wasn't good.

"It was the promise and fascination of becoming like God," said Myla.

"They were already like God, my brother," Adaam-Mir said impatiently. "This story has never made sense to me."

"Adaam-Mir, if you are going to understand the sons of Adam, you must stop thinking rationally. Much of what they do makes no sense. It is the way of this world. Men and women and children sell their souls to Satan either to get what they already have, or to get what they can never have."

"And these?" said Adaam-Mir, with a sweeping gesture of his hand.

"They want God without God," said Myla.

"God *without* God?" Adaam-Mir shook his head. He knew that Myla was about to share with him another ridiculous truth about the sons of Adam.

"They want to be like God—" began Myla.

Adaam-Mir interrupted. "But is this not the great plan of God? It was always His plan."

"Yes," Adaam-Mir. "It is the mystery unveiled in the blessed book. But, my brother, the sons of Adam want to be like God without serving God. They want to be like God through their own power."

"But they have no power, my brother," said Adaam-Mir. "What power they have comes either from the blessed Creator or Satan. How can they *possibly* seek to be like God through a power that doesn't exist?"

"Adaam-Mir, the deceiver manifests himself to these people in many ways. He convinces them through various philosophies and beliefs that they have tapped into a power within themselves...or within the universe."

"A power within themselves," said an astonished Adaam-Mir. "This is the same lie he told us, my brother."

"Same lie. Different audience. Same tragic results," said Myla with sadness. "ESP, psychic phenomenon, spiritual awakening, higher consciousness, whatever. Different names for the deceiver's power."

Adaam-Mir looked at the snakes with a frown. "And these coiled serpents? They will enter all?"

"Not everyone will receive a serpent immediately," said Myla. "Some people are more open to Satan's power than others. They can expose themselves once and come under terrible bondage. Others can go much longer before they are paid the wages of their rebellion."

"I would not take such a gamble," said Adaam-Mir.

"Neither would I," said Myla. "But people who are blinded by pride, arrogance, rebellion, or ignorance don't see it as a gamble."

"They do not *see* at all, my brother," said Adaam-Mir.

*****

"You guys did some chants and stuff, and something went into your spine? That doesn't sound right, Mom?" said Sharon with alarm.

"I didn't say something went into my spine, Sharon," said Barbara. "I know what you're saying. Everything's not a demon. I said I felt something press against my back. I said it felt like something went into my back, and now it hurts."

"You felt *something* press against your back while you were doing yoga. You felt something go *into* your back while you were doing yoga. Now your back hurts." Sharon looked at her father. Then her mom. Then back to her father.

"Sharon's not saying you have a demon, Barbara. I'm not saying you have a demon," said Edwin.

"What are you saying?" she asked defensively.

"Sharon's right. Something's wrong with this," he said.

"With what? A muscle strain? Really, Edwin, this is why people think we're nuts," said Barbara.

She had a point there, thought Edwin.

"When did you start thinking everything is a demon?" she asked.

"Come on, honey," Edwin coaxed. "You know I don't think everything is a demon. I'm still getting used to this demon stuff." Edwin cast a furtive micro glance at Sharon—at least, he thought it was furtive. "But I've been reading...and praying. Going back through the gospels. And listening to some You Tube videos by some guy named Derek Prince."

"You Tube videos?" Barbara looked at Edwin and Sharon. "You looked at a You Tube video and now I have a demon."

"Mom, you were doing yoga when it happened," Sharon pleaded.

"Barbara, I don't know what happened to your back. I just know that I don't like the idea of having yoga classes at the church," said Edwin.

"When did this happen? You knew we were planning yoga sessions and you said nothing." Barbara's face was tight with anger.

"I didn't like it when I heard it, Barbara. But I didn't know enough about it to say anything," he said.

"And now you do, Edwin? Now you're an expert on yoga," said Barbara.

Sharon knew the discussion had just escalated. It was time to leave, but she couldn't.

"I went online and read up on yoga, and kundalini yoga in particular. I read some testimonials of people who practice it," he said.

"Dad," Sharon beamed inside, "you did?"

Barbara heard Sharon's excitement. It only added to her sense that they were ganging up on her.

"Yeah," he said. "These people even say it's dangerous. They talk about this kundalini power like it's something that can drive you crazy."

"Oh, Edwin! I've heard enough," said Barbara.

"Listen to him, Mom. Please," begged Sharon.

"Don't both of you get on me," demanded Barbara.

"I'm not getting on you," said Edwin.

"That's the truth," snapped Barbara before she knew what she had said.

It got quiet.

The spirits that blocked Edwin's communication with Andrew at the ball park lowered their curtain, separating Sharon from everyone else.

"Uhhh, I'm running late. I'm supposed to hang out with Rob and his sister. I'll be back in a couple of hours." Sharon left, hoping that she was reading too much into her mother's words.

Chapter 26

The pressure was on.

The fornication squad hadn't done anything except torment Sharon with explicit sexual dreams. This had been immensely satisfying, but watching her toss and turn in her sleep and unconsciously pant like a dog in heat could not compare to watching a thorn deliberately choose sexual pleasure over Christ. There was only so much pleasure that could be experienced by taking advantage of a sleeping beauty. (And they couldn't *really* do that!)

But they had made accelerated progress with Rob. The sexual demons that had been with him for years revealed to the fornication squad that his resistance had never been this low. He had gone from simply looking at nude pictures, pornographic videos, and spying on his sisters to adventurously trying to act out some of the things he saw in videos.

This was a line he had told himself for years he wouldn't cross. But he had also told himself that he'd never go beyond looking at still photos, and now he had looked at thousands of videos. Surprisingly, he had found that he was fascinated by images and videos that showed women being raped, hurt, and even killed in a sexual context.

Like so many others at the bottom of the quicksand pool of pornography, he had discovered to his horror that it was easy to get into, but apparently impossible to get out. He was only seventeen, and yet he had been a slave for nearly five years. Unlike others who had gradually become slaves, he had been denied the luxury of a slow descent into depravity.

His first exposure to pornography had been like a fish's fateful introduction to a hook hidden by a fascinating lure. One bite and he was hooked. He had been shocked by the hook, and defiantly, then desperately, fought and pulled against the force that was pulling him out of his environment. To his dismay, he had discovered that the more he pulled, the more he found he was resisting an irresistible force. Every exertion of his was met by the patience and skill of the force pulling the hook in his mind.

Eventually, mental exhaustion and spiritual fatigue reframed his fight against the pornographic hook from one of fighting to be free to one of fighting for the delusion that he was still fighting to be free.

Rob was at the crossroads—again. He knew which road he'd take. The one that terrified him. It had terrified him whenever he had allowed a moment of such dark calculations. For it would mean no more pretenses. No more lying to himself. But this was a choice under duress. The urges were now overwhelming. Something was driving him.

And there were the voices.

Rob sat at his computer and watched. His face dark. His eyes angry. But not because a young lady was being violated on his screen. And not because the men who were doing it would end her life to get a final, sick rush. No, his face was dark and his eyes were angry because this was who he was. He didn't know the girl in the video. But whoever she was, she deserved what they were doing to her.

*****

No one knew what the Mighty Bashnar had planned for Rob and Sharon. No one knew why he was standing behind Rob, or even that he was in Rob's house. (Unless some angel was spying on him. They had a way of popping up when they were least expected.)

The Mighty Bashnar felt his excitement building. It was similar to what he felt when he had raped and killed those women in Florida through a serial killer he had inhabited. He had enjoyed it so much that when his puppet was caught by the police, he helped him escape from jail. But prayer finally caught up with his murderer, and he lost him to the death penalty.

The Mighty Bashnar thought back on those glorious moments of murder. He closed his eyes and extended both of his heavy arms. He took in deep breaths and slowly exhaled as he mused. Their terror. Their cries. The sounds of skulls being crushed as he slammed hammers or clubs or dumbbells against flesh and bone.

He remembered the blood. *Oh, the blood!* So red. Oozing from the gashes, the ragged openings of flesh done by his hands through his dupe. Oh, that he could do this more often. Some he had killed and violated later. Others he had kept alive, to play with them. To taste the terror in their eyes. To hear them beg for their lives. To hear them say, "You don't have to do this." To hear them say, "I'll do anything. Just let me live."

To be able to be like God for one moment. To take the life of a son or daughter of Adam!

Then there were the explosive moments of orgasmic carnage. He recaptured those moments and let old feelings become new again. He puckered his lips and blew out a long, slow breath that brought him close to a climax of evil satisfaction.

Lovers, sitting in a car in the park, in the dark of night.

Murderer, emptying his gun into those unsuspecting lovers.

It wasn't often that a demon of the Mighty Bashnar's kind could directly invade a child of Adam. There were so many variables involved, and so many inherent dangers. The reward had to justify the risk of making himself vulnerable to enemies who may catch him weakened upon his exit. Invading Rob to get to Sharon was worth the risk.

Rob looked at the movie on his computer screen, but he didn't see it. His mind was on how far he had fallen. He thought about the tiny surveillance cameras he had been using. He thought about the ones he had used on his own sisters.

The Mighty Bashnar smiled at the timing of this thought of perversion. He placed both hands on Rob's head and stepped inside of him.

Rob gasped when he felt it. His chest convulsed a couple of times, then settled. It jerked suddenly. Then he felt a tearing, like something large being squeezed into something small.

Something had stepped inside of him. *Someone* had stepped inside of him. Someone mean. Whoever this person was who had invaded his body was evil. It was the essence of evil. It had never been good. It could never be good. And it hated all that was good.

Rob felt the presence move around inside of him. The moving, however, wasn't in his physical body. It was in his mind and personality. He felt this thing doing something like driving stakes in the ground. Rob got the feeling that this thing was claiming him. He shook his head and jumped up and rushed to the bathroom.

He looked in the mirror.

There was no white. No blue. His eyes were totally red.

*****

Sharon rang the doorbell.

Rob opened the door. He smiled. "Hey, Sharon, come in. I have a surprise for you."

*****

Michael ordinarily would have smiled when they told him. He appreciated coldness. He appreciated a heart of stone. Business required it. He was a coldhearted, ruthless murderer who took what he desired. But he had three adorable children. He couldn't imagine throwing his kid's bones in the streets. This preacher wasn't worthy of children. Michael's contempt of this man grew. If this creep didn't care about his own kids...

"Just threw them in the street? His own son." Michael was livid. He whispered into Lenny's ear. "Doesn't fear me. Doesn't care about his kids. I want this animal taught a lesson. Something that'll stick with him."

*****

Barbara was tight-lipped, but dinner still had to be served. She didn't appreciate being told she had a demon. She also didn't appreciate Edwin's sudden antagonism toward an exercise program. Why couldn't they have yoga at the church? *Sharon. Oh! I love her to death, but that girl can be soooo weird at times. Edwin follows her like a puppy follows his master.*

"Dinner's ready," she yelled lightly.

"It certainly is," said one spirit of infirmity. "I don't think I can wait." He turned and went upstairs to Andrew's room. A few others looked at one another as though they couldn't believe they hadn't thought of that themselves. They followed the eager spirit upstairs.

Andrew turned off the water and dried his hands. He put the towel across the bar and looked at his hands and wiggled and stretched his fingers. His hands were tingling. He opened and shut his hands several times. The tingling slowly went up his wrists and momentarily stopped at both elbows before traveling up to his shoulders.

Andrew moved his arms with several motions, checking, then shaking his arms, as though he could shake the tingling out. He left the bathroom looking at both hands, still stretching his fingers, and pressing on shoulders that had suddenly become painfully sore.

Edwin's mind was heavy with thoughts when he heard Barbara call them for dinner. The house had been vandalized. Not burglarized. Vandalized. They had been singled out. Someone had left a threatening note on their door. Presumably, these same people had dug up his little son's grave. *Oh, God, don't let Barbara find out.* He had undoubtedly stepped on some crazy people's toes. But whose?

He didn't preach anything controversial. Well, he had tried to keep up with Jonathan some. He had dabbled at preaching some charismatic stuff, but he would've been surprised had someone been offended enough to dig up his son's grave. *And they cursed. What church person would say "Don't f— with us"?* What could they possibly be talking about?

"Hey, what's wrong with your arm?" Edwin asked Andrew as he pulled back a chair.

This got Barbara's attention.

"I don't know," he said with a grimace, moving his shoulders back and forth. "My hands started tingling. Now my arms are sore."

"Where's your neck brace?" Barbara's question was more of an order.

Andrew got up to go get his brace without saying anything.

"I shouldn't have to remind him to wear his brace," she said to Edwin. "I noticed that Sharon wasn't wearing hers, either." Barbara noticed Edwin's preoccupation with scratching. "You have a rash?"

"I don't think so," he said. He unbuttoned his sleeve and rolled it up.

"Let me look at it," said Barbara. She got up. "There's a little patch here that looks a bit discolored."

"Really? I don't see it," he said. "But it really itches."

"How long has it been itching?" she asked.

"Just started," he said.

"Hmp," she said. "I think we have something for rashes."

Edwin smiled slightly. Things had been tense between them since his episode a couple of days ago. It had been four days since his attack. He'd have to try again soon. But for now it was nice to see her show concern for him. "I'll put something on it after dinner. The food smells delicious. It's the stroganoff, isn't it?"

The fence that guarded Barbara's anger lost a few planks. She loved to cook, and she loved it when people appreciated her cooking. She smiled. "Yes. Nothing fancy."

Edwin and Barbara smiled at one another.

"Andrew," said Edwin, calling him upstairs.

He didn't answer.

"Andrew, food's getting cold," said Edwin.

"What is that?" said Barbara.

"What?" asked Edwin.

"That sound. The knocking sound," she said.

Edwin stood up and turned his ear toward the staircase. He heard it. It wasn't knocking. It was more like thumping. "Andrew," he called out apprehensively. When he didn't get an answer, he darted to the stairs and hopped up two at a time. At the top of the stairs, he heard commotion in Andrew's room.

Their house had been vandalized. His son's bones had been dug up. He had been threatened. Edwin was sure someone had broken into the house and was assaulting his son. Adrenaline hurled him inside his son's room to fight off the intruder.

But there was no intruder. Andrew was on the floor thrashing wildly. Only the whites of his eyes showed. His body bounced up and down as though being rapidly pulled up and slammed repeatedly onto the floor. Edwin saw in a moment that the thumping sound was actually his son's foot kicking the wall. "Barbara," he yelled, "call 911!"

"What's wrong?" he heard her frantic question.

"It's Andrew. He's having a seizure," said Edwin.

*****

Barbara couldn't wait until they got home to talk to Edwin privately. She had to ask now. It was eating her alive. "Why is this happening?" Her question broke the difficult silence.

Edwin glanced back toward Andrew.

"It's okay, Edwin. Andrew's fourteen." A short pause. "I'm sure he wants to know, too. Why is this happening to us?"

"The doctor said seizures can happen to anyone at any time," said Edwin.

"I was there, Edwin. I heard what the doctor said. I'm asking *you*, my husband, why is this happening to us?"

"Barbara, I think we need to talk about this later," said Edwin.

"Dad, I want to know," said Andrew. "It's not just the seizure. It's everything. It's me and Sharon both getting knocked out at the same time on our stairs. What are the chances of that happening? And our house. Now this. What if I've got epilepsy? What's going on?"

"You don't have epilepsy, son. It was just a seizure," said Edwin. "You heard the doctor say we shouldn't jump to conclusions. They're going to run tests on you to see what's going on. And we'll have the bloodwork results back soon."

"Dad, that's what epilepsy is. It's seizures." Andrew sounded frightened. "Harold's dad has epilepsy."

"He does?" asked Edwin.

"Yeah. That's why they're so poor, Dad. He can't keep a job," said Andrew.

"They're not supposed to fire you for stuff like that," said Edwin. "The American with Disabilities Act—"

"Edwin," Barbara spoke sharply, "can we talk about our son and our family and not about what employers are supposed to do with employees with epilepsy?"

Edwin looked straight ahead. He didn't like his wife's tone of voice one bit, and she'd hear about it when they got home.

"Something strange is going on, Edwin." Barbara's tone was noticeably less cutting.

Edwin didn't know what answers his wife expected him to provide. But he agreed with her and Andrew that something strange was going on. How could any one family have such a string of bad luck in a few days?

"Maybe we're under attack," said Edwin. He spoke in a low voice, almost like he was ashamed to let such nonsense come out of his mouth. Neither Barbara nor Andrew said anything. The silence made Edwin wish he could snatch those Jonathanesque words out of the air.

"Under *attack*?" said Barbara. There was no doubt that she felt the same way Edwin felt about his words.

"You mean like Paul?" asked Andrew.

Edwin looked in surprise at Andrew in the rearview mirror.

"Who's Paul?" asked Barbara.

"He was an apostle, Mom," said Andrew.

"Yeah, like Paul," said Edwin.

"Makes sense, Dad. That could be it," said Andrew.

Edwin wondered at the irony of hearing his wife automatically dismiss the possibility of a biblical answer. She had been raised in the church, and had been a Christian all her life. Yet, his fourteen-year-old son accepted, without any resistance whatsoever, the possibility that they were being attacked by the devil.

He also thought of the irony that he was the one having these thoughts. When did he start taking these stories seriously? When did he stop looking at them as historical events recorded solely to provide teachers and preachers with lesson plans to be taught within a non-miracle framework? Even though he had been exposed to Jonathan's miracle ministry, and even though he had been used by God to work miracles, he still felt like an outsider to the miraculous.

He had seen a lot in the last year, but in many ways he was as baffled—and in some ways more baffled—by this miracle and prophetic stuff as he was before Jonathan came into the picture. But how could he deny what he knew to be true? Even if he didn't totally understand it all? Wouldn't that make him like the children of Israel in the wilderness? How was it possible to not believe God after seeing him part the Red Sea? *I don't know what's going on, Lord. But I don't want to be like those people in the wilderness,* he thought.

Immediately, clear, forceful thoughts pushed into Edwin's mind. *Now with whom was He angry with forty years? Was it not with those who sinned, whose corpses fell in the wilderness? And to whom did He swear that they would not enter His rest, but to those who did not obey? So we see that they could not enter in because of unbelief.*

It was that voice.

Edwin remembered the few times he had heard it. He remembered how he had responded. He summoned his strength and decided that he wasn't going to make that same mistake. If this voice was the Holy Spirit speaking to him—he thought fearfully about the alternative—he needed to take heed.

"Edwin, this family needs rest. We haven't rested in days. What do we have to do to enter His rest?" said Barbara.

Edwin's head snapped around toward Barbara. "What did you say?"

"Edwin, watch the road," she said.

"What did you say?" he asked again. His heart speeding up.

"I said what do we have to do to get some rest?" she said.

"No. You said, 'What do we have to do to enter His rest.'"

Barbara was puzzled. "That doesn't even make sense, Edwin. Whose rest?"

"Yeah, Mom, that's what you said," added Andrew.

Now Andrew, thought Barbara, shaking her head. She let it drop. She'd talk to him later.

"Andrew," said Edwin.

"Yeah, Dad," he answered.

"When did you read about Paul being attacked by Satan?" asked Edwin.

"After me and Sharon got knocked out," he answered.

"That was Sunday," said Edwin. *He went to the word of God immediately. I'm just now going to the Word. How did he know to do that?* "How did you know to look for the answer in the Bible?"

"Dad, that's what we're supposed to do. We're Christians," said Andrew matter-of-factly.

"What answer?" asked Barbara. "To what question?"

"The stuff that's been going on, honey. A messenger of Satan was sent to persecute Paul wherever he went. Satan tried to destroy him by using people to attack him," said Edwin.

Barbara let out a loud breath. She didn't try to conceal how she felt about this kind of talk. She was not going to get a straight answer.

They drove several minutes in silence.

Andrew's nose drew up. Something stank. The windows were closed. He looked at his mother. She looked disturbed. She glanced back at him. Andrew shook his head once and nodded toward his father. Barbara looked horrified.

"Edwin," said Barbara, "did you—?" The pungent smell rushed down her throat, gagging her. "Oh, Edwin!" She pushed the window button and hung her head out the side.

Andrew couldn't hold it any longer. He burst out laughing until he hurt his neck. "Ooohhh...owwwww, my neck," he said between laughter and gasping for fresh air. The thing that made this even funnier to Andrew was this was the first time anyone in their family had passed gas in public. "Oh, Dad, you're killing us."

Barbara didn't share Andrew's humor. This was disgusting. What kind of example was Edwin setting for their children?

Edwin sat stone-faced, looking out the front window as though he was in shock. This made Andrew laugh even louder.

Two things happened when they arrived home close to midnight that turned a bad night into a nightmare.

One, when Edwin got out of the car, Barbara and Andrew saw that the smell in the car wasn't simply a passing of gas. It was a total blowout. Edwin had had a complete and very messy bowel movement that was fit for a beast. They watched him walk in silence with his legs spread far apart.

Two, Sharon was not at home.

Chapter 27

Elizabeth checked the thermostat before going downstairs. It was a bit warm. She entered the kitchen and saw a note on top of the granite island in the center of the large kitchen. Next to the note was Jonathan's phone. She picked up the note and read it.

> *God told me to leave you alone until He deals with you. He said you and He have something to work on. I'll contact you when I hear from God. Still praying. Still fasting. Still fighting the good fight. Your love, Jonathan.*

Elizabeth gasped. For more than one reason.

First, God had only told Jonathan twice since they had married to suddenly leave her high and dry like this to go pray intensively somewhere. He would never have left like this without God telling him to do it.

Second, he could be gone for days or even weeks. Although she had wondered how she was going to look him in the eyes after trying to get the Reiki lady to pray for her mom, that problem was now delayed to a future date. But as difficult and shameful as it was going to be, she would have rather faced Jonathan than to be alone now. *He couldn't have chosen a worse time,* thought Elizabeth.

Third, he had said he would be gone until God dealt with her. What did that mean? Her eyes carried the thoughts of fearful consequences of her actions. *He and I have something to work on?* Oh, she hoped he didn't *work* on her the way He had *worked* on Samson. *He chastens those whom He loves,* she recalled.

The fourth reason why Elizabeth gasped was because the moment she read the note, a bone-chilling cold descended from the ceiling. It felt like a blast of arctic air was draping over her body one inch at a time. It started at the top of her head and ended icily at the bottom of her feet. She felt frozen. It seemed to be more than a mere inexplicable and sudden change of temperature. The cold carried a message. It *was* the message.

Elizabeth gasped again.

Somehow she knew the cold represented her relationship with God. *But how could this be?* she wondered, as her befuddled mind temporarily forgot that she had asked a demonized woman, a witch, to use Satan's power to heal her dear mother. She remembered her sin. *I love the Lord. I made one mistake,* thought Elizabeth. *And I did it for Ava. I did it to save Ava's life.*

Ava would rebuke you sternly for this. She would rather die than go to the devil for help, came the forceful impression into Elizabeth's mind. It was like a voice shouting from behind a door and walls that muffled its volume.

Elizabeth looked at Jonathan's phone. *I can't call him.* She glanced around the kitchen. It was freezing in there. She went toward the stairs. Halfway up the stairs, she stopped and abruptly turned around. She stilled her breathing so she could hear better. Nothing. She turned back around and went up a couple of steps and stopped again, turning sharply, looking down in every direction.

She looked warily at the main floor. Jonathan *had* caught someone breaking into their home. But even though she looked over the bannister, her concern wasn't down there. It was on the stairs. It had felt as though someone was directly behind her, nearly stepping on the backs of her heels as she walked.

Elizabeth shook her head. She was just spooked because of what she had done with the Reiki lady. She was almost at the top of the stairs when she felt a light stroke go down her back.

"AAAaaaaaaahhhhhh!" she screamed. She fell forward as she tried to get away on her hands and knees from whatever had touched her. Her fingernails scraped the hardwood floor as she scurried frantically to find traction on its slippery surface. Something pulled lightly at an ankle and let it go when she kicked. Elizabeth was on her butt, scooting backward, looking in the direction of the breathing her terrified ears clearly heard. This felt like what she had been through in Haiti.

"Who are you?" she screamed at the invisible presence. She wanted to get up. To get up and run away. But fear had made her legs like jelly. She scooted backward as far as she could go. Looking. Looking. Looking.

She couldn't see it, but she knew something was standing there. Something evil. It was peering at her. She knew it. "What do you want?" she yelled, with her back against the wall, hugging her knees.

It came closer.

Elizabeth was bawling. Why wasn't Jonathan there with her? Why was this happening? "Leave me alone," she begged.

It lightly pulled her foot.

She kicked at it. She got an idea. Why was she letting this thing mess with her like this? She was a child of God. She had authority over demons. She had cast out demons with her husband all over the world. He had shown her how. "In Jesus's name, leave!" she demanded.

Controllus was amused. He opened his arms wide, with his palms upward. He looked around. "Where are they Elizabeth? Your mighty angels?" He tugged at her ankle again. She felt delicious. What a sensation it was to break through the barrier and actually touch one of these daughters of Adam.

She kicked at whatever had pulled her ankle. "In the name of Jesus! In the name of Jesus! In the name of Jesus!" she screamed desperately.

One of the six council demons who was there with Controllus joined in. "In the name of Jesus. In the name of Jesus. In the name of Jesus." He moved his arms like a conductor directing a symphony. "Everybody now."

The other six council demons joined. Controllus laughed and waved his hands like a conductor, too. "In the name of Jesus. In the name of Jesus." He suddenly stopped laughing. He reached down and grabbed her leg and lifted it up, dragging her forward a few feet.

Elizabeth kicked wildly. "Jeeeeeeeeeesuuuuuussssss, help meeeeeeeeeeeee!"

The fun was over. Controllus's face showed his hatred of her. He jerked and swung her leg from side to side. When he finished, he threw it against the wall. "That name is *not* yours to use." He spat his words at her. "You came into my world." He pounded his chest. "My world. You come into my world and call on Jesus? You call on him like he's going to help you. I'm a demon. A demon," he screamed, "and I know more about your Lord than you do. Pathetic. Just pathetic, Lizzy.

"Did you think you could collaborate with *the enemy* without penalty? Did you think God would make an exception for you?" Controllus appeared to calm down as he thought of his question. *Never fails. The more gifted or favored a child of God is, the more she thinks she can violate the enemy's law and get away with it.*

Controllus glared at Elizabeth. "Lizzy, for the life of me, I don't know why he hates me and my kind with such special hatred. But he does. He does. He curses us above all others. And everyone who consorts with us are cursed." The angry, philosophical demon spit a big wad of slime onto her face. "That includes you."

One of the council guard demons whispered into the ear of the leader of the council demons. The leader turned to Controllus. "We can do more?" he asked with dirty intentions.

Controllus's eyes widened at the new and rare possibility. He *had* touched her leg.

Seven demons looked hungrily at Elizabeth's shaking body.

A brilliant white light shone from heaven directly onto Elizabeth and the demons closest to her. The demons not directly under the light jumped back. Controllus and two council guard demons were directly under the light. They scurried out of that light as though they were roaches being sprayed with poison.

One after the other, four towering, massive angels exited the light. They weren't as bright as the light, but they were bright. Controllus and the others recognized this class of angels. They were a strange breed. They were mercy angels.

Demons thought them strange because the name didn't fit what they truly were. They were anything but mercy angels. Instead, they were ferocious, volatile, and exceedingly thorough killers. They didn't talk much. But then that was a trait of all angels.

Yet this class of angels at times seemed to have no mouth, except when they used them in battle to rip a demon's neck open. The angels that stepped out of the light had those obscenely large mouths. There were only four of them, and there were seven demons. But their numerical advantage was offset by the incredible size of the angels, and the fact that a more appropriate name for mercy angels would've been *annihilators.*

One of the mercy angels walked toward Controllus with two long swords. Controllus didn't notice the peculiarity of the swords because his eyes were fixed on the angel's large mouth. But the council guard demons saw it. They saw it on all of the angels' swords.

A blade came out of the top of the handle. Ingenious. Instead of one long sword for distant fighting, and a dagger for close-up fighting, they had two long swords with daggers built into each. Even their boots were weaponized. They had blades coming out the front!

"The precious one will not be violated," said the angel. He looked down at Controllus. He wasn't waiting for an answer. For this was no question. It was a certainty.

The six council guard demons watched Controllus. They didn't like him. Yet they would not hold his silence against him this time. To say anything under such circumstances would not be brave. It would be stupid.

The other three large-mouthed mercy angels looked down at the other six demons. Their gazes appeared manic to the demons. Message sent. Message received. *Don't violate the woman.*

"How can you call her precious? She has sinned. She has touched the thing that God hates," said Controllus.

The blow from the towering angel against the witchcraft spirit's face was faster than should have been possible for an angel his size to deliver. Its force spun the demon's body in a circle and dropped Controllus in an awkward, crumpled heap. His knees were under his belly. His chest and face were on the floor, and his big rear poked up, like a sleeping baby.

"When he awakens, tell him Elizabeth is precious because the Lord says she is." The angel had something else to say. "Tell him the only reason I did not kill him and put him in everlasting chains of darkness in the *Dark Prison* is because the Lord is not through with him yet."

The angels left.

So did the six council guard demons.

Elizabeth got up and ran to her bedroom.

Controllus was still crumpled on the floor in his sleeping baby position when the Mighty Bashnar entered and stood over him.

*****

Elizabeth was in her bedroom, but not in the bed. Whatever had attacked her in the hallway seemed to be gone. She wanted to get in the bed and pulled the covers over her head and cry until she couldn't cry any more. But she was afraid to get in bed. She had gotten a feeling that that thing wanted to rape her. She was not getting in that bed.

Instead, she sat trembling on the floor against a wall in her walk-in closet. The light was on and she was surrounded by hanging clothes, shelves of clothes, and shoes everywhere. Mercifully, the enclosed space of the cozy room lessened her fears a little.

Elizabeth's knees were pulled up to her chest. She hugged her legs and thought of the precariousness of her position. She felt like a person clinging to a piece of floating debris after a shipwreck. And that is what this was. A shipwreck.

The floating debris was her hope that Ava would recover, and now that she also would recover. And what about her and Jonathan? What would this do to their relationship? As flimsy as her hope was, it was all she had. The only alternative was to turn it loose and be sucked into the depths of this sea of darkness and ruin that was pulling at her. She had to hold on and believe that although the safety of land was nowhere in sight, she would miraculously reach it before it was too late.

But why was she here? What had caused the wreck? How could she be strong one moment and so weak the next? How could she go from seeing God work miracles of healing through her hands to asking an occult healer to heal her mother? Where was her faith? How had it failed her so easily?

She thought of Peter. One moment he had told Jesus, "Even if I have to die with You, I will not deny You." Then within a few hours he was saying, "I never knew the man." He had even cursed at the little girl who had refuted his claim of not knowing the Lord.

Lord, what is it about us that makes it so easy to deny You? Why is it so easy for us to stray? After all I've seen, after all You've done for me. You rescued me. Gave me a new life. Gave me a mom and a husband who loves and protects and adores me. Elizabeth burst into tears. *And this is how I repay You.* She rocked back and forth in the shameful realization that she had committed spiritual adultery. *Oh, God, how could I? I see why Judas hung himself. I'm not fit to live.*

*****

He was walking through dry places, seeking rest, but not finding any. The ease at which a demon could find a human home depended on many things. What kind of spirit was he? To what geographic area was he assigned? What prayer activity was in the area? What prayer cover did the intended victim have? What kind of church was the intended victim a part of? What kind of natural or spiritual resistance would the intended victim offer the demon?

This spirit of suicide had been viciously and unjustly kicked out of his house weeks ago. Now that he thought about it, he should have seen it coming. Natalie had always been depressed. Compliments of her habit of focusing on her failures or on what she didn't have or on how unhappy she was, and how her state in life would never change.

Suicide thought fondly of Natalie. *You made it easy for me. You loved to compare yourself to others. Always trying to be what you weren't instead of embracing who your creator called you to be. Natalie, when you judge yourself by a false standard, you'll come up lacking every time.*

The spirit's fond memories floated away when he was reminded of the carelessness that had made him a wandering bum. A homeless demon, tormented by a restlessness that only a demon could understand.

Natalie had grown up in the church and had always called herself a Christian. So Suicide didn't consider it dereliction of duty to assume she'd go through the motions. Where he messed up, he recalled with bitterness, is when she started believing the cursed book. But again, how could he have known she was starting to believe it? Should he have taken her growing obedience as a sign?

Yet even this behavior wasn't proof that something was amiss. For Christians routinely went on righteousness and obedience spurts much like fat people went on diets. They'd listen to a sermon or read a book or something similar and get all roused up only to return to their old ways when the excitement of the moment died down.

The problem was Natalie didn't listen to a sermon or do anything that would've brought attention to herself. She simply sat down with the cursed book one day and said she was tired of living in defeat. She told her creator that she was going to find every place in the New Testament that talked about her. She called this accepting who she was in Christ.

Suicide twisted his yellowish, jaundiced face.

Looking back now, he had to agree with his superiors that he had been an idiot. He should have known that the moment Natalie started believing what the creator had said about her, he would lose his grip on her. And that's exactly what happened.

By the time Suicide knew what had happened, it was too late. Natalie had memorized and meditated on portions of the cursed book so much that he was chased out. Literally.

One day Suicide had taken a stroll in Natalie's mind. He noticed things looked different. Odd. For one, the place was cleaner. There was still some scattered litter here and there, but it wasn't like before when there were piles of trash everywhere. He had also noticed that the walls were clean. His graffiti was gone. Years of work gone. Just like that.

Then he turned a corner in her mind. His narrow mouth opened and dropped his long chin in shock. The whole neighborhood had been razed to the ground and rebuilt from the ground up. Suicide's beloved ghetto of dilapidated buildings were gone, as were his beloved rats that used to scurry boldly about the streets they owned.

Suicide recalled how bewildered he was at the sight. He would never forget the feeling. He couldn't. It was too closely linked with his eviction.

It was then that he heard a voice from the sky shout, "There he is!"

Suicide had turned and saw a terrifying sight. Even now he marveled that he had actually been chased by the Lord Himself. Why would the God of heaven pay such attention to a lowly spirit of suicide? Why would Almighty God Himself come to Natalie's rescue?

Those were questions he may never get answered. But one thing was for sure, someone on a white horse had taken off after him. Thinking about it still caused Suicide to break out into a foul sweat. The rider had eyes like a flame of fire, and on his head were many crowns. He wore a robe that looked to have been dipped in a red liquid. Suicide remembered that as the figure got closer, he saw something come out of his mouth that looked like a sword. And there was writing on his clothes. *King of kings and Lord of lords* was written on his robe. This name was even written on his bared thigh.

Suicide's demon associates refused to believe the details of his story, but who else did they know of who dressed like that? As far as he was concerned, he had been chased by the Lord God Almighty Himself down the street, around the corner, and clean out of the mind of a nobody daughter of Adam.

He had done his best to reclaim his home. He had even solicited the help of several other demons more wicked than himself to go back with him to Natalie. They'd establish a stronghold with walls so thick they'd never be breached. But they ran into a problem. Natalie hadn't gotten lazy as they had hoped she would. She instead had continued her practice of reading and memorizing the cursed book. She prayed and worshipped like a disgusting fool. And worst of all, she didn't just read and memorize the cursed book. She obeyed it.

But that was all history. Today was a new day, and he had just heard what might indeed be an invitation. Someone had just said something that bordered on a request for death.

I see why Judas hung himself. I'm not fit to live, Suicide heard Elizabeth say. *Oh, goodie. I love it when people curse themselves.*

*****

Elizabeth listened to the voice coming through the telephone. *Brain swelling...body weak...prepare for worst...*

The message was clear, but Elizabeth's brain garbled the message. "I'll...I'll be right there," she said with a spinning head.

*****

Suicide looked at the witchcraft spirit lying on the floor. *What is going on here?* He looked at his side and gasped. "My darkness!" he said. Someone had chopped off the demon's hand and left it there beside him. Suicide backed up, looking around warily. Who would do that to a witchcraft spirit? He wasn't going to wait around to find out. He looked at Elizabeth. "I'll be back," he said.

Chapter 28

Elizabeth stood at the bedside of her mother. Mom was so pretty, even now, with part of her beautiful, long black hair shaved off to make way for the surgeon's knife. Elizabeth knew *scalpel* was the more technical term, but *knife* more accurately described the brutality of what had happened to Mom. This was more of a back alley *crime* of life rather than a neat, controllable *event* of life.

She had prayed and prayed. She was weak from fasting. There was nothing left to do but continue the same. That's what Jonathan was doing. That's how Ava lived her life. And both of these wonderful people had proven repeatedly that holding on to God in faith for the impossible was the smartest thing to do in a crisis. But Elizabeth didn't feel smart right now. She felt hollowed out by tragedy. All shell, no innards. Like she had been to a taxidermist.

This fight had been brutal. There was no word to describe how tired she felt. Not just physical tiredness, but a tiredness of the mind and spirit. It was as though the batteries of her life had played out and she had found a way to function on the momentum of necessity. But every action depleted her even more. She was a starving woman reduced to eating herself for energy.

Finally, she could kiss and stroke and tell her mom she loved her no more. It was time to leave. She lightly held Ava's hand. "We have to hold on to God, Mom. You're going to be healed."

Elizabeth left the room bouncing back and forth from feeling like a woman of faith for encouraging her mom and boldly declaring in the face of death that she would live, to feeling like a hypocrite for mouthing words she didn't believe. *But she did believe them, didn't she?*

Elizabeth walked down the long, brightly lit hall of the critical care unit toward the elevators. She was actively trying to push the doctor's pessimism out of her mind. *With men these things are impossible, but with God nothing shall be impossible,* she repeated silently. She was lost in her mental struggles when she arrived at the elevators and came out of her cocoon.

She saw a lady waiting for an elevator. Elizabeth wasn't sure, but the lady appeared to have seen her and turned away. "Madeiline," said Elizabeth.

The Reiki healer didn't look up.

"Madeiline," Elizabeth repeated, touching her arm.

The lady walked away without ever giving Elizabeth eye contact.

"Madeiline," Elizabeth called out to her. Elizabeth stood there stumped. "I'm sorry for your allergies."

The lady didn't stop walking. Actually, she quickened her pace. Without turning around, she said loudly, "I don't have allergies."

Elizabeth watched in chastened silence until her would-be healer disappeared around the corner. *What was that all about?* she allowed herself to wonder, even though she had a strong suspicion.

*****

Elizabeth drove toward home wondering whether she should go home. *Something was in that house.* She pulled off the highway with no destination in mind. But there was one destination she wasn't going to. Home.

She was still fasting, but maybe she could stop somewhere and get some juice. *Good. Cracker Barrel. That'll do.*

Elizabeth sat by the window. She smiled at her grand view of the parking lot and watched with delight as a mother walked hand-in-hand with her little daughter. Sweet. Another hand-in-hand. This time the two hands were husband and wife. She could tell because the three little ones bore the physical traits of them both. Family. Nothing was as beautiful as family. Warmth cascaded through her. It felt good. A welcome change from what she had been feeling the past four or five days.

Elizabeth looked up at the server. She smiled at her. "How do you pronounce your name?"

"Ah-ee-sha," said the server.

"I thought so," said Elizabeth. "I like to properly pronounce people's names. Aisha, I'm a Christian. May I briefly share something with you?"

The young lady seemed eager to hear. Perhaps because it was always a good idea to be friendly to the person who hopefully would leave you a tip. Or maybe it was because she thought Elizabeth was beautiful. "Yeah," she smiled.

"Thank you," said Elizabeth. "I believe the Lord wants me to tell you that your lips are beautiful. They're not too big. He made your lips." She put out her hand and the young lady laid her fingers across Elizabeth's palm. "Thank you, Aisha. The Lord wants you to know that you're not ugly and there's nothing wrong with your hair."

The server squeezed Elizabeth's hand. She looked at Elizabeth through eyes that now held water. Her bottom lip trembled as her mouth opened. She said nothing. Her tears carried her thoughts.

Elizabeth put the young lady's hand to her mouth and kissed the back of it. "You are beautiful and you were made for God's glory."

The lady stood there with closed eyes and a trembling lip. She opened her eyes. "Thank you. Me and my boyfriend had a fight and he said some mean things."

"People can say really mean things, Aisha. We can't stop them from saying mean things, but we don't have to believe them. Always let God's opinion of you be the one you go with." Elizabeth smiled at her.

"Now you thank God for those big, pretty lips of yours and that wonderful head of thick hair."

The server laughed through her tears. "Okay." She stepped away and stopped and turned. "Can I hug you?"

Elizabeth got teary-eyed. "Of course, Aisha."

They hugged.

"Where do you go to church?" asked Aisha.

Elizabeth reached in her purse. "Here." She handed her a card. "Oh, let me put my cell phone on there." She wrote down her number. "Call me any time."

Aisha smiled. "Okay. Thank you," she said, and walked back to the kitchen.

*****

"Did you see that?" said Controllus to the council guards. "Even now! Even now!" he angrily swung his nub. "She belongs to me, and still the enemy uses her. What about the agreement?"

Controllus saw the tension in the eyes and on the faces of his six borrowed guards. He turned to see what they were looking at.

"You mean *my* agreement?" said the Mighty Bashnar.

"What are you doing here?" demanded Controllus.

"You looked like you could use a hand," he said, with a straight face.

Controllus heard the laughter behind him. He spun his head and glared at the guards. Their laughter continued. He snarled at them and turned back to the loathsome warrior spirit. "You have jokes."

"I see you don't like them. You're not clapping," he said.

The six guards found this hilarious. They made no effort to conceal their laughter.

"I didn't know you were a comedian," spat Controllus.

The Mighty Bashnar was cool. He bent his head in an exaggerated way and looked at the witchcraft spirit's nub.

The six guards waited for another joke.

"Michael Jackson wore one glove," said the warrior spirit.

The guards erupted in laughter.

"What do you want?" screamed Controllus.

The Mighty Bashnar waited for the laughter to die down. He stepped forward. The guards yanked their swords and daggers out. "What I want you can't give."

They watched the bold demon disappear into the horizon.

"Controllus should change his sword to his left side," whispered one of the guards. The guards laughed.

Controllus whipped his head around. "Something funny? Forget him. We have work to do here."

*****

Elizabeth sipped her orange juice and pulled out her iPad. She went into a Bible app. She went over several Scriptures that dealt with waiting on God. One stuck out.

> *And shall not God avenge His own elect who cry out day and night to Him, though He bears long with them. I tell you that He will avenge them speedily. Nevertheless, when the Son of Man comes, will He really find faith on the earth?*

They had been crying out to God day and night.

...Though He bears long with them. It hadn't been long in an absolute sense. It had only been five days. But it felt much longer.

He will avenge them speedily. If a day to the Lord was a thousand years, and a thousand years as one day, what did He consider speedy? This thought didn't help.

That last sentence was sticky. It wouldn't go anywhere. *When the Son of Man comes, will He really find faith on the earth?* Elizabeth had heard Jonathan preach on this a hundred times. God was saying that sometimes it takes a long time to get an answer in prayer. People should cry out for as long as it takes. God's question was, When He came with the answer, would the person still be in faith?

Elizabeth thought of herself. Many Scriptures came to mind, but one passage that had helped her and Jonathan many times nudged itself to the front.

> *Therefore do not cast away your confidence, which has great reward. For you have need of endurance* [Elizabeth liked to use the word *patience*], *so that after you have done the will of God, you may receive the promise: "For yet a little while, and He who is coming will come and will not tarry. Now the just shall live by faith; but if anyone draws back, My soul has no pleasure in him."*

Elizabeth wasn't confused, but she was having a hard time reconciling Jonathan's words with these words. Jonathan sounded like he was preparing her for Ava's death. But these Scriptures were telling her to hold on. Why hold on if she's going to die anyway? Could Jonathan have been wrong? Yes, but how many times had he been wrong?

Lord, just tell me plainly, Elizabeth prayed.

*****

Controllus moved in for the final phase of his plan. He knew he had to get her to move before God spoke. This was usually the best time to seduce Christians.

*****

Elizabeth left a big tip and went to the counter to pay. The line was long and only one person was behind an apparently broken register. Two women behind her were talking to one another.

"That was amazing," said one of them to the other. "Pam, how did she know that?"

"She was in that lady's business, wasn't she?" laughed the other woman.

"You think she was planted in the audience?" asked the woman.

Pam shook her head quickly with a crinkled nose. "No. I don't work for her, and last night she called me out."

"She did?"

"Yeah." Pam looked around playfully, giving the impression that this was the end of the conversation.

"What did she say to you?" the lady asked.

"Who?" said Pam.

"You know who. Did she say anything about you know who?"

Pam chuckled. "Oh, you mean the fake." She made a face and slowly shook her head. "Yes, and yes."

"She did? He's married, isn't he?"

"As married as can be," said Pam.

"I knew it," the friend said with a gush.

"You're going to love this," Pam toyed.

"What?" Her friend was eating this up.

"His name isn't Richard. His mom isn't sick. And he doesn't travel for his job." Pam lowered her head and raised her eyebrows. "His name is Kareem. His mom is doing *just* fine. And the reason he doesn't travel for his job is *garbage men don't travel for their jobs.*" She sang the last few words. Pam thought about Kareem hanging off the back of a garbage truck. She said with a laugh, "Oh, I guess he does travel for his job."

"A garbage man? Oh...my...gosh. She told you all of this?" The lady pondered her own situation. "How do you know she's right?"

"Ever heard of the Internet?" said Pam.

The friend went from reluctant skeptic to eager believer. She looked at the counter and the flustered lady behind the register. They had to get back to the conference. She got out of line and went to find the manager.

Elizabeth heard the whole conversation. She turned and smiled at the lady named Pam. "I couldn't help but overhear your conversation. That's a fascinating story."

The lady laughed. "*Kah-reem's* a fascinating liar," she said with a laugh. "Men will tell you anything, won't they?"

Elizabeth smiled. "Some will, yes."

"And we believe them," said Pam.

"We want to believe the best," said Elizabeth.

"Girlfriend, that can get you in trouble," said Pam.

"Did this happen at church?" asked Elizabeth.

"At the big Episcopal church," she said.

"Episcopal?" said Elizabeth.

"Yeah. Which way did you come here?" the lady asked.

"From the interstate," said Elizabeth.

"You would've passed it on your left. Can't miss it. Takes up the whole block," said Pam. She could see interest in Elizabeth's eyes. "You should come. Maybe God's got something for you."

Maybe God's got something for you.

"The lady's got a master's in theology, but you wouldn't know it. She's real down-to-earth. You'd like her. Starts in about half an hour." The lady smiled.

Elizabeth hummed her contemplation. "Maybe I will," she said, fully intending to check it out.

*****

Controllus watched with glee as Elizabeth turned into the church parking lot. "What did I tell you?" he said rhetorically to his borrowed guards. "A lamb to the slaughter."

If the witchcraft spirit was looking for praise from Prince Krioni's guards, he'd be waiting a long time. But the guards did look on with keen interest and a reluctant admiration for a one-hand demon who was both smart enough to manipulate a powerful woman of God, and dumb enough to mouth off to a mercy angel.

"Deeper and deeper she goes," said a triumphant Controllus.

*****

The meeting was held in a large sanctuary. Maybe room for two thousand people. It looked as though three hundred people were there. Most people were bunched toward the front. Elizabeth didn't look for the lady who had invited her. She sat down in a row that only had a few people. She looked around. Something felt a little odd.

She shrugged it off as her dropping in a meeting alone not knowing anything about it except that she had overheard a conversation about a minister operating in the gifts of the Spirit. She pulled out her iPad, ready to look up any Scriptures the preacher might refer to.

In a little while, a woman from the front row walked briskly up the few stage stairs. She wore a snazzy, red skirt suit and white blouse. The scarf she wore was a nice accent. Elizabeth liked it.

"Haven't we had fun?" she said to the audience.

Exuberant clapping broke out.

Elizabeth smiled and shifted in her seat as she looked around at the happy faces. It was always good to see people excited about the word of God.

"Are you ready for the spirit to move?" she asked.

More clapping. Some whistles. "Yes," shouted others.

"Oh, you are a hungry bunch of seekers," she said. "Okay, Sheila's ready to come on, but before she does, I want to remind you to visit her book table in the back of the room. She also has a few slots still available for private readings. I'm sure they'll disappear fast, so you better hurry."

Private readings? thought Elizabeth. *She must be some kind of writer to have people willing to pay for an author's reading.* Elizabeth enjoyed going to literary events and hearing authors read portions of their books, but she couldn't think of any she liked so much that she'd pay to hear them read. Then she reminded herself that she and Jonathan had gone to some paid literary events at the *Atlanta History Center.*

"Okay, I'm going to get out of the way so the spirit can move. Wooooo-hoo!" she said, waving her hand as she left the stage.

The audience clapped as Sheila Rawlinson came onstage. Her plain, nondescript clothing was in stark contrast to the immaculately dressed woman who had introduced her. Her slow pace was also unlike her fast-walking, energetic announcer. But this was probably due to her age. Elizabeth watched with concern as the lady made it up the few stairs. She walked over to a chair and table and sat down. She looked carefully over the audience.

"Two-hundred and sixty-seven, Glen," she said to the book table guy. "I want the names of those seven people who didn't come back." Her voice was as strained as her journey up those three stairs.

Laughter from the audience.

She picked up the bottle of water on the table. Her first couple of attempts to open it were unsuccessful. She looked at the audience and put the bottle down. "Glen," she called to the book table guy again before trying and succeeding at taking the top off of the bottle, "never mind. Treating an old lady like this." She shook her finger at the lady who had introduced her. "Connie, you came dangerously close to a lawsuit. Were it not for those beautiful shoes... Isn't she splendidly dressed?" she asked the audience.

The audience clapped.

Elizabeth had sat through hundreds of sermons. She knew a master of the stage when she saw one. This old woman was a master. The audience loved her and she knew it. Elizabeth found herself being pulled into the woman's orbit of humor and age that presumably had made her wise.

The woman put the bottle of water to her mouth and took a swallow so long, it could have qualified as a comedy skit. The old woman didn't stop until the tall bottle was empty. She put the bottle down emphatically.

"Aahhh," she said. "Connie, where's the restroom?"

The audience loved it.

"Just kidding," said the old woman. "I can hold it for five more minutes." She smiled at the smiling crowd. "Oh," she said, waving her hand, "hi, y'all." She waited a few seconds. "The energy in Atlanta isn't as high as it used to be. Of even a year ago when I was last here. There's been a shift. But the energy in this room today is high. We should be able to tap into the spirit's divine mind as powerfully as we did last night."

Elizabeth's curiosity was roused. Her large eyes narrowed with questions.

The old woman lifted her hand. Someone dimmed the lights, leaving a spotlight on her. The lights were so low that Elizabeth almost couldn't make out the faces of people. This was an odd way to preach the word.

Without a que, everyone starting chanting, "Divine spirit, come. Divine spirit, come. Divine spirit, come." Over and over and over and over. "Divine spirit, come. Divine spirit, come. Divine spirit, come."

Elizabeth didn't join in. Something in her rebelled against participating. She listened for a few minutes, looking around. Everyone sat in their seats with their hands lifted with open palms. Nearly three-hundred people were calling on the Holy Spirit to come. So why did she feel so out of place?

"Receive the divine spirit," the woman encouraged. "Do you feel it?"

It? thought Elizabeth. She and Jonathan weren't fans of people calling the Holy Spirit an *it* as though He were a force and not the third Person of the trinity. But she told herself not to get too much in a huff about it. There was no need to judge people harshly for an honest mistake of semantics.

"It's here," said the old woman. "Open your soul to the divine consciousness."

Elizabeth felt a chill. *Divine consciousness? What's going on here? Oh, God, not again. You've got to be kidding me,* she thought.

"Someone here has had a miscarriage. In your third month. Mary. Your name is Mary. You and your husband tried for years to have a baby. You conceived and lost the baby."

"Aaaaaaaahhhh," a lady's scream cut through the darkness.

The sudden scream startled Elizabeth. But what unnerved her more was the old woman's voice. It sounded like her, but it wasn't her.

"That's meeeeeeee," said a woman's strained voice in the darkness. "I lost my baby," the lady cried out.

Elizabeth was torn between leaving—*something was wrong*—and staying—*what was going on with this miscarriage?* The light cut through the darkness and confirmed her misgivings. *The Holy Spirit called an it. Divine force. Readings. These aren't author readings. They're psychic readings. I'm in some kind of spiritist meeting!*

"I'm getting out of here," she said, not completely under her breath. She got up and walked quickly down her row. When she turned into the aisle in the darkness where she was an unknown stranger, she heard the woman from the stage say with a voice that was hers, but a personality that was not, "Elizabeth."

Elizabeth's walk-run came to an immediate halt. Her eyes were wide with shock.

Controllus watched anxiously.

The moment the shock loosed the muscles in her legs, Elizabeth ran toward the door.

"Elizabeth," the voice said authoritatively, "if you stop, I will answer your questions about Ava."

Elizabeth slowed. *She loved her mom desperately.* But the moment she stopped, she felt something push her forward toward the door. She didn't resist. This was the Holy Spirit. *Oh, thank you, Jesus!* She bolted from the building as though it were on fire.

Chapter 29

Word from the hospital was not good. There was a good chance that Ava had suffered brain damage. How much? They didn't know. Their best prognosis was dismal. The only viable options they saw were to keep her on life support or to take her off life support and see if her body was strong enough to sustain itself. That best case scenario, however, still left them with Ava having brain damage.

But there was another *best case* scenario. One that transcended the laws of science, biology, and medical technology.

Jonathan had been praying and fasting four full days. He hadn't heard anything from heaven yet. This didn't discourage him. He knew from the Scriptures and from experience that he shouldn't let God's silence negatively affect his faith. After all, that's what it meant to walk by faith. *There would be times when the silence would be exceedingly, even excruciatingly painful and debilitating.* He wouldn't be taken down by silence. He'd continue to attack this stronghold of death until it broke.

The place he had chosen to conduct his attack from was a friend's large, luxury cabin in the Blue Ridge Mountains of north Georgia. It was big enough to sleep ten people. So it was perfect for Jonathan's tendency to walk as he prayed.

He drank some more water and sat the bottle down. He stood up with his Bible opened to Mark 11 and walked through the cabin reading Scriptures out loud. He liked to say this was him going on record. It was for the benefit of heaven and hell. He wanted everyone to know where he stood.

"I come against you mountain of death in the name of Jesus. Come out!" he began his attack.

*****

A harried line of demons bumped into one another as they rushed back and forth along the long trench that ran alongside the stronghold walls. Some wore helmets, but most didn't have that luxury. Besides, helmets didn't do much good when a thousand-pound boulder fell on you. And they certainly didn't help if you were so unlucky a demon as to be on the receiving end of a direct hit from an incoming missile.

Death walked along the high, thick walls of his stronghold. They weren't merely thick. They were impenetrable. Impregnable. Impossible to breach. *These walls were inspected and certified as 99% prayer proof.*

Death surveyed the damage to his impenetrable, impregnable, impossible-to-breach walls. They were being breached! Demons were scattered everywhere. Panic was in the air, along with missiles and angels. Even lightning. Lightning strikes! Death cursed. What was next? Would the enemy hurl diseased cows over his impossible-to-breach walls?

He looked at the plumes of smoke that rose over his smoldering stronghold. *Ninety-nine percent prayer proof,* he thought cynically. Death was incensed at his predicament, but his anger did not exceed his intelligence. There was no such thing as a one-hundred percent prayer proof stronghold. Even those strongholds that had stood the test of time—at least until now—had not been certified one-hundred percent prayer proof.

For you never knew when you'd run into a lunatic child of God who acted like this Jonathan. Or worse—the thought was absolutely hideous and fearful to think upon—if there were two or more united in tenacious prayer.

Death shuddered at the thought of Christians united in prayer. He looked to his left. A small dot in the sky. His eyes bulged. It was a small, *blue* dot. A prayer missile! There was no cover on the top of the wall. He ran as fast as he could to reach the closest ladder. He grabbed the two top beams and jumped in the air and swung his legs toward the ladder.

The missile hit before death's feet found the rungs. It landed at the outside edge of the wall, about two hundred feet from the ladder. Massive chunks of stone exploded into every direction.

Death opened his eyes. His ears rang so badly he felt vibrations in his head that made his teeth tremble. He pulled up his dangling legs and found a resting place on a ladder rung. *Ninety-nine percent proof,* he thought. *It's always the one percent you have to look out for.*

Death made his way to his situation room for a damage assessment. The damage was as he had seen himself. Extensive. How was one person able to inflict such damage on a stronghold of this magnitude? Death's only hope, he knew, was to outlast the attack. This plan almost always worked. And just to make sure it worked for him, Death would make repairs as quickly as possible. This would prolong the battle and hopefully wear out the man of God.

A voice thundered in Death's situation room. It was so loud and powerful that the table trembled and rattled itself a few inches from its place. Death shot to his feet. So did the demon officers who sat around the long table.

Death wondered if this voice was heard only in his bunker. Or if it had reverberated throughout his entire stronghold. He hoped not. It would be bad for morale.

*****

Jonathan turned his Bible to Joshua 6. He pointed his finger at the sky and almost yelled as he read the story of the fall of the walls of Jericho. "I know you hear me, Death. Your walls are coming down!"

*****

The hours passed as Jonathan energetically prayed for Ava. He still had not heard from God, but he was determined to pray through. Yet even his determination couldn't stop his sleep deprived body from turning a nap between prayer sessions into a six-hour slumber. His eyelids didn't move until he felt something tapping him hard on the forehead.

A slit formed in his flittering, burning eyes. He was so tired. He must've been dreaming. He saw two figures, one on each side of the bed. Jonathan's eyes closed. *Just a little more sleep.*

One of the masked figures unplugged the portable clock radio next to the bed. He gripped it and slammed it hard on the sleeping man's face.

Sleep didn't lessen the pain of a one and a half pound clock radio being slammed down on his face by a two-hundred and twenty-pound man who enjoyed this kind of thing. Jonathan jerked and flailed his arms as he sat up in a pained daze. He grabbed his throbbing face. His eye hurt even more. The edge of the radio had sliced hard directly on his eyelid.

Jonathan looked to his left and right with the one eye he could see out of. Both men wore ski masks and gloves. Both of them had guns with silencers. This didn't look like a robbery.

The men didn't say anything.

Neither did Jonathan.

After a few awkward moments one smiled under his mask. "You're not going to ask us what we want?"

"I figured you'd get around to that," said Jonathan. He rubbed his fingers over his forehead and face. Generous amount of blood. *Must've cut me open pretty good.*

"You've got a big mouth," the other thug added.

"God has blessed me," said Jonathan.

The guy with the clock smirked. "He's blessed," he said to his accomplice. "Watch our blessed friend here while I make the call." He walked out of the room. When he returned, he turned the light on and pointed the phone at Jonathan. “Look up,” he ordered, with that kind of amusing tone perfected by armed crooks with a sense of humor.

“Do you want me to smile?” asked Jonathan.

“Yeah. That would be good,” the thug answered.

Jonathan smiled into the camera. “This doesn’t look good, Mr. Bogarti. Me sitting in bed smiling at you. You on the other end probably smiling at me.”

The smile under the camera man’s mask evaporated. He snatched the phone down.

“How the—” The other thug stopped himself. He looked anxiously at the thug with the phone.

The thug with the phone walked quickly out of the room. He returned after getting a cryptic earful from Michael. “Get up.”

“Now?” asked Jonathan.

“Yeah. Now,” he yelled.

Jonathan got off the bed and walked toward the door. “Downstairs?”

“Where else we’re going to go?” snapped the thug with no sense of humor.

Jonathan started walking slowly down the stairs. “I hope you didn’t come here in a stolen car. That’ll make it easier for the cops to catch up with you.”

“Shut up.” It was the humorless thug again.

“You didn’t notice the cameras when you drove in, did you?” Jonathan turned around just in time to see the last motion of the humorless thug’s gun crash against his head. He fell down the rest of the stairs.

“Hey!” the phone thug yelled to the ticked off thug. “We gotta bring ‘em in. How much talking can he do with a broke neck?”

“That’s the point. None. This preacher’s got a big mouth.” He glared at the crumpled man at the bottom of the stairs.

The other thug stepped over Jonathan and looked through the window for cameras. “I don’t see any cameras.”

"Would he have told us if there were cameras out there?" said the angry thug. He stood over Jonathan and jerked him onto his stomach. "What? No jokes?" He yanked his hands behind his back and put a plastic tie around his wrists. "Get up."

They walked Jonathan to the back of the car and opened the trunk. The humorous thug taped his mouth. The other said, "You try any of that TV stuff and we'll kill you. You got that?"

Jonathan nodded and got into the trunk. When it slammed shut, he started praying.

*****

Captain Rashti looked at him with admiration. He was one of a kind. "Your wounds were grievous," he said, looking at the side of Enrid's neck and at the marks on his chest and leg. "You can be totally healed in the presence of the Lord."

"I bear these marks in my body for the glory of God and the sons and daughters of Adam," said Enrid.

"I understand. It's a great honor. The Lord of glory bears in his body the marks of His struggles for the sons of Adam." Captain Rashti hadn't seen the long scar on the angel's face.

Enrid saw him looking at it.

"More glory," the Captain said with a faint smile. "Enrid, I have another mission for you. Nothing as glorious as assassinating two ruling spirits for the Mighty Bashnar."

Enrid's eyes brightened. "What is it?"

"It's Jonathan," said the captain.

*****

Vivian's exquisitely painted eyes were locked onto the large television that hung on their bedroom wall. She and Michael had to get going, but the news story was fascinating and touching. Girls had been locked up for years and used as prostitutes.

In another part of the house, Michael looked at the screen on his phone. He didn't say anything. Hard to intercept words not spoken. He nodded instead.

Michael entered the bedroom with a bounce in his step. Compliments of a wife who for the past few days had been making love to him as though she were trying to pay off a million dollar debt. And compliments of seeing that preacher sitting on the bed bleeding. Today had been a good day for lust and business. Now it was time to take care of the business of lust.

Michael glanced at his wife as he put on his watch. Vivian didn't watch a lot television. "What's going on?"

"It's terrible," she said. "Poor girls. Locked up for years."

Michael stiffened in his thousand-dollar suit. "Yeah?"

"I don't know what I'd do if some sick monster kidnapped our daughter and used her like this."

They both watched as the FBI escorted a parade of handcuffed men into awaiting cars. Michael looked intently at the men's hanging heads.

"All of them should have their balls cut off," said Vivian with venom. She looked at her husband. "We have a daughter. I swear I'd personally cut off the balls of anyone who hurt Isabella or Priscilla."

"Perverts," said Michael. "Sex is everywhere. Why would somebody do something like that?"

"Because they're monsters," she said emphatically.

Mike noticed the passion in her voice.

An angel spoke in her ear.

"Those men in handcuffs are only in handcuffs because they're the low men on the totem pole. They couldn't do this without protection. The real monsters are the ones you don't see. There's someone behind the scenes making money off these poor girls."

"Always is," said Michael.

"Our girls dance because they want to." Vivian didn't know why she said this. It didn't fit.

"We're not making anyone do anything," said Michael, sitting down next to his wife. "Our girls make a ton of money doing what they want to do. Some of them are helping their families. Some of them are going to school. Look at Terri. And Gena. Those girls are gonna graduate without owing one dime in student loans."

"We're not like those men," said Vivian.

Michael heard the question in her statement. He hugged his wife with one arm. "Those men are monsters. We care about our girls." He looked at her with the soft eyes of an enraged murderer and kissed her tenderly on the forehead. "I'm going to take care of some business before I go in. I'll see you at the club."

*****

Jonathan had been in the trunk of the car for hours. Wherever he was, it was secluded. They had driven down a long, pot-hole filled dirt road. He hadn't heard anything at all. Not even the thugs. But he knew they were there.

*****

Michael Bogarti had chosen a spot that had served them well a few times. An abandoned house deep in the woods. He had never visited personally, but he had seen videos of the place. And, of course, he had taken precautions—extra precautions, since he would do this job himself.

He walked toward the car with a man at each side. All three of them wore ski masks. Two carried guns. Rick carried a gun and a large bag. Lenny carried a gun and a gas can. Michael looked at the trunk of the car that the preacher was in as he approached. His eyes wouldn't leave that trunk. He was going to close out this deal tonight.

The two thugs who kidnapped Jonathan stood there waiting on the approaching three men.

When Michael got there one of the thugs started to say something, but Lenny cut him off with a finger to his own lip. It had already been decided that no words would be spoken.

Mr. Bogarti had come to take care of business, not to socialize. He'd cut this pig's tongue out for talking too much. He'd cut his eyes out for the way he had eyeballed him on the phone. Then he was going to gut him like a pig. Those were the exact words he had whispered to Lenny just before they had gotten into the car: "I'm going to take that pig from the trunk of the car and gut him."

Rick took an oversized plastic jumpsuit out of his bag. He handed it to Mr. Bogarti. After he put on the jumpsuit, Rick handed him another. He did the same with plastic for his shoes. Then Mr. Bogarti put on two plastic head pieces.

The two thugs had heard of Mr. Bogarti's paranoia, but this was ridiculous. Ridiculous to them. However, to a businessman who understood how a drop of blood or a microscopic piece of human tissue or a fiber off of this or that could send him to prison, he preferred the ridiculous ritual of wearing two plastic suits.

The inside plastic suit would contain his DNA and make sure that none got on the outer plastic suit. The outer plastic suit, the one with the preacher's blood on it would be burned here on the spot. Later, Mr. Bogarti would burn the inner plastic suit.

Mr. Bogarti was suited. It was time.

Rick handed him the knife and the crude tool he'd use to pry open Jonathan's mouth. Mr. Bogarti's scowl burned through the plastic. This preacher was never going to tell his wife about his business. Neither would that other preacher.

Michael heard an odd sound from the trunk. He motioned to one of the thugs to open it.

The trunk popped. The man raised it. He looked inside and opened his eyes wider than they'd ever been before.

A pig squealed and jumped out and ran down the long dirt road as though he had overheard a conversation about how good bacon tasted.

Everyone watched that pig until it was out of sight. They turned back to face one another.

The man who opened the trunk frowned in shock and looked at his accomplice, then at the man in the plastic suit. “Mr. Bogarti, Mr. Bogarti, I don’t know how this happened.”

Rick and Lenny pointed their guns at the men. Both men pulled off their masks. They were now unnecessary.

Lenny took both men’s guns. He gave one to Rick.

Michael removed the plastic hoods and his ski mask. “Rick, give me his gun.”

He gave it to him and backed away. Lenny also backed away from the men. They both had been with the boss long enough to know what was coming next.

“Where’s the preacher?” Michael asked the thug who had taken the clock radio to Jonathan’s face.

“Mr. Bogarti, I don’t—”

Michael lifted the gun and pulled the trigger, cutting short the man’s answer. He looked at the remaining bug-eyed thug. “Whose idea was it to put a pig in the trunk?”

“Mr. Bogarti—” The thug thought about what had just happened to his accomplice when he said he didn’t know. The thug’s lungs filled with rapid breaths of air. What could he say?

“Never mind,” said Michael. “Where’s the preacher?”

This thug had never been on this side of terror before. His face showed the panic that had brought him so much amusement when he had seen it in others he had victimized. “We had him.” He pointed at the open trunk and jabbed his shaking finger with every word. “We—had—him—handcuffed—in—that—trunk! We had him, Mr. Bogarti.”

“I know you had him. I saw him on the phone. Where is he now?” Michael asked.

The thug’s miserable life was coming to an end. He saw it in the hardness of Mr. Bogarti’s face. “We tied ‘em up and put him in the trunk, I tell you. I saw him go in this trunk. He was in this trunk crying out to Jesus until we made him shut up. We opened the trunk and cracked him in the head and told him to shut up. Mr. Bogarti, we did not leave this car." The thug looked at Michael's face for the slightest hint of hope.

"Mr. Bogarti," said Lenny, "can I ask him something?"

Mr. Bogarti pulled back his stare from the man. "Yeah."

"That was disrespectful," said Lenny. "And stupid. Why would you do something like this? Somebody pay you to do this?"

"No, man! Nobody paid us nothin'. I'm telling you, man. I don't know where that preacher is, and I sure as get out don't know where that pig came from.

"Where's the preacher?" said Michael.

"I don't—"

Michael shortened his answer with a bullet to the forehead. "Now let's find that preacher before Vivian finds out what's going on."

*****

The Mighty Bashnar had left Sharon to personally witness this dagger's tongue being cut out. He had escorted the thugs to Jonathan's cabin. He had seen them beat him and knock him down the stairs. He had seen them tie him and put him in the car. He had seen them open the trunk of the car and hit him in the head. He had seen them watch that car like their lives depended on it. And still, he and his servant, Michael, had watched a pig jump out of the car and run down the road.

The Mighty Bashnar looked around. Who else had seen this? He would be the butt of every joke if this ever got out. He didn't see anyone. But what consolation was that? Obviously, someone had seen what had happened. Some angel.

How? How? How were these blasted angels able to do things like this? he thought. His eyes darkened. *Jonathan may be gone, but I've still got Sharon!*

The Mighty Bashnar left with a furious roar.

Chapter 30

It would've been a gross understatement to say Edwin and Barbara hadn't slept all night. They hadn't breathed all night.

Sharon was gone!

They had left with Andrew to go to the hospital and had returned to an empty house. They called everyone there was to call. No one had seen or heard from her. The police had told them they'd keep an eye out for her and the vehicle, but since at the time she was only a few hours late, they'd wait a few more hours before calling it an official missing person case.

Edwin and Barbara had gone ballistic and insisted that their daughter was missing from home. She was not simply late coming home. The police didn't find it helpful that their daughter had told neither of them where she was going. Maybe this wasn't an oversight.

After the police left their home, Edwin acknowledged the grim facts that precious time was being wasted and his daughter was in trouble. She didn't have a flat tire. She hadn't run out of gas. She was in serious trouble. He grabbed his keys.

"Where are you going?" Barbara asked, with puffy eyes that showed little white.

"I'm not waiting on someone else to find my daughter." He walked determinedly toward the door.

"Dad, I'm coming," said Andrew.

"Me, too," said Barbara.

"Barbara, you need to be here in case someone calls," he said.

"Edwin, I can't—" started Barbara.

Edwin raised his palm. "Barbara, you need to stay here." His voice was low and firm.

"Andrew, you need to stay with your mother." Edwin cut off the well-meaning pushback he saw in his son's face. "Your mother needs a man here to help her while I look for your sister." He looked at them both. "I'm going to find her and bring her home. Call me if you hear anything."

He was out the door before they could object further.

*****

The Mighty Bashnar was torn between taking his wrath out on Sharon and tormenting her weak, worthless father. Her torments were most exhilarating, but they had not satisfied as he thought they would. Just when he had done something to her through Rob that should've brought the most fiendish pleasure, he heard that pig squeal.

He couldn't get that pig out of his mind.

Every time that pig squealed in his mind, it only added to his bubbling frustration that dealing with this Rob was turning into a crap shoot. Getting him to do to Sharon *exactly* what he wanted done was requiring more effort than he should've had to expend under the circumstances.

He had authority from heaven to attack this family. He had a sex pervert who was potentially murderous. He had a beautiful young girl tied up. He backed up in his thoughts. *That's where the problem was.*

Sharon was sitting in a chair with her cuffed hands draped over the back of it. A chain was snaked over the handcuffs, under the chair, and around her waist. She couldn't go anywhere without taking the chair with her. But he had told Rob to *tie* her to the bed, and instead she was cuffed and chained to a chair.

He had ordered Rob to take this beloved daughter of heaven and to reenact every humiliation of his depraved mind. He had ordered him to leave her clothed with nothing but the faith they would tear from her soul. He had ordered him to beat and torture her to within a breath of the life she painstakingly submitted to her God.

The wretched heifer should have been bleeding and moaning in agony, trembling in shame at her dishonorable treatment. But what had she really suffered at the hands of her demented kidnapper?

True, Sharon was chained to a chair.

But was she bleeding and moaning in agony? No. The most he had done was pinch her until she cried and screamed into the tape he had over her mouth.

Was she trembling in shame at her dishonorable treatment? No. There had been no dishonorable treatment. Except for his pinching. And he seemed reluctant to do even that.

Was she clothed with nothing but her hideous faith? No. Except for her open blouse, there she sat as though she were on a date with a naughty nerd.

To Rob's credit, he had put the neck tourniquet on her. He had even twisted it a few times around her neck. But something made him stop every time. The slighted warrior spirit didn't know if it had been the desperate pleading of the thorn's eyes, the weakness of his would-be murderer, or Rob simply desiring to prolong the game as long as possible.

The warrior spirit appreciated what it felt like to play with captured prey. But this pretender hadn't even done the simplest of tasks. The Mighty Bashnar had ordered him to at least tip the young girl's chair over. This would increase her sense of helpless.

But there was another more sinister purpose in this task. The warrior spirit had dealt with reluctant killers before. He had broken through their resistance by getting them to obey little things. Tipping chairs one moment. Strangling women the next.

Another more troubling thought entered the Mighty Bashnar's mind. He knew that Sharon was praying. She was always praying. He admitted that even he couldn't make her stop praying. But what if heaven was double-crossing him? What if they were answering her prayers in violation of the agreement? That could be why his pervert wasn't acting like a pervert.

He looked at Rob. He gave *pervert* a bad name. This was no way for a pervert to treat a tied up girl!

The Mighty Bashnar floated above the house. He'd attack Sharon's worthless father and come back for her later.

*****

Just a little while after the Mighty Bashnar left, Rob looked at Sharon with a long, glazed stare. He walked over to her and slammed his hands against her shoulders. The chair tipped backward and Sharon fell against the floor.

She looked up at the ceiling, praying harder than she had ever prayed in her life.

*****

Edwin had only driven around for twenty minutes before the Mighty Bashnar caught up with him. He brought with him more spirits of infirmity.

"Looking for your precious daughter, worm? I'll give her back to you wrapped in the same package I gave you little Christopher. You miss him, I know. You'll miss Sharon even more." The warrior spirit looked at one of the demons with him. "Strike him in the bowels," he ordered. A demon wrapped himself around Edwin's intestines and squeezed. "Strike him in the bladder," he ordered. A spirit squeezed Edwin's bladder.

Edwin jerked and doubled over. His head almost hit the steering wheel. He raised his head in disbelief. It had happened again. It was happening now. He couldn't stop himself. His mouth dropped open in horror.

The Mighty Bashnar's lips curled, but the laughter of his demons filled the darkness.

*****

Barbara stopped and listened. *Edwin? He's only been gone a little while. Oh, did he find her?* She ran to the door and pulled it open. His face was not happy. "What—?" Barbara stretched her neck looking behind him. "Why are you back so soon?" she asked, as he walked past her. He was walking like a cowboy again. *Oh, God, not again.* She intercepted Andrew and walked him into another room.

Edwin grabbed a plastic garbage bag and went upstairs. In less than half an hour he was walking out the door with an expression of stone. He had a Bible in one hand and a plastic garbage bag in the other.

"Edwin?" said Barbara, as he walked away.

"I'm going to get my daughter," he answered. Andrew was right. This was not a coincidence. He was under attack. They were under attack. He lifted the Bible half-way and said it again, but this time he wasn't talking to his wife. He was talking to whoever else may be listening. "In the name of Jesus, I'm going to get my daughter."

*****

The demons with the Mighty Bashnar looked at him in bewilderment.

"Why are you looking at me with those dumb looks? He's a worm," declared Bashnar. "Wait for around ten minutes, after he gets away from the house. Then strike him again. We will strike and strike and strike! Do you understand?" His question wasn't really a question. It was chastisement.

"Yes, Mighty Bashnar," they all answered.

Ten minutes later they prepared to strike.

Edwin looked forward with steel eyes. "I rebuke you, Satan, in Jesus's name." Edwin's voice was low, but determined.

The demons didn't just hear the thunderous sound. They felt its crushing power shaking their bones. They held onto one another, trembling violently. They felt the darkness around them being pulled out of place. Jolt after jolt after jolt.

The Mighty Bashnar refused to believe what was happening. He stiffened his body and told himself this was impossible. The worm could not shake his world. But this didn't stop his teeth from rattling or his thick bones from feeling the power of those words hurl through the darkness like the wave of power from a nuclear blast.

Within a few seconds the rumbling was over.

The warrior spirit wasted no time. "Strike! Strike! Strike!"

The demons grabbed his intestines and bladder and squeezed. They looked at their agitated boss. He expected results. But both demons knew that no matter how hard they squeezed, nothing was going to happen.

The Mighty Bashnar pushed his neck forward and looked the worm up and down. "Where is it? Where's the mess?"

"It's all gone," said the demon on the intestines. "We pushed it all out the first time."

"Yeah," said the bladder demon. "There's nothing left. He's empty."

The Mighty Bashnar looked at the worm's face. He didn't see fear. He didn't see indecisiveness. Could it be that the worm had turned into an adversary?

Chapter 31

Edwin had to do something. Driving was something. But Atlanta was a big place. He couldn't drive up and down every street. He felt a tide of helplessness rising irresistibly, threatening to drown his hope.

He resisted.

Sharon was out there, and he was going to find her.

A sudden sunrise at midnight. *Yes! Why didn't I think of that before?* He swerved the car over and came to a screeching stop, making a parking space. He called his wife. "Barbara," he said to her, "Rob. It's gotta be Rob. Yeah, that guy. Look on the side of the refrigerator. His address is on there." He waited a torturous twenty seconds or so. "No. No. I don't want to call him. If he knows where our daughter is—" He cut the sentence off. He didn't like where it was leading.

He looked behind him and pushed hard on the gas pedal, jumping in front of a car that would've hit him had he not taken off so fast. Edwin glanced back at the car in the rearview mirror. *Seconds mattered.*

Every red light was a curse. Every stop sign a menace. Some, Edwin the pastor impatiently waited on. Others, Edwin the father violated. Considering the size of Atlanta, and its notorious traffic, it didn't take long to get to Rob's address, but it felt long. All that mattered now to

Edwin was, *Am I too late?* His mind hadn't yet allowed him to define what the event was he was trying to prevent.

Edwin looked up the hill on his right as he drove up Rob's street. It just now dawned on him that it was Wednesday morning. School. Rob would be at school. What about his parents? Maybe someone was at home.

What if no one's at home?

Edwin drove up the long driveway and parked his car. Not that he could tell by looking at the outside, but the house had an empty look. *That doesn't mean no one's there. She could be calling my name right now.*

Edwin got out of the car and quietly pushed the heavy SUV door shut. He looked at the large trees that provided shade to the house. He looked at every window for movement. He walked toward the front door knowing that he was getting into this house one way or another.

He looked through the long, narrow window on the side of the door. Nothing. He rang the bell and didn't wait before knocking on the door like a man looking for his missing daughter.

*****

Rob's room was really the entirety of their large basement. His parents had thought it a good idea to give their wonderful son as much privacy and space as they could afford. Their stellar educations had provided stellar careers that—along with uncanny business investments by his parents—had provided Rob anything he desired.

Rob was the perfect son. Smart. Mature. Obedient. Never any trouble. That's why his dad didn't think twice about turning a business trip to Japan into a vacation for him and his wife. *He really was a good boy.*

The good boy and the Mighty Bashnar stood behind the trembling girl. Rob slowly pulled the tape off of her mouth. Everything had been done slowly to prolong the pleasure. But now it was time to reenact and experience the same thrill he had seen in his snuff porn videos.

The thing inside of him didn't want the sound of Sharon's gagging muffled under a piece of tape. Its ears wanted to hear the sound of life leaving her throat.

Rob and the Mighty Bashnar slowly twisted the neck tourniquet.

"You don't have to do this?" Sharon pleaded.

His words were without emotion. "Yes, I do."

"Oh, but he does," said the Mighty Bashnar.

Those three words took away the shadow of hope she dared to hold onto. She accepted that she was going to die. She closed her eyes and prayed.

The tourniquet tightened.

More.

More.

More.

Rob couldn't tighten it further. He held on to the handle until the compulsion inside of him released him. He dropped his arms to his side, drained, depleted.

There was very little distance between tipping chairs and strangling girls. The Mighty Bashnar stepped out of Rob and fell before the young woman. Fortunately, he fell with his head facing the girl. He looked at Sharon's lifeless head hanging limply. *Wonderful.* He looked at Rob with new respect. And new hope. "Finally, I have my murderer."

In a few minutes, the Mighty Bashnar regained his strength. He made his way to his feet. This unjust weakness that the enemy imposed upon demons of his strength—even though it was momentary—who entered humans was one of the main reasons he did this so rarely.

Rob and the Mighty Bashnar looked above them. Someone was at the door. Rob ran upstairs to his parents' bedroom and got his father's gun and put it in the back of his waistline.

*****

Edwin's pounding had crossed the line of politeness. He saw through the side window that someone was coming.

The door opened. A young man that fit Sharon's description of Rob stood before him. Tall. Handsome. Muscular.

"I'm Sharon's father," said Edwin.

A quick and relaxed smile removed the momentarily stunned expression on the young man's face. "I'm Rob." He laughed and ran his hand through his hair as he said, "But you already know that. Nice to meet you."

"She's missing," said Edwin.

"Missing?"

Edwin watched Rob look quizzically at the ground, shaking his head.

"Yes, missing. She didn't come home last night. When was the last time you saw my daughter?" Edwin's expression matched the insinuating directness of his questions.

Rob didn't want to be caught in an easy lie. He tried to recall his last phone conversation with her. "I don't know." Rob thought about it. "It could've been—"

He thought about it too long. Edwin pushed past him and walked inside.

Rob walked behind him. "Mr. Styles, what are you doing?"

Edwin stood in the large foyer. He scanned every direction. "Sharon," he yelled.

Rob's eyes grew large. He darted to the front door and looked outside to see who might've seen Edwin come in. He closed the door and ran back to Edwin.

Edwin's eyes were hard. "You look nervous."

"Mr. Styles...you're...you're intruding. You're acting like I had something to do with Sharon's disappearance. Would you please leave?"

Disappearance. That was a strange way for this young man to refer to his daughter. "You can call the police," said Edwin.

"Mr. Styles, I don't want to call the police."

Edwin stared into Rob's eyes. "I didn't think so. Where's my daughter?" he asked, stepping forward.

Rob stepped back. He weighed his options. "Mr. Styles, you *need* to leave." He sounded more like a man than a young man.

"Why aren't you in school?" Pause. "I'm not leaving here without my daughter," answered Edwin. "Where is she?"

They locked eyes.

The Mighty Bashnar was straining against Rob's weakening will. This was his chance to get the worm and his daughter. *"Kill him!"* he shouted repeatedly.

"This is the last time I'm going to ask you, Mr. Styles."

"This is the last time I'm going to ask you, Rob," said Edwin, meaning it.

Check his room," said the angel.

"Where's your room?" asked Edwin.

Rob made up his mind. "Downstairs," he answered coolly.

"Which way?" he asked.

"You sure you want to do this?" Rob asked.

Edwin didn't see a young man who he thought may have something to do with his daughter being missing. He saw a *man* who may have had something to do with his daughter's disappearance, and one who was acting as though he did. "You sure you want to try to stop me?"

"Around the corner," Rob pointed to the right.

Edwin went around the corner.

Rob followed.

Edwin looked at him.

Rob pointed to a door. "I live in the basement."

Edwin opened the door. He flicked on the light. "Sharon" he yelled down the stairs."

Rob came forward and stood a couple of yards behind Edwin. "You see, Mr. Styles, there's no one down there. I don't know where Sharon is. If I hear from her, I'll let you know."

Edwin looked hard at Rob.

Rob didn't wilt. He had killed once. He'd do it again. His face was as hard as Edwin's. "Would you feel better checking my apartment?"

"Yes, I would," answered a determined dad.

"Go on."

Edwin went quickly down the stairs.

Rob took the gun from his back. He lifted his shirt and put it in his front waistline. He followed casually down the stairs.

Edwin got to the bottom of the stairs and looked both ways. Rob was right. This was an apartment. "Sharon," he called.

"She's not here, Mr. Styles," Rob said from behind him.

Desperation gripped Edwin. He turned to Rob. "If you've done anything to my daughter, I'll kill you."

There was no need to follow Sharon's father. He'd know when he found the body. That's when he'd shoot the intruder who had broken into their home. It would turn out to be a tragic accident. *Desperate father looking for his missing daughter breaks into boyfriend's home. Boyfriend kills father mistaking him for a burglar.*

Rob went to the refrigerator and got out a bottle of water. He went to the TV room and sat in an oversized leather seat. He put his feet up on a large coffee table. "I'm in here, Mr. Styles." He took a drink and waited for Edwin to open the right door.

He saw Edwin go to the closed door. The man stopped and looked at him. *Go on in, Mr. Styles.* He pulled back his shirt.

Edwin turned the knob and pushed the door partly open.

Rob gripped the gun.

Edwin's phone rang. He snatched it out of his jacket pocket.

"Edwin, they found the car!" It was Barbara.

"Where?" yelled Edwin.

Rob watched Edwin turn and run up the stairs. He got up and went to the door that Edwin had partly opened. He pushed it all the way open and stepped inside and looked to the left at the dead girl in the chair. "You almost had company, Sharon."

Rob ran upstairs. He went to his front door to catch Mr. Styles. He was grabbing the car door handle. "I told you she wasn't here," said Rob.

*****

The men who had been following Edwin wondered why he didn't come out with his daughter. They knew she was in there. But that wasn't their problem. That was the problem of the men who were supposed to have been watching the girl.

The men following Edwin rolled slowly past the parked car with their accomplices in it. They rolled down the window and talked as they drove by. "He doesn't have the girl. She must still be in there."

One of the men in the parked car put in a call to the guy standing a few feet from Mr. Bogarti. The guy received the bad news with a hard face. He whispered something into Mr. Bogarti's ear, whose face now mirrored his own. Michael stiffened momentarily. He had a disappearing preacher, and now it seemed he had a disappearing girl. He whispered back to the man.

The guy sitting in the parked car received his orders and looked up at the house.

*****

Enrid received his orders and looked down at the parked car.

*****

Rob dragged the extra-large suitcase up the stairs. He was strong, but he had to rest on each stair. Once he reached the top, he stood still, looking around and stretching his right hand. *What else do I need to do before I leave?*

He rolled the luggage to the garage and put it on its side inside of the car's trunk. He pushed the garage door opener. It began its cranking sound. Sunlight rushed in as the wide door lifted. Rob smiled. He had done it. He had finally satisfied the powerful, tormenting urge and had embraced his true self. He had killed. And if he were careful, he'd be able to do this forever.

*****

The man in the parked car saw Rob's car coming down the driveway. He pulled his leg back into the car and shut the door. "Where does he think he's going?" he said, as Rob's car turned left and away from them.

The driver turned the key. A clicking sound came from under the hood. He cursed and snatched out his phone. He called the same guy he had spoken to earlier.

The man listened in angry disbelief. "Battery? That's what you want me to tell him?" He gave the man some instructions and hung up. The man walked toward Mr. Bogarti. Michael saw the man's scowl as he approached.

"What now?" asked Michael, his dark eyes showing his impatience. "The house disappear?"

He whispered. "The guy with Sharon's on the move."

"What's the problem? Follow him."

"That's the problem, Mike. Tony's battery is dead."

Michael pulled his neck back and dropped his head a little. "Tony's *battery* is dead?"

"Yeah. Said he hears a clicking sound when he turns the ignition," said Rick.

Michael could hardly believe it. "He hears a clicking sound," he responded. Disgust. His tone was filled with absolute disgust.

"Since they can't follow the boy, I told him to get up there and check out the house. Maybe the girl is in there," Rick added.

"Or maybe she's with him," said Michael. "We *need* that girl."

"I understand," said Rick. He made a phone call.

*****

Tony and Carlos walked up the long driveway. They walked at a normal pace, talking to one another and laughing and gesturing for the benefit of any nosey neighbors. But they weren't going to trust that their little act was going keep someone from calling the cops. So once they got to the door, they broke the side window and entered without hesitation. Tony ran upstairs. Carlos searched the first floor.

Nothing.

They stood in the kitchen. Carlos opened the door and scanned the garage. He closed it.

"Downstairs," said Tony. "Stay up here. Let me know if we get any company." He flicked the light and trotted down the stairs. The place was quiet. He checked everywhere. No one was down there. He walked toward the stairs and opened the door to the last room he hadn't checked.

He stopped cold. The girl was slumped over, chained to a chair. He pulled out his gun and stepped out of the room and scanned the place again. He didn't find anything. He went back to the girl and lifted her head. Her neck had a reddish-purplish bruise around it. He stared at her forehead. "What the—?" He pressed on the side of her neck with two fingers. The girl was dead.

They needed to get out of there. Fast.

Carlos took a couple of quick steps toward the door and stopped. He turned and looked at the girl's chest, above her bra. Why didn't he see that before? This guy was sick. He thought about taking a picture for the boss. But the last thing he needed was to have a picture of a murdered girl on his ex-con phone. He ran up the stairs.

Tony looked at Carlos's anxious eyes.

"Sharon's dead. We gotta get out of here," said Carlos.

*****

Rob's euphoria was greater now than it had been when he was turning the tourniquet around her neck and her head had finally dropped to her chest. He closed his eyes and exhaled deeply.

Beeeeeeeeeep! Beeeeeeeeep!

The car's horn behind him rushed him through the new green light. Rob went through the intersection and passed by a police car that had been guided to this gas station by angels. The police car waited for a chance to exit the gas station. Rob watched it from the corner of his eye. He was met by the very next red light. The police car turned into traffic and came to a stop directly behind him.

Just great, Rob cursed his bad luck.

The officer on the passenger side sipped his hot chocolate. "Man, what you talkin' about? The Raiders been sorry forever. You keep dreaming."

The officer driving had a mouthful of trash-talk hanging out of his mouth when he looked at the license plate. *Are you serious?* he said to the great detective in the sky. He pointed at the car directly in front of them. "Jay, check *this* out."

"Come on. Come on," said an impatient Rob. The light finally turned green. He was careful to look both ways before pressing on the gas. He drove a block. The cruiser was in back of him, maybe six car lengths. Rob looked for speed limit signs as he drove.

Flashing lights.

Rob's heart tried to burst out of his chest. His panicked, wide eyes looked into the rearview mirror. They were directly behind him with their lights flashing. For a moment he thought about trying to lose them. But that was stupid. This wasn't TV. But what could he do?

Wait a minute. Maybe I don't have to do anything. They don't know anything. How could they? Just play it cool, he thought. Rob started slowing down.

"Keep moving," he heard the cop say over his speaker.

Rob obeyed the officer's directions. This went on for several blocks. Each time Rob tried to pull over, the officer said, "Keep moving." Rob told himself that this was probably a good thing. They could've made him stop at any time and they didn't. So whenever they were through checking whatever they were checking, they'd whiz by him and he'd be on his way to Lake Lanier.

"Turn here," the cop ordered.

Here was off the main street and heading east toward a school on his right. Rob slowed down.

"Keep going. We'll tell you when to stop."

Now something didn't seem right. Rob looked at the elementary school. *Probably got some rule about stopping in front of a school,* he thought.

They drove past the school and continued several blocks until they ordered him left, down a street with woods on both sides. In the distance, there appeared to be some kind of factory.

"Turn here and stop. Do not get out of the car."

Turn where? There's nowhere—a gravel road? Why not stop on the street? Rob's mind raced back to the house. What was this about? They couldn't have found out so quickly. He turned down the road, parked, and turned off the ignition. Both cops got out and approached the car on opposite sides.

The gun! I still have the frickin' gun! he remembered. Now he was nervous. He didn't have a concealed weapons permit, and they were too close now for him to take it out of his waist and put it in the console.

They went through the driver's license and registration routine.

"Did I do something wrong, officer?" Rob asked.

"Do you have a weapon in the car? Mr. Cheney."

"No."

"Where are you going?" the cop on his side asked.

"Lake Lanier. We've got a place up there."

"What about school?" asked the cop.

Rob thought he'd be a lot cooler than he was. He wondered if they could see how nervous he was. No answer to the cop's question came to his mind.

"We were notified of a missing girl. A Sharon Styles. You know her?"

Rob's face got hot. He looked straight ahead. No way was he going to look that cop in the eyes.

The other cop said, "Mind if we look in your trunk?"

That's when Rob's mind went off its axis. It tilted hard, sending his thoughts scrambling. Gravity was gone. He couldn't get his footing.

"Mr. Cheney, do you mind if we look in your trunk?" The cop did not sound like no was an acceptable answer.

Beads of sweat tickled Rob's forehead on their paths to his cheeks. He didn't hear his own answer. "No." He popped the trunk.

Rob looked in the rearview and side mirrors. The cop at the passenger window looked at Rob. The cop in the back looked at the large piece of luggage. He reached for the luggage.

"Gun!" the cop at the trunk heard his partner yell.

Boom!

He ran around to the driver's side in a crouch. He was a nervous breath away from pulling the trigger. The driver was splattered and slumped over. The other cop had his gun pointed at the driver.

"What happened?"

"He shot himself. By the time I saw he had a gun it was too late."

"He didn't kill himself for nothing." The cop hurried to the trunk and unzipped the luggage. "Ray, you're not going to believe what's in this suitcase."

Chapter 32

Detective Leonard looked the girl over. Pictures had been taken. Evidence gathered. He could take his time. She was an attractive white teen. Long blonde hair. Few marks on the face. Busted lip. Dried blood under the nose. *Clean kill,* he thought. *Strangulation. Nothing messy*. He was tired of messes. And he was *really* tired of finding the bodies of dead young women. *Retirement couldn't come soon enough.*

As far as murders went, there was nothing extraordinary about this one except for the name tag and writing on the poor girl's forehead. The killer had written *Sharon* on the girl's forehead and stuck a name tag on her chest with her name on it. *Why would he do that?* Oh, there was one other obvious thing that stuck out. Her blouse was open, but she was fully clothed. *Now why did you do that? You could kill her, but you couldn't rape her? Did you rape her and put her clothes back on? Did you try to rape her and couldn't get it up? That's why you killed her? Because you're impotent? We're going to find out you sick—"*

"Detective Leonard," said one of the officers.

He looked at her.

"We found something on his computer," she said. She looked at him with a look of surprise. "He left it up."

"A gift from a killer. Nice of him," he said.

There was no surprise that Rob had a bunch of porn on his computer. Men who killed young girls almost always had porn on their computer. It was surprising, however, that he had picture after picture of teenage girls with the same name. What was it about this name that had put a hook in his jaw? *Is that your mother's name? Your sister? Is that it? You got a crush on your sister? Elementary school teacher?*

"Who are you?" the female officer asked a man coming fast down the stairs like he had a right to be there.

Detective Leonard went to the bottom of the stairs.

"I'm her father," said Edwin.

The female officer put her hands up and pressed against Edwin's chest. It was awkward. She didn't want to do it, but he couldn't be down there.

"Officer Williams, it's okay. It's okay. Everything's been done." Detective Leonard looked at her sadly. "He's her father. He's *here*."

Her face softened.

"I'm Detective Leonard. We talked on the phone."

Edwin's eyes were red. He looked at the detective as though he were battling to make his tongue obey him.

"She's in here, Mr. Styles." The detective went into the room first.

Edwin took slow, dreadful steps to the door. Each step felt like he was crucifying himself. Crucifixion would've been easier than seeing his daughter dead. He stopped just short of where he could see Sharon.

"Mr. Styles, we can do this at the morgue. You don't have to see her like this." The detective knew he couldn't stand to see his own daughter like this.

Edwin's love pressed past his fear. His heavy leg moved forward. He entered with his eyes skidding over the floor at his feet. He stood there in a mummified state for several moments, unaware of anything but the swooshing of his life as it went down the drain.

The detective put his hand on Edwin's shoulder to steady him. "Mr. Styles?"

Promise me you'll serve God no matter what happens to me, Sharon's words resurrected and burst through the soil of his pain. His head was still bowed. *I will. I will. God, I'm not going to let this stop me from serving You.*

Edwin lifted his head and made himself look at the body. His mouth gaped open. A low, coughing sound came out.

The police looked at one another and lowered their heads.

"Ooooooooooohhhh my Gooooooooood!" Edwin wailed and fell to his knees.

*****

The cop car turned and rolled slowly toward the hollowed out shell of a long gone factory. They drove around the back and stopped near outside stairs that went up six floors. The driver got out and went to the trunk. He hoisted the heavy suitcase and put it on the ground. He looked around in every direction. The field of grass was nearly as tall as him. They could be anywhere watching. One thing was sure: someone *was* watching.

The cop put the luggage where he was told to put it, under the stairwell. He had searched Rob's pockets for a key. He left that key on top of the luggage. There was a plastic container under the stairs. He took the top off and found two envelopes inside. Ten thousand dollars each. Mr. Bogarti didn't mind this payment. The package was worth much more than twenty thousand dollars. And, besides, he knew these two. At least half of this money would be spent in one of his clubs.

The luggage was there for four hours before a car pulled up to the stairwell and a guy grabbed the bag and put it in the back of a Suburban. The Suburban drove to a covered garage and put the bag in another vehicle. That vehicle drove to one of Mr. Bogarti's unregulated business locations.

A man accompanied another who rolled the luggage down a long hall and into a small room with a bed in it. One of the men spoke into one of the holes that Rob had drilled into the luggage. "I'm going to unzip this suitcase. If your eyes aren't shut tight when I do, I'm going to slit your throat. You understand?"

There was a muffled grunt.

The man hit the bag hard with the palm of his meaty hand. "You hear me?"

"Yes," said a terrified female's voice. She tightened her eyes. When she heard the zipper, she started sucking hungrily for air.

The man opened the big bag and looked at the handcuffed girl's eyelids. Squeezed tight. "Good girl." He tied a blindfold on her and lifted her up. He tossed her on the bed.

"What's your name?" the man asked gruffly.

Her lips trembled so badly. "I...I...I...for...give you."

The man looked at the other man, smirking. "She forgives me." He reached down and grabbed a fistful of hair. He jerked her head up. "What's your name?"

Lord Jesus, give me strength. "My name is Sharon."

He pulled her hair tighter in his hand. Sharon winced. "We don't want to hear your mouth, you understand?"

"Yes."

"Sir," he said.

"Yes, sir."

The man whispered something in her ear and nibbled it.

Sharon gasped.

"But only if you're good," he laughed.

The heavy door closed hard. Sharon heard the sliding of a bolt. She lay on a mattress—a *mattress*—blindfolded, with her hands cuffed behind her. She felt more helpless now than when she was chained in Rob's basement or when she was stuffed in a suitcase. She didn't know where she was, and no one knew where she was. She already felt herself going crazy. She started quoting Scriptures.

I will never leave you nor forsake you.

Lo, I am with you always, even to the end of the age.

Behold, if you make your bed in hell, I am there.

A verse pushed itself into her mind. *The Lord prepares a table before us in the presence of our enemies.*

"Oh, God," Sharon prayed softly, "please take care of me. Don't let that man do that to me. You took care of Daniel, and he was a slave. You took care of Joseph when he was in prison. I'm in a prison, Lord. Please—" She began to cry heavily, but she dared not let that disgusting man hear her. She muffled her pain. "Please, help me to be faithful to you even now."

Terrifying moment after terrifying moment passed. Sharon remembered the other girl in Rob's basement. "I'm sorry, Lord, for only thinking of myself. Please help the other girl escape."

Sharon's body shook with terror when she heard the bolt on her door slide.

*****

Barbara didn't wait for Edwin to get to the house. She ran outside when she saw the car coming up the driveway. "Edwin," her troubled eyes said what her mouth couldn't.

His eyes met hers. He grabbed her arm and looked at her silent pleadings. "I went back. The police found a dead girl in Rob's basement. It wasn't our Sharon."

Barbara clutched her chest and began gasping for air. She burst into tears and fell into Edwin. He rested his cheek atop her head as her heaving rocked him. He held her tightly and joined her tears.

"I don't know who the poor girl is in Rob's basement," said Edwin. "They found her strapped to a chair, strangled."

Barbara sucked in a horrified breath. "Oh...oh...oh...Edwin, where's our Sharon? Where's our baby? My God, what if he's hurting her? What if he's killed her?"

Edwin pulled back. He held both of Barbara's shoulders firmly, reassuringly. "Sharon's *not* dead."

Barbara's tearful face anguished even more. Her lips trembled as she spoke. "You don't think so, Edwin?" She wanted to believe him. She *needed* to believe him.

"She's not dead." He sounded like a man with inside information.

Barbara grabbed his face. "How can you say this? Tell me. Tell me. How do you know she's not dead?"

Edwin looked at his wife's pained face and desperate eyes. In that moment, he felt the weight of being husband and father. *Protector.* He was supposed to *protect* his family. Christopher was dead. Andrew now suddenly had epilepsy. Sharon was in the hands of a killer. He had been going through his usual self-doubts and fears. And here was Barbara, the beautiful woman who had trusted him with her life, looking him in the eyes and begging him to somehow be in this moment what he had never really been in the entirety of their marriage. *She wanted him to be the leader of the family.*

Edwin rested both of his large hands on the sides of her wet face. "Sharon's not dead because God's not through with her yet. Sharon's not dead because love never fails."

Barbara shook her head, crying with a closed mouth. She wanted to believe this. Sharon was only seventeen. *How old was the girl they found dead?*

"Honey," said, Edwin, "I'm not just saying this. Somehow I know that this is going to turn out alright. Somehow God is going to get the glory from this."

Barbara didn't know why he was talking like this. It didn't sound like him. It sounded more like Sharon, or Jonathan. "Like Christopher? Like God is getting glory from our little boy dying?"

Her statement squeezed the air out of Edwin's lungs. He had to consciously make himself breathe. "I...still don't have an answer for Chris." His voice was light. "But I know Sharon is alive, and I know she's coming home."

"Do you think this monster is hurting her?"

The spontaneous surge of courage that had enabled him to reassure his wife had just as spontaneously disappeared. He *knew* in his heart that Sharon was coming home. *But in what condition?* She probably was being hurt. But he knew he couldn't say this.

"Barbara, we have to be strong. We can't focus on the cross. We have to focus on the resurrection. I'm going to pray until she comes home." Barbara was going to say something. Edwin cut her off. "Call everyone in the church. It's automated. Carmen can show you show. It's one call. Tell them what happened. And tell them I said to read *Acts 12* and to come to church tonight ready to cry out to God."

"We're just going to pray?" asked Barbara.

"You want to see your daughter alive again?"

"Of course I do."

"Then pray," he said, and walked away. "I'm going to the garage. I've gotta be right with God when I stand before the church tonight."

"To the garage? Sharon says that's how Jonathan prays."

Edwin stopped. This time the mention of Jonathan's name didn't make him angry. He looked at his wife. She needed him to be the man he was called to be. "I know." He disappeared into the garage.

*****

Krioni-na listened to this conversation with fascination and vicarious dread. So much had happened so quickly.

Prince Krioni was undermining Bashnar with some success. The witchcraft spirit had done enough with getting yoga into the church, and with manipulating Elizabeth, that the self-important Mickey Mouse Bashnar would never get the glory he so craved, even if the whole Atlanta revival went down the toilet today.

Yet, that psychopathic warrior spirit had managed to beat these Styles vermin to a pulp. He had even come close to killing them with that carjacker. The family was in shreds. Everything was in disarray. There were tears and confusion everywhere. *And now he had Sharon.*

Krioni-na was only an observer spirit. He didn't fight angels. He didn't attack people. He watched and he wrote. That was all. Like a reporter of the sons of Adam. But what he *did* didn't change what he *was*. He was one hundred percent demon, top to bottom. He hated God, and he hated what God loved.

That meant he hated the sons and daughters of Adam. And it meant despite his role as observer, he especially hated the Sharons and Jonathans of the world. For they, to put it in the simplest of words, made God happy.

It was this last musing of the observer spirit that made him question the wisdom of both the prince and the warrior. From his perspective, it appeared that despite what apparent advances they were making against the revival in general and the Styles and Banks in particular, they could all—including him—be worse off now than before the *Job Strategy* and Prince Krioni counter strategy had begun.

True, great damage had been done. A crime family was riled up. Jonathan was on the run. Elizabeth had been compromised. Andrew was sick. Sharon was locked up. Barbara was demonized. Edwin was sick.

Edwin.

The Mickey Bashnar's so-called worm.

Instead of crumbling under the weight of the onslaught, he was turning to God in prayer. And to make matters eternally worse, he was mobilizing the church to pray. Krioni-na knew what this meant.

He had had the misfortune of recording episodes like this. Episodes where saints who were supposed to fall away from God because of their trials had instead grown closer to Him than ever before. The very things that had been designed to destroy them had been used to exalt them.

One can put a thousand to flight. Two can put two thousand to flight.

A terrifying thought entered the observer's dark mind. *What if God was behind this so-called Job Strategy? What if God was using them for His own purposes? Like when Joseph was sold into slavery only to later be revealed as God's method of saving Israel from starvation. What if they were being played again? What if this was the cross and resurrection all over again?*

This would mean an unleashing of heavenly power that could sweep away some of their most cherished strongholds. *If this happens,* he shuddered at the thought, *I can find myself on the front lines, fighting angels and thorns and daggers.*

But who could he tell? The Mighty Bashnar? Prince Krioni? Which of them would admit that God was using him to strengthen the church so it could destroy greater works of darkness? He shook his head in dejection. *Why did I ever believe Lucifer's lie? How could we have ever thought we could rebel against God and win?*

*****

The first several minutes of Edwin's prayer could only be accurately described as a burst of anguish that used some words. He had never cried so desperately, even about Christopher. With Chris, he had cried about what he had lost. Even as he had cried about his son, although he didn't see it this way then, there had been an odd relief in knowing that he was crying about something that couldn't be changed. *Christopher was dead.*

But now he was crying and anguishing about what he *could* lose. What he *could* lose? Not knowing. It was hard to explain. Perhaps it couldn't be explained. But not knowing was more difficult than knowing.

Was Sharon dead? He didn't know.

Was she being hurt? He didn't know.

Would he ever see her again? He didn't know.

There was a seed of faith in his heart that whispered, *Sharon is alive.* But there was a gaping hole in his chest that exposed a half-beating heart that screamed with a bullhorn, *Sharon is dead, and you'll never see her again.*

"Please...please, don't let anything happen to Sharon. Lord, please. I love my daughter. I love her. I love her. I love her."

When the last words fell from his mouth, he fell to the floor on his knees. He raised his face with closed eyes to the ceiling. His tears weren't tears. They were unbroken lines of liquid pain that coursed down his face, gathering at the nape of his neck. But no amount of crying, no amount of wailing, no amount of yelling or demanding or pleading removed even the slightest bit of pain from his tortured mind and soul. He was being impaled. *In unrelenting, unending waves.*

Could the worse tortures of hell be any worse than what he was feeling?

"What...can...I do? Is there anything? Anything I can do to help my daughter? God," he screamed, and waited for the lump in his hurting throat to go down, "what do You want from me?"

Everything.

The thought was soft, light, almost imperceptible, except that it had just shredded him into a million raw pieces. Each piece exposed everything previously hidden by the skin of pretense, religion, and impure motives.

Everything? God wanted everything?

"Lord, I don't know what that means." Edwin searched his heart as best he could. "I went to seminary. I tried to learn about You. I've done everything I know to do. I even pray for the sick now. Lord, I even cast out demons." He shook his head back and forth. "And I hardly know what I'm doing. I'm trying, Lord."

Edwin raised up on his knees. His back erect, head lowered. He hadn't been honest. He hadn't done the best he could. He had done the best he could while living in fear. He was throwing spears at a lion from a mile away. True, he would never be eaten by the lion, but he'd also never strike the lion from such a great distance.

A movie flashed across his mind. It came and went with the speed of lightning. He was a contestant in a foot race. The setting was like the Olympics. Tens of thousands of people were in the stands. Edwin ran a full lap and was comfortably in the lead. On the second lap an old man offered him a wheelchair. Edwin jumped in the wheelchair and started turning the big wheels as fast and as hard as he could. But the harder he worked, the farther behind he got. The movie was over.

Edwin pondered the vision, if that's what it was. It had come and gone so fast that it couldn't possibly be considered a vision. *Is this what Jonathan gets?* Somehow he knew that the race was life. He thought about the first lap of the race, when he was leading. He was happy. He jumped up and down playfully as he ran.

Edwin thought more on the vision. Tears rolled down his face as the understanding became clear. This was a kid running the race of life and having fun doing it. Then an old man had given the kid a wheelchair. He had turned the child into a cripple.

Edwin immediately knew what this meant. The weight of the revelation doubled him over. He didn't cry. He moaned. Deeply. Painfully. From the depths of his soul. *The old man with the wheelchair is Uncle Ted. Lord, it's Uncle Ted. I was just a little boy...a little boy.* Edwin's deep moans and pain competed with the coherence of his thoughts. *He did this to me. He did this to me,* he screamed within. *He made me afraid to be seen. He made me a cripple.*

Get out of the wheelchair. The thought sliced through Edwin's self-pity.

Huh? Get out of the wheelchair? thought Edwin. *But I was just a little boy.*

You are no longer a little boy. The thought was a mixture of being nearly indistinguishable from the other random, competing thoughts and being so penetrating that what it lacked in volume it made up for in authority. This thought *knew* him.

"What do you want me to do, Lord?" Edwin said aloud. "How do I get out of the wheelchair?" The answer dropped into his heart before he had finished asking the last question. "Lord, no," he gasped. But again, Edwin knew before he finished his protest that he would do it. "I want a new life, Lord. And if this is what it takes to get it, I'll do it. I forgive Uncle Ted."

Edwin waited for the lifting of the weight. The spiritual release. The ripping off of the straight jacket. This didn't happen. He smelled the aroma, but he didn't taste the victory. "I forgive him, Lord. I forgive him. What more can I do?"

"But I say to you, love your enemies, bless those who curse you, do good to those who hate you, and pray for those who spitefully use you and persecute you, that you may be sons of your Father in heaven."

Edwin was stunned at the Holy Spirit's violence. God was stripping him naked of even the most sheer refuge of the flesh and slamming him onto the cross of crucifixion.

Love Uncle Ted?

Bless Uncle Ted?

Do good to Uncle Ted?

Pray for Uncle Ted?

Edwin thought bitterly about a part of this Scripture. *Pray for those who spitefully use you...* Uncle Ted had spitefully used him. Repeatedly. His assault on him had released a barrage of homosexual spirits against him. He had never given in to the vile thoughts that had intermittently come upon him like sudden, violent storms. But it wasn't right that he should've had to fight for something that was his by birthright. His sexual identity.

And now he not only had to forgive this man, God was apparently requiring him to take his forgiveness to an impossible level. He was telling him to act out his forgiveness with works. *Oh, God, why not just tell me to jump in front of a moving train?*

I AM, God answered.

*****

The demons who watched Edwin were well beyond stunned. For this condition could be experienced one moment and recovered from the next. No, what the demons felt was more existential. That is, forgiveness, or more accurately, the kind of forgiveness God was leading Edwin into, was the type that not only destroyed strongholds. It was the heavenly quality that destroyed the ground upon which strongholds stood.

This kind of forgiveness threatened the very existence of the dark kingdom. It was the kind that caused Jesus to give Himself as the sacrifice for the sins of the world.

Once this horrifying news was relayed to Prince Krioni, he put the entire Georgia region on the highest state of alert and wasted no time in mobilizing a formidable army to prevent Edwin from entering this level of forgiveness.

Sirens blared throughout the region.

*****

The Mighty Bashnar knew time was running out. He had to move with even greater speed and devastation.

Chapter 33

Sharon jumped up from the bed when she heard the bolt slide back. On the bed was the *last* place she wanted to be if this was that disgusting man. Her hands were still cuffed behind her and she was still blindfolded. She took several awkward steps backwards until her back met the wall.

The door opened and closed.

Sharon's back pressed hard against the wall. Rapid breaths escaped her open mouth as her chest bounced noticeably up and down.

Noticeably.

Whoever entered the room said nothing. Sharon tried without success to slow down her heavy breathing. She waited with trepidation to feel the man's hands. He had told her what he would do to her when he returned.

She cried out desperately for help under her breath. *"Oh God. Oh God. Oh God. Oh God."* Sharon tried. Oh, how she tried to make herself stop crying, but her eyes wouldn't obey. She listened for the man. She heard nothing but her own heavy breathing. She thought she heard something and jumped.

She wanted to say something, but should she? Maybe if she said nothing, he'd leave. She waited in silence, afraid to do anything that would make him touch her. But, finally, the silence became unbearable. She didn't know what this man was doing or where he was. Was he still near the door? Was he a couple of feet from her?

She was wearing a skirt, and Rob had not allowed her to button her blouse before stuffing her in the suitcase. Her open blouse. Was this man looking at her lustfully? *Thank You, Lord, for not letting Rob take my bra.* She tried to stop the nervous breaths, to stop making her chest bounce. *Please, Jesus, don't let him. Don't let him. Don't let him.*

Her attention snapped to her legs. She had considered more than once to throw this skirt away because of its length. *Oh, God, I'm so sorry for not listening to Your precious Holy Spirit. I represent You. I should not be dressing like this. I don't want to be a stumbling block.* These thoughts bubbled up from her heart without effort.

Sharon jumped.

Someone was there. She heard something. Then she heard someone let out a short blowing sound. *Oh, God,* Sharon moaned in her heart. An involuntary moan slid between her lips.

The man exhaled cigarette smoke and smiled. "Do—"

Sharon gasped at his voice. It was that same man.

"You're afraid. You don't have to be afraid of me—if you're obedient. Some of our girls must be taught obedience. Are you an obedient girl, Sharon? Or will we have to teach you to obey? We give all of our girls a choice, you know?"

Sharon's breaths were faster and harder. She hated herself for it.

Gasp. The man was standing only inches from her.

"You are going to show me before I leave your home—"

Home? thought Sharon fearfully.

"—whether or not we have to put you in obedience school."

Sharon knew she shouldn't ask, but she had to. She had to know what kind of place she was in. Her voice tremored as she asked, "Sir?"

The man smiled at the beautiful young girl in the short skirt and open blouse. "Yeah."

"What's obedience school?"

"You don't want to know, Sharon." The man didn't like Sharon's hair hanging over her chest. He swept her hair behind her.

His slight touch sent waves of helplessness and fear through her.

"But you will know if you don't pass the test."

"What test?"

"Open your mouth."

Sharon's lips trembled vigorously. She opened her mouth.

"Wider."

She did.

He took a long drag off his cigarette and blew the smoke into her mouth. Sharon gagged badly. She coughed forward. Her forehead went into the man's chest. "You touched me, Sharon."

She raised her head. "I'm sorry."

"You don't have to be sorry, Sharon. Friends should be able to touch one another."

His words froze her.

"You just passed the first test, Sharon."

She was still frozen.

"Ready for another test?" he asked.

God... "Yes, sir," she answered weakly.

"Good. You moaned earlier."

"I did?" asked Sharon.

The man smiled. "Oh, yes. You did. You most *cer-tain-ly* did."

Sharon waited.

"Do it again," he ordered.

"Moan?" she asked, almost crying. Her mouth opened and closed a couple of times, nervously licking her lips each time. She knew she could get in trouble for crying, but she let herself cry. She pushed the tears from her eyes.

"I'll tell you the one thing about obedience school that you need to know, Sharon. It can be extremely painful. Pass my tests and you don't have to go to obedience school. Understand?"

"Yes, sir."

"Good. For some reason, I like you. That's why I'm giving you a second chance."

"It's God's favor."

"What did you say?" the man asked.

"I'm sorry. Umm...I didn't—I wasn't trying to—"

"Did you say God's favor?"

"Yes," Sharon whispered, but not because she tried to whisper. She whispered because she was confused and afraid and shocked, and because she didn't know if she was about to be raped, and because she was broken. Her voice couldn't carry the weight. "God loves me."

The man didn't hear her. He moved his ear closer to the young girl's full, trembling lips, until he could almost feel the moisture of her breath. "What did you say?"

"God loves me," came the whisper.

The man smiled. "Really? He has a funny way of showing it. I love you, too. Now moan."

*****

Sharon hadn't stopped crying and praying and searching her heart since the man had left her room. She knew no one deserved to be in a place like this, but she couldn't help asking God what she had done to deserve this. *I love you, Lord. You know I do. If I have sinned against You, I'm sorry. If I've sinned against anyone, I'm sorry. Please don't hold my sins against me.*

Sharon jumped off the edge of the bed. She thought she heard something. She waited until she was sure no one was opening the door. She sat on the edge of the bed. "No, Lord, I want to kneel before You." When her knees touched the concrete floor, a thought came to her mind. *But this happened that the word might be fulfilled which is written in their law, They hated Me without a cause.*

Sharon gasped. This time for joy. Then she cried. "Lord, I thought I had failed You. I thought I had sinned against You."

"Why else would you be here, Sharon?" The Mighty Bashnar's voice came out of nowhere, pushing aside her peace. "You have failed him. You are being punished for your sins."

Sharon's head went to the left, then the right, as she weighed both thoughts. "No. No. That's not true. I know that's you, Satan." She reached into her heart to find a Scripture to refute this thought. A passage came to mind that she had memorized shortly after becoming a Christian.

> *He has not dealt with us according to our sins, nor punished us according to our iniquities. For as the heavens are high above the earth, so great is His mercy toward those who fear Him. As far as the east is from the west, so far has He removed our transgressions from us. As a father pities his children, so the Lord pities those who fear Him. For He knows our frame; He remembers that we are dust.*

The thorn's eyes were blindfolded, but the great warrior spirit saw the fire in them.

"Get out of here, Satan, in the name of Jesus," she ordered.

The Mighty Bashnar instinctively pulled out his sword and dagger and spun in a circle. He remembered the agreement and smiled under his ugly face. He looked derisively at the thorn. He remembered Samson. How the playboy prophet had faced him that eventful day thinking He still had the power of the Holy Spirit to help him. It had been a pleasure putting out his eyes. Now he would get even greater pleasure ripping this girl's faith from her wretched heart.

The demon put his weapons away.

It happened too fast to know what had happened until after it happened.

One sword. Two blue flashes. Across the Mighty Bashnar's wide chest. He snatched his weapons and roared at the invisible attacker. "Show yourself, angel," he roared.

He did. Suddenly. In a flame of fire. He was the fire.

The Mighty Bashnar was too proud to regret his words. But he was too much of a warrior to not be awed by what was facing him. *What kind of a beast are you?* he thought. He had never seen such an angel. *Is God still creating angels?*

The fire angel walked toward him.

The Mighty Bashnar stood his ground as long as his pride and tolerance level for heat allowed. This was only a couple of moments. He backed up only as much as he had to. If at any moment the fire lessened, he would pounce on this angel who had dared to cut him. But the fire didn't lessen.

"Sharon is My choice servant. She belongs to Me."

The warrior spirit gazed into the mouth of the mysterious angel. Were there swords coming out of this angel's mouth? "I have an agreement." (Those were swords!)

"Leave My servant," said the fire angel.

The warrior spirit stiffened in defiance. There was a reason he was called the *Mighty* Bashnar. He didn't run from—

The Mighty Bashnar knew it happened because he felt the slices all over his body. But he hadn't seen a beginning or ending of the attack. The fire angel was motionless before him. Except for the sword in his mouth. *But the sword hadn't moved,* thought the warrior spirit as he backed away. He told himself he wasn't running. He was reassessing the situation. And he couldn't do that if he were in a hundred pieces.

*****

The man walked softly to Sharon's door and looked inside. She was on her knees with her face toward the ceiling. She looked to be praying. He watched her for a few minutes. This girl was a strange one. He jerked hard on the bolt. He saw her jump to her feet and back against the wall.

Sharon had no reason to be any less afraid than the first time the door opened. She heard the door close. She couldn't tell whether anyone had entered. If someone was there, was it the same man who was there earlier? Was it someone else?

She found herself hoping it was the first guy, then wondering why she would want that awful man to come back. He had made her moan for what seemed like forever, but at least he didn't touch her. "Who's there?"

Something struck her hard on the side of her face. She spun and fell on her side on the concrete floor. Strong hands grabbed her around the front and back of her throat. They lifted her off the floor and hung her up in the air. Sharon felt like her neck would crush under the pressure. Her legs dangled in a panic.

The person slammed her face-down onto the bed. He buried her face into the mattress. Sharon struggled for air, but her nose and mouth were pressed so deeply into the mattress that breathing was impossible. She knew was going to die. But just before she passed out, the man stopped. Sharon turned her face to the side and sucked air into her deprived lungs.

"Why are you doing this?" she gasped.

Someone pushed her shoulders down, while another sat on her legs.

There were two people in the room!

Sharon could've died from fright. Someone raised her skirt above her hips. Something smacked hard against her bare butt. Again and again and again. She screamed as loud as she could. This went on forever.

The people stopped beating her. She heard them walk toward the door.

"I forgive you," she cried.

Two people walked out the door. The one with the thick paddle went back.

Sharon let out a deathly cry when the wood struck her butt again.

The door closed.

She heard the bolt slide shut, but this didn't mean they had all left. She lay on the bed too terrified to move. Under her breath, she said, "I forgive you."

*****

Ten minutes after Sharon was beaten and the men had left her room. Someone coughed.

Sharon's eyes bulged under the blindfold. She had thought someone stayed behind. "Please don't beat me any more," Sharon begged.

The door opened and shut.

A couple of minutes later she heard the outside bolt slide hard against the metal. She hated and feared this sound. Sharon lay the side of her face on the mattress. She was trying to hold on to her faith, but she was so afraid she couldn't think straight. She braced herself for more beatings. Or worse. And there was now no doubt. *Worse* was coming.

The man looked at the handcuffed girl lying on her belly on the bed. Even with her blindfold, he could see her hopelessness. This was good. Hopelessness equaled brokenness. Broken girls were obedient girls. Every one of their girls had this look. "Sharon, what happened?"

"They beat me." Defeat was in her voice.

He looked at her. "You're a mess. Here, let me pull up your panties." He did. "There must've been a mistake. There's another girl going through obedience school. The guys went to the wrong room. I'll tell them they need to be more careful. And I'll talk to the others to make sure there are no more mistakes. Okay?"

"Okay," she answered with hopeless resignation.

"It gets a lot worse than spanking, Sharon." He rubbed Sharon's head and wiped tears from her face. "Only disobedient girls need to go to obedience school. You keep walking the straight and narrow and no one will bother you. That's in the Bible, isn't it? The straight and narrow path and the broad path?"

"Yes sir."

"I'm going to go now."

"I forgive you," said Sharon.

"Now why do you feel I need forgiveness, Sharon?" He said this rubbing her head.

"It was you."

"What was me, Sharon?"

"You're one of the people who beat me." Sharon sounded like she was in a trance.

The man smiled. He bent down and kissed the side of Sharon's head. "I'll be back in a little while to take you on a tour." He stood up and headed for the door.

"Sir?"

"Yes, Sharon?"

"I'm praying for you."

The man looked at her. He had been wrong. She wasn't broken. This wasn't shocking. Some girls broke almost immediately. Others took a little time. But they *all* broke. She wasn't broken because she still had hope. And she still had hope because of her faith in God.

Once they took her faith, she'd fall into line like the others.

*****

Sharon didn't know how she knew. She just did. She raised up and sat on the edge of the bed. *Someone was coming.*

The man looked in Sharon's room. She was sitting on the bed. He slammed the bolt open. She didn't move. She didn't even look toward the door. That was a good sign. She was accepting her predicament. *Good girl.*

The door opened. "Sharon, you don't have to be afraid. It's me," said the only voice she knew. "How's your bottom?"

She hesitated. She didn't want to talk to him about her butt. "Sore."

"Stand up."

She did.

"Turn around."

She did.

"That's good, Sharon. You didn't hesitate. That's a sign of obedience." He looked at her butt as though he were her doctor. She was almost all blue. "I'm not going to lie," he said, touching the parts that looked the worst. "That's pretty bad. But it can get a lot worse, Sharon. You understand? A lot of girls are beaten much worse than that. Some are beaten every day. Or every few hours. It depends on how quickly they learn to obey. You just have to do what you're told."

She heard everything he said, but his words were passing through a filter of shock. Her mind tried to shut down to the reality of what had happened and what was happening. *This was not happening to her.* But when the man pulled up her skirt and examined her like she was his property, reality slapped her out of her self-induced stupor. *Something died inside of her.*

"Sharon, I think we're going to get along fine. I think you're going make a lot of men happy."

Sharon fought to not pass out when she heard his words.

"You're going to make us a lot of money. If you stay with us."

Sharon widened her eyes under the blindfold. *If I stay?* She wanted to scream, *What do you mean, if I stay with you?* But she was afraid to ask.

"It's all up to your father, Sharon."

She didn't say anything.

"Go on. You can ask me," the voice coached.

"What do you want from my father?"

"Something you Christians preach about. Repentance. He has to change his ways."

Sharon tried unsuccessfully to make sense of this.

"It'll all come together soon enough, Sharon," he said. "I told you I was taking you on a tour."

Sharon's trembling returned. She didn't know what this *tour* was, but she knew it was evil. She felt him putting something over her head and around her neck.

"This is a leash, Sharon. You'll wear it whenever you come out of this room. Whoever your master is will lead you wherever you're supposed to be. You'll only take it off when you're working, unless your work requires you to keep it on. Remember I told you that I like you?"

Sharon willed herself to answer quickly. "Yes sir."

"Girls don't walk anywhere. You crawl on your hands and knees until you earn the right to walk. I brought some knee pads and mittens for you. It'll protect your knees and hands." He put them in her hands. "Do you want to walk on this tour or crawl?"

"May I walk?" she asked.

"That's not how it's done around here, Sharon. If you want anything of your master, you have to kneel first."

"You want me to get on my knees?"

"That's the only way to kneel, Sharon. From your knees."

Sharon dropped her head.

"And Sharon?"

"Yes sir," she answered, with her head still bowed.

"There's another rule."

"What?"

"If you crawl, you'll have to do it without your clothes." She couldn't see his smile.

"I have to take off my clothes?" Each word came out like they were teeth being pulled without anything to deaden the pain.

"Your choice, Jesus girl."

Sharon kneeled. "Sir, may I please walk?" The tears had returned.

He lifted her up. "Of course, you can. I told you I like you, right?"

The terror had returned to Sharon's bones in all its dread. "Yes...yes, sir."

The man looked at Sharon. "You're a Christian."

Sharon didn't say anything. She didn't know whether he was making a statement or asking a question.

"Doesn't the Bible say something about kneeling to other gods? Isn't it a sin? Idolatry or something?"

Myla and Adaam-Mir placed their hands on her shoulders.

"Yes. The Lord Jesus is God, and besides Him there is no other," she answered.

"Why'd you kneel to me?"

"I didn't kneel in worship to you, sir. I kneeled because I didn't want you to make me take off my clothes."

The man smiled. "What if I told you to kneel to me in prayer if you want to walk out of this room with your clothes on?"

Sharon followed his voice and got on her knees at his feet. "Sir, I don't know who you are, but God does. One day soon you're going to stand before Him to be judged of your sins. You'll answer for beating your wife and neglecting your two sons. You'll answer for stealing money from your sick grandmother. That was wrong. She trusted you, and you stole everything. God will require payment for every sin. Repent. Turn from your sins. I forgive you for what you've done to me. God will forgive you, too, if you only repent and live for Him."

The man had tried to move away from Sharon the moment she had mentioned him beating his wife and neglecting his two sons. *How'd she know that?* But he couldn't move his feet. They felt like they weighed five hundred pounds each. Same thing with his arms.

Sharon didn't know the man couldn't move. She looked up toward him with her blindfold. "Sir, I had no idea places like this really existed. I thought they were only on television. I'm so sorry that you have given yourself to evil. Think of how many lives you've destroyed. God will not let you get away with this forever."

Alex.

Sharon's bowed. Her head touched one of the man's lower legs. "Alex, God knows everything about you. And no matter what you do to me, you can't run from Him. Please give your life to Jesus," she pleaded.

Alex looked down at her with wide eyes. "Who are you? Who do you work for?"

Sharon shook her head. "What do you mean?"

"How do you know my name? How do you know those things about me?" Alex thought about this. Even if she was working for someone, she wouldn't know this stuff.

"God must've told me. I didn't even realize what I was praying until I was through."

"God?"

"Yes, I'm a prophetess?"

"A what? A prophetess?" He tried to move. He still couldn't. *What's going on?*

"A prophetess speaks for God."

He tried several times to move. He could move his head, but nothing else.

Sharon waited in silence for him to say something. He didn't. "Alex, I've never been so scared in all my life. I can't stop you from beating me or raping me or whatever evil thing you decide to do. But I want you and Satan to know that I will never pray to you or anyone other than Jesus Christ. Now if you insist that I have to pray to you to keep my clothes—" She closed her eyes under the blindfold. *God, help me.* "Take them. But God won't let you get away with this."

"You don't have to do that, Sharon."

"I don't?" she asked, hoping that he wasn't playing cruel games with her.

He shook himself. He was still stuck. "No. I changed my mind."

She didn't want to so easily let herself be manipulated, but she burst into tears at the faint hope that God's grace had reached into this dark place to protect her.

Alex looked down at the crying girl. He had two huge problems on his hands. One, he couldn't move. Two, one of their girls knew his identity. He had an answer for what to do about the girl. But why couldn't he move? How did he fix that? *Am I sick?*

He watched this Jesus girl bawl at his feet forever. This was no problem. The place was full of crying girls. Some girls, that's all they did was cry. Before, during, and after they worked. No matter what you did to them, they cried. Nobody was going to think anything by hearing the Jesus girl cry. But what would happen if someone came in and found him standing there paralyzed and this girl calling him by name?

He looked down at Sharon. *This girl is going to pray forever. Oh what the— "*Hey, Jesus girl. Sharon."

She continued to lean her head against his leg without looking up. "I don't mind if you call me Jesus girl. I would rather be called Jesus girl than Sharon."

"Uhh, Je—Shar—Jesus girl," he said.

"Yes, Alex," she said, looking up.

The man's body was stuck, but his memory worked fine. He whispered, "Sharon, do me a favor, okay?"

"Okay, Alex."

"Another chill shot up and down his body. "Don't call me Alex. If anyone heard you call me that, one of us would be killed."

Now Sharon froze. "Oh."

"Or best case scenario, you'd be shipped someplace overseas where they love pretty white girls. You understand."

"I understand."

Alex was totally embarrassed, but what alternative did he have. He couldn't stand there forever. "I need to ask you another favor."

Sharon looked up, grimacing from the effects of the beating. "What do you want?"

Alex hesitated. He shook his head in disbelief at his situation. "I can't move."

Sharon stood up. "What do you mean?"

Alex shook his humiliated head again from side to side. "I mean I literally can't move my hands or feet." He exhaled heavily. Sharon smelled the tobacco on his breath. "I must've had a stroke."

"You mean you *really* can't move?"

"I *really* can't move."

Sharon dropped her head and turned and found the bed. She lay down on her side and began to cry. Her crying grew stronger.

"Hey," said frozen Alex, "what's wrong?"

Sharon found a place between crying breaths. "You're—you're—you're still the same person."

Alex grimaced. "What? What are you talking about—I'm still the same person?"

"Oh, God, I thought he had changed," cried Sharon. "I thought You had touched his heart."

"Hey," said Alex with a raised voice, "evidently He touched more than my heart. Look, as soon as you started that stuff about Barbara and the kids—"

"Who's Barbara?" Sharon asked, still crying. "She's your wife?"

"Yeah," he blew out a *stupid* breath, "I don't believe this. I told you my wife's name."

"My mom's name is Barbara," said Sharon. "It's okay. God knows everything about you anyway."

"Yeah, but *you're* not supposed to know anything about me."

Sharon stopped crying. "I thought you had changed. I thought you had changed your mind about making me take off my clothes because you knew it was wrong. You didn't change your mind. God froze you."

"You're wrong, Sharon."

"Right," she said. "And soon as you're no longer stuck, you're going to beat me again and make me walk around naked with a leash around my neck like I'm a dog. I hope God never unfreezes you. You're evil!"

Alex rolled his eyes. "I'm serious. I changed my mind right before I got stuck."

"Just because I'm your prisoner doesn't mean I'm stupid." She whispered, "*Alex*."

"Listen, I don't know what to say, alright? I'm evil, okay? I admit it. All I'm asking you is to do something about this."

"Then what?" she asked.

"Then what *what*?" he said.

"You know what. This is wrong, Alex. Are you going to let me go?"

"Sharon, I...."

Sharon heard it. She shook her head and let out despondent breaths. "You would if you could, but you just work here. Right, Alex?"

His voice was low. "Right, Sharon."

Sharon screamed and screamed and screamed again. It wasn't right. Why should she have to pray for him? Why should she have to do good to evil people like this? If God had mercy on this man, he was just going to hurt her again. *Why, why, why do the righteous have to suffer like this? When will You judge the wicked, O Lord? When will you stop them?*

Alex looked and listened. They had never had one like this before. He looked at the door. He thought he heard someone. "Sharon," he whispered, "will you help me? Will you ask God to let me go?"

Sharon's chest heaved up and down from her crying. "Ask Him yourself." She went back to crying.

Alex let out a nervous breath. "God, will you please let me go."

Immediately he was released.

Alex left the room as though it were on fire. He slammed the bolt shut and roughly wiped his face.

*****

One hour after Alex left Sharon's room, he returned and told her she may not see him again. He didn't know why he told her this.

A little while after Alex left Sharon this second time, the bolt on her door slid back. The door opened. She didn't move from where she was lying. Someone roughly put her on her belly and pushed the back of her shoulders into the mattress until she felt like her bones would break. Someone sat on her legs. Up went the skirt. Down went the paddle.

Chapter 34

Elizabeth was not going back to that house alone. She had had enough of being manhandled by demons. She called Barbara and was devastated to hear that Sharon was missing. Elizabeth didn't tell Barbara why, but she asked whether she could stay with them until Jonathan returned. Barbara enthusiastically agreed. "Will you pray for us when you come?" Barbara begged.

Elizabeth readily agreed. Yet as soon as she had ended the call, she wondered how she'd be able to pray for anyone. She needed someone to pray for her. Once Elizabeth arrived, she entered a house that was filled with as much darkness and heaviness as was in her own soul.

Barbara closed the door and nearly collapsed into her arms. "She's gone, Elizabeth. Our Sharon is gone. We don't know where she is."

Elizabeth hugged her tightly. Barbara's wails were heartbreaking. It was almost enough to make Elizabeth forget about her own problems—almost. "They're going to find her. Sharon's going to be okay. God will take care of her." Elizabeth rocked Barbara. Her eyes were hollow as she stared without focus over Barbara's shoulder. *Is God taking care of Mom?* Elizabeth resented the unwelcome thought, but she couldn't deny it an audience.

Andrew walked solemnly into the foyer. His energy gone. His face sad. "Hi, Elizabeth. You came to pray with us?"

"Yes."

"Dad and Mom's got everyone praying for Sharon." His tone didn't reveal faith or unbelief. He had just stated a fact.

"That's the best thing we can do right now, Andrew, is to pray. We can change this situation. We just have to..." she stopped her voice from breaking, "ahum, we just have to believe God and pray."

"Do you think God will help my sister?" Andrew asked Elizabeth, his eyes looking deep into her soul.

Elizabeth opened her mouth. She hesitated. She couldn't say, *I don't know. I hope so.* "Yes," she answered. She wasn't consciously lying. She was merely a drowning woman reaching for a twig in the hopes that whatever saving quality that couldn't possibly be found in the twig could miraculously be found in the desperate act of reaching for it.

Andrew hugged Elizabeth. "Thank you, Elizabeth. Dad says Sharon is coming home, too. I'll go get him." He was only a few steps away when he fell to the floor and started violently thrashing and contorting.

"Edwin!" Barbara screamed frantically. "It's Andrew again."

Andrew was on his back. His legs kicked like angry pistons. His hands were clutched rigid, smashing against the hardwood floor. Barbara got on her knees and thrust her hands under his head. She still couldn't keep his head from banging hard against the hardwood. She grimaced as his head and her small, delicate hands crashed against the floor.

"Edwin!" she screamed again.

Elizabeth got on her knees on the other side of him. She put her hand on his chest. "Let him go in Jesus's name," she ordered.

Immediately Andrew stopped thrashing. His face turned toward Elizabeth. Only the whites of his eyes could be seen. He looked at her as though he were studying her. "Darkness. I see darkness. Only light can overcome darkness. You have no authority over me."

Before either of the women saw it coming, he snatched Elizabeth's neck with both hands and shook her as though she were made of straw. She and Barbara tried desperately to pry his hands loose. He was like a pit bull.

"Andrew, let go. Let go." Barbara tried with all her might to pull his hands from around Elizabeth's neck.

Elizabeth's hands dropped limp as Andrew jerked and snatched her up and down and from side to side.

"Andrew, you're killing her. Stop it!" screamed Barbara.

He didn't.

Edwin came around the corner. "In Jesus name, Satan, stop!"

Andrew's hands fell to the floor, and Elizabeth rolled over on her side. He lay motionless. His eyes rolled back.

Barbara looked at him. She looked at Elizabeth. She looked at Edwin. He kneeled down and placed two fingers on her neck.

"She's alive," he said.

Barbara's mouth was as wide as it could open. "You told *Satan* to stop."

Edwin didn't say anything.

"Andrew has a *demon*? The shaking is a demon?"

"Apparently so," Edwin answered, examining them both.

"A *demon?*" Barbara said incredulously. "Then why couldn't Elizabeth cast it out?"

"I don't know."

"He almost killed her," she said. "I don't understand. He said, 'I see darkness. Only light can overcome darkness. You have no authority over me.' Why would the devil say something like that to Elizabeth? Doesn't she have authority over demons? Why didn't he listen to her?"

Edwin looked at the unconscious Elizabeth. That was a good question.

*****

The men sitting in the car could hardly believe their eyes. It was him. The black preacher. Just walking down the street like he owned the city. He turned and looked at them before he went up the other preacher's stairs. He waved at them.

"There he is," said one.

"Did he just wave at us?"

"No wonder the boss wants to smoke him." The man started to open the door.

"No. No. No," said the other man. He looked at the postal worker and the FedEx truck. "He ain't going nowhere. Let's wait until it gets dark."

*****

The doorbell rang.

Edwin opened it.

"Edwin, it's customary to smile when a friend who has been beaten and kidnapped and freed by an angel comes by to see you."

Edwin didn't smile. "A lot's going on, Jonathan. Come in."

Jonathan stepped in and saw Andrew and Elizabeth lying on the floor. "What—?" He rushed to his knees beside them. "What happened?"

"Andrew almost strangled Elizabeth to death," said Barbara. She was totally flustered.

Edwin wished she hadn't put it in those words.

Jonathan looked at Edwin. "Edwin?" He turned back to his wife.

"It's—I—let's get them to the family room. We can talk there," said Edwin.

Edwin carried Andrew. Jonathan carried Elizabeth. Edwin sat Andrew in a chair. Jonathan put Elizabeth on her back on one of the sofas.

"What's going on?" asked Jonathan.

"Everything, Jonathan," said Barbara.

Jonathan saw that Barbara was barely with them. "Calm down, Barbara. Take a deep breath." She did. "Take another one." She did. "Now just start at the beginning."

"Sharon's been kidnapped," she rushed.

Edwin squeezed Barbara's shoulder. "She's been missing since last night. We haven't heard anything. The police found our car, but that's all. No sign of Sharon."

Jonathan felt his insides drop. He slowly sat in a chair and looked straight ahead at the wall. He didn't say anything.

His silence unnerved Barbara more than she had been. She looked at Edwin.

Edwin looked at Jonathan's face. It suddenly looked dried out, like every ounce of water had been sucked from it. "I went to her boyfriend's house—"

Jonathan snapped out of his trance. "Rob."

"Yeah. I went to his house. He said he didn't know where she was. I was searching his house when Barbara called and said they had found the car. I left. But I went back to his house. The cops were there. They had found a dead girl in his basement."

"Oh, God," said Jonathan. "And Sharon?"

"No sign of her. Nothing. But Rob had written Sharon's name on the dead girl's forehead. And he put a name tag on her with Sharon's name on it. They said he had some kind of obsession with Sharon, or Sharons, anybody named Sharon—if they looked like her."

Jonathan tried to recall if he had overlooked anything about this guy.

"What?" said Edwin.

"I had a word for him when I met him. I told him something about watching out at—no, no. I told him to be strong in the late hours. I told him that he could move any mountain that he didn't enjoy. I had kind of gotten a picture of him struggling with pornography."

"Did you tell Sharon?" Barbara felt this was something he should have told her.

"No, Barbara. I'm sorry. It wasn't as clear then as it is now."

Barbara blew out a hard breath and left the room. "She would never go out with someone who watches pornography," she said on her way out.

"I would've said something had I known, Edwin."

"I know," said Edwin.

Elizabeth started coming to.

Jonathan stroked her cheek until her eyes opened.

"Jonathan," she said excitedly.

"I'm here, Liz."

She raised up. They hugged.

Barbara returned. "I'm sorry, Jonathan. I know you love Sharon."

"Like she's my own."

Edwin heard this. Instead of being jealous, he was grateful. "We all love her, and we're going to get her back."

Jonathan heard the faith in Edwin's voice. It removed some of the shock and despair he felt. "That's right. We're going to get our Sharon back." He felt awkward bringing up something other than the crisis of Sharon being missing. But there was still the issue of finding his wife laid out on the floor and being told that his friend's fourteen-year-old son had strangled her until she passed out. "What happened, Liz?"

Elizabeth rubbed her neck. She didn't seem to know where to start.

"Andrew has been having epileptic fits," Barbara began.

"Andrew? Epilepsy? I didn't know he had epilepsy," said Jonathan.

"He didn't until last night," said Barbara.

"It started Sunday," said Edwin to Jonathan.

"The epilepsy started last night, Edwin," said Barbara.

"The attack on *us* started Sunday," said Edwin. "Jonathan, more bad things have happened to us since Sunday than have happened since we've been married. Someone broke in and vandalized our home. Tore up everything. Andrew fell down the stairs and knocked himself out. Sharon went to help him and fell down and knocked herself out."

"Wait a minute. At the same time?" asked Jonathan.

"Maybe a minute apart," said Edwin. "We went to the hospital and almost had two wrecks on the way back. I drove through two red lights."

Jonathan had a thoughtful look.

"Jonathan," Edwin looked at him intently, "the lights were green."

"They were red, Edwin. I saw them both times," said Barbara.

"I saw green, Barbara." He turned back to Jonathan. "On the way home we stopped at Kroger's. We got carjacked." He put up his hand. "Wait a minute. There's more." He looked at Barbara with an embarrassed expression. "I'm suddenly incontinent. I can't control my bowels or my bladder."

"He made an awful mess, Jonathan." Barbara frowned her face. "Just awful. Twice."

"And...then..." he rolled up his sleeve, "this thing started yesterday. It was a little rash and now...."

"Edwin," Barbara gasped. His arm was red and scaly from the wrist to the elbow. "We have to get you to the doctor."

"Doctors can't help what's happening to us."

"You can't just let that thing spread."

"I'm not going to let it spread—none of this. I'm going to stop it." Edwin's eyes were determined. "I'm going to stop it all, Barbara."

"How?" she asked.

"I'm going to attack. We all are."

Barbara furrowed her eyebrows in thought. "*Attack*? What are you talking about, Edwin? Attack what?"

"We're going to attack what's attacking us. Satan. We're going to attack Satan."

"Edwin!" Barbara screamed, "our little girl is out there somewhere. Our family is in shambles, and you're talking about attacking Satan?" Barbara emphasized each word with her hands. "*What...is...wrong...with you*?"

Edwin's eyes flashed. He raised a balled fist. "That is *exactly* why we're going to attack. Sharon is out there somewhere—only God knows what's happening to her." The dread of his daughter's circumstance extinguished his fire. He dropped his fist. His head followed. He glazed at the floor. *My daughter needs me.* He raised his head and looked intently at Barbara. "We're being attacked by Satan."

His voice was low and even. "He's trying to overwhelm us the way he overwhelmed Job."

Barbara knew her husband meant well, but she was way beyond frustrated. This was the wrong time to go off fighting demons or to expect God to do what they should be doing. Shouting into the air wasn't going to tack one poster to a telephone pole. And they couldn't expect God to do a press release for their daughter. She looked at Jonathan with the faint hope that he'd say something practical.

He did.

"Barbara, we need to do everything we can to get Sharon back. I'll call Daphne Krugle at the television station. You remember her. She'll be glad to help us. Let's get a good picture of Sharon and get it circulated. Let's get everyone at the church to use their social media to spread the word. Twitter. Facebook. Whatever. You never know who knows what."

Edwin looked at Jonathan. *Thank you,* he thought.

"But Barbara," said Jonathan, "Edwin's right. This isn't a coincidence. Too much has happened in too short a period for it to be a coincidence. We're going to do everything we can." He looked at her reassuringly. "*Everything* we can in the natural to get Sharon back. But we have to go to God as never before. We have to do as Edwin says. We have to fight."

Barbara covered her face with her hands and tried to rub the stress away.

Edwin hugged her closely to his body. "It's going to be okay. We have to trust God." He pulled back and cupped her head in his hands. "Trusting God doesn't mean being passive. Job came out of his trial by fire because he trusted God even when it didn't make sense. He praised and worshipped when it didn't make sense. He maintained his integrity when it didn't make sense. We're going to do all of this. And we're going to use the other weapons of our warfare."

"What other weapons, Edwin?" asked Barbara.

"Aggressive, persistent prayer. The name of Jesus. Our authority in Christ. Anything and everything until we get our baby back."

Barbara didn't disbelieve the miraculous. How could she? She had seen it continually for the past year. It was just that she saw it as some kind of mystical lottery. Sure, people did win it. Lots of them. Their church was filled with people whom she knew for a fact had won it. But you couldn't build your life on the fanciful hope that you may win the lottery. "Okay," she answered, hoping faintly that her precious daughter would win God's lottery.

Jonathan was stunned speechless. What had happened to Edwin?

Edwin saw the question in his eyes. "Barbara, I'm going to take Jonathan to my office. I need to talk to him alone. You and Elizabeth can watch Andrew?"

Neither Barbara nor Elizabeth, especially Elizabeth, looked eager.

"He may be out for a while. We'll be right down the hall if you need us."

"Okay," said Barbara.

The men went to Edwin's study. They sat.

"You're wondering what happened to me. Fire has a way of making people jump out the windows of tall buildings," said Edwin.

"You've jumped?"

"Well, more like I was pushed. I can't stand by and let Satan take my family." There was a moment of reflective silence. "Look, Jonathan, I need to ask your forgiveness."

"For what?"

"I've been jealous of you. My family is in love with you. At first I didn't mind. It was cute. But the more they gushed on you, the more I resented it. I resented it because you are what I want to be. Every time they made a big deal over you, it reminded me of my own deficiencies."

"Edwin—"

"Hear me out, Jonathan. My family loves you primarily because you believe whatever God says, and you're not afraid to risk it all. You don't care what people think. And I think this is why God does so much for you. Sharon is like that, too. She's like in another world. *I want that, too.* I'm tired of being on the outside of what God is doing.

I'm tired of being afraid, of just existing. I want to live." Edwin exhaled deeply. "Anyway, I needed to confess this. I hope you can forgive me."

"Well, I don't know, Edwin. I understand everything you said, but I'm having a hard time with you not mentioning being envious of my good looks and engaging personality. They've never said *anything* about me being good-looking?"

"No."

"Barbara wouldn't tell you. I'm sure Sharon has said something, though."

"No." Pause. "And *that*, Jonathan."

"What?"

"No matter what the circumstance, you don't let it get to you. You can probably crack jokes before getting your head chopped off."

"Not if the guy with the axe is cross-eyed."

Edwin's weary face managed a half-smile. "There's something else. A few days ago somebody called and said I was sticking my nose into their business. They tacked a picture to our front door. It was a picture of Christopher's grave. I and Sharon went to the cemetery close to midnight. They dug up his casket and left his bones next to the hole. What kind of people would do something like that?"

Jonathan sat up straight. "I think I know."

"Who?"

"The kind of people who kidnapped me and kept me locked in a car trunk for hours."

"Wha—how—locked in a trunk? When did this happen? How'd you get away?"

"Some guys dropped by the house to send me and Liz to heaven. A guy came through the window and I knocked him out with an iron. Got him to talk. Well, actually my bride got him to talk."

"Liz got him to talk?"

"Christian women. They have their ways. Some guy named Michael Bogarti is not in my fan club." He patted his eye. "He gave me this. Seems that he lost a little money when the FBI closed down that mansion place."

"Why'd he come after you? Ava was the one that really pushed that."

"Who knows? Maybe because I've been so vocal about the sex trafficking industry in Atlanta. Or *maybe* it was the sex trafficking special I did with Daphne Krugle. You know that was right after the mansion deal."

"Why is this guy not in prison?" asked Edwin.

"He lives in the shadows."

"We've got to believe God to bring him out of the shadows and into the light."

"Amen, brother."

"Jonathan," Barbara was at the door, "Elizabeth's got something to share with us. It's about her and Andrew."

Chapter 35

Elizabeth looked at each person with beautiful, but sad eyes. Andrew had revived, but didn't recall anything that happened. He sat across the room, which was quite fine with Elizabeth. Jonathan had tried to sit beside her, but she hadn't let him. Instead, she sat in a chair alone. She glanced at Edwin and Barbara and lowered her head briefly before looking up. Her lips were tight with tension. Her eyes watery with shame.

Elizabeth spoke haltingly, her speech made difficult by the weight of her crimes. "I've sinned against the Lord, against my husband, and against all of you. The reason I couldn't help Andrew, the reason I couldn't cast out the spirit is because of the darkness the demon saw in my soul. My Ava...my mom is sick. She's at death's door. The doctors have given up. Jonathan and I have been praying and fasting," she wiped a cheek free of water, "but, well, it is not going well for Mom."

Elizabeth looked reluctantly at her husband. She knew this would hit him like a train. "I lost faith in my husband, who has never lost faith in me. I lost faith in my Jesus, who has done nothing but love me." She shook her head in disbelief. "He rescued me from a terrible plight, from a life of humiliation and cruelty. A life of slavery. I see now, His gift became my God. He used Ava to deliver me. I love her with all of my heart. How could I not love her? She took this abused orphan and made me her daughter. When I saw that I was going to lose her, I sought the help of a witch."

Barbara gasped. "Oh...my...Lord."

The train violently hit Jonathan with all of its irresistible force. Something like a cough carried pain out of his mouth. Somehow the train had cruelly not killed him. It had left him instead in a mangled mess of shredded flesh, exposed organs, and grotesque parts.

Edwin rushed to one knee in front of Jonathan. He pushed him back from falling over.

Elizabeth burst into tears.

Barbara's first instinct was to hold her, to comfort her. Her second instinct, and the one that prevailed, was to not hug someone who had just come from a witch. She had seen Jonathan and Edwin pray for people who had been involved in witchcraft. It was always like watching a horror movie. *She was having absolutely nothing to do with witchcraft.*

"Andrew, go get Jonathan a water," said Edwin. "Sit back, Jonathan." He helped his friend back onto the sofa.

"I'm sorry, Jonathan," said Elizabeth.

The water came. Jonathan drank it like it could save his life. "Thank you, Andrew."

"We're glad you're here," said Andrew.

"It's my favorite place." Jonathan looked at Elizabeth. "Besides home. Come here beside me."

She jumped from the chair and nearly slid on her knees between his parted legs. She looked up at him with closed eyes and wailed as though she had been shot. Jonathan bent forward and clutched his screaming wife.

"I'm sorry. I'm sorry. I'm sorry," she screamed repeatedly.

"We'll get past this, Liz. I'm with you, baby."

"I love the Lord," Elizabeth moaned.

"I know you do." He rocked his wife. "And the Lord knows you do." Jonathan held the back of her head and pressed her into his chest. He held her and rocked her for about half an hour. Finally, her cries died down.

"Help me up, Jonathan," she asked.

She sat beside him. They held hands.

"I had gone to see Mom. I was having a terrible pain in my eye. It spread to my face. It was debilitating. A lady whom I had just met offered to pray for me. It wasn't until after she had laid hands on me that she disclosed she was a Reiki healer."

"Aghhh," grunted Jonathan. "Were you healed?"

"Yes. Immediately. Spectacularly so."

Jonathan grunted again.

"What's a Reiki healer?" asked Barbara.

"You've heard of black magic...white magic, bad witch, good witch?"

"Yes."

"Witchdoctor?"

"Yeah."

"Well, the Reiki healer and the witchdoctor are cousins. One lives in a jungle. The other in a skyscraper. Same employer—Satan." Jonathan turned back to his wife. "You didn't know the lady was a witch, Liz."

"Jonathan." She said his name like a child about to confess to breaking something. "I saw the lady again. I couldn't get the healing out of my mind. I tried. I really did try. And all the while Mom was getting worse. Then when you began to talk as though you knew Mom was going to die...."

Jonathan remembered. It all made sense now. The Lord had told him to leave his wife alone so He could deal with her. This was His work. He had tried her faith by delaying His answer and by separating them. The Lord didn't want Elizabeth to be able to hide behind his faith. He recalled how God had done the same thing with King Hezekiah. He had left him to see what was in his heart. He remembered how God had given Abraham Isaac and later asked him to give him back to the Lord.

"Jonathan, do you think I can ever be restored? Not *forgiven*. I know God will forgive me," said Elizabeth, humbly, but with a confidence birthed and nurtured by years of walking with God. "But do you think I can ever regain the sweetness?" She began to cry again. "I broke His heart, Jonathan. I went to His enemy because I felt He was moving too slowly. It was the golden calf all over again."

"Yes, Liz. *Yes*. I don't know why He loves us. I don't know how He loves us. I only know that He does, and that for some ridiculous reason that we'll probably never understand, He's crazy about those who fear Him." He rubbed her face. "Remember what the angel told the women at the tomb when Jesus rose from the dead? 'Go tell the disciples, and Peter, that He will meet you in Galilee.' Peter had denied Him. Had left Him when He needed Him most. But the Lord didn't hold this against him. He knew Peter loved Him. He knows you love Him."

They hugged and cried together.

She looking knowingly into her husband's eyes. "There are still consequences of my sin."

He looked knowingly into her eyes. "There are still consequences." He looked at Edwin. "I'm going to need your help."

Barbara left the room.

*****

"Look. There he is again." Jeff had worked for Mr. Bogarti for a long time. He wasn't new to the game. But he was new to marks who knew they were being hunted walking down the street as though they weren't. *Hey, if you want to make our jobs easier, fine.*

"Not a care in the world. He's almost skipping. I don't like him." There were few people that Billy did like. "I see why *Someone* wants to kill him with his own hands."

Jeff looked at Billy. "But *Someone* says we can kill him if we have to." His smile showed his preference.

"Why is he walking?" asked Billy.

Jeff scanned the streets. It wasn't dark yet, but no one was out." It would be easy enough. Drive alongside him. Empty his magazine of fifteen hollow point bullets. Jump back in the car. "I'm tired of screwing with this guy. Let's end this."

"What...is...he...doing...now?" said Billy.

"Jogging?" Jeff chuckled at the middle-aged man with the noticeable belly. "*He's* jogging."

Jonathan had begun a little trot. Suddenly he took off in a sprint.

"He's running," said Jeff in shock. It wasn't the fact that he was running. It was the speed. The guy who looked as though he couldn't walk up a flight of stairs without stopping for air was running like an Olympic sprinter.

The car burned rubber accelerating. Both men watched Jonathan in awe. This was happening too fast to figure it out. They just had to keep up with the guy with the missile up his butt.

Jonathan darted across a street with a four-way stop sign. The car darted across the intersection seconds later. They were gaining on him. Jonathan took a sharp turn and ran up a home's steep driveway. Near the top, he made another sharp turn and ran back towards the street with the four-way stop sign. He ran across the tops of several lawns.

Jeff hurled the car into a driveway on the left. He shifted into reverse and tried in vain to not burn rubber. The object was to shoot this rabbit without a bunch of folks looking. He sped down the street towards the corner.

"There he is," said Billy, pointing to their mark. He was standing at the top of a lawn at the corner. It was like he was waiting on them. "Go. Go. Go," he pressed the driver.

Jeff drove through the stop sign and made a right. Billy had his gun out. No one was on the street. That preacher was going down *now*.

The car slowed down. Where was the preacher?

Jeff's mouth dropped open. "That can't be him."

"Where?" said Billy, looking at his side of the street.

"There," said Jeff, pointing directly ahead. "That cannot be him."

Billy looked ahead and blinked his eyes several times. "What the heck? How'd he—?"

"Something ain't right, bro. Something ain't right." Jeff looked at the figure who was at a standing trot. He was already at the end of the other block. He faced them. "What's he doing?"

"He's playing with us, man," said Billy.

"How can he run like that? Nobody can run like that."

"He can," said Billy.

The car continued its slow roll toward the bouncing figure.

Jonathan took off straight ahead. The next block had a small park to the left. It was two blocks long, two blocks wide. He ran to the end of the first block. The car gained on him, but only temporarily. Their mark looked over his shoulder and kicked it into another gear.

"Billy, what's going on, man! He can't run like that! Nobody can run like that."

"Get him, Jeff!"

"I'm trying to get him. This dude's running like an animal." He pushed the pedal hard.

Jonathan turned the corner of the second block. He was at the end of that block before the car turned the corner. The car chased Jonathan around the park two full times.

"We ain't catching him," said Jeff. "Nobody can run like that."

"What are we going to say?" asked Billy.

"Nothing. We're not saying nothing about nothing. This never happened. Let's get out of here before somebody calls the cops."

"Look," said Billy. "He's doing jumping jacks."

Jeff frowned and pushed hard on the gas.

Jonathan slowed down and let them catch up just enough to stay encouraged. He turned down this street, ran up another, trotted here, trotted there. The men's egos followed the tireless man until finally his steroids or adrenaline or whatever he was taking ran out. The guy was tired. He looked exhausted. Of course, he was exhausted. How could he not be? They had chased this guy for at least half an hour, clean into another neighborhood.

They watched him take slow, heavy steps into an empty house that was being built in an undeveloped cul de sac. It was the only house there. *Perfect.* The guy could hardly make it up the stairs. The men looked at one another. They communicated without saying anything. Jonathan was most definitely going to be shot—many times. But first he was going to get the butt whipping of his life.

Jeff was the driver, but he was first out of the car. He was the one who this preacher had made a fool of. Billy was right behind him. He pushed the door shut.

The men walked silently from the large living room to the kitchen. They opened doors. They found nothing.

"That's some kind of coffee you been drinking," said Billy to the man in hiding. "Have to get me some of that."

"I don't think it was coffee. I think it was speed. Some kind of super speed," said Jeff. "Come on out, preacher. Let's talk about it."

He wasn't on the first floor.

They heard a cough in the basement.

The men smiled.

Jeff led the way. "Should've known you weren't up those stairs," he said to the man in hiding, wherever he was. "You looked mighty tired trying to make it up those few stairs outside."

"Well, lookey here," said Billy. He stroked his long, brown beard. "Here's our rabbit."

Jonathan was doubled over on one knee. He didn't look up. His breaths were labored.

Jeff stepped forward. "You owe me gas money."

"Stand up, preacher," said Billy. "We want to make this a fair fight." He smiled at Jeff.

Jonathan didn't move.

Jeff buried his boot deep into the belly of the bent over man. The man didn't seem to know that a large man had just kicked him in the gut. The man said something under his breath.

"What did you say?" said Billy.

The man raised his hands over his head while he was still on one knee. He lifted his face toward the ceiling. "For the glory of God and the sons of men."

Jeff landed a blow across Jonathan's jaw. It should've broken it. Jeff's blows had broken many jaws. The man apparently had not been told that he had been struck in the face.

Billy backed up. "I've had enough of this, bro." He pulled out his gun and squeezed off three quick rounds.

The man's eyes opened. He stood up slowly.

Jeff and Billy watched the man come off his knees and stand. What they saw made them want to run, but made it impossible to run. Each moment of the man's ascent from being on his knee to standing up unveiled a transformation. Before their very eyes they saw a man change into something they could never describe.

What stood before them resembled a man. This thing was tall. It was big. Yet it was big in another way. The size that stood before the two killers seemed large enough to put the universe in his pocket.

The being's body glowed with something like an intense rainbow. But rainbow may have been the wrong word. Rainbows make people feel good. The colors that emanated from this being didn't make Bogarti's men feel good. It made them feel dirty and unworthy to be in his presence.

Both men looked in its eyes. They did not choose to do this. They were compelled. His eyes were not red as fire. They were red *with* fire. The men looked into the fire and saw the horrors of hell. The real horror of it was that they saw themselves there being tormented forever.

An overwhelming sense of helplessness rushed into both men. They fell down as though they were dead men. They couldn't move, but they could hear.

"When you persecute My servants, you persecute Me. I put before you life and death, blessings and cursings. Choose life that you may live."

Enrid left the men in a crumpled heap.

*****

There was a lot to do. Edwin and Jonathan conferred with one another in Edwin's study.

"Liz is in deep, Edwin. She's in real deep."

"God can get her out. I've learned that from you, Jonathan."

Jonathan was complimented by the reassuring smile on his friend's face. He detected something new. Edwin was smiling not because of his confidence in him, but because of his confidence in God. Edwin was not the man he was a week ago. Jonathan's left cheek took a slow turn toward its own smile. *Satan, looks like your little plan has backfired. You meant these trials for evil, but God has used your fire to develop and purify my friend's faith.*

"I know God can deliver, Liz, Edwin. That's not my concern."

Edwin waited for the rest.

"Witchcraft is different. It's not like other sins. I don't mean to be vulgar, but," Jonathan tilted his head with a look of worry, "it's like having sex with the devil."

Edwin's head pulled back like he had just sniffed a whiff of something awful.

"Witchcraft is spiritual intimacy with Satan. It is becoming one with him. It's worship in the reverse. The person who goes to a psychic or a fortune teller or what have you, they are getting in bed with the devil. That's why God hates it so much. It's the reason why he used Israel to destroy whole nations. Remember Canaan?"

"Yeah."

"Remember what He said about why he wanted them destroyed? Edwin, I've quoted these Scriptures to congregations all around the world:

> *When you come into the land which the Lord your God is giving you, you shall not learn to follow the abominations of those nations. There shall not be found among you anyone who makes his son or his daughter pass through*

> *the fire or one who practices witchcraft, or a soothsayer, or one who interprets omens, or a sorcerer, or one who conjures spells, or a medium, or a spiritist, or one who calls up the dead. For all who do these things are an abomination to the Lord, and because of these abominations the Lord your God drives them out from before you.*

"Edwin, that's in—"

"Deuteronomy," Edwin finished.

"That's right," Jonathan smiled. "You do have a few letters behind your name, don't you?"

"It's not how much you know. It's how much you understand and believe...and *do*," said Edwin.

"I knew there was some reason why I like you. I couldn't quite put my finger on it, but there it is."

Edwin was thinking about Canaan. "That explains it. I'd often wondered why God—well, I'll just say it—why He was so ruthless with them. I knew He had to have some good reason for ordering the extermination of whole nations. Hmm. *It was witchcraft.*"

"Yep. Good old witchcraft. People don't know what they're getting into when they mess with that stuff. Most folks won't ever sacrifice an animal to the devil or attend a séance. But they'll do other dumb things. Stuff like astrology. Iridology. Palm reading. Acupuncture. These are baby steps to bondage. May take longer, but they'll get you there."

"Acupuncture? Letting someone stick you with tiny needles? *That's witchcraft?*" asked Edwin.

"Seems harmless enough, right? Like, who would've thought eating a piece of fruit would've led to this wonderful world of mayhem we have?" Jonathan looked at Edwin. "That fruit didn't have *War* or *Famine* or *Poverty* or *Murder* on the label. Satan is like that. A cute puppy that bites like a lion and swallows like a python."

"But *acupuncture*?" said Edwin.

"It's like a lot of things. On the surface, harmless. Beneath the soil, poison. Most people think of witchcraft as someone casting spells." Jonathan chuckled. "*That's* witchcraft, no doubt about it. Haiti. Me and Liz had a time in Haiti. Those folks can cast a spell. I'd love to take you there some time," he said with a grin.

"I just bet you would."

"Satan is tricky, Edwin. You can't always judge him by the clothes he wears. Take acupuncture. On the surface it's just someone sticking tiny needles in you to relieve pain or to help you stop smoking or whatever. But what's the philosophical basis of the practice? The building may look good, but what about the foundation?

"The foundation is the ancient Chinese belief that there's a mystical energy force in the body that must maintain perfect balance or all heck breaks out. Acupuncture supposedly calibrates the balance by sticking needles in *just...the...right...spots.*"

"I can see the quackery. Where's the witchcraft?" asked Edwin. "Okaaay. The mystical force," he answered his own question.

"That would be the one," said Jonathan. "Any time there's a mystical this or that, look for the spirit of witchcraft. Any time there's astrology involved, look for the spirit of witchcraft. If there's any kind of divination—I don't care what name it goes by—look for the spirit of witchcraft. Horoscope. Tarot cards. Fortune tellers. Readings. Ouija Board. Crystal ball. Any supernatural source of power or knowledge that doesn't come from the Lord Jesus Christ and His precious Holy Spirit comes from the spirit of witchcraft. It comes from Satan."

Edwin was silent. He loved Jonathan. Just today he realized that he loved this man more than he knew. His envy of him had been ridiculous, but rational. This was a perfect example. Jonathan was adamantly—some would say *fanatically*—opposed to anything that even remotely looked like witchcraft. And he didn't mind it if society placed him in the crazy category. That kind of courage and devotion to God, it was something to covet.

"Edwin, I catch a lot of flak for calling things witchcraft that don't look like witchcraft. For instance, yoga."

Edwin stiffened.

"Every time I talk about yoga, people throw a fit." Jonathan reminisced. "Well, not everywhere. Some pastors are hard on it. God bless 'em. But some preachers have yoga classes in the church." He looked at Edwin. They looked intently at one another. "Yoga in the church. *Can you believe that?*"

"What's wrong with yoga in the church?" inquired a woman.

Edwin and Jonathan looked up at Barbara in the doorway. She had seemingly popped out of thin air.

"Nothing if you want to fill God's church with witchcraft spirits." His tone was a bit abrupt. "I'm sorry, Barbara. I didn't mean to be curt."

Edwin's face strained to mask his anger. "Barbara has invited a kundalini yoga master to hold sessions at the church. Haven't you, dear?"

Barbara knew that look on her husband's face. "Yes." Her answer was unsteady.

"Yoga sessions at the church?" asked Jonathan.

"Yes. I believe the guy comes on Tuesday and Thursday mornings." Edwin looked at Barbara. "Do I have the days correct?"

"Yes." Her voice was even. It was obvious in her voice and face that she and Edwin weren't in agreement over this.

"A *kundalini* yoga master in God's church," said Jonathan rhetorically.

"Kundalini. That's right," said Edwin. He looked at Barbara with a half-grin.

She didn't share the feeling.

"On Tuesday and Thursday mornings, as in Tuesday *yesterday*?" asked Jonathan.

"Yes," Barbara answered defensively. "He's a delightful man. There was nothing hocus pocus about him."

Jonathan said nothing. He stared at the wall as though he were looking at a movie. "I gotta go," he said.

"Where are you going?" asked Edwin.

"Take care of Liz for me."

"What? Take care of Elizabeth? You have to leave now?" asked Edwin.

"Yes. Now." He called for Elizabeth. She and Andrew came. "Liz, Edwin's going to take care of you. I'm on assignment." He turned to Edwin. "Edwin, Liz has opened the door to witchcraft. I trust you to free her from this thing."

"What thing?" asked Barbara. "She asked God to forgive her. Isn't that enough?"

"It's not about forgiveness, Barbara. It's about open doors. You drink poison and ask God to forgive you, He will. But you still need your stomach pumped. Edwin, witchcraft is stubborn. It will fight you until you think you're not anointed. Don't worry about how nasty it gets. Get them all out of my wife."

Edwin looked at him, wondering.

"Please," said Jonathan. He looked at Edwin with pleading eyes. "I need you to help my wife. You can do it. You're not the man you used to be."

Edwin looked at Elizabeth. She had witchcraft demons. He looked at Andrew. He had epilepsy demons. He looked at Barbara. She probably had some kind of yoga demons. One of him. Three people needing deliverance. *Lord, I don't know how, but my eyes are upon You.*

"I'll take care of Elizabeth."

Jonathan smiled with watery eyes. "I know you will, Edwin."

"And I'll take care of everything with a bad foundation," added Edwin.

Jonathan didn't let himself look toward Barbara. "Good." He gripped his hand and spoke emphatically. "You are not the man you used to be."

"Where are you going?" asked Elizabeth.

"I don't know yet. The Lord hasn't told me. It's about Sharon. That's all I can say."

Chapter 36

"Sharon is alive. Keep praying for her."

Click.

Barbara almost choked on hope. The man hung up before she could say anything. "Edwin," she screamed and ran into his study. She thrust the phone into his chest. "She's alive. She's alive. Someone—a man called and said she's alive and we should keep praying."

Edwin grabbed the phone and looked at it hopefully. The calling number was blocked.

Alive.

He walked toward the family room. Elizabeth and Andrew were on the way to his study. He motioned them to follow him. Barbara followed like a little puppy.

"Sharon's alive. Someone called and said Sharon is alive," he said.

"Oh, my God," Elizabeth cried. "Thank you, Jesus."

"Sharon's alive?" asked Andrew.

"I don't know who called. But our Sharon is alive because God told me she's alive. And we're going to get her back. He looked intently at his wife. "We are going to do *everything* to get her back."

Oh, had she known what her husband meant by *everything.*

"Now," Edwin lingered, looking at each person, "we've got a few hours before we go to church. We have a lot of things to do between now and then. A lot of dying. A lot of resurrecting. First, the dying."

Edwin started tapping numbers into his phone.

Everyone watched with intrigue.

Edwin locked onto Barbara's eyes. "Hello, Jessica?"

Barbara's eyes narrowed. She tilted her head. *I know he's not calling my sister.* She listened in horror, and when it was too much to take, she walked over to her husband and hung up his phone. "What are you doing, Edwin? She is not welcome in my house."

"This is not *your* house, Barbara. It's the Lord's house."

"Should I go into another room?" asked Elizabeth.

"Yeah," said Andrew, standing up.

Edwin and Barbara answered simultaneously.

"Yes," said Barbara.

"No," said Edwin.

Elizabeth and Andrew sat in awkward silence.

"Edwin, you know what she did to Christopher. To us." She looked at him knowing he should understand.

"I know what she did, Barbara. Honey, we all know what she did. She dishonored our son and humiliated our family."

"Then how could you, Edwin? How could you ask that woman into our home?"

Edwin knew exactly how his wife felt. He knew her pain. It had not been enough that they had lost their child. No, crazy Jessica had grabbed their son out of his casket before anyone could stop her in an insane attempt to raise him from the dead. When he tried to stop her, she wrestled with him for Christopher's body. In the struggle, their little boy's body dropped to the floor. Yeah, he knew exactly how she felt. *He felt the same way.* But he had to obey God despite how he felt.

"How can I ask Jessica into our home? Honestly, Barbara, I've always disliked your sister. You know that. She's arrogant, self-righteous, and sanctimonious. She's got God in her little genie's bottle. Whenever she wants Him to do something, she gives it a little rub and out He comes to do her bidding. She's got a simplistic formula or answer for everything. There's nothing about your sister I like. But when she did what she did to our little boy, *I hated* her. I hated her until Sharon got kidnapped."

Now there was a *really* awkward silence in the room.

Edwin answered the burning question on everyone's mind. "We've been attacked by Satan. The only person who can get us out of this mess is God, and we can't ask Him to help us if we refuse to forgive Jessica. We can't go to God with unforgiveness in our heart unless we're there to repent."

Barbara looked at Edwin with a tired, deflated expression. She walked to the sofa with drooping shoulders and sat down. She rested her elbows on her knees and buried her face in her hands and softly cried.

Andrew was staring at his own shoes.

"Andrew, I wanted you to hear this because you're almost a man. You're going to have your own family one day. You need to know how to lead them. And Andrew," said Edwin.

"Yes, Dad."

"You need to know that there's no place for unforgiveness in the life of a child of God. We can choose who we like and dislike. But we don't get to choose who we love. If you want to walk with God, you have to love others the way He loves us. He said, 'If you do not forgive men their trespasses, neither will God forgive your trespasses.' You understand, son?"

"Yeah, I understand." Andrew lifted his head. "Dad, I have a confession to make."

Edwin looked around. Barbara raised her head. "What is it, son?" he asked.

"I think I hate Aunt Jessica."

Edwin didn't know what to say. He had never considered how the funeral fiasco had affected the children. He looked at Barbara. Her face showed the same surprise.

"I see now that I have also harbored ill feelings toward your sister, Barbara."

Elizabeth, too?

It was as though the gauze had been pulled back and Edwin could see the ugliness of the wound. Infection had set in. If left to fester, death would swallow life.

"We have to cry out to God with all of our heart." Edwin pleaded with his eyes as he looked at his wife. "But we can only pray in confidence, *if our heart does not condemn us.*"

Barbara was torn between what she felt and what she knew she had to do. It was a huge tug of war. Her heart was the rope. "Oh, God," she muttered.

"You can do it, Mom," said Andrew.

"I want to." Her hands came down from her wet face. "I just can't."

Edwin looked at her. "You're going to, Barbara."

She looked at him, holding her face, trying to get strength from his newfound strength.

"Do you know why?" he asked.

She looked with a pained expression that looked to be holding back an outburst of tears.

"You're going to forgive Jessica because you love God and because you love your daughter. You're not going to let anything stand in the way of your daughter coming home." Edwin's words were tender, strong, and confident. "And," he bowed his head and shut his eyes tight. When he opened them, they were filled with water. "Since I'm the head of this family, I'm going to set the example. I forgive Jessica. And I forgive my uncle Ted."

Barbara and Andrew had no idea he had an uncle named Ted.

"When I was young, my uncle raped me. Several times. It started when I was six. The last time he did it, I was eleven. I've lived with this shame for all these years. I've lived with a tormenting, hollow feeling in my soul." Edwin thought about stopping here, but he told himself that he wasn't going to live with *any* more dark secrets. Somehow he knew the power of the sin committed against him was its secrecy. *He was going to break that power now!*

"It doesn't happen very often—not as often as it used to—but I've had to battle homosexual thoughts ever since Uncle Ted first molested me." He saw the surprise in Barbara's eyes. Surprisingly, he didn't see this in Elizabeth and Andrew. "I've had to battle the accusations that he raped me because I wanted him to, because there was something feminine about me. But that's not true. It's not true now, and it has never been true. He raped me because he's a sick, depraved pervert.

"Well," he blew out a breath, "if I can confess this to all of you, and if I can forgive this pathetic human being, we can forgive Jessica."

"Dad, thank you for sharing that with us."

Edwin gave a slight grin to his son. He was a fine young man. He wasn't Sharon—no one was Sharon—but in his own way, he was an incredible kid, and he loved him dearly.

Edwin held out his phone to Barbara. He spoke softly. "I need you to call your sister. Tell her that we need her assistance."

Barbara looked at Edwin for a few seconds before moving. Andrew and Elizabeth watched anxiously. She looked into his eyes. His gaze lifted her to her feet. She went to him like a child just taking her first several steps and fell into his arms.

"Oh, Edwin, I'm so sorry. Why didn't you tell me?" She held him tightly, rubbing his back, and offering encouraging words through her tears.

After their long embrace, Barbara took the phone and called Jessica.

They all watched as she spoke into the phone.

Barbara lowered the phone. "She's crying," she whispered to them.

Everyone smiled.

"Have you eaten?" Barbara asked her sister. "Good. We've got some leftover beef stew and rice. I'll have it ready for you."

They finished talking.

"How do you feel, honey?" asked Edwin.

"Like a load has been lifted from my shoulders."

"Good." He kissed her on the forehead. "When she gets here, I have to go see my uncle Ted."

"Dad, you're going to go *see* him?" asked Andrew. "Where is he?"

"He's in a nursing home in Atlanta."

"In Atlanta? I didn't know you had any relatives here," said Barbara. "What if he doesn't want to see you?"

"I didn't have any relatives here. He was dead until I forgave him. He sort of doesn't have a choice but to see me. He had a stroke that left him in a bad condition. He's paralyzed and he can barely talk. If I can't get in the room, I can't get in the room. God told me to go see him. My part is to go. His part is to open the door."

"Can I go with you, Dad?"

Edwin smiled. "I'd love for you to come with me."

In a short while, the doorbell rang. Edwin, Andrew, and Barbara went to the foyer. Barbara opened the door.

Jessica stepped inside. She jerked twice and held her side. She doubled over and screamed, "Glooooooooraaaaaaaaay to the Most High God," and began speaking in tongues.

*****

The car came to a stop in the visitors' parking area of *Rosemont Way*. This had been the home of Edwin's uncle for the past two years. Edwin and Andrew got out and walked toward the building.

"Dad, why does Aunt Jessica jerk like that?" asked Andrew.

Edwin felt his throat constricting the closer he got to the entrance. "She says it's the power of God."

"God ever jerk you?"

Edwin swallowed and massaged his throat. A slight itch cascaded over him. His whole body suddenly felt the way it did when his foot fell asleep and he had to kick the ground several times to get the blood circulating. "No."

Andrew jerked a couple of times.

Edwin looked at him strangely. "What are you doing?"

"Nothing. Just trying to see what that feels like."

"One Aunt Jessica is enough for any family. The good Lord knows how much we can bare."

Andrew laughed. "She's funny, Dad.

Edwin looked at his amused son. He gave a long nod. "That's one word you could use to describe her."

They got closer to the door. It was getting harder for Edwin to breathe.

"Hey, Dad," said Andrew. He stopped walking.

Edwin happily stopped. "What's up, Andrew?"

"I wanted you to know that I'm a Christian now."

"What do you mean, son? You've always been a Christian—since you were a kid."

"I don't mean that kind of Christian," said Andrew.

Edwin looked at his son, waiting for more.

"Kids do what their parents tell them to do. Then they grow up and do their own thing. Like my friend, Keith. He was a Christian. He went to Christian school until he got to high school."

"He's not a Christian anymore?" asked Edwin.

"No. Really, Dad, I don't think he ever was. I think he just went along with whatever his parents told him. They wanted him to be a Christian, so he was a Christian. But when he got to regular high school it wasn't enough to stick. He had enough Jesus to make his parents happy, but not enough to keep him when he got to high school."

"Do you think he should've stayed in Christian school?" asked Edwin.

"You can't hide forever, Dad. Sooner or later we have to face the real world."

That was a profound thought. "Humph. What about you?" asked Edwin.

"I think I didn't know what it meant to be a Christian, I mean a true Christian, until I saw you and Mom forgive Aunt Jessica. I mean, I believed God was real and stuff, but I know how you and Mom felt about Aunt Jessica. Then when you told us about your uncle—*Man, and you're going to forgive this guy!* I just," Andrew looked at his dad and smiled, "now I know God is real."

Edwin looked at his son and contemplated what he had said. He wouldn't let this slip from his memory. It was something he'd have to teach from the pulpit.

But for now he had to find a way to live without air. He hadn't anticipated this kind of struggle. He had already mentally forgiven his uncle. He was here simply because he felt God had instructed him to take his forgiveness to a deeper level. *But the closer he got to the door, the less he was able to breathe.*

*****

The Mighty Bashnar was in a position he hated. He was reacting.

His powerful hands wrapped desperately around Edwin's neck, squeezing as hard as possible. He stood before the man he still stubbornly—Controllus felt *insanely*—considered a worm with one leg braced behind him. But no matter how hard he dug into the earth with his powerful back leg, he still slid backward as Edwin walked. He couldn't let this worm enter this level of forgiveness. *This was the realm of God.*

*****

The receptionist told Edwin and Andrew that they could go back to Ted's room. God had definitely greased the path. The lady acted as though Edwin was a VIP. But instead of going directly down the hall to get to Uncle Ted, Edwin walked unsteadily back to the seating area.

"Dad, you okay? You want some water or something?"

Edwin shook his head. "Yeah." His voice was scratchy.

Andrew hurried to the water machine and got a flimsy cup of cold water. He watched his father's troubled eyes as he drank. "Dad, you can do this."

Edwin smiled and frowned at the same time. "I didn't know it would be this hard."

"What he did to you, Dad...I mean, there's not a lot of people who would forgive somebody like this."

"Yeah," said Edwin, massaging the front of his neck, "now that I'm here, I only hope I can go through with it."

"You can, Dad. I know you can. Jesus will help you."

Edwin took a few deep breaths. "Yeah, you're right." He pushed himself up. "Let's go."

They got to Uncle Ted's room and stopped at the door before anyone inside could see them. Andrew placed his hand on his father's shoulder. "Lord Jesus, I ask you to help my father. This man raped my dad. I don't know if I could do it, Lord. I don't know if I could forgive someone who did something like that to me. I don't even know if I can forgive this creep for what he did to my dad. But Dad wants to forgive him. Please help him. In Jesus's name. Amen."

Andrew looked up. "Ready, Dad?"

Edwin looked at his surprising son. "Ready. Are you ready?"

"Ready."

"Ground Zero," said Edwin.

Father and son stepped into the room. The room was dimly lit, but it was clean, even cozy-looking. They looked at the man, then at one another.

Edwin stepped forward. He gazed at the figure in the twin bed. This was definitely Uncle Ted, but he looked nothing like what Edwin remembered. The last time Edwin saw him was also the last time Uncle Ted raped him. That was three decades ago. Time and two strokes had exacted a terrible revenge on the old man. The old man who wasn't nearly as old as he looked.

Uncle Ted the child molester had been tall, muscular, and good-looking. He had long, brown hair that sat on his shoulders. He had piercing blue eyes. Eyes that used to bore into Edwin's soul and reduce him to less than nothing.

Uncle Ted the old man was skinny, and there was absolutely not the slightest hint that he had ever hosted a good look. The vultures of time and disease had done more than eat away the evidence of a handsome face. They had left in its place a face frozen stiff with an expression that seemed to be looking at a truck about to run him over. His long, brown hair had not only turned gray, it had turned loose. But not with any decent organization. Patches of it here and there had fled and had left Uncle Ted's head looking like a badly kept lawn. One with mineral deficient soil that only allowed small, disarrayed growth.

His eyes.

Uncle Ted's eyes were technically there, but they were no longer piercing. They were empty, vacant, like a house with tattered curtains, but no tenants. And although they were still blue, it was questionable whether they worked, or whether they simply followed sounds.

Edwin walked to the left of the bed. "Ted," he said. His voice didn't convey confidence.

The old man's face turned toward Edwin.

"It's Edwin. Your nephew. And I've got my son with me—Andrew."

The old man's mouth was frozen open, with half his top lip arched high, exposing teeth. He obviously heard Edwin.

"I'm not going to be here long." Edwin glanced at his son. "I'm here because of the things you did to me."

The old man grunted.

"Dad, I think he said something," said Andrew.

The old man's eyes narrowed.

Edwin looked into Uncle Ted's eyes. It was only a hunch, but he thought he saw defiance. Maybe even hatred. This brought up something that Edwin hadn't considered. What if Uncle Ted wasn't sorry? What if his uncle still blamed him for the rapes?

Edwin felt anger rise in his chest. He looked down at the paralyzed shell of a man. He looked at his son. His son's words bubbled up above the anger. *Now I know God is real.*

Andrew nodded encouragement.

Edwin took the encouragement and provided some of his own. He pulled up one of Sharon's favorite passage of Scriptures.

> *But I say to you, love your enemies, bless those who curse you, do good to those who hate you, and pray for those who spitefully use you, that you may be sons of your Father in heaven; for He makes His sun rise on the evil and on the good, and sends rain on the just and the unjust. For if you love those who love you, what reward have you?*

It was hard to see how anyone other than the Lord Himself could have these Scriptures as their favorites. As Edwin looked into the tortured face of his rapist, the monster who had stolen so much from him, the one who had caused him such pain, two things were certain. One, he wasn't the Lord. And, two, he wasn't Sharon.

He could just as easily snatch the pillow from under Uncle Ted's head and suffocate him as he could forgive him for what he had done. Edwin walked out of the room before he did the unthinkable. Andrew followed close behind.

Edwin stopped at his son's urging.

"Dad, I know what—no, I don't know what you're feeling. But I know you've got to forgive this guy."

Edwin turned his back to Andrew and stepped away. He stared at a picture on the wall without seeing the picture. "I know. But I *can't* forgive him. I hate him."

"Dad, that's why God told you to come here. If you didn't come, you would've deceived yourself into thinking you had forgiven him. I guess that's why Sharon's always saying we have to do something good to people who hurt us. If we can't do good to our enemies, I guess that means we haven't forgiven them."

Sharon was missing, but here she was speaking through his son. Edwin's eyes watered. "I can only forgive this man if I see him as God sees him," he said, turning around and patting his son on the shoulder.

"You can do it, Dad. I know you can."

Edwin bowed his head. "Lord, I see now why you told me to come here. I haven't really forgiven this man. I can't do it in my own power. Please open my eyes so that I can see him as you see him. Maybe then...." He opened his eyes and raised his head.

"Andrew."

"Yeah, Dad?"

"You're an incredible kid. I love you, and I thank God you're my son."

Andrew felt his eyes suddenly emitting water. He knew his father loved him. But he had never felt that he loved him the way he loved Sharon. Until now.

"Come on, son." He hugged him sideways. "Let's do this."

They stepped back into the room.

"Ted," Edwin looked at his son, "*Uncle* Ted, I'm a preacher. I have a church. I have a wonderful wife and three wonderful children. One is in heaven. I'm here because above all else, I'm a Christian, a servant of Jesus Christ. He's forgiven me of every sin. And because He's forgiven me, I forgive you."

The old man jerked and grunted. His eyes glared. It was unmistakable now. He was angry.

Edwin saw the anger. He hugged Andrew to his side and kissed him on the top of his head. "My son needs to see me forgive you from my heart." He paused. "I do. I forgive you for raping me."

The old man repeatedly jerked his anger at Edwin.

"It doesn't make a difference how you feel about me. Uncle Ted, I forgive you." Edwin felt the Holy Spirit pulling him deeper into the character of Christ. "And more than that, I love you."

The old man jerked and jerked and jerked. His eyes glared hatred at Edwin.

Edwin went to the side of the old man's bed. The man couldn't turn his head all the way around to face Edwin. He grunted angrily as his eyes strained to see Edwin.

Edwin pulled the cover up to his uncle's neck. He took the old man's head in his hands and bent down and kissed him on the forehead. "I forgive you, Uncle Ted."

Edwin looked at his son. He could tell Andrew was proud of him. "Let's go, son."

They walked toward the door.

The old man grunted something.

"He's saying something, Dad."

Edwin and Andrew stopped and looked at the old man.

"Sor-ry," he said. A tear slid down the side of his frozen, but less tortured face.

Chapter 37

The Mighty Bashnar knew this meeting with Prince Krioni and the Council of Strategic Affairs was coming. It became a strong possibility once the deplorable angel, Enrid, rescued Jonathan from his killers and left a pig in the trunk. It became an inevitability when the worm forgave his uncle. That kind of development would have been posted throughout the dark kingdom.

He paced the dark hallway near the door to the waiting area of the council chambers. The obligatory planned delay of calling him into the room didn't bother him this time. There were more important matters to consider than the prince's silly games.

An administrative demon tried not to stare at the wounds of the famed warrior spirit. *He looks like he was shredded,* he thought. He humbly beckoned him and nervously watched the warrior spirit walk to and stand before the big door.

This time there was not the usual bellowing, "You may enter," from the prince. Instead, the door opened from the inside. The Mighty Bashnar stepped in and was immediately met by six armored and heavily armed castle guards. "You will be relieved of your weapons."

The administrative spirit had been present on two occasions where warrior spirits had chosen to die for what they considered an honorable death rather than give up their weapons. On both occasions the warrior spirits had been killed, but not before killing many more than they should have been able to kill. *It was amazing what those warrior spirits could do.* The clerk gripped his desk and leaned toward the door.

The Mighty Bashnar looked at the six. Their weapons were already in their hands, and their armor ruled out any instant kills. But there was a possibility. Their eyes. The helmets they used had wide openings for their eyes instead of small grates. *Who chose these helmets? He should be beaten,* thought the Mighty Bashnar.

The warrior spirit saw the battle before the battle. His fingers were too thick to go through the helmet's eye holes. But his long claws were not. He could gouge the eyes of two guards either on the left or the right before anyone knew what happened. That would leave four. A strong back fist across the helmet of the guard standing next to the second blinded guard would stun him just long enough to pull out his—

"That would leave three of the six, Mighty Bashnar," said Prince Krioni. "Blind two, strike one. That would leave three."

The Mighty Bashnar looked to his right at the prince on his elevated platform. He could not contain his surprise.

Prince Krioni looked at the warrior spirit with a sneer. "You are a warrior spirit, no? The battle before the battle. Blind two, strike one. *That...leaves...three.*" This was an immensely satisfying moment for the prince and a jarring one for the warrior spirit. "There is a reason I am a prince, warrior spirit." The prince shuffled some papers that didn't need shuffling. "There are twelve others who haven't introduced themselves yet. And look behind you, mighty one, in the waiting area. Six more. All dressed by the same wonderful tailor. What is it going to be warrior spirit?"

He hated the prince, but he was a student and fan of good strategy. The prince had taken adequate precautions. He would certainly lose this battle. He chose to offer up his weapons. But he didn't choose this because of the certainty of losing the battle. He did it for his great name. If he died now, he would go down as a failure. The prince would see to that. No, he had to live to fight Jonathan and Edwin another day. Plus, he still had Sharon.

The Mighty Bashnar stepped forward and peered at each of the six masked demons in front of him. "I permit you to retrieve my weapons."

They did so.

"Step forward, Bashnar. You may look upon me." The prince was anxious to get on with it.

The Mighty Bashnar looked around. Normally there was only the council and whoever was cursed enough to stand before it. But today the place was packed. It was standing room only. He looked at the equipment posted around the ceiling.

The swine is broadcasting. The Mighty Bashnar's eyes and nose flared. Had he known the prince had planned to make a mockery of him throughout the dark kingdom, he would never have surrendered his weapons.

The prince flicked his fingers at a demon who whispered something into his ear. "Warrior spirit, you have been summoned here to give an account of the Atlanta revival and your Job strategy."

"May I speak, great prince?"

"I am told you are full of words."

The Mighty Bashnar said nothing.

"Go on. Go on. Speak. That is why we are here," said the prince.

"I am the Mighty Bashnar. *Mighty* was conferred upon me because of my great exploits. It is a title created and awarded by the father of darkness. It is a title that compels respect from all levels of darkness."

The prince smacked his lips and shook his head in irritation. He looked at the audience. "For the record, we respect the title *Mighty.* It is a great title," he said hurriedly. "Anything else Bashn—"the prince smirked—"I'm sorry. Anything else, Mighty Bashnar, before we begin our inquiry?"

"No. Respect has been satisfied."

The prince looked at the warrior spirit with a dropped head. He rolled his eyes. "Respect has been satisfied," he muttered derisively, shaking his head. This warrior spirit's pride had no limits.

"Mighty Bashnar, you appeared before this council and prevailed upon us to request of heaven special permission to attack the Atlanta revival rebels with extreme ferocity." The prince again shuffled papers that didn't need shuffling. He looked up. "You assured us that this so-called *Job Strategy* would put an end to this revival foolishness. Has it, *Mighty* Bashnar? Has it put an end to the Atlanta revival? Has it destroyed *any* of its chief culprits?"

"No."

The prince waited for more. The warrior spirit was offering nothing else. "That is it? Just *no*?" The prince's big fist slammed on the table. "This council deserves more." He motioned to the unseen audience. "The darkness—those watching these proceedings deserve more."

The Mighty Bashnar said nothing.

"You are the *Mighty* Bashnar, are you not?" spewed the prince.

"I am the *Mighty* Bashnar."

"Mighty Bashnar, where are the mighty results?"

The warrior spirit looked at the prince with cold eyes, but he said nothing.

"Okay, mighty one. Oops, I did it again. I meant to say Mighty Bashnar." The prince opened a folder. "Since you seem to have lost your voice, I will recount for the sake of all who are interested in this Atlanta revival disease what has happened since you received special authority to destroy it.

"First, what was life like before the *Job Strategy*? It was bad. This cannot be denied. This church and its band of misfits had been a constant source of light. They rescued hundreds of people from our clutches."

This statement caused a lot of nods of agreement and some whispered comments in the room's audience.

"But," the prince knew he was being broadcast; he paused for effect, "they...were...contained. They could only go so far. They were like Jesus before he sent back the Holy Spirit. Limited to tormenting us only in Israel. But, Mighty Bashnar, where are we now that you have employed the great *Job Strategy*?"

The prince put a piece of paper on top of another. "Aaahh, here. Here is where we are. Let's start with the man you consider a worm. Edwin. The pastor. Weak. Double-minded. Timid. Discounted most of the Bible. Reluctant and ambivalent second-stringer to the dagger, Jonathan."

The outbreak of talking surprised the prince. "Quiet," he ordered roughly. "The dagger isn't in the room." The chattering ceased. "Now where is Reverend Worm?" He motioned to a demon. He came to the front and dropped two balls and chains before the Mighty Bashnar. "Do you recognize these two chains?"

The Mighty Bashnar looked at them. "Yes."

The prince saw that he wasn't going to expand his answer. "You should. These are the chains of unforgiveness that were attached to your worm. I emphasize *were* because obviously they are no longer attached. The reason they are no longer attached is because of your brilliant plan to kidnap Sharon."

"I hate her," a demon's voice shrilled above the others.

"I hate her, too," yelled out another demon.

"She is a pain in the dark area," agreed the prince. "We all hate her. Now shut up. We have work to do. Where was I? Yes. You kidnapped Sharon. Certainly we can all agree that the darkness would be a much better place without Sharon. But unfortunately this only pushed your worm into deep prayer." The prince looked at the audience. He spread his hands before him. "So instead of breaking this son of Adam, you gave him reason to seek God as never before. Brilliant plan!

"These chains. These were our secret weapons. You knew that as long as he lived in unforgiveness, he was blocked from God's grand plan for his life. But *Mighty, Mighty* Bashnar, what did you do? You punished the man so much that he ran to the light. How can we keep people in darkness if we chase them to the light?"

"What would you have us do, great prince? Leave them alone?" said Bashnar.

"I agree. It's a bad position to be in. Damned if we do this. Damned if we do that. Terrible predicament." The prince stretched his neck forward. He jabbed his finger as he spoke. "But knowing our predicament, you failed to take precaution. You were so intent on destroying Edwin that you overlooked the obvious."

"What would that be, great prince?"

"The obvious reasons, Mighty Bashnar—and there are two—is that for some fiendish reason our enemy takes pleasure in using the weakest of his vile dogs to bring him the greatest glory." Something exploded inside of the prince. He slammed his fist on the table. "Have we learned nothing from the death and resurrection of the Lord? Was he not at his weakest on the cross? Did we not celebrate and dance and exchange gifts when he died? And how long did our party last? Have you forgotten, Mighty Bashnar? It didn't even last three full days?"

The crowded room was deathly silent. The prince was known for his cool. So this display of anger was magnified.

"Mighty Bashnar, I believe you have sullied the *mighty* title," said the prince.

So this is what this is about? You want me to be stripped of my title. The Mighty Bashnar looked at the two chains with their attached balls of metal. They could be formidable weapons.

A demon followed the warrior spirit's eyes. He motioned to a large demon who hurried to the chains and dragged them away.

The prince continued. "I believe you have been used by the God of heaven to strengthen those whom you promised to destroy."

The room erupted in chatter. The prince did nothing to stop the talk. This was good for the broadcast. He let the talk go on until he saw that it apparently wasn't going to die down on its own. "Order. Order," he said nonchalantly. "Order," he said a little more forcefully. "We must face the cruel facts. The man Edwin is not the worm he used to be. He has grown up. He's no longer splicing and dicing the

Bible and choosing which parts to believe, which parts to reject. He has even forgiven the man who molested him." The prince shook his finger at the audience. "This kind of forgiveness can be our undoing.

"And Sharon. You did succeed in getting Rob to kidnap her. But then what? What did you do once you had her?" Prince Krioni looked at the audience. He lifted his fingers and mimicked his point. "You pinched her."

The demons roared in laughter. This is what the prince wanted. He wanted this arrogant, proud warrior spirit humiliated in front of the entire dark kingdom.

"Now to be fair—and we're all about being fair—your killer wasn't able to kill Sharon, but you do still have her. Where is she, Mighty Bashnar?"

"She is my prisoner. I have her locked in a room near a private airport. I am using Michael Bogarti."

The prince looked around the room nodding his approval. "Michael Bogarti is a good man. What have you done to the girl?"

"She has been beaten."

"Beaten?"

"Several times," said Bashnar.

"Michael Bogarti runs several of our sex slavery businesses. Am I right?"

The Mighty Bashnar looked at the prince. His eyes fought to turn black. "You are correct."

"So I'm sure the young girl has been violated." The prince pretended to look at some papers.

"No."

The prince dropped the papers to his desk for effect. "No? I'm sorry, Mighty Bashnar. You did say that you and Michael Bogarti have Sharon locked in a room. But she has not been violated?"

"Yes, we have the girl. No, she has not been violated."

"This is unbelievable, Mighty Bashnar. Why in darkness has she not been violated?" Prince Krioni looked at the audience. "If we can't violate a girl who is in the custody of our sex slavery people, when can we violate her?"

The Mighty Bashnar heard the audience behind him laugh. He knew that this same laughter was happening throughout the world wherever demons were watching. It was almost worth it to rush the prince. But he had little chance without a weapon.

He read something. "I'm sorry, Mighty Bashnar. I overlooked something. It says here that you, and I quote, 'spanked her booty.'"

Demons howled with laughter as though they were in a comedy club. The prince, himself, tried unsuccessfully to contain his laughter.

The Mighty Bashnar tried to ignore the laughter, but this was impossible. The laughter wouldn't go away. When it seemed to die down, another demon would burst out in hideous cackling. Then another would join, until the whole room was on the laughter train all over again. The warrior spirit swore to himself that even if he died trying, he would murder this prince.

The prince lifted both hands to the audience. "Please, please, let's not laugh at the Mighty Bashnar. This is a tough booty. I'm sorry. I meant to say it's a tough business."

A demon directly behind the warrior spirit and separated by only ten feet of open space and one row of seats screeched with laughter until it seemed his lungs would burst.

It happened too fast for anyone to respond until it was too late.

The Mighty Bashnar turned and flew through the air, knocking down two castle guards. He landed on the laughing demon and smashed his face with a powerful fist. This put the demon to sleep. The warrior spirit stretched his hands. Long claws jutted out. He roared in fury as his hands feverishly ripped the flesh from the demon's face and throat. That's what the warrior spirit was after. *His throat.*

The Mighty Bashnar yanked the disrespectful demon's neck bone out. He looked at the mound of flesh and bone in his hand. He then looked at the horrified audience that was now within his reach.

A club smashed into the Mighty Bashnar's skull. He woke up in chains, seated before the prince.

"Forgive us for the chains, Mighty Bashnar, but we can't allow you to dismember every disrespectful demon. You've made your point, I suppose."

The Mighty Bashnar was chained, but he felt better now. Everyone in the dark kingdom had seen him protect his honor. *How could he have ever been accepted in the presence of another warrior spirit had he not done so?*

"We left off with Sharon before—oh, forget it. You say she is your prisoner, but I wonder who is the prisoner. She is in our custody, but the worst thing to happen to her is she has been beaten. I read here that not only has she not been violated, she's clothed. How can we have her in such a vulnerable state and she sits there in her room fully clothed and untouched?"

"The enemy has not honored the agreement," answered the Mighty Bashnar.

"Since you brought it up, let me be the first to inform you that your authorization was revoked."

The warrior spirit knew that his special permission wasn't indefinite. But this news came as a shock. "When did this happen?" asked Bashnar.

The prince frowned. "Does it matter? Does it matter one bit whether it was two o'clock or three o'clock? It's over. It's been revoked. Here's what matters *Mighty* Bashnar. It happened within minutes of Edwin forgiving his uncle. Do you now see why I believe heaven owes you a paycheck? You've been working for them for the past week."

The warrior spirit was reeling from having the rug pulled from under his *Job Strategy*. He couldn't deny the prince's charges no matter how humiliating it was to admit that his idea to destroy his enemies was really God's idea. God had used him to drive his people to him.

"I see it in your face, Mighty Bashnar. You see now. Edwin was weak; now he's strong. Sharon is in prison, but she's infecting everyone there with that hideous love and forgiveness of hers. Andrew was just another inconsequential Christian teenager. We were going to get him later on. Now, honestly, he could turn into another Sharon—oh, my darkness. Barbara...well, Barbara was Barbara. Now what do we have? Even she has entered forgiveness. What do you think the enemy is going to do with her? Well, we'll all be around to see it, won't we?

"Aahh, our favorite dagger, Jonathan. He was a terror before this *Job Strategy* fiasco. What do you think he's going to be now? You and your pig debacle! Elizabeth. She had idolatry in her heart before the *Job Strategy*. Guess what? She doesn't any more. Then there's Vivian."

The prince looked at the audience. "Our own Vivian! How could such a thing happen? Before I answer that, let me give you the whole picture. Not only has Vivian turned on us, but what about Alex? And Jeff and Billy? Do we see a trend here? All of these people came into contact with the presence and power of God because of one thing. One thing, Mighty Bashnar."

The prince looked out into the audience and asked rhetorically, "Anyone know what that one thing is? Oh, no one? Allow me. *J-o-b Str-te-gy.* The enemy has used you to perfect his people through trials by fire. That was the second obvious thing you overlooked. *Things we design for evil, God is able to use for his own purposes.*"

The prince gathered his papers into one folder. "Based upon the evidence I have presented, the council will vote on whether or not to request of the father of darkness that you be stripped of your *Mighty* title."

The Mighty Bashnar knew this was coming. Yet it still shocked him to hear the thought spoken. When would the council meet again to vote? *Maybe I can do something between now and then to prevent this vote? Or at least to persuade our father to reject this humiliation.*

"How do you vote?" said Prince Krioni. "Yea, to request the Mighty Bashnar be stripped. Nay, if he is to keep his title."

The Mighty Bashnar's shock increased. They were voting *now*?

"Destruction?"

"Yea."

"Chaos?"

"Yea."

"Hades?"

"Yea."

There was only one vote left. Ordinarily, council matters required only three votes to do something. But a request to have the *mighty* title taken from him required five. The only vote left was that of his friend Crucifix.

"Crucifix?"

Crucifix answered without hesitation. "Yea."

The Mighty Bashnar was having the closest thing to a panic attack a demon could have. He heard something like a train's horn blaring in his ears. He fought to remember where he was. The floor beneath him started moving. He held tightly to the arms of the chair to keep from falling.

The prince stood up. "Mighty Bashnar, are you okay? You look faint."

The famed warrior spirit didn't answer. He heard the prince's words, but they were indecipherable.

The prince looked at him with a smirk. "I wanted to ask you when you entered my chamber, but I felt it would have been inappropriate. But now that the meeting is over. What happened to you? You're sliced every which way. You didn't tangle with the fire angel, did you?"

"Fire angel," the Mighty Bashnar mumbled.

"I thought so," said the prince. "Only you would stay to fight the fire angel. You were probably intrigued when you saw him. He is a fascinating angel. Fire. Swords coming out of his mouth. Great warrior spirit, do you know why that particular angel is so intriguing?"

The Mighty Bashnar tried to stop the confusion and focus.

"That's no angel. It's the Lord. I would suggest the next time you run into an angel of fire with a sword coming out of his mouth that you go in the other direction. Oh, when you leave here, you may want to catch up with Edwin and Jonathan and try to salvage what you can. They have terrible things planned for this evening."

Chapter 38

Vivian sat, seriously pondering something she would have considered utterly ridiculous only a week ago. Miracles were for Hollywood, the gullible, and those either already in psychiatric hospitals or on their way. But so much had happened since she had gone to that charismatic church—her research gave her this name—that she could no longer relegate such things to only foolish or deranged minds, unless she was admitting to being one of the two.

If Vivian was nothing else, she was as she had been told all her life by grade school teachers and university professors. She was exceptionally bright. She not only had a sharp memory. She had an understanding mind. As one professor told her, "You think top-bottom and bottom-top."

That was his way of saying she had great deductive and inductive reasoning skills. She could start with a big observation and determine how this big fact affected the little facts. Or she could start with the little facts and let them steer her to the big fact. According to Dr. Philyaw, some people had one predisposition or the other, or perhaps an unimpressive mixture. But she was one of those rare ones who excelled "top-bottom and bottom-top."

Vivian had been doing a lot of bottom-top thinking. All of the little things—but they really were big in their affect—that had happened since Sunday had pushed her to one inevitable conclusion.

Jesus Christ was alive and more accessible than she had ever dreamed.

One little thing was that something had told her to go to that strange church.

Another little thing was that that young girl had told her things about herself she could not have possibly known without God telling her.

Another little thing was that when the preacher put his hand close to her forehead, she had felt a bolt of power surge into her body and knock her down.

Another exceptional little thing—if she could call it that—was the video of what happened to her as she was on the floor. *What bizarre behavior and contortions. Why had she slid like a snake? Why did her tongue shoot in and out of her mouth like that? Why did she roll around on the floor?*

Another little thing was that from that day until now, she had been speaking in some unknown language when she was alone. She knew it was a language. It had all the characteristics of one. Although she had no idea what language it could possibly be. One thing was certain, however. *It was lovely and deeply satisfying.*

Another little thing was there were still unexpected surges of energy that shot through her body. Sometimes it caused her to jerk.

Another little thing was there was an inexplicable joy deep in her heart. She—and a few of their girls—had discovered her smiling widely at them. Prior to the past Sunday, Mrs. Bogarti was definitely not known for smiling at or around the girls.

It was something linked to this last little thing that led Vivian to think about asking God to heal her daughter. It wasn't cancer or muscular dystrophy or spinal bifida, but it was something that no five-year-old girl should have to live with. It was amblyopia. Better known as lazy eye.

Their precious Priscilla was perfect in every way. She was beautiful, playful, and smart. Her features were keen, like her mother's. Her face looked as though it were sculpted rather than grown. Her hair was dark and lovely and long. It bounced when she ran. She was nearly always radiant.

Nearly always.

Amblyopia was called lazy eye because of how the condition affected the appearance of the eye. The nerve pathways between Priscilla's left eye and her brain were not adequately stimulated. This caused her brain to favor the right eye. The result was the little angel's left eye appeared *lazy.* And worse, it wandered.

The doctor's remedy was for Priscilla to stimulate the weak eye by wearing a patch over her strong eye at least four hours a day. There was no medical reason to believe this treatment would not succeed. However, each time Priscilla put the patch on, something happened to her little spirit. She said she felt like an ugly pirate.

Her radiance turned dim whenever the patch was on, and was not restored until it came off. Vivian's heart was pierced every day that Priscilla called herself ugly. *That* was every day. And her sense of being ugly soared whenever she was around other little girls. This posed an especially acute problem, since Priscilla had so many beautiful little friends and girl cousins. *Her little girl should not have to bear such a problem at this young age.* Maybe she didn't have to.

Vivian thought about the irony of her conversation with *Lollipop,* birth name, Crystal Madison. Crystal had danced for them for a few years. Yet Vivian hadn't spoken more than a dozen words to her in all that time, and she certainly had never smiled at her. But when Vivian had seen her late the night before, she had an irresistible urge to smile widely at her and stroke her arm.

This small act caused the girl to break down in tears. Crystal told her that she had visited a church a few times. Her last two visits were because of what happened on her first visit. One of their preachers, a guy named Jonathan Banks, called her out of the audience and told her some things about herself that he couldn't have known.

He also told her to tell her mother to immediately have her breasts examined. He said the devil was trying to kill her mom, but that if she went to the doctor now, they could stop the cancer. Even though her mother had just had an examination a few months prior, she went to the doctor. They found the cancer. This was a fascinating story, but it was what Crystal said next that gave her hope for her little girl.

Crystal talked to the preacher afterward and told him that her roommate was really sick. She asked him to remember her in prayer. The preacher surprised her by telling her that her roommate's name was Joy, and that she was her lesbian lover. He also surprised her by offering to go to her apartment to pray for her girlfriend. The preacher and his wife went to Crystal's apartment that night.

Crystal disclosed to Vivian the reason she started crying when she smiled at her and rubbed her arm was because she had had two vivid dreams about her. In both, she was told to share this story with her. She had been afraid to approach her because she was known to be so professional and aloof.

When Crystal shared this story with her, Vivian asked, "This preacher came to your house to pray for *your female lover*? What kind of preacher would do that?"

"Yeah, and what kind of God would pick a lesbian out of a crowd and tell her to warn her mother that the doctors had missed a cancer in her breast?"

This story caused Vivian to ask Crystal a question that she had been asking herself since Sunday. "How does this encounter with God affect your dancing?"

"Mrs. Bogarti, I've thought about it. The money's too good to give up. There's nowhere else I can make this kind of money. I guess I'm greedy. Maybe when I'm older."

Vivian appreciated *Lollipop's* honesty. "Let's hope you live long enough to get older." Vivian was surprised at the spontaneous statement which came out of her mouth like a galloping horse with no rider.

This recollection brought her again to the same crossroads that had left her literally trembling several times since Sunday. *What was she going to do with this new God of hers?* There was no way she could serve God and continue to make a living selling sexual lust.

Vivian battled away from those troubling thoughts and focused on another troubling thought. Priscilla's lazy eye. Would this preacher be willing to pray for her daughter?

*****

This had only happened to Jonathan two times in his entire ministry. Now it had happened twice more in two days. He knew that supernatural transportation was written about in the Bible.

Enoch was transported from earth to heaven. Elijah had supernaturally outrun a chariot. Plus, he was later transported to heaven in a chariot of fire. Ezekiel had been transported a couple of times, maybe more. Philip the evangelist baptized a guy and came up out of the water in another city.

Jonathan knew all of this. But knowing something and experiencing it were two different things. There was no way to get used to being stuffed in a trunk, and watching the trunk open and looking into the face of an angel and being led off to freedom the way Peter had been freed from prison in the book of Acts. Nor could he get used to being in one place one moment and blinking his eye or taking a step and being in another place the next moment.

Jonathan looked around. Well, at least the Holy Spirit had dropped him off in an affluent neighborhood. He looked behind him. Beautiful, huge homes. He turned back around. Same thing.

Guess I'll just walk in the direction I landed, he thought. He walked past two homes. When he got to the third, he heard, "Here."

"Well, at least they'll know I'm not a Jehovah's Witness."

*****

The nanny looked at the monitor. A man stood outside the high gate. "Yes?"

"My name is Jonathan Banks."

"Good evening, Mr. Banks. How may I assist you?"

"I'm here to see someone."

"Who are you here to see, Mr. Banks?"

Nice accent, thought Jonathan. "I haven't the faintest idea. But it has something to do with Sharon Styles."

Hazel looked at the smiling, waving man. She pushed a couple of buttons on the high-tech monitor system.

"Vivian, there's a man at the gate who says he doesn't know who he is here to see. However, he says his name is Jonathan Banks, and it has something to do with Sharon Styles."

Another little thing. No, actually a big thing.

Vivian snapped out of her momentary shock. "Let him in, Hazel. Oh, has Priscilla had her bath yet?"

"Yes."

"Don't put her to bed just yet. Mr. Banks is a preacher. He's here to pray for Priscilla."

Vivian continued to sit. She needed to give herself a few minutes to ponder these strange occurrences. She looked out of the huge window into the darkness. The trees offered no explanations.

Jonathan was ushered by the nanny into a large, formal living room. He and she sat. They exchanged small talk until Vivian entered the room.

Jonathan stood.

Vivian extended her hand with a cordial smile. "Reverend Banks, welcome to our home. It's a pleasure and a surprise to meet you."

Hazel looked at Vivian and got the nod. She left the room.

Jonathan shook her hand. "My pleasure, Mrs..."

"Bogarti."

Lord, tell me You did not do this to me? "Bogarti?"

Vivian gently pulled her hand.

"Oh, I'm sorry," said Jonathan. *Probably not a good idea to ask you if your husband is here,* he thought.

She smiled politely. "Please be seated, Reverend Banks."

They both sat.

"I go by Jonathan," he said with a smile.

She looked at him with an inquisitive, gender-neutral smile.

Okaaay, and I can call you Mrs. Bogarti, he thought. "You said you were surprised to meet me. You were *expecting* me?"

"I was not expecting you, but coincidentally I was thinking of you just when you rang the doorbell."

"You were thinking of me?"

"Reverend Banks—"

"Jonathan, please."

Vivian smiled. "Jonathan, you don't know *why* you're here?"

"No. But I'm sure I'll know shortly."

"Hmp. I've never heard of such a thing."

"I think it's the company I keep," he said.

She turned her head.

"Nothing. It's just that God has an incredible sense of humor."

She had no idea what he was talking about.

"Mrs. Bogarti, how do you know me?"

Jonathan's question made her feel better. It was concrete. Something that could move them past this awkwardness. "One of our employees told me that she visited your church."

"I don't have a church, but I speak at a lot of churches. Which one did she see me at?"

"Glory Tabernacle."

Jonathan smiled. "Edwin. He's a good friend of mine. He's the pastor there."

"Do you recall speaking to a Crystal Madison?"

"Lollipop," said Jonathan.

This had the effect of someone tapping on a car brake too hard. It jolted Vivian slightly. Jonathan saw that it kind of threw her.

"All the girls have stage names," said Jonathan.

This preacher was peculiar. "Yes, they do."

"Lollipop fits better than Crystal," he said.

Vivian looked at this preacher, not knowing what to make of him.

"I mean for the business she's in," he added.

"The business she's in, it doesn't bother you?" asked Vivian.

"It bothers me a lot."

"And yet you went to her apartment to pray for her girlfriend. Why?"

"She was sick," replied Jonathan.

"But *why* did you go?"

"Oh," Jonathan chuckled. "Mrs. Bogarti, you mean why did I go to the home of Lollipop the stripper to pray for her sick, lesbian lover?"

"Yes, that is precisely what I mean."

"I'll explain this to you over a glass of tea."

"Pardon?"

"You look like the kind of woman who would have *Oolong* tea."

Vivian didn't smile outwardly, but she found she wasn't offended by this man's forwardness. "I do have *Oolong* tea."

"You probably have *Ginseng*, also."

"Yes. I have an assortment of white, green, and black teas."

Jonathan smiled and motioned with his hand. "Lead the way."

They went to the kitchen and drank tea and talked for half an hour. Vivian found this man deeply intriguing. One moment he was witty and light. The next he was blunt and serious. He weaved in and out effortlessly.

"And where is your daughter?" asked Jonathan.

By now Vivian's reserve and arm's length cordiality had been breached. The man sitting at her table was no longer a strange stranger. He was the preacher who had been sent by God to pray for her daughter. "I'll get her," she said, with excitement in her voice.

Hazel entered the kitchen holding Priscilla's hand.

Jonathan looked at her and gushed. "Oh, aren't you a precious little girl."

Priscilla put up her little hand and bent her fingers back and forth several times in a wave.

"Say, hi Reverend Banks."

The little girl smiled widely and said, "Hi, Jonathan."

"You know me," said a smiling Jonathan.

Vivian looked at Hazel. "You told her Reverend Banks' first name?"

"No," she answered.

"Then how does she know it?" Vivian thought out loud.

Priscilla ran to Jonathan and hugged him. "The angel told me his name."

Vivian had never seen her daughter hug a stranger. She didn't stop her. She looked at Hazel, then at her daughter. "You saw an angel?"

The little girl shook her head.

"When baby?"

"Last night when I went to bed."

"You had a dream?"

"No. I wasn't asleep. The angel tucked me in and said a man named Jonathan was going to come and talk to Mommy so that God could fix my eye. That's why I'm happy."

Jonathan looked at Vivian and smiled.

She returned the smile with a hand over her mouth. Her dark eyes held water.

Jonathan held Priscilla's face in his hands. "I'm going to ask you a very serious question, okay?"

The child nodded her head.

"Did the angel call me fat?"

Priscilla laughed. "No," her little voice peaked.

"Are you sure? He didn't say anything about me being overweight?"

"No, Jonathan," she answered again with a long laugh.

"Well, probably because I've been fasting the past few days. Me and your mommy will talk, okay?"

"Okay," said Priscilla.

"Do you think she really saw an angel?" asked Vivian.

"I'm sure she did," said Jonathan. He looked up at Vivian. "Before we talk any more about your angel, I need to talk to you about my friend's angel. She's missing. Her name is Sharon."

Chapter 39

"Mrs. Bogarti, I believe the Lord sent me here for more than one reason."

"You do? Oh, I'm sorry, Jonathan. Where are my manners? Please call me Vivian."

Jonathan smiled. "Your manners are as impeccable as your tea. Thank you, Vivian." He sipped his tea. "My friend, Edwin. His daughter, Sharon, is missing. She didn't come home last night. She's seventeen. We think something bad has happened to her."

Vivian's face showed motherly concern. She didn't know what to say. Her heart raced to her own children—especially Priscilla. If something happened to her, she'd die. "I'm sorry, Jonathan. Have the police—?" She stopped and thought. "Hazel said you were here to talk to me about Sharon Styles. This is the preacher's daughter. Why would you want to talk to *me* about her?"

Vivian's attention was diverted. She listened. "Mike, is that you?" she called out. "Excuse me, Jonathan. That sounds like my husband."

"I'll be here enjoying my tea," he said.

She left the kitchen.

"Lord, this would be a most opportune time to do that little thingy You do. You know, the *I Dream of Jeannie* thing." Jonathan listened as intently as he could. He couldn't make out what they were saying, but then it went dead silent. "Okaaay, I think I know what that means," he said.

Michael Bogarti walked slowly into the kitchen, behind his wife.

"Mike, this is Jonathan. He's one of the preachers at the church I visited last Sunday."

Jonathan smiled and stood with his hand extended.

Mike's hand didn't come up immediately.

Vivian noticed.

Michael noticed that his wife noticed. He raised his hand and shook. "Nice to meet you." He looked at his wife. "I thought I recognized his face."

"I'm sure you have. I get around." Jonathan sat down.

Vivian asked Michael if he wanted tea. He didn't hear her. Only his eyes were working now. Seated at his table in his house drinking his tea and being served by his wife was the man he had been trying to kill.

"Mike?" said Vivian.

"The tea's delicious," said Jonathan to Michael. "I've already had the jasmine *Oolong* and the *Golden Monkey* black tea."

Michael's back was to his wife. He wanted to look directly into this arrogant preacher's eyes. He wanted him to look into his eyes and see that he was dead. He couldn't because the guy was so caught up in his tea. He gave the suicidal tea sipper a hard half-smile, half-grin. "You like *Golden Monkey*? Think I'll have some."

"I also like *Pig in a Trunk*. What about you, Mike? You ever had *Pig in a Trunk*?"

"That's an odd name for a tea," said Vivian.

"It's rare. A backwoods concoction. Some folks would kill for it, though. I guarantee you, Mike. If you ever have it, you'll never forget it." Jonathan drank the last of his tea. "But, Vivian, I'd choose your *Golden Monkey* over two pigs in a trunk."

Michael wondered whether his hatred was seeping through his façade. Vivian knew him so well.

Vivian smiled. "I'm normally impervious to flattery, Jonathan."

"Well, for good reason. The world is so full of hypocrisy," said Jonathan, looking at Michael.

"Yes, it is," she said, putting Michael's tea on the table.

They all sat around the table.

"Mr. Bogarti, the Lord sent me here tonight. I'm still sorting out why. I think I've got most of it, but knowing the Lord, there's probably a surprise or two in store for me." He looked at Michael. "And probably for you. Both of you."

Michael didn't want his tea, but he sipped it. Vivian was exceptionally perceptive. She'd pick up on the slightest oddity. "Oh, why's that?"

"Before you got home, I was just about to explain to your wife why I came to her for help."

"What kind of help?" asked Michael.

"A missing girl. A girl named Sharon. She's my friend's daughter and my adopted niece. She's a wonderful human being. The godliest young person I've ever had the pleasure of knowing. And now she's gone."

"That's terrible, but how does this involve Vivian?" Michael asked.

He was straining to keep his cool. How much did this preacher know? What did he want? Was he here to tell Vivian whatever it was that he knew or thought he knew? It didn't make a difference whether this preacher had all the facts or not. If he accused him of taking Sharon or of being involved in sex trafficking, he could never prove it.

Michael cursed in his mind. *He doesn't have to prove it!* The accusation itself would be enough to cause suspicion in his wife. Vivian wasn't one of those women who believed the best about her man until forced by overwhelming facts to face the truth. She knew he was greedy. She knew he was an extortionist. She knew he was a murderer. She knew he was an adulterer. It would not be difficult for her to believe he was also a kidnapper and sex trafficker.

"The past few days have been terrible for us. It all started when that mansion place was raided," said Jonathan.

Michael looked puzzled. "What mansion?"

"The one with the girls," he said.

"The girls?" he muttered, looking at Vivian for help. He started nodding his head. "Yeah...yeah, the prostitution place." He looked at Vivian. "You remember. We saw it on television."

"I remember. What does that have to do with you, Jonathan?" asked Vivian.

Michael felt sweat dripping from his armpits down both sides. He knew he couldn't take his suit jacket off. He even felt sweat dripping down the back of his head onto his neck. Thank God, none had dripped down his face.

"I'm involved in some efforts to stop sex trafficking. I also work with some people who rescue girls from their pimps."

"You do that kind of work?" said Vivian.

Jonathan was surprised at the sudden light in her face. Why would a woman in her business be giddy about someone who fought sex trafficking?

"I do all kinds of work, Vivian. Anything that helps God and hurts the devil."

"That's got to be dangerous," said Vivian.

"Very," said Jonathan. "Since that mansion came down, someone broke into our home and tried to kill us."

Vivian was shocked.

"God protected us," he said, looking at Michael. "The guy's in jail. But then I guess the Lord saw I was bored. I went off somewhere to pray. A couple of guys kidnapped me. They were planning to kill me," Jonathan looked at Michael, "but the Lord protected me. I got away."

"How'd you get away?" said Michael.

"Have you told the police?" asked Vivian.

"No, I haven't. God's got this thing under control. I've been in worse situations." Jonathan looked at Michael. "I think He has taken a special interest in going after whoever is after me and my friends."

"That's interesting," said Michael.

"It'll be even more interesting to see how God finishes this guy off," said Jonathan.

"And Sharon?" said Michael.

"I believe whoever is after me has Sharon."

"Why do you think so?" asked Michael.

"Vivian, you've got to hear this." Jonathan looked at Vivian and Michael as though he were about to share a secret. His voice was low. "A few days ago someone broke into Sharon's home and trashed it while they were at church. Later that night a guy called and told Edwin to mind his own business. To make sure they made their point, these people tacked a picture of Edwin's dead three-year-old son's grave to his door. Edwin and Sharon went to the cemetery. Guess what they found?"

"What?" asked Vivian.

"Someone had dug up their son's bones and laid them next to the grave."

Vivian gasped and put her hand to her mouth.

"What kind of people would do something like this?" Jonathan asked.

"That's sick," said Michael. "I've never heard of anything like it before. I think you should call the police. Somebody who would do that would kill your friend's daughter. I mean if the two are related."

Michael's words stilled Jonathan. He looked at his would-be killer as innocently as possible. "You think Sharon's life is in danger? You think they'll kill her?"

"Hopefully, she's still alive. But anyone who would dig up a little boy's body to send a message is sending a pretty serious message. You probably don't want to do anything else to antagonize these people. Keep things low key. You don't want them to smuggle her out of the country. Or worse, kill her. These people sound like they'll do *anything?*"

"They do, don't they?" asked Jonathan.

"I think Mike's right," said Vivian.

Jonathan looked at her. "It's just hard to do nothing." He smiled. "She's a remarkable young lady."

"Mike, she's the one who pulled me out of the congregation. She's the one who told me to forgive my sister." Vivian communicated the rest with her eyes.

Michael could hardly believe his ears. *The girl he had locked up was the one who had told his wife to forgive him and his sister.* The business jungle wasn't fair. It was a shame that the girl who had gotten him back in the sack with his wife had to pay the price because her folks had stuck their noses in his business. *But business was business. She had to pay.*

"Jonathan, I'm certainly available to help." Vivian opened her palms. "I don't see how, though."

"Maybe there's a way," he said.

"Anything," said Vivian.

"Your business...." said Jonathan.

"Yes?" answered Michael.

"People know people who know people. Maybe someone has heard or seen something. You never know. You think it would be possible to show a picture of Sharon to your girls? It's a longshot, I know."

Vivian answered eagerly. "Yes, we can do that."

Michael let out a long, slow, simmering breath. "Sure."

"Listen," said Vivian, "let's move into another room. I'm going to go get the children and let them say good night to Daddy. We'll take care of Priscilla, and let Hazel tidy up the kitchen."

She led the men into a room, closed the door, and went upstairs.

*****

Michael Bogarti. Extortionist. Sex trafficker. Murderer.

Jonathan Banks. Miracle-worker. Prophet. Preacher.

The men's eyes locked.

"We have a problem," said Mr. Bogarti.

"A problem you can fix," said Jonathan.

"Look, I don't know how much time we have before my wife comes back downstairs. So I'm going to make it clear for you."

"I wish you would," said Jonathan.

"You say one thing to Vivian about me having anything to do with *The Mansion* or Sharon and she's dead. Is that clear enough for you?"

"No, Mike, it isn't. You're obviously better at kidnapping and selling little girls than you are at making yourself clear. Who's dead? Sharon or your wife?"

Mr. Bogarti raised his finger, held it for a moment, then waved it at Jonathan. His eyes were tight with murder. "That smart mouth of yours. I don't know how you got out of that trunk, preacher, but you better be glad you did."

"What did I miss, Mr. Bogarti?"

"You missed me cutting out your fat tongue."

"But I didn't miss you murdering your own men."

Michael froze momentarily. He thought for a second. "You were there. You had to be."

"More like God was there," said Jonathan.

"God!" spewed Mr. Bogarti. "You and this God—"

"He's complicated things, hasn't He?" Jonathan jumped in. "Seems like your wife has taken a liking to Him. That probably came as a surprise to you. I know I'm surprised."

Michael peered at Jonathan with a pointed finger. "Preacher, if you ever...*ever* want your preacher friend to see his daughter alive again, you better hope Vivian never finds out anything about me and my other businesses."

"And what if she does? I know, she finds out and Sharon's dead. But what about *her?* She's not like you. You're a reprobate, depraved scoundrel, marked for eternal damnation. You and your money are going to hell. But Vivian has found God. She'll never go along with sex trafficking. Matter of fact, not only would she not go along with it. I think she'd divorce you. What do you think, Mike?"

Mr. Bogarti stared at Jonathan. He reached into his inside holster and pulled out a gun. He tapped his open palm with it. "I swear to

God, preacher, I will kill you, your wife Elizabeth, Edwin, Barbara, Sharon, Andrew—"

"Must've touched a nerve," said Jonathan.

Mr. Bogarti put his gun back. He needed to keep his cool. He couldn't have Vivian walking in and seeing him sitting there with his gun out.

"You'd lose the children," said Jonathan.

"Shut up," said Mr. Bogarti. "Nobody's taking my kids."

"This life of sin. This love of money. You're willing to choose it over Vivian? Over your children? You have a beautiful family. You're already rich. Why don't you stop? Just stop right now. Walk away from it."

Mr. Bogarti looked at Jonathan with contempt. "Just walk away? Give everything I worked for to someone else?"

"Mr. Bogarti, let the girls go. Every girl you've got locked up in some hell hole, let them go." A picture so faint it was nearly indiscernible appeared in the back of Jonathan's mind. He looked oddly at Mr. Bogarti. "I just saw Pharaoh. You're Pharaoh. You're a vessel of destruction, chosen to fight against the Almighty for His glory."

"What?" spat Mr. Bogarti.

"Your whole kingdom is coming down," Mr. Bogarti. "You're going to lose everything. Your wife. Your children. Your—"

"I swear, I'll kill anybody who tries to take my kids."

"Your wife just wants to serve God, Mr. Bogarti."

Michael leaned forward in his chair. "You like clarity. I will make this so clear that even you can understand it. Nobody's taking my kids from me. If you care anything about Sharon, if you care anything about Vivian, if you care anything about anybody, you will keep your mouth shut."

Jonathan pushed back in his chair.

Michael pushed back in his chair.

"We still have a problem," said Jonathan. "A problem you can fix."

Michael said nothing. He had said too much to this preacher already. At the appropriate time, he'd give this fool a crystal clear communication. A bullet in his hollow head.

"You've kidnapped God's little girl. He wants her back."

Mr. Bogarti's eyes were ice. "Tell him to come get her."

"Your judgment has come out of your own mouth," said Jonathan. "God is going to give you a sign that He rules in the affairs of men."

Michael's expression was dark. His lip turned up in disgust.

"I walked here, Mr. Bogarti. I don't have transportation home. Would you be so kind as to ask a couple of your men to give me a ride? Vivian doesn't need to know about your kindness."

The darkness left Michael's face like a fast receding shadow.

"Jesus Christ died for your sins, Mr. Bogarti. He sacrificed Himself that others may live. That you may live. The Lord wants me to demonstrate this love to you so you will have no excuse when you stand before Him on Judgment Day."

"What do you have in mind?" asked Mr. Bogarti.

"Simple. A life for a life. I give you my life for Sharon's life. It's what the Lord did for you."

"A trade. How would this work. I release Sharon, then you get in the car? I don't think so, preacher."

"I do like that idea, but I can see why you wouldn't be a fan of it," said Jonathan. "Here's what you're going to do. You're going to get Sharon on that phone before your wife comes back. If this doesn't happen, deals off."

Michael could've screamed. Oh, how he wanted to blow this preacher's brains out. That would come soon enough. He pondered the offer.

"Vivian's been gone a while. She should be back any moment with those precious children of yours."

Michael snatched out his phone. He looked angrily at Jonathan as he spoke into the phone. "Now! Right now, Alex! Get that girl to the phone."

Within two tension-filled minutes, Sharon was on the phone. Mr. Bogarti thrust it out to Jonathan.

Jonathan snatched it. "Sharon?"

"Jonathan? Oh, Jonathan!" Sharon screeched in shock.

"Are you okay?"

"No, Jonathan," she cried. "This place—this place—what they do to the girls."

"What about you?" Jonathan asked anxiously.

"They beat me, Jonathan. They beat me over and over." She sounded pitiful and afraid.

"Give me my phone," Mr. Bogarti demanded with a curse word.

"Sharon, keep praying." Jonathan looked into Mr. Bogarti's eyes. "Your heavenly Father is coming for you." He handed the phone over.

Mr. Bogarti hung the phone up and stuffed it in his pocket. He opened the door.

Both men sat down and stared at one another while they waited for Vivian. It was still a good while before they heard the children approaching.

Jonathan watched Mr. Bogarti hug two of his children. He was either a wonderful actor or he loved those kids. He hugged and kissed them like he was about to go off to war. And they loved their daddy. For some reason, Mr. Bogarti didn't introduce him to his children.

"Where's your mom?" he asked his son.

"She's sick. I think she threw up, Dad."

Mr. Bogarti looked at Jonathan as though it was his fault. He kissed his son on top of his head. "Tell your mom I'll be right up."

His son and older daughter walked out as Priscilla walked in. Jonathan watched in amazement as this murderous pimp's face lit up when he saw his daughter. She looked at him and smiled and put her head down and shuffled a few steps without lifting her feet. She wore angel pajamas.

Mr. Bogarti opened his arms. "Come here, baby."

Priscilla smiled by pushing down hard on her little lips. Suddenly, she took off running and landed in Jonathan's lap.

"Ohhhh, what have we here?" said Jonathan. "You're an angel."

Mr. Bogarti had never experienced anything like this moment in his life. It was akin to being raped. He watched this man hug his daughter and put those big lips on her forehead. He saw himself pointing his gun at this man and emptying his magazine. That moment would never come soon enough, but it was coming.

Jonathan looked at Mr. Bogarti and smiled. "Kids, they love me." He looked at the little girl and whispered in her ear. "I think the angel's going to come back soon and fix your eye."

Michael appeared to be about two seconds away from biting through Jonathan's clothing and eating his heart. Jonathan had seen (and experienced) looks like this before. This was a wonderful time to defuse the situation. "Don't you have a phone call to make?"

Michael snatched his phone out and gladly made the call. Two of his best killers were on the way to show Jonathan Banks some serious kindness.

*****

Mr. Bogarti walked his guest to the door and onto the porch. He looked at him coldly. "My men are parked on the street."

"You're not going to let her go, are you?" asked Jonathan.

"If you believed that, you wouldn't get in the car. Why would you sacrifice yourself if you thought I was going to double-cross you?"

"I'm getting in the car because God told me to, Mr. Bogarti. Besides, I told you God wants you to see His love in action so you'll have no excuse when you bust hell wide open."

"Why are you giving your life for this girl? You screwing her?"

"I'm giving my life because Jesus gave me His life," said Jonathan.

"I see," said Mr. Bogarti. "When you see him, tell him I said I appreciate it."

"And Mike?" said Jonathan.

"What?"

"You couldn't possibly understand my love for Sharon. Do you know why?"

"Please, educate me Mr. Banks."

"Because you're a thoroughly depraved and disgusting human being."

"You have a nice ride," said a smiling Mr. Bogarti. He watched until he saw Jonathan open the back door of the waiting car and step inside. *Good. One down. Now he could do whatever he wanted with Sharon. Kill her. Work her. Or ship her off.* He closed his front door and carried a wide smile with him up the stairs.

*****

The car door closed.

"Oh, my God!" screamed the man in the backseat when he saw who he was seated next to. He jumped out of the car and ran off into the night.

Jonathan looked down at the man's gun. He had left it on the seat. He looked at the man in the front seat. The man was looking back at him in terror. Jonathan tried to make out what the man was trying to say through his chattering teeth.

"Shhh—shhh—man...sir...I didn't know! God almighty, I swear I didn't know." The terrified man spoke into his lap as though he were afraid to look at Jonathan. "I'm sorry for hitting you and kicking you, man." He spoke quickly, as though he only had a few seconds to make his case. "Billy—he's the one who shot you. I didn't shoot you. Is that deal still on the table?"

Jonathan was as confused as the man was terrified. He didn't answer.

The man took his gun out. "I'm putting my gun on the back seat. Is that okay, man? Is that okay?" Jeff was nearly crying.

"Uuhh, yeah,you most certainly can," answered Jonathan.

Jeff slowly stretched his hand toward the back seat with the gun in his hand. "I ain't trying nothing," he pleaded.

"Okay, I promise not to hurt you," said Jonathan.

"Is that deal still on the table?" Jeff begged.

"The deal," repeated Jonathan.

"Yeah, man, you said life or death, blessings or cursings. Is it too late, man?"

Jonathan tried to look into the man's face for some clue as to what was going on. The man had his chin buried in his chest. He looked determined to not look at Jonathan. "Why won't you look at me?" he asked.

The last time Jeff had looked into what he thought were Jonathan's eyes, he had looked into the bowels of hell. He had literally seen his own soul being tormented beyond description. "Ohhhh, my God, man! Don't make me look into your eyes again. Look—look, can I just have the deal?"

"Life or death?" asked Jonathan.

"Yeah," Jeff sniffled.

"Yeah." Jonathan looked out the window in the direction where Billy had disappeared. "And tell your friend he can have the deal, too."

"I will, man. I will." Jeff opened his door.

"Wait," said Jonathan.

The man froze. He answered with a trembling voice. "What, man?"

"Where's Sharon?"

"I swear on those red eyes, I don't know anybody named Sharon."

Jonathan looked at him intently. "If you see Sharon, you help her. You hear me? Or the deal is off. Anyone who hurts that girl will have to deal with God. And tell that to your friend."

"God? Oh—" Jeff cursed.

"Now I was told you gentlemen would provide me transportation."

"Take the car," Jeff nearly begged.

"I'm going to church," said Jonathan. He didn't know what was going on, but whatever God was doing appeared to include him not getting shot. That was just dandy. "You're free to come."

"Naw, man, I mean *sir.* I got a lot of thinking to do."

"Life and death, blessings and cursings," said Jonathan.

"Yeah, man, I gotta get my act together."

"Well, I can't argue with you there. Go on and join you buddy."

Jonathan was going to say something else to the fellow, but he was already sprinting in the same direction that his friend had gone. Jonathan got into the front seat. It was time to go help Edwin and the church pray this man's kingdom down.

Chapter 40

Sharon couldn't sit. Her bottom was raw from the beatings. She didn't want to be on the bed because this is where they beat her. But standing hadn't helped her that much either. A man had come into the room three different times.

Each time he had told her to do something disgusting. Each time Sharon answered, "In Jesus's name, no." And each time, he slapped her to the floor and immediately left the room. But the last thing he always heard before he left was Sharon saying, "I forgive you." Whoever this man was, he had told her this would continue until she begged him to let her do what he had demanded.

Sharon had been stronger than she had ever thought she could be. But her terror was real. She thought of the other girls. Someone had taken her on what they called a tour. She stayed blindfolded until they arrived at particular rooms. There someone put her head in a vise-like device that fixed her line of sight straight ahead. They'd put her head in it and take off the blindfold. She never saw who was leading her about. But she could see everything else.

The things they did to the girls were repulsive. She knew she'd never be able to get these images out of her mind. She'd never get the sounds out of her ears. She'd never forget the hopelessness or the blank, zombie-like stares in the girls' eyes.

The men who did these things to them couldn't have hearts. They couldn't be human. How could a human being treat a defenseless girl worse than an animal? Sharon felt herself on the verge of throwing up more than once. Miraculously, she did not, and this was good for her. For one of the men told her she would clean the floor with her mouth if she did throw up. *Oh, God, where are you?*

Sharon leaned against the back wall of her dark room thinking about an odd thing she had seen on the tour. The men had put her head in the wooden clamp. She had looked straight ahead. At first she saw the same heart-wrenching scenes of girls and young women being brutalized. Then suddenly the room got blurry, like a television with a bad reception.

When it cleared, she saw herself standing on the bodies of girls in chains. She had a Bible in one hand and she pointed at a large crowd with the other. Fire came out of her mouth as she spoke. Then the vision faded back to the reality of violated bodies and empty eyes.

She had been too traumatized to think past the bodies in the vision. But now in the darkness of her room, with nothing but the constant, throbbing pain of her raw butt to keep her company, she dared to let herself interpret this vision with faith. Faith led her to two Scriptures.

The first to come to mind was Jeremiah 33:3. *Call to Me, and I will answer you, and show you great and mighty things, which you do not know.* Sharon knew the background of this promise. Jeremiah the prophet had received it one of the many times he was in prison for serving God. The Lord had given His servant such a great promise even though he was in prison.

Sharon thought of how often it seemed God went out of His way to show Himself strongest when His people were at their weakest. She thought of her situation. She definitely qualified. She had never been so weak or so vulnerable. God was obviously telling Jeremiah even his prison couldn't stop the Almighty from showing Himself strong to him if he could make himself see past the prison. *Was that what God was telling her? Believe past the prison? Ask as though there were no prison?*

The promise was beautiful. It could have brought a smile to Sharon's face. It would have, were it not for the fact that strangers were routinely pinning her to the bed and raising her skirt and beating her raw. The only thing that had stopped them from raping her was for some reason they had not chosen to do so.

The beautiful promise of calling unto God from the prison might have caused the flickering spark in her soul to catch fire had it not been for the ugly fact that a beast of a man had come into her room three times and had demanded sexual things of her. Her face was swollen from resisting. And he would return. She knew he would. She also admitted shamefully that she could not honestly say she was strong enough to keep resisting. *God, help me.*

The second Scriptures that came to mind were the most startling. They also helped in a way the previous Scripture did not. These were Hebrews 2:17, 18.

> *Therefore, in all things He had to be made like His brethren, that He might be a merciful and faithful High Priest in things pertaining to God, to make propitiation for the sins of the people. For in that He Himself has suffered, being tempted, He is able to aid those who are tempted.*

The first Scripture was telling her to look beyond her prison. Honestly, she wasn't there yet. She was living from moment to moment, wondering when she would be raped. Wondering when she would be thrown into one of those rooms with the other girls. She knew this was wrong. She knew she should believe her Heavenly Father. *Hadn't He made Jonathan call?* But that thrilling phone call was immediately tempered by another beating. *Lord, forgive me for my weak faith.*

The second Scriptures, however, were giving meaning to her present circumstance. Even though Jesus was God, He came to earth and became as she was—in all of her weaknesses—so He could be a faithful high priest. She didn't understand all of the theology of these Scriptures, but this didn't stop her from being strengthened by them.

Perhaps she'd never understand every reason why God had allowed her to be kidnapped. But she did understand the obvious message of these Scriptures. She had entered into the sufferings of Christ. Like He had done before her, she had been reduced to the level of those whom she wanted to help. Now she smiled. It was only a fleeting vapor of a smile, but it was one, nonetheless.

She remembered how her heart had burned within her when that lady, Amanda, had talked about the horrors of sex trafficking. She had felt an instant connection with her. She had also felt that she should do something to help them. Now she understood. That night she had an option. She could get involved while the adrenaline of the moment was upon her. Or she could make a mental promise to herself to get involved, get distracted by the cares of the world, and let it slip her mind.

Now she would never forget about *those* girls. For they weren't *those* girls any more. The girls were *her.* Their fears were her fears. Their humiliations were her humiliations. Their beatings were her beatings.

Sharon got on her knees and looked up to the heavens. She didn't hear the man approach her door. Nor could she see him looking in through the small window. This was the man who had been trying to slap her into submission.

Sharon's smile cut through the physical and spiritual darkness in her room. She didn't yell, but she didn't whisper either. She thought of Daniel bravely praying after the king had threatened to throw anyone into the den of lions if they prayed to anyone other than the king. Maybe she would never get out of this horrible place. Maybe she would join the full humiliation of her sisters. But she knew now that she was suffering as her Lord had suffered. The devil wasn't in control. The Lord was in control. *Her precious Lord was in control even now.*

"Lord, I am sorry for resisting your will. I'm sorry for hating my persecutors. I know now why I'm here. I didn't do anything bad. I didn't miss your will. I didn't make you angry. I'm here because you love these girls..." She paused. "And because you love the men who are doing these awful things to—" Sharon was going to say *them*, but with deep satisfaction, she changed it to "us."

She cried, knowing she was in God's will. "Us. Us. Us. I'm one of the girls. Who am I, Lord, that you would choose me for such a mission? I'm not worthy to be used by You. I'm not worthy to be granted such an honor as this.

"Lord, the people who are beating me, I ask you from my heart, will you please bless them? They don't know your love. They don't know your wrath. And Lord, the guy who has been coming into my room, I'm so sorry for hating him. I don't have a right to hate anyone. Maybe if someone had prayed for him earlier in life, he wouldn't be so evil now."

Sharon heard something and gasped.

Fear jumped on her like a mugger springing out of the dark.

The door opened.

Her throat constricted. She tried unsuccessfully to swallow. *Oh, Jesus, help me to love.* "Whoever is there, will you please take off my cuffs just so I can lift my hands to my God? I want to worship Him. Please. I won't touch my blindfold. You can put them back on afterwards. It's just been so long since I've lifted my hands to Him."

The silence was shorter than it seemed to Sharon. Whoever was there wasn't going to do it. The tears that rolled down her face showed her disappointment. She got off of her knees. "You don't have to throw me on the bed. I lie down in Jesus's name."

The man watched Sharon lie on her belly. Over and over she softly said, "Thank You, Jesus. I love you, and I love this man."

The door closed.

This meant nothing to Sharon. Her door had opened and closed many times. Sometimes whoever was there left. Sometimes they didn't. She wouldn't worry about it any longer. They were going to do whatever they did. She was going to serve her God no matter what they did.

She smiled to her God and waited.

In a few minutes, the door opened. She heard the footsteps stop at her bed. Someone touched her handcuffs. "You can't touch your blindfold."

"I won't," Sharon promised. She stood to her feet and shocked the man by hugging him around his thick arms.

He looked down at the girl who was squeezing him.

"Thank you. I won't take long," she said.

Sharon got on her knees and worshipped God as though her mystery persecutor wasn't in the room. It lasted only about two minutes. But it was her most powerful worship time ever. In a way beyond words to explain, she felt this was the *first* time she had worshipped her God in spirit and in truth.

Sharon finished worshipping the Lord and again hugged the man who had kindly allowed her to lift her hands to God. She turned away from him with her hands behind her back. The man waited much longer than necessary before putting the cuffs back on.

"Are you hungry?" he asked her.

"Hmp? Oh, I'm"—she was going to say *starving*. She wasn't starving. She had seen one of the girls who was disciplined by being deprived food—"yes, I'd like some food, if you can. I don't want you to get in trouble, though."

"Do you have any allergies?" he asked.

"No," she answered.

"Do you like your water cold or room temperature?"

"Room temperature, please."

"I'll be back."

He returned with a plate of spaghetti and meatballs, corn on the cob, a piece of French toast, and a bottle of water on a large tray. He started to set the tray on the bed, but thought better of it. That bed had seen a lot of dirty action. He turned the wooden chair toward the back wall and set the tray on it. He put on a black mask.

"Sharon, will you stand up?"

She did.

He turned her toward the back wall and guided her to the chair. He picked up the tray and sat her down. He put the tray on her lap and took off her blindfold from behind. "It's nothing fancy. Just spaghetti."

Sharon looked at the food and burst into tears. She heard the Scripture so loudly in her heart that it almost sounded to come from the man. *You prepare a table before me in the presence of my enemies.*

"This is the best meal I've ever been offered," she said genuinely. "Thank you."

"Take your time," said the man, taking off her cuffs. "Just don't look around."

"I won't. Just knowing you're there is enough."

The man behind the mask squinted his eyes.

*****

The Mighty Bashnar looked at this spectacle the way a man condemned to die by hanging looks at the noose that awaits his neck. What was going on? Sharon was the only thing he had left that could possibly stop the prince from taking his title. He had come here to see her suffer with his own eyes. To see her die. Instead, she was being served spaghetti by a man who should've been violating her.

Clang. Clang. Clang.

The Mighty Bashnar whipped his head around. His face showed his distaste of what he saw.

Controllus was there with eight guards. He had picked up another two once Bashnar had showed his behind at the council meeting. The clanging sound was the witchcraft spirit striking a pot with a spoon.

"I would've clapped to applaud your victory here, but, well, you know." He stretched his neck and looked at Sharon's plate. "Meatballs? Not meat *sauce*?"

His eight guards laughed. One of them offered some insight. "I'm sure the meatballs aren't ground round or ground chuck."

The Mighty Bashnar turned and slowly pulled out his dagger and sword.

"No need to get personal, Mighty Bashnar," said Controllus.

"Is that still his name?" mocked one of the guards.

The guards went through another round of laughter.

The Mighty Bashnar started a slow walk toward them.

"Okay, we're not here for this. We were just passing through, Mighty Bashnar, to witness for ourselves your great Job strategy. Edwin and those folks are praying their hearts out for this girl. We were just wondering how that was affecting things over here. Now that we see we've interrupted supper, we'll be on our way."

Controllus and his group left holding their sides as they convulsed with laughter.

But the Mighty Bashnar wasn't going anywhere until Sharon the thorn was dead.

*****

Sharon finished her meal. The blindfold was put back on her and she was put back in handcuffs. She lay on her side on the bed and fell asleep. She awakened when someone opened the door to her room.

Chapter 41

Edwin looked at Barbara, Elizabeth, Andrew, and—God help him—Jessica. They were in one of the church classrooms. First, he'd somehow deal with delivering Andrew, Elizabeth, and Barbara. Barbara, surely not without a fight. Then he'd go out into the main sanctuary to join Adam and Sherry Chriswell. They had been leading the church in prayer for Sharon literally all day.

Everyone was seated except Jessica. She walked around like she had ants in her pants. She just couldn't sit still. Edwin tried to ignore her antics and comments. If she weren't jerking, she was blurting out something in tongues.

"Are you sure, Andrew?" Edwin asked.

"Yeah, I'm sure. I mean, as soon as you forgave your uncle and kissed him on the head, I felt it leave." The *it* of which he spoke was the epilepsy.

"The epilepsy left you when I asked forgiveness?" asked an incredulous Edwin.

"Yeah, Dad, I guess so. I felt it getting weaker inside of me the closer we got to his room. When you left his room the first time, when I got you some water, I felt it get stronger. I guess it was because you were having a hard time going through with forgiving him. But when we went back to his room and you forgave him, it felt like something yanked him out of the top of my head. I even heard a popping sound."

"A popping sound? Like a real popping sound?" asked Edwin.

"Yeah."

Jessica looked like she would burst if she didn't say something. Edwin reminded himself that they were all now one big, happy family. He also reminded himself that Jessica did not grate on his nerves. "Jessica, you have something you want to say?"

"Sometimes the sins of the fathers cause curses upon the children," she said in one quick breath.

Edwin had been prepared to smile politely through his annoyance. He was surprised that not only had Jessica not annoyed him, she had actually said something that made sense. Weren't they all suffering because of Adam? Didn't King David's son die because of his sin with Bathsheba? Of course, he couldn't look at this as a simplistic formula that answered every mystery. But he could see how it was possible that a parent's actions could open the door to negative consequences for the family.

"Thank you, Jessica. I can see that."

She wasn't used to being thanked by Edwin for her theology. She smiled.

"And, Jessica?"

She looked at him expectantly.

"Thank you for saying "sometimes" instead of putting it out there as a law or a formula."

"Oh, I've grown, Edwin. I know everything's not a demon, and I know we can't control God. I'm not into formulas any more. I seek God."

Edwin wasn't expecting that. *Wow! Miracles do happen,* he thought. He smiled at her.

She returned his smile. Suddenly, she jerked to the side with her hand on her lower back. Her face grimaced. "Glory to God," she shook her head. "But we still have to use our authority."

Edwin grinned at Andrew. "Yes, we still have to use our authority." He looked at Barbara and Elizabeth. "That leaves you two."

Elizabeth didn't smile, but her natural beauty presented her expression as a smile. Barbara certainly didn't smile.

"That leaves us two *what*?" she asked.

"For deliverance, Barbara. The yoga," said Edwin.

Barbara's eyes rolled without her help. "Edwin, are we going to go there again?"

Elizabeth's and Jessica's eyes widened. "You do yoga?" they both asked.

Barbara looked at them. "Now don't you two start on me. Jessica, you just said everything's not a demon."

"Right. Some things aren't, and some things are. Yoga is a demon," she said.

Barbara turned to Elizabeth. She looked at her hoping for her usual thoughtfulness and well-balanced perspective. "Elizabeth?"

"Barbara, Jonathan and I have cast out yoga demons all over the world," she said. "Yoga's not just stretching. You have to look at its roots. The roots are antichrist, occultic. It's in the Hinduism family. What's the worldview of the yoga tradition?"

"We meditate. We stretch. We breathe. We don't say anything about God one way or another. It's *not* religious. How can stretching be of the devil? I don't mean to offend anyone, but this is ridiculous. Everything's not a demon." Barbara looked at her sister. "You said so yourself."

"If you're so sure yoga's not a demon, you wouldn't mind us telling it to come out, right?" asked Jessica.

Barbara frowned and shook her head. "What are you saying, Jessica? Edwin, do you understand what she's saying?"

Jessica answered. "What I'm saying is you should let us come against this thing in Jesus's name. If there's nothing there, there's nothing there. If something's there, we'll make it come out."

Barbara had had it. "Edwin, Sharon is still out there. We have to get her back. I think we should be with the others out there praying for our daughter to come home. It doesn't make sense that other people are out there praying their hearts out while we sit in here and chase shadows."

Edwin's voice was tender. "Honey, let us pray for you. Jessica's right. What's the worst that can happen? Nothing's there, nothing's there. Something's there, we get it out. You're right. Sharon's out there. We can't have anything standing in the way of our prayers being answered."

"Mom," said Andrew, "Joshua and Israel conquered Jericho with a miracle. But when they went to fight a little city, they lost because one guy stole some clothes and stuff."

"That's right," said Jessica. "We have to get the sin out of the camp before we face the devil."

Barbara looked around. She was outnumbered. Even Andrew had gotten in on it. And if there was the slightest chance they were correct, she didn't want to do anything that could jeopardize Sharon's safety. "Go on. Let's pray so we can join the others."

*****

"What are we going to do now?" asked Yoga.

Witchcraft stepped forward. Yoga had opened the door, but the stronghold belonged to him. "Yoga, you're panicking already? They haven't even begun."

"They're about to begin, Witchcraft," Yoga answered with cynicism. "We're talking seconds here."

Witchcraft looked at those who comprised the stronghold. Antichrist. Hinduism. Kundalini. Back Pain. Darkness. Idolatry. It wasn't as formidable as he would've liked, but it was strong. The battle would no doubt be bad, but they had to hold on to Barbara. She was a pastor's wife. Pastor's wives were some of their most effective servants.

"Our plan is to say nothing. Do nothing. Respond to nothing. Keep our mouths shut. Hopefully, they'll interpret our silence as proof that we're not here." Witchcraft looked at Yoga's fear-filled face. "What? What do you want to say?" he asked impatiently.

"And if they make us respond? If they keep the pressure up and we're not able to pretend any longer?" asked Yoga.

"Yoga," said Witchcraft condescendingly, "what do we always do when this happens?"

Yoga shook his head. There was no need to answer. It was the same old thing. You finally get a good home, and then some two-bit Christian kicks you out and you're homeless.

Witchcraft continued. "Then we fight. Intimidate whoever's attacking. If that doesn't work, intimidate Barbara. Tell her you're going to kill her. Choke her. Anything. Just get her scared enough to make them stop praying for her. But remember this: Our greatest weapon is deception. Do your best to make them think we aren't here."

*****

"Can I do it, Dad?" Andrew asked.

Edwin paused. He looked at everyone. "Well, I guess so. I don't see why not."

"They're going to use the boy," said Darkness to Idolatry. He sounded pleased. "He's only fourteen."

"And how old is the Holy Spirit who lives inside of the boy?" asked Witchcraft. "How old are the angels who'll come to help this boy? Will the fire bolts that are unleashed upon us be any less scorching when he commands us to leave? Really Darkness, I expect more from you."

Darkness lowered his head. He looked ashamed.

Andrew looked around the room. He was nervous. He had never done this before. But he saw Dad and Jonathan do it all the time at church.

"Don't be afraid, Andrew," said Jessica. "You got the Holy Ghost, right?"

"Yeah," he answered tentatively.

"That's all you need. They'll listen to you," she said.

"Oh, I wish she'd shut her big mouth," said Kundalini.

Back Pain inconspicuously shuffled himself to the back of the group, then slowly slid away from them. Crowds attracted fire strikes. Better to make himself a smaller target.

"Just pray for me, Andrew." She glanced at Edwin. "We really need to get to the auditorium."

"Let us know if you sense or feel anything out of the ordinary when Andrew prays for you. Okay, Barbara?" said Elizabeth.

Elizabeth's smile tempered Barbara's irritation. "Okay," she answered.

Andrew got on one knee before his mom and placed his hand on her forehead.

"Open your eyes," said Jessica. "The word says watch and pray. You don't want to get boxed in the nose, do you?"

Andrew frowned. "Noooo."

"Go on, Andrew," Barbara encouraged.

"In Jesus's name, if there are any yoga demons in there, I command you to come out," commanded Andrew.

The demons looked around. They didn't see or hear anything out of the ordinary. A couple of them smiled.

Barbara looked at Andrew and smiled. "You did fine." She looked around. "Can we join the others now?"

"Mom, that was just one time."

"Okay, Andrew, try it again." She let out a heavy breath. "Then we're going to pray with the others."

"I can only pray one more time?" he asked.

"Son, we need to go pray for your sister," answered Barbara.

"In Jesus's name, come out! Come out! Come out!" he yelled.

His shouting startled Barbara and she jerked because of this.

"There it is," said Jessica.

"There is *nothing*," retorted Barbara. "He scared me half to death with that screaming. Must you scream like a madman, Andrew?"

"I'm sorry, Mom. It's just that you said I could only pray one more time. So I wanted to make it count."

"Well, it counted, Andrew. My ears are ringing." Barbara stood up.

The demons looked at one another, surprised at their good fortune. That was it? That was the deliverance session? A few shouts?

"Glory to God," shouted Hinduism. He started dancing a jig, kicking his legs and flailing his long arms awkwardly."

Idolatry smiled at his close friend's dance. His gift was obviously not rhythm. "Stick to deception, my friend. Dancing is not your calling."

"And deliverance isn't Andrew's," he said, bouncing from side to side with his hands in the air.

Nearly all the demons laughed and celebrated their good fortune. They loved so-called deliverance people who got discouraged after a few minutes. This wasn't even a few minutes. It was just a handful of shouts.

Witchcraft wasn't laughing with the others. He had a bad burn on his face that was the result of laughing too soon in a deliverance battle. He took a final skeptical look around. Nothing. *The battle really was over.* He allowed a crusty smile.

Back Pain was the lone holdout. He stood apart from the others watching their jubilation. *Something wasn't right.* He looked up into the darkness.

There was a faint whizzing sound above.

Every demon looked up with scared eyes. By the time their eyes locked onto the fireball in the sky, it had landed on Back Pain. It hit him in the shoulder. He fell to the ground and screamed. He was fortunate that it was a small fireball. It had only burned his back, shoulder, and arm.

Barbara took a few steps toward the door. Her belly jutted forward as she screamed and grabbed her back. She fell backward onto the floor before anyone could catch her.

"What's going on?" said Jonathan.

Everyone looked up.

"Jonathan," said Edwin, "Andrew's been taken care of. Barbara and Elizabeth still need prayer."

Jonathan kneeled down. "Go on to the auditorium. We'll take care of Barbara." He looked at Elizabeth. "And Elizabeth."

"I'm so glad you're here," Elizabeth said almost in tears.

"Thanks." Edwin looked at Jessica. *Forgiveness is more than words,* he told himself. "Jessica, come with me. We've got some demons to cast out. I've got a church full of people who have been doing yoga."

*****

Edwin looked out over the huge audience. Many of them weren't members of his church. They were simply people who cared about a missing young girl. He breathed in their support and continued his explanation of why he needed to cleanse God's church before they continued in prayer for Sharon.

"This is God's church. There is only one sovereign pastor of the church. His name is Jesus. I didn't die for the church. He did. So please hear me when I say this. I have the honor, privilege, and responsibility of being entrusted by Him and you to serve as your human pastor. Part of my responsibility as your pastor is to help you understand the words of the Lord.

"It is also to help you stay away from harmful doctrines, heresies, and practices that would compromise your walk with the Lord." He dropped his head and looked within himself for a few moments. "I've recently failed in this task." He looked at the audience, slowly scanning faces as he spoke. "I've failed by allowing the spirit of witchcraft to come into our church. I've done this by permitting yoga sessions to be held in our building."

"Glory to God, pastor!" a lady yelled out.

"Preach it! Preach it!" a voice from the back said.

There were also some bewildered expressions from people he knew had no idea why Christians shouldn't be involved in yoga.

"I'm not going to spend a lot of time going into what yoga is and isn't. Not tonight anyway. We're here to pray my daughter home. And there's not a moment to spare. But I will say this. We're followers of the Lord Jesus Christ. Hindus and Buddhists and Muslims and atheists don't apologize for who they are. I'm not apologizing for who we are. We believe Jesus Christ is the only way to heaven. We believe all those who reject Him will suffer eternal punishment. We believe that any doctrine or worldview that conflicts with one hundred percent devotion to Him is one hundred percent wrong.

"Yoga is wrong. Its origin is idolatry. Its foundation is antichrist. Its destination is witchcraft. It has no place here in our church. And as long as I'm your pastor, there will not be another yoga session sponsored by this church or located in any building that belongs to us.

"Now I know that some of you here this evening may have participated in one of our yoga sessions. First, I ask you to forgive me for allowing this in our church. Second, I ask that anyone who has ever participated in yoga please come forward to be prayed for. I'm asking you to join with us in public repentance to the Lord for yielding ourselves to occult influences, and for opening ourselves to the spirit of witchcraft."

People from all over the auditorium started to trickle up front.

*****

Controllus looked as though his mouth had been cranked open with a car jack. He was not only losing people who had recently come to him through the yoga sessions. He recognized some of the faces as those who had been in partnership with him for years.

"There's Bobby! What in darkness is he doing here? And what's he doing going down there to the altar to be prayed for?" Witchcraft was incensed. He knew exactly what would happen. Bobby would go down there for one thing and God would shake him loose of all kinds of bondages.

Controllus looked at his guard detail. "He's taking all of my people."

The guards were nonchalant.

"All of them," said an anxious Witchcraft. "There are fortune tellers down there. I'll have to answer for this?"

One of the guards commented while looking at his nails. "You should be more careful."

Clang. Clang. Clang.

Controllus and his eight guards looked in the direction of the sound.

The Mighty Bashnar stood there with a pot in one hand and a spoon in the other. "I could have celebrated your victory by clapping, I do have two hands, but I thought since you like pots and spoons, it would be more appropriate to—" He hit the pot again. *Clang. Clang. Clang.*

"This is as much your undoing as it is mine," said Controllus.

"I don't think so, witchcraft spirit." The Mighty Bashnar slowly floated away. "I still have Sharon."

"Not for long, Mighty Bashnar! Do you not remember what happened when the church prayed for the apostle Peter to be freed from Herod's prison? Have you not seen this church praying for Sharon? You won't have her for long!" yelled Controllus.

This dumb witchcraft spirit is right for once in his worthless life, thought the Mighty Bashnar as he flew away. *I have to destroy her now!*

Chapter 42

The healing angel had been waiting over a full day for permission to touch Priscilla's eyes. He had authorization from the Creator to heal her once her mother submitted fully to His will. He wanted this to happen quickly. It was his nature to heal.

Yet it wasn't merely on account of his driving instinct to restore sons and daughters of Adam to health that made him want this to happen soon. It was also because the Creator in His infinite goodness and wisdom allowed healing angels to experience in rapturous joy what the sons and daughters of Adam experienced in relief. Healing for one. Joy for the other.

He followed Priscilla, waiting for Vivian to take up her cross.

*****

Michael was anxious. Something was wrong. He hadn't received any word, cryptic or otherwise, about their big mouth preacher. Jeff and Billy were very good at the business of killing. So he knew that jerk was dead. But why hadn't someone told him something?

He bounced between looking at the news, reading the *Wall Street Journal*, and glancing at Vivian as she prepared a late breakfast. He had stuck around because she had been throwing up since last night.

"Honey, why don't you let Hazel do that?" He offered this knowing that Vivian wasn't a fan of other women cooking for her husband. It didn't make a difference that this was part of Hazel's job description. It was ridiculous for Vivian to be like that, but he liked it. How many guys had a woman as beautiful and smart as she was who was too jealous to let the hired help cook her husband a meal?

"No, I'll do it, Mike," she answered.

Ego stroked. Michael smiled.

The television news reporter commented on the body of a man with a gunshot to his head found in a car. This wasn't what snapped Michael's head up. What snapped his head up was when the reporter spoke of a hidden camera in the car that produced a video of two cops looking in the dead man's car and pockets and walking away without doing anything, except taking a large suitcase from his trunk.

Vivian heard the television, but it was just another killing until she saw the look on her husband's face. It was more than curiosity. She turned back around and moved things around on the stove and counter. The next story took away some of the nausea that had filled her belly and chest since last night.

The pastor from that church was telling the reporter that the church had been praying all night for Sharon's return. Behind him stood the preacher who had come to their home the night before.

"That's that preacher. That's Jonathan Banks," said Michael, without hearing his own words, but Vivian heard them.

Vivian put her husband's food on the table and stood by his side. They both stared intently into the large screen. Sharon's father and mother begged the community to keep praying and to provide any tips, no matter how ridiculous they may be.

"They're still praying. They prayed all night. They think Sharon is still alive. What do you think, Mike? Do you think this girl is still alive?"

Michael had to pull the television's tentacles from around his throat. He looked at his wife. His eyes were glazed with confused thoughts. *His men had Jonathan tied up in a locked trunk. Somehow he had gotten away. Last night he watched him get in the car with two people who not only were good at killing, they enjoyed it. But here he was on television.*

He looked into Vivian's face and studied her.

"I hope she's not dead," said Vivian.

The preacher hadn't told her. Good! He wasn't as dumb as he was arrogant. "I hope she's not dead either," said Michael. "Maybe the posters will help."

Vivian lowered the television's volume and sat at the table with Michael. She placed both her hands on top of his and squeezed. She lowered her head and began to pray before he knew what she was doing.

"Lord Jesus, this poor girl is missing and her family is tormented by her loss. If she is still alive, we humbly ask You to free her so that she may continue to provide such wonderful assistance to those who desire truth."

Michael thought Vivian was through praying. He opened his eyes.

"And Lord Jesus, we ask that if this young lady is being held somewhere against her will that You will lift up your mighty hand against the wicked person who has taken her. Amen."

Michael hadn't reclosed his eyes. He watched her as she prayed and met her eyes when they opened. "I've never heard you pray like that before."

"I have never prayed like that before. Not for a stranger." She sipped her coffee. "But I have prayed this way for my daughter's eye for years."

He smiled. "*Our* daughter's eye." A spirit of unbelief whispered into his ear. After a few moments, he said, "You have prayed like this for years and He hasn't answered your prayers." He sipped his coffee. "Do you think He will answer your prayers to free this girl if He hasn't answered your prayers to help our little girl?"

"Until Sunday I never knew that I could know God. But now that I've tasted of His goodness and have experienced His mighty power..." she shook her head, "I do. I believe He will help them both."

Michael wondered as he looked across the table at his wife.

Vivian prayed as she looked across the table at her husband.

"We'll see," he said.

They both turned when they saw Priscilla shuffling toward them with her head lowered. She held her eye patch in one hand and a children's Bible story book in the other. Michael smiled with an open mouth. "My baby. Come here, Priscilla." She shuffled toward him and he scooped her up. "Aahhh, that's my girl."

"Why did you take your eye patch off, Priscilla?" asked Vivian.

Priscilla's face was buried into her father's chest. "The angel told me to open my eye wide so he could blow God's breath into it. He smelled good."

Michael rubbed her back and smiled. "The angel smelled good, baby? Like Mommy's cakes? Aahhh," he said, snuggling into her little neck.

"The angel said I don't have to be a pirate anymore because Mommy picked up her cross."

"Priscilla," Vivian lifted her little girl's face, "open your eyes, baby."

Priscilla opened her eyes and laughed. "See, I don't have to be a pirate any more."

"Oh, my God! Oh, my God! Oh, my God!" That's all that would come out of Vivian's mouth.

"What?" Michael held Priscilla in front of him. "Look around, Priscilla."

She turned her head in every direction.

"No. No," said Michael. "Hold your head still. Don't move it. Now look around with just your eyes."

She did. "See, Daddy?"

He lowered her to the floor.

"Oh, my God! Michael, her eye," Vivian put her hand to her mouth and cried, "God healed our baby!"

"Can I have an ice cream pop?" Priscilla asked whoever may be listening.

Michael walked a few steps away, shaking his head. He spun and walked back to Priscilla. He kneeled and palmed her head in his hands.

"Look around with your eyes, Priscilla. Push in every direction. Up. Down. All around." He let her go.

"Can I have an ice cream pop, Daddy?"

"Oh," said Vivian. She got an ice cream pop out of the freezer and opened it for her. She picked her up and squeezed her."

"I can't breathe, Mommy."

Vivian laughed through her tears. "I'm sorry, baby. Mommy's just so happy. Mommy's so happy you don't have to be a pirate any more."

"Daddy, are you happy?"

"Yes, I'm happy," he said.

"You don't look happy, Daddy. Mommy, Daddy doesn't look happy."

"He's happy, baby. He's just surprised that God healed you."

"Is Daddy shocked? He looks shocked."

"Yes, Daddy's shocked. But that doesn't mean he's not happy." Vivian didn't know what to do. She wanted to scream, shout, dance, run. She held Priscilla tightly and rubbed her back and released some of the energy by walking with her from room to room. She finally returned to the kitchen.

Michael was on his phone. He ended the call. He sat down and motioned for Vivian to give him Priscilla. He sat her on his lap facing him and bounced his leg up and down. He watched her eat her ice cream. But he watched her eye more. "What did the angel look like?"

"Friendly."

Michael glanced at Vivian. "Friendly? That's nice to know. Was he tall or short?"

"He was tall. And he had a shiny face and shiny clothes. He told me to tell you something."

Michael looked into Vivian's eyes for a few seconds. He looked at Priscilla and smiled. "What did the angel say to tell me?"

Some of Priscilla's ice cream pop was dripping down the side of the cardboard. She licked it. "Got it, Daddy!"

"You got it, baby. Now what did the angel tell you to tell me."

"He said He knows who you are and where you are. He said He's going to visit you because you have something that belongs to Him." She took a big lick and looked at her daddy. "He said you asked Him to come get it."

*****

Michael felt sick. He couldn't explain Priscilla's eyes. He couldn't explain the coincidence of her being healed just when he and Vivian were talking about God answering Vivian's prayers. (Was she really healed? She looked healed!) He couldn't explain that Houdini preacher. He couldn't explain why no one had contacted him. He didn't like to do this, it was risky. But he had to contact someone. Even if it meant checking his businesses in person.

He went into his home office and closed the door. He logged in to his computer. He needed to assure himself that all was well. He punched in the insanely difficult passwords—three layers of protection. He didn't smile, but he was satisfied that no one—not even the FBI—would be snooping in his files any time soon.

Even if his computer were confiscated, they'd get nothing. They'd get nothing because nothing was on his hard drive. His precious files were on two servers in two different locations. Each could be remotely wiped clean. He also had an encrypted external hard drive that was kept in a safe place. A place not in his home.

Michael looked at file after file of high definition video and clear audio of powerful men, and even women, enjoying his unregulated inventory. Judges, politicians, attorneys, police chiefs, detectives, powerful regulators, even an FBI agent. Looking at his insurance policy made him feel better.

This good feeling hit the ground like a kite driven by a violent wind when neither of his trusted assistants, Rick and Lenny, answered their phones. *They always answer their phones,* he thought. This was an inflexible rule. Something was monumentally wrong.

*****

Sharon was lying on her side on the mattress. She looked straight ahead into the darkness of her blindfold. She had worshipped the Lord and thanked Him with tears for letting her enter His sufferings. But now only minutes later, the door had opened again. Instead of bravely embracing whatever Satan had devised against her, she was trembling so badly that she felt like she may fall off the side of the bed.

Oh, God, I'm sorry for being afraid. Please don't let them beat me again. I can't take any more, she pleaded.

"Faithful Sharon, a daughter greatly beloved. Do not be afraid."

This wasn't Alex. And it wasn't the man who had fed her. She didn't answer the strange, new voice.

"Satan has meant this great evil to destroy you, but your heavenly Father has meant it for the salvation of many. You have been purified in the fire. It was necessary that you enter the sufferings of your Lord that you may walk in the power of His resurrection. Faithful Sharon, your tears and prayers have been presented before the Creator for an everlasting memorial."

Sharon didn't move. What was this man saying? Who was he? Why did he talk so strangely? If he knew the Lord, what was he doing here? "Who are you?" she asked.

"I am Myla. I am sent from the presence of the Almighty because of your prayers for the girls and your love for your persecutors."

Sharon's mind raced. It bounced from one Bible story to another. Was she talking to an angel? "You're an angel? You came for the girls."

"Yes. We have come for the girls. Your father and the church did much damage to the stronghold by persevering prayer. But we were not authorized to come until you prayed for your enemies. Love of your enemies is the purest form of godliness. God is love. He who walks in love, walks in God, and God walks in him."

"Sir, when may I go home? When can I and the girls leave this place?"

"Stand, Faithful Sharon."

She stood and faced the voice.

"Behold," said the angel.

Sharon's eyes were shut tight behind the cloth. This didn't stop her from seeing the angel who stood before her in battle dress. He glowed with the glory of heaven. The light that flowed from him coursed through her body and soul and spirit, connecting her to the Father. She knew instinctively that the light that came from the angel didn't originate with him. He was like the moon that radiated only the light it received from the sun.

"Today your tears and prayers and forgiveness will free these daughters of Adam and will expose and destroy the mighty."

"Sir?"

"Yes, Faithful Sharon," said the angel.

"I love the Lord. He is precious to me," said Sharon.

"Everyone knows you love Him and will do whatever He desires. It is why you were chosen. Now, the time of judgment is at hand. But God will give you all those who will hear your words."

"But what if they don't listen?" she asked. "Can they have more time to repent?"

"God will not always strive with flesh. If they will not heed your words today, they will face His judgment today. Do not be afraid. Whether you live or die, you are the Lord's faithful servant. I must go now."

Sharon watched the light grow dimmer until it and the angel were gone. The moment the last glow of light disappeared, the handcuffs fell from her wrists in several pieces.

Sharon gasped and put her hands in front of her. For a moment, she was afraid to remove the cloth from around her eyes. But she remembered the words of the angel that she belonged to God in life or in death. She removed the blindfold.

She looked around the small room. What horrors had this room seen? How many girls and women had been brutalized in this room? How many tears had fallen here? How many girls had prayed for God to help them? Why had she been shown mercy and the others had not? She knew these were questions that would not be answered until Judgment Day. But it didn't lessen the grief she shared for her sisters in bondage.

She turned. Were Sharon's eyes playing tricks on here? She blinked hard a few times and walked to the table that could not have been here before the angel appeared. It was extremely ragged and was about three feet high and reached from the left wall to the right wall. It blocked the door. On top of it was a golden candlestick with seven arms. Each of the seven were lit.

There was a large brass cup with a liquid in it. Was it wine? It looked like wine. Sharon put her nose to the large cup and sniffed. She couldn't tell. Whatever it was smelled fresh. Next to the cup was a large loaf of bread. Was this stuff for communion?

Sharon looked at the last item on the table. She had no idea what this was. It was the size of a large microwave oven. It was a sculpture of two angels with outstretched wings. *Two angels? Two angels? Two angels? The mercy seat! Was this a replica of the mercy seat?*

She sat on the bed. What was going on? What was she supposed to do with this stuff?

In a moment, someone looked inside the small window. Her eyes met his. His eyes bulged. The door opened. A man with a mask stood there saying nothing. He appeared to be weighing whether he should slam the door and run away or step inside.

"Please come in," said Sharon. "I have to talk to you."

The man looked at her hands. He looked at the pieces of handcuffs on the floor.

"The angel of the Lord. He broke the handcuffs," said Sharon. "If you want to live past today, listen to me."

The man looked up and down the long hall and pulled the door shut behind him.

"Are you the man who fed me?"

He didn't answer immediately. "Yes," he answered tentatively.

"Thank you." She looked at the masked man. She saw fear in his eyes. "You don't have to be afraid. The Lord has sent His angel to free me and the girls." She waited. "He is coming to destroy His enemies."

The man let out a heavy breath and rubbed his hand down over the mask. He grunted and let out several heavy breaths.

"Do not be afraid. He has given me all who will repent and cry out for mercy. That is what this stuff is for. This table, I think, represents the cross that my Lord Jesus was crucified on. That's why it's so ragged. And I think the red stains represent His precious blood."

She pointed to the other items, touching them ever so lightly, reverently.

"This is the mercy seat. This is the bread that represents His body that was broken for you. This is the wine that represents His blood that was poured out for you. You will not leave here alive today unless you believe that Jesus Christ is the Son of God, the Savior of the world.

"You must turn from your sins and believe the gospel. You must live for Him." She looked at the bread and wine. "If you do this, then I will give you some bread and wine in His name. This is called communion. He told His followers to take communion as often as they thought about Him dying for their sins."

Sharon could see the eyes surrounded by the black ski mask. *He wanted Christ.*

"Do you believe what I have said? Do you want the Lord?" she asked.

"I heard a voice," he said. "I was in the head, and I heard a voice. It said, if you want to live, go see Sharon. Do whatever she commands. Do you want me to free you?"

"No. I am already free. I want you to free yourself. Do you want the Lord? Will you turn from this wickedness?" she asked.

"Yes," he said.

Sharon smiled with tears. "Please kneel before the Lord and tell him in your own words that you believe He is the Son of God and that He died for your sins, and that He rose from the dead. Then ask Him to forgive you. When you finish, we'll take communion. Then go get everyone who works in this filthy place and tell them to come see me."

The man got on his knees and started praying.

"Wait," said Sharon. "What is your name?"

"Chuck."

"Chuck, we have to take off our masks when we come to the Lord. Please take yours off," she said tenderly.

The man pulled off the mask.

Sharon looked at his face. It was wet with tears, and it still held some fear. She laid her hands on top of his. "Thank you for being kind to me. And thank you for choosing life. Let's hurry. God's judgment is coming."

Chapter 43

Michael personally went to three of his clubs and two of his restaurants before arriving at their *Man Land* club. It was in the heart of Atlanta and was the premier adult entertainment club in the southeast. Everything was normal. *Everything except for the fact that no one involved in his unregulated businesses could be found!*

He went to one of the employee rooms—not the dancers' room—that had a television. Everyone in the room was silent as they watched the screen. Big shots were being rounded up by the FBI for their involvement in sex trafficking. They had the district attorney, Mike Torre. They had Winston Birch, the Atlanta mayor's chief of staff. They had two chiefs of police and a host of lower law enforcement detectives and officers.

Mr. Bogarti tried in vain to appear to watch out of mere curiosity, but this was impossible. It was impossible because reporters were discussing video and audio that was only on his servers. No one had access to this but him. *But someone obviously did have access to his servers!* Someone was trying to take him down.

He watched as much as he could before rushing to the office he maintained at *Man Land*. There was nothing on the videos that could implicate him. But it was only a matter of time before people raced to cut deals for the name of the supplier of the girls.

Mr. Bogarti scurried up and down every street and alley of his mind. Who had done this to him? Who could've done this? He made himself stop thinking like this. It didn't serve any purpose now. He could figure out who the traitor is later. Right now he needed to buy some time.

Buying time.

Mr. Bogarti was a businessman who dealt with hard facts. He had never fancied luck or expected sunshine to come from a storm. The storm was coming. Buying time was nothing but hoping for sunshine. But what else could he do? The FBI could be at his house now. His phone could be tapped. They could be on their way to get him at this very moment. Any way he looked at this, the storm was coming and his video umbrella was gone.

I'm going down, he admitted. His thought wasn't pitiful. It was determined. He was going down, but not alone. The big mouth preacher and his other preacher friend were out of his reach. But he knew how he could still touch them both.

Sharon.

He was never going to see his precious children again. They would never see their precious Sharon again. He would die before he ever went to prison. She would die before he made sure he didn't go to prison.

He left *Man Land* to go murder Sharon.

*****

The building and surrounding acreage was enveloped in thick darkness. It was darkness caused not by the absence of sunlight, but by the concentration of evil in and near the structure. The darkness was compounded by years of hopelessness and despair. It mixed with the evil and produced a darkness like the blackest smoke and just as suffocating. This smoke of hell gave the building the appearance of being on fire, only without the flames.

The man who approached the building wore white linen. He wore a container that was strapped over his shoulder and back. In his right hand he carried a brush. His mission was to put the mark of the Lord upon everyone who had obeyed Sharon's words.

He entered the darkness without regard to the swarming spirits who screeched violently at his appearance. He knew and they knew he was not alone. Absent from sight, but not absent from the man's sides, were fierce mercy angels.

The man entered each room and examined its occupants for faith in Christ. Most rooms had no one who could receive the Lord's mark, even among those who were being exploited. In one such room, there were two girls and one woman, all being used to satisfy the depraved lusts and dark imaginations of the men and women who used them. Despite the hellish activities, he could not put the Lord's mark upon them. For though they wanted freedom from their torments, they did not want freedom from their sins. He left in the hope that he would find someone who wanted true freedom.

The man with the pouch looked through the thick darkness at the light that came from a room. Its brightness told him it was Sharon's room. He walked toward it. Demons hissed and screeched and swiped their claws at the man, although from a distance far enough away that they knew it wouldn't provoke the mercy angels who were hidden in invisibility.

Alex was on his knees being served communion by Sharon. Chuck stood by him with his hand on his shoulder. The man with the pouch smiled and opened its wide top. He dipped the brush inside and pulled it out and pressed it against Alex's and Chuck's forehead. He smiled at Faithful Sharon and left the room.

The man with the pouch returned to Captain Rashti. "I have marked all who have obeyed the words of God's friend, Faithful Sharon."

Captain Rashti turned to Myla, Enrid, Trin, Adaam-Mir, and several other angels within his inner circle. "It is time. The prayers of the saints and the sins of the wicked are filled to the full." He looked down a long line of angelic warriors and lifted his hand toward one who carried a trumpet. He thrust his hand downward.

The trumpet's sound filled the air.

The mass of angelic warriors rushed away in three directions to destroy the strongholds of the ruling spirit of the sex slavery kingdom of Mr. Bogarti.

*****

Sharon almost couldn't believe it. This was like something out of the Bible. Joseph had been sold into slavery and later thrown into prison, and God had exalted him to be second-in-command of the Egyptian empire. Daniel had been taken as a slave to serve the king of Babylon, and God had exalted him to a position of great authority. Like them, she had been taken as a slave only to be later exalted by God. *Oh, Lord, truly Your ways are higher than our ways,* she thought.

Yet as unbelievable as this was to be leading her abusers to the Lord, she was crushed that there weren't more. "There's no one else, Chuck? Are you sure? Did you tell everyone?"

Chuck looked at Alex as he answered Sharon. "Yeah, everybody knows."

Alex knew what Chuck was thinking. He was thinking the same thing. This wasn't church. You couldn't do what they had done and simply go back to your pew. This was a criminal business. If you were not for it, you were against it. Someone probably had already called Mr. Bogarti.

"What's wrong, Chuck?" asked Sharon. "Why are you looking at Alex like that?"

"Our boss, Mr. Bogarti. He's not going to like this. It'll be a miracle if we make it out of here alive," he answered.

Sharon looked at him, wondering. "Bogarti?"

"Yeah," said Chuck.

"I prayed for a lady on Sunday named Vivian Bogarti," said Sharon.

"You...prayed...for...Vivian?" asked Alex.

"Yeah," said Sharon.

"Wait a minute," said Alex. They couldn't be talking about the same Vivian. "This lady is about forty. She looks maybe thirty-five. Beautiful. Long, dark hair. Classy. Really expensive clothes and jewelry."

"Yeah. That's her. She came up to be prayed for. She had two guys with her."

Alex and Chuck looked at each other in shock. What kind of coincidence was this?

"She prayed for Vivian," Alex said to Chuck. "She prayed for Vivian."

"God really touched her," said Sharon.

"God touched Vivian?" said both men.

"Yeah. She fell out on the floor and was delivered. She got filled with the Holy Spirit."

Neither man knew what Sharon was talking about.

"She was really blessed," said Sharon.

"Well, I'll be," muttered Alex.

They sat in silence for a minute.

"Alex, Chuck, I think you should go."

"What do you mean?" asked Alex.

"You can't stay here. It's going to end soon," said Sharon.

The men looked at one another.

Chuck spoke for them both. "Sharon, the only way we're getting out of here is if we shoot our way out. They're not going to just let us drive away."

Alex shook his head. He wore a heavy expression. "Besides, the things we've done to the girls..." Wasn't this the story of his life? He wasn't making any excuses for what he had done, but it had always seemed that the only choices before him were bad ones.

"You can start over," said Sharon.

"Somehow I don't think the government's as forgiving as you and God," said Alex.

"They're not," said Sharon. "But you're not asking the government. You're asking God."

The men didn't say anything to this.

"Have any of the girls seen your faces?"

"No. We always wear a mask," said Alex.

"Then go. Leave while you can," said Sharon.

"I want to. God, knows I want to," said Alex. "I don't want to go to prison. But, Sharon, this doesn't seem right. The way we hurt the girls. The things we've done. Then just walk away to live our lives, like nothing ever happened."

"It's *not* right, Alex. It's mercy. Mercy is for people who have done wrong. And I'm not asking you to walk away and live your lives as though nothing ever happened here. I'm asking...really, God is asking that you live the rest of your lives in debt to Him for the mercy He has shown you. In the Bible, there was a guy named Saul who put Christians in prison. He had them tortured. He even had them put to death. But God saved him and used him mightily. He didn't put him in prison the rest of his life."

"Start over," Chuck thought out aloud.

"The governor and the President have power to pardon criminals. So does God. I can't speak for him. But maybe He's giving you that kind of second chance. If not, you'll find out soon enough. Leave now and see what happens."

The men looked at one another.

"Sounds a lot better than prison," said Alex.

Chuck couldn't wrap his head around this kind of mercy. *But what if God was willing to give him that kind of second chance?* "That it does. But we still got the issue of how do we get out of here?"

"We walk by faith, not by sight," said Sharon. "Don't try to figure out everything. Miracles happen when you believe God no matter what the circumstances tell you. God can get you past the other guys. Hey, that would be a good sign, wouldn't it? That He's giving you another chance."

Alex looked at Chuck, then back at Sharon. "Okay, let's go."

"I'm not going, Alex. God wants me to stay with my sisters."

"What!" exclaimed Alex. "No way. You don't go, I don't go."

"Me either," said Chuck.

"I am going. Just not when you go. The Lord wants me to walk out with my sisters."

"How—?" began Chuck.

Sharon interrupted him. "We walk by faith, not by sight. I'll find out God's plan after I obey it. Now go before it's too late. Just leave as though God has cleared the path for you."

Find out God's plan after she obeyed it? That didn't make sense to either man.

The sight was incredible. A seventeen-year-old girl. Two large, hardened criminals. She encouraged them as though they were her frightened little kindergarten sons going to school on the first day.

Chuck kissed her on the forehead. "Thank you, Sharon. If God gets me out of this mess, I'm going to live the rest of my life helping girls like this." He patted her hand. He was unashamed of his tears.

Alex hugged Sharon. He was so ashamed of how he had treated her that he couldn't speak. Tears rolled down his rugged face.

Sharon looked at him and smiled. "Mercy, Alex. It's all about mercy."

This only made it worse for him. He squeezed down hard on his jaws. He put his large hands up to his face as though he were praying. He let out a large breath and cried. His body rocked as his emotions declared his guilt.

Sharon wiped her eyes. "Go. Please go while you can."

She pushed both men to the door and watched them walk down the hall. She wasn't anxious as she watched, but she was curious. She wondered what was grabbing their attention and causing them to stop and gaze into different rooms. Finally, they turned a corner and were gone.

*****

Alex sat in his car. He was only a few miles from where he had left his own angel. Sharon. She was the strangest and most wonderful person he had ever met. They couldn't make one better than her even in Hollywood. He seriously wondered whether she was a real angel.

Why not? After all the stuff that girl did, and him getting frozen, and that furniture in her room, it was harder to believe she wasn't an angel than to believe she was. But just in case she wasn't a real angel, he made a couple of phone calls.

Chapter 44

Sharon walked down the same hall that Chuck and Alex used to leave. Her steps were slow, tentative. She was walking by faith, but as she had learned through this experience, walking by faith did not mean your faith wouldn't be tried by fire.

She walked past two closed doors. They were rooms like hers. She looked inside and saw no one. She approached the next room, which was open. She encouraged herself and stepped into the doorway. A man was lying on his back on a cloth sofa. He was grimacing in pain.

"Help me," he said.

Sharon took a couple of tentative steps forward. The man was covered in open, wet boils. His face and neck, his arms and hands, nothing but boil after boil. There was literally not another place where a boil could erupt. Sharon looked around helplessly. What could she do?

"Please, help me," the man begged.

Sharon instinctively stretched out her hand. She heard in her spirit, "If you see a man sin a sin unto death, I do not say that you should pray for it."

She pulled her hand back in tears. "I'm sorry," she whispered. She backed away in fear. Her lips trembled as she asked, "Why didn't you come to my room? God would've given you mercy. God would've given you mercy had you only humbled yourself and asked," she cried, as she hurried away.

In room after room, she found the same thing. Men sprawled out, covered in boils. *That's what Chuck and Alex were looking at.*

Sharon made her way back down the hallway and passed her room. She stopped and stared inside. The table was gone. So was the mercy seat, candle, and communion elements. "Lord, what....?"

She continued down the hall. She recalled sitting at Jonathan's feet with her family totally mesmerized at his stories, wondering which parts were true and which were embellishments. Now she knew that truly the Lord was the same yesterday, today, and forever. *She served the God of the Bible.*

Sharon reached the section of building where the girls were locked up. Room by room, she said, "In the name of Jesus," and opened the doors.

More than once she had to physically pull girls out of their rooms. The men had played so many psychological games with them that they didn't know whether or not they were being tested for loyalty.

"I don't want to be beaten," begged one girl pitifully as she pulled against Sharon.

This one was the smallest Sharon had seen. She let out a loud groan and picked the little girl up. "In the name of Jesus Christ, I free you. You're going back home to your parents."

Sharon looked at a girl who stood still in the hallway. She was maybe a couple of years older than Sharon. She seemed to not know where to go. "What is your name?"

"Succulent," she answered.

This brought more tears to Sharon's eyes. She squeezed the young girl she was carrying. "No. *Your* name. Not the name these monsters gave you."

"Eliana," answered the girl. The sound of her name in her ears seemed to awaken something in her.

"Eliana, the Lord Jesus Christ has freed you. Now go and free the others. God has stricken all of the men with boils. They can't hurt us," said Sharon.

Eliana didn't move. "You are Sharon. God's friend. I saw you two years ago."

"What? Two years ago? What do you mean?" asked Sharon.

"Two years ago I was taken."

"You've been here two years?" asked Sharon in horror.

"No. Not here. I am from Russia. I was kidnapped two years ago in Russia. I worked there until I was traded a month ago."

"You said you saw me two years ago," said Sharon.

"Yes. I am a Christian. Three days after the men took me, I had a dream. This, what you are doing here today, I saw it in a dream two years ago. The Lord told me to hold on." The girl started crying. "He told me that He would come for me."

Sharon felt the little girl's head resting on her shoulder. She looked at this stunningly beautiful Russian girl. She looked at the others. Some were running, bolting for freedom before they woke up from their dreams and reentered their nightmares. Others walked, slow and tentative at first, until it dawned on them that they really were free. They then joined the running.

"Eliana, I am going to take care of this girl. Go and free the others. Free our sisters."

"I will free our sisters," she said.

*****

One of Michael Bogarti's cars was a hundred and fifty thousand dollar Mercedes Benz SL63 AMG Roadster. The right girl could pay for a car like this in a year, at the most a year and a quarter, if she was managed properly. This was the car he drove to the hospital.

This hospital wasn't a real hospital. It was called the hospital because of how it looked and because it had been a small hospital around twenty years ago. Now it was used to house girls before they made it to one of the permanent sites, or before they were shipped off somewhere. This freed up space at the permanent sites. Where the big money was made. It was all about efficiency.

The hospital was surrounded by a ten-foot stone wall. There was an east and west entrance. Both entrances had around the clock guards. The entrance gates were on wheels and did not open or close without a guard. The gate was open.

Mr. Bogarti looked into the large windows of where the guard was supposed to be. There wasn't one. He hit the horn. No one answered. Just like there was no one answering his phone calls. He cursed and drove past the empty guard house. It didn't matter that something was wrong. That's why he was here. *Everything* was wrong.

The boil-covered guard was lying on the floor with a high fever and fighting unconsciousness. Each time he dozed off, he saw monsters clawing at him. The car's horn jarred his heavy eyes open, at least for a moment, but he couldn't answer whoever was trying to get his attention.

Michael knew he was in the beginning of the end, or the middle of the end, or somewhere in the death spiral of his empire. But he wasn't ready for what he saw coming toward him. He slowed his car and stared with bulging eyes out the front, then out the side window as several girls walked toward the gate. They looked winded.

His magazine carried fifteen bullets, and he had another one. He could shoot them. Even if they ran, he'd get them all. He stopped the car. He watched them start running again. His hand reached for the gun.

"Ah, what's the point? It's over." At least the FBI wasn't there. If they were, the girls wouldn't be trying to find a way out. He pressed the gas.

Michael's car came to a slow stop about a hundred feet from Main Door East. He watched a trickle of girls burst through the door and run down the long street toward freedom—and toward the cops. He didn't have long.

Where was Sharon? A faint hope rose that he had not counted on. If he found her soon enough, maybe he could kill her and get out of there before the cops arrived. He had a stash of cash that would let him live right for at least a few years. He'd relocate and get another unregulated business going. Girls who needed managing were everywhere. *He just might come out of this thing alive and on top after all.*

He got out of the car and quickly made his way through the door. He walked down the hall. All of the girls' doors were open. Those that weren't, were empty. He looked inside a room where at least one of his guys would be. Two of them were there. On the floor. Gasping.

Michael stood over one of them. "What the—?"

The suffering man found strength and reached for Michael's leg. Michael jumped back. He didn't know what this thing was that was on Dennis. Whatever it was, he didn't want it on him. He looked at the other man. He looked worse than Dennis. Both men looked as though they had been exposed to some kind of killer chemicals.

Michael pulled out a handkerchief and put it to his mouth. He'd breathe through it until he knew what he was dealing with. He turned away to go find Sharon. He stopped and went back to Dennis. He stooped down, but not close enough for the man to touch him.

"Where's Sharon?" Michael asked through the handkerchief.

The man looked up with glazed eyes. "Sharon? The Mexican?"

"No. Not the Mexican. The white girl. The preacher's daughter. She came in—"

"Se…se…se…"

"Seven? Is it room seven?" Michael asked the dying man.

"Yes." His voice was a faint whisper. *"An…gel. Watch…out…for…for—"* The man used the last little strength he had to push out the last word. *"Angel."*

Michael stood up with a scowl. "I'm sick of hearing about angels." He left the room with his gun in his hand.

*****

Sharon walked down the long hall with her new friend, Kimberly, still wrapping her legs around her waist. She couldn't put her down. She was so little. So adorable. And, praise God, because she had just arrived, still so innocent. She knew she had been taken from the store. But she still didn't know what kind of place she was in.

Sharon twisted from side to side as she walked. "How old are you, Kimberly?"

"Six."

"You're six. Six years old."

"Yes." She put up six fingers for Sharon.

Sharon stopped. She put Kimberly down and got on one knee. "Jesus. Jesus." She cried between her words. "She's six. Kimberly's only six years old. Oh, God, what were they going to do to a six-year-old? What if I had not come here? She would—oh, my God, it's too horrible to even say."

When Sharon looked up, Kimberly was smiling. Every tooth beaming. "God sent you here to get me."

Sharon wiped in vain to dry her face from tears that wouldn't stop. "How do you know God sent me here?"

"I asked Him to send someone to take me back home."

Sharon looked into Kimberly's little face, full of trust. *I asked Him to send someone to take me back home.* Just like that. She asked God to send someone. A Scripture came to mind. *Except you become as a little child, you shall in no way see the kingdom of God.* Now Sharon really understood. Trust.

"Can I call you Mommy?" Kimberly asked.

Sharon picked the precious girl up again. "Yes, you can call me Mommy until we get you to your mommy." She headed for the room. She didn't know how long she had to wait, or even what she was waiting for, but she felt strongly in her spirit that she was supposed to wait in her room. She thought about the room they had kept her in. Room seven. God's number. The number of completion and perfection.

She smiled peacefully as she walked toward *completion.*

*****

Michael heard the noise coming from the room at the end of the hall. Room seven. He was going to complete this. He began to trot toward the open door. He entered the room with his gun raised. The little girl turned around to see what Mommy was looking at with her mouth wide open.

"Daddy!" the little girl yelled. She wiggled away and ran to Michael.

Michael was frozen, but not because of an angel. He was frozen in shock because Vivian and Priscilla were there instead of Sharon. He tried to quickly lower his gun.

Vivian watched with a wide mouth as his arm slowly lowered.

"Daddy! Daddy! Daddy!" Priscilla hugged his leg.

Michael shakily put the gun in his inside holster. He and Vivian looked at one another. She couldn't speak. Neither could he.

"Daddy, why were you pointing a gun at me and Mommy?"

"I—" No words would follow.

"Is it a play gun, Daddy?" she asked, looking up and smiling.

"Vivian," he groped for something to say, "I don't—what—?"

She had had more time to process this possible scenario, but now that all of the evidence had been capped with him showing up as the star witness, she was in a daze. Her mind wasn't working. All she could understand was that her husband and the father of her children was a sex trafficker. He had kidnapped the girl who had freed her from hatred and unforgiveness. The one who had led her to Christ. A fearful thought entered Vivian's mind.

"Is she dead? Is Sharon dead?" she asked her shell-shocked husband.

He shook his head lightly. He felt as though he had been in a head-on collision. He was now standing outside the mangled car and wondering who he was and what planet he was on. "No," he answered. "She's not dead."

"*What*...are you doing, Michael?" she asked.

"I don't understand," he said. "What are you and Priscilla doing here?"

"Michael, what are *you* doing here?" She tilted her head and cried with her mouth closed. "What is Priscilla's *father* doing here?"

The stupor was still sitting on Michael's brain, but the disjointed words and thoughts were slowing down enough for him catch and connect some of them.

"This is one of your businesses you didn't want Jonathan to tell me about?" She saw the anger rise in his face. "He didn't tell me, Michael." Now a question rose in his face. "You told me."

"What are you talking about, Vivian?"

"You remember when we discussed the whores you were sleeping with?" asked Vivian.

Michael looked down at Priscilla.

"It's really too late to be concerned about what your daughter hears about you," said Vivian. "I'll try, but I won't be able to keep the truth from her for long."

He looked at her with pain in his face.

"I told you that I would take precautions." Pause. "Since you had proven undeserving of my trust." Vivian wiped an eye. "I did. I heard everything you and Jonathan discussed."

Michael's eyes focused on the things he had said.

"I heard everything." Vivian broke. "*Everything,* Michael." She shook her head. "Everything. I heard you tell him that you had Sharon."

He looked at his wife, fearful of what she may still say.

"I heard you threaten her safety."

Michael closed his eyes and grimaced. He knew what she would say next.

"I heard you threaten *my* safety. You threatened my safety. The mother of your children."

"That's why you were sick? It's why you were throwing up," he said.

"Yes. It's an appropriate response to hearing your husband discuss his willingness to kill you."

Sharon was standing with Kimberly a few feet from the door. She had heard nearly everything. She stepped into Vivian's view.

Vivian looked at her. Jonathan followed Vivian's eyes and turned around.

"I'm Sharon," she said simply. "Hi, Mrs. Bogarti. It's good to see you again. Hello, Mr. Bogarti. Can I take Priscilla so you can talk?"

Michael didn't know how to respond. How much of this conversation had this girl heard?

"Yes," said Vivian. "We would appreciate the privacy." She got up and went to Priscilla. "Give Daddy a big hug."

Michael got down on one knee and hugged his daughter for a long time. He kissed her on the forehead. "Daddy loves you. You can go play with Kimberly."

Sharon's and Michael's eyes met. He had slipped. He looked at Vivian. She caught it, too.

Vivian took Priscilla by the hand and walked her into the hall. Her back was to Michael. She looked at Sharon and mouthed *Run!*

Sharon smiled. "I'll take care of them. We'll have fun."

Vivian went back into the room.

Sharon walked both little girls away several feet and said, "Wait here." She went back to the room. "Mr. Bogarti, I could've left with the others. I didn't because God wanted me to stay. I think part of the reason he wanted me to stay was to be here when you arrived. I think he wanted you to hear me say I forgive you. I forgive you for kidnapping and abusing me. I forgive you for coming here to kill me."

His face raised as he looked at her.

"I figured that's the only reason you would be here."

He said nothing.

"Mr. Bogarti, you've hurt a lot of people. But even now God will forgive you if you sincerely turn your life over to Him. Repent. Turn from your sins. Believe in Jesus. Serve Him. He can give you true life."

His expression didn't change.

"Mr. Bogarti?"

He looked at her with a little of the attitude that had brought him there to kill her.

"There's a story in the Bible about a farmer who didn't serve God. One year he had a very good crop. He said to himself that he would use his new wealth to build bigger barns. But do you know what God said to him?"

Mr. Bogarti didn't answer.

"He said, 'You fool. Tonight your soul will be required of you.' I don't know why. I just felt that I should share that story with you."

Sharon turned and took the little girls away.

"Michael, that's the girl you came here to kill," said Vivian. "She's so full of God's love. How could you ever lay a hand on a girl like this?" Vivian thought of the little girl that Sharon led away with Priscilla. "But then anyone who can hurt a girl like Kimberly can certainly hurt a girl like Sharon. You don't have a heart."

"We are in the sex business!" he yelled. "You are in the sex business!"

***

The Mighty Bashnar descended. He knew the danger. If one of his enemies caught him in a weakened state... He couldn't be concerned with this. It was a risk of war. His title and honor were at stake. He stepped inside of his servant.

***

Michael's face hardened. "Did you have anything to do with my videos getting out?"

"What difference does it make, Michael?"

He slapped her to the sticky floor. "It makes every difference!" He peered down at the daughter of Adam. He saw light coming from her. "You revealed the stronghold. Didn't you! You exposed my darkness!"

Vivian's head had hit the floor hard. Her face felt like it was on fire from Michael's slap. Her head was bleeding on the front side.

Michael snatched her from the floor and jerked her up in front of him.

She felt as though she were made of straw. She was physically hurt, but she was more shocked and terrified that he had hit her.

"What did you do, daughter of Adam?" he growled.

"Yes!" she screamed. "When I found out you were cheating on me, I put a program on your computer that records your key strokes. I went into your files. I sent them to the FBI and CNN."

He growled each word like a beast. "You did what?"

"It's wrong," she said.

"I am your husband," he growled.

"But he is my God," she snapped back defiantly.

Michael looked at her with pure black eyes.

Vivian struggled to get away, but his grip was iron.

He reached inside his suit jacket and put his hand on his gun holster and immediately fell to the floor.

Vivian stumbled backwards until her back met the wall. She looked down at her husband's still body.

Michael felt it grip him before his body hit the floor. For a second, whatever power had invaded him allowed him to look at his body on the floor and to look at his wife before it yanked him downward. He was disoriented. What had happened? He was on the floor. The floor that was above him. How high above him? Feet, yards, miles, light years, a universe away, a dimension away? But he was here. Wherever *here* was. And *here* was changing by the microsecond.

There was no way to tell how far he had gone down. He looked around and could see nothing distinguishable. For in every direction there was nothing but thick darkness. He felt the darkness whip against his body.

His body.

He touched himself. He had a body. *But I left my body,* he thought. The next thought was cruel in its utterance and final in its declaration.

I'm dead. I'm the fool Sharon spoke of. I rejected God's mercy and now He has required my soul.

Something pushed his head in the direction to where he was speeding. There was a distant glow in the darkness. The atmosphere got hotter each moment that he looked at the glow. Hotter. Hotter. Hotter. Scorching.

Michael screamed into the darkness. At first his screams were all that he heard. Then his screams were joined with other screams that came from the direction of the dark glow. Suddenly, he was standing outside of a huge wall. A creature appeared at his side. It gripped the back of his neck and his bicep. Its grip was bone-crushing.

The huge gate opened. A pale white figure was waiting.

The demon that gripped Michael spoke. "This is Michael Bogarti. The Lord extended shameful and despicable mercies to this man."

The pale demon approached Michael. His face was close to his new eternal prisoner. "Obviously, you rejected His mercy."

"Nooooooooooo," screamed Michael, as the demon put a clamp around his neck and led him into hell. "This is a mistake."

The demon shook his head as he pulled Michael deeper into his new home. "No mistake, tough guy. There's only mercy and judgment. You don't want mercy, you get judgment." The demon clicked his tongue and laughed a long, haunting laugh that seemed to never end.

*****

The Mighty Bashnar crawled on his hands and knees away from Michael's body. He collapsed onto his belly, totally depleted, unable to move anything. He'd only need a few minutes to recover his strength.

Krioni-na had been watching from a safe distance. When he saw the warrior spirit approach Michael, he wondered if perhaps he had stumbled onto a once in a lifetime opportunity. It appeared he had. He stood over and behind the Mighty Bashnar.

The Mighty Bashnar's eyes looked around as much as possible. "Who is there?" His voice carried the weakness he felt in his body.

Krioni-na reached into his boot. He pulled his dagger and buried it several times into the warrior spirit's thick back.

"Uggh...uggh...uggh...uggh."

Krioni-na would give him one for the road. He stuck the blade in slow and twisted it back and forth. He loved the sound of the warrior spirit's muscles being torn.

"Ugggggghhhhh."

The wounded warrior spirit felt something close to his face. He heard a loud pop, then a long hissing sound. His eyes widened. Was someone passing gas on the Mighty Bashnar? He sniffed. His eyes turned black with murder. Murder that he couldn't commit until his strength returned.

Krioni-na floated away. He was careful to not sing until he was safely away.

Controllus saw everything that Krioni-na had done, but his guards didn't. He had told them to wait for him while he took care of some business. They made wisecracks about whether or not it was safe for him to go out alone since the Mighty Bashnar was in the area. Fools! That was exactly why he didn't want them with him. What he had to do had to be kept a secret. He didn't need to get on the warrior spirit top ten hit list, or any of their lists if he could help it.

He hurried to the Mighty Bashnar and stood behind him. He pulled out the warrior spirit's right arm. He looked at his enemy's mammoth paw and smiled.

Whack!

He picked up the Mighty Bashnar's right paw and tossed it across the warrior spirit's body. He lifted Bashnar's big head and turned it to the right as he stepped to the left. He almost said, "Good," and had to stop himself. He stretched out the spirit's other arm.

Whack!

Controllus threw the hands in some bushes and flew away to join his guards.

Chapter 45

Prince Krioni established a new precedent by moving the Mighty Bashnar's meeting from the famed chambers of the Council of Strategic Affairs to the Hall of Darkness. It was several times larger and could handle the unprecedented crowd.

Everyone knew that such a surprising move of venue was not for the benefit of the crowd, but for the benefit of Prince Krioni. He hated the Mighty Bashnar. He knew that many demons shared his hatred. There wasn't a hall in all the dark kingdom that could accommodate all of this warrior spirit's enemies. But the prince had made sure that as many as possible would be able to witness this humiliation.

All five council members sat on an elevated stage, as did the badly wounded Mighty Bashnar. The council sat together, centered near the back wall of the wide and very deep room. The Mighty Bashnar sat alone, at an angle. This allowed the council members—today it would be only Prince Krioni who would speak—to have eye contact with the warrior spirit as they spoke.

The Mighty Bashnar's ankles were chained to the floor. There was also a large chain that went around his waist and wrapped through the insides of his thighs. It was also affixed to the floor. Hopefully, this would contain his unpredictable murderous tendencies.

The Mighty Bashnar's eyes told the audience nothing.

Controllus had a front row seat. He stared at the warrior spirit, hoping that he could will him to look his way. The warrior spirit's eyes finally settled on him. Controllus lifted his arms high and clapped his one hand against his wrist. He then lifted his good hand over his right eye and did a military salute. His mightiness didn't show anything in his face, but that was fine with Controllus. He knew he was seething in futility.

"We are here to present the final ruling from our dark father concerning the title of *Mighty,* which was won by the warrior spirit, Bashnar. Details, if anyone should desire them, can be found in the official record, which will be published later. For those of you who can't wait, there are handouts in the lobby.

"Now, let's proceed. Mighty Bashnar, first we would be remiss if we did not express our sympathies for your grievous wounds suffered in the battle for Atlanta. I imagine it is not an easy thing to lose both of your hands. And for a warrior spirit of your legendary stature whose legend is owed in no small part to those formidable weapons...*which...you...no...longer...have.*" The prince shook his head. "It must be a handful contemplating such a loss."

There was a smattering, but loud, eruption of laughter around the great room. Controllus was part of the smattering.

"What?" said the prince. "Why the laughter?"

An administrative spirit seated at a table on the main floor spoke. "Great prince, your reference to a handful."

More laughter. Partly for the reference. Partly for the lyrical, screechy voice of the clerk.

"Oh, darkness," said the prince. "I meant no hand. Ugh, I mean harm. I meant no harm." He looked with pleasure at the laughing demons. "Enough. It is time for the declaration."

He picked up a piece of paper and read. He didn't need the paper. He had read the words so many times that he had them memorized.

By order of the Lord of Darkness, let it be declared and established from the moment of public proclamation of this official declaration by the Chairman of the Council of Strategic Affairs, the great Prince Krioni, that the spirit known as the Mighty Bashnar, of the fierce warrior class, be stripped of the title Mighty.

Let it be known that this edict comes after overwhelming evidence that the demon formerly known as Mighty Bashnar did fail in his primary task of destroying the Atlanta revival enemies.

Let it be known that this same spirit failed in his secondary task of either seriously impeding or compromising the Atlanta revival.

Let it be known that the lofty plans and actions of the demon formerly known as the Mighty Bashnar did fail most notably because of a shameful ignorance of the ways of our great enemy.

Let it be known that this same demon did ignorantly work for and further the plans of our great enemy by recklessly using persecution tactics that instead of destroying the Atlanta revival, or compromising its main proponents, did instead expose their hidden weaknesses and flaws, purify their faith, and drive them to the very God they were to be separated from.

Let it be known that the failures of this demon are so magnificently deplorable that the strategies, tactics, execution, and results, as well as the lessons learned from these results, are to be recorded in the History of Exploits and Defeats.

Let it be known that the following are lessons to be recorded:

First, the enemy is able and apparently enthusiastic and committed to using the weakest of his children for his grand purposes. Adequate safeguards must be maintained to prevent them from understanding this.

Second, persecutions and hardships that we devise for evil can have the opposite effect of purifying the faith of the enemy's children if they filter their hardships by looking at them through the words and character of God.

Third, the power of forgiveness is as lethal a threat as ever and has the capacity in its irrational behavior to soften the hardest hearts and to destroy strongholds previously thought unassailable. A person walking in the kind of forgiveness that goes beyond the utterance of words to the action of kindness toward an enemy is Spirit-filled and cannot be controlled.

Fourth, focused and fervent prayer, especially such prayer offered by two or more in agreement is as it always has been—the avalanche and tsunami of the Lord, which sweeps away everything in its path.

> *Fifth, the enemy grants his mercy unjustly and undeservedly to the most vile of his servants and ours. They must never be allowed to understand his eagerness to show mercy—even though he has withheld it from us.*
>
> *Finally, that demon spirit formerly known as the Mighty Bashnar, unless he should show such brilliance worthy of the Mighty title and be reinstated to his former glory, shall from this point on be known as Bashnar the Less.*

Prince Krioni finally had Bashnar where he wanted him. He spent the next two hours playing perfectly the role of the judge who spoke on behalf of offended justice and a slighted community. Finally, he grew tired of his own words, although he felt they were quite impressive.

"You have nothing to say of your miserable failures and how you helped to purify the Atlanta saints through trials by fire?" asked the elated prince. "No defense of your failed plan to use politicians and special interest groups to get the church off track? Nothing about your ridiculous ploy to get Barbara into politics? *Really, Bashnar the Less, what would that have done even if you had gotten your way?* You have nothing to say? Fine. Then there is yet one thing to do before you are escorted out into the street."

The prince stood and raised both hands. The other council members joined him, as did everyone else in the great hall. Bashnar stood and defiantly raised his arms and pressed his forearms together to form an X.

"The spirit formerly known as the *Mighty Bashnar* is now *Bashnar the Less!*" yelled the prince.

The audience echoed. "The spirit formerly known as the *Mighty Bashnar* is now *Bashnar the Less!*"

"Make sure we get a close-up of him as he's led away," Prince Krioni instructed the clerk, who relayed the instructions. "Now get this cripple out of here."

Several armed and still wary guards escorted Bashnar toward the center aisle. He had to walk past Controllus. Controllus stood and crossed his raised arms at the forearms to mock the disgraced warrior.

Bashnar never broke his stride. His left leg swept from the floor in a circular motion. The inside of his hard, meaty ankle slammed against witchcraft's jaw.

Controllus hit the floor so suddenly he appeared to have never been standing. His face absorbed several violent kicks and stomps of protruding claws backed up by hundreds of pounds of pressure before anyone could stop the warrior spirit.

Controllus could hear nothing that Bashnar growled. His days of hearing had passed. This didn't stop Bashnar from speaking to his lifeless body. What he had to say was as much for the audience as it was for the garbage at his feet. He looked at Controllus with totally black eyes. "I am a *waaaarrior* spirit. *Waaaarrior* spirit. I told you I would kill you at the moment of my choosing." He looked up. "Now take me to the *Dark Prison.*"

*****

The spirit of death looked with regret from a great distance at the smoldering ruins of his so-called *certified* stronghold. Rubble and demons were strewn about. Ava was out of her coma and out of danger and already causing problems with her prayers. *Oh well,* he thought with exasperation, *hopefully I can find another home soon. There must be someone in this hospital who doesn't have anyone praying for them.*

*****

Jonathan and Elizabeth walked down the long white hall of the hospital. "I never want to go through anything like that again in my life," said Elizabeth. "I felt like I was going to die in those deliverance sessions. It was so painful. Why do you think it took so long to free me?"

"God knows us, Liz. He never passes up a good teaching moment. Flesh has a tendency to take for granted the things it gets too easily. I don't know why we're like that. We just are."

Liz smiled for two reasons as they got closer to Ava's room. One, because she got what Jonathan said. Diamonds and gold were highly valued because of their scarcity. Some things required greater effort. *Seek and you shall find,* she mused. *The greater the value, the greater the search.* And, two, because they hadn't come to the hospital to visit her mom. They had come to take her home.

*****

Captain Rashti and his angels returned to the hill that overlooked the valley. He looked down at the farm house. The little girl with the heart condition and with spirits of infirmity hounding her wasn't out playing. He wondered about her fate.

Adaam-Mir saw the captain looking at the farm. He had learned a lot about the captain, and the sons and daughters of Adam, and spiritual warfare. But there was so much more to learn. "What will happen to the little girl?" he asked.

"I don't know," he replied.

"Can we do anything for her?" asked Adaam-Mir.

The captain looked at the door of the house for several seconds before answering. "That is a matter between the Creator and the sons and daughters of Adam to decide."

*****

Edwin stood before the Sunday morning congregation. He looked out over God's flock with a new determination that could be seen in his eyes and face. His family was on the front row. His *entire* family. He looked at Sharon. He felt his chest filling with praise. He wasn't a shouter. It wasn't his personality.

"Glory to God!" he shouted, with his mouth pointed to the ceiling. "Glory to God! Glory to God!"

Sharon looked at the tears that flowed from her father's eyes and ran onstage and held him with her head on his chest. Barbara immediately joined them. Andrew gave it a few seconds before he went up.

Edwin hugged Barbara on one side and Sharon on the other. Andrew held his sister.

The congregation stood and clapped. Someone ran to the drums and started banging. Adam Chriswell trotted to one of the guitars and made it praise God for bringing Sharon home. His wife, Sherrie, joined him. She grabbed one of the microphones. She was an incredible vocalist, that is, when she wasn't overcome with emotion and crying, which she was right now. Sharon broke from her father and made a dash for the piano.

Jessica eyed the pandemonium like a fish out of water. She wasn't meant to be dry. Something hit her in the side. She knew what that *something* was. It was the Holy Ghost. *Oh…it…was…on…now!* "Glooooooraaaay!" Jessica shouted and took off out of the aisle and ran around the inside of the church.

Evidently several people had been waiting for someone to make the first move at running. Two ladies wearing hats that competed for wildness took off in separate directions.

Edwin rejoiced and laughed and cried as he watched thousands of people praise and worship their wonderful God with abandonment. He spotted Jonathan and Elizabeth. "Jonathan, get up here. You helped bring Sharon home. Elizabeth, you too. Get up here."

They came up holding hands.

Jonathan cut loose with what Edwin guessed must have been a pent up Pentecostal dance.

"Wow, Dad, Uncle Jonathan can go. I didn't know he could move like that," said Andrew.

Jonathan heard him. "I can't move like this," he said.

Edwin went to the microphone. "No. No." He waved his hand. "Don't stop. We prayed too hard. Keep praising Him!"

Sharon looked at Barbara with a big smile. "Mom, is that Dad?"

Barbara's hands shot up over her head. She started bouncing up and down with her eyes closed. "Thank you, Jesus! Thank you, Jesus," she said repeatedly with tears.

Sharon put both hands to her face. *"Oh...my...God!* Mom? Mom?" Sharon dropped to her knees and began to have her own crying praise fit.

Edwin continued. "What the devil meant for evil, God meant for good!" He found 1 Peter 1:7-9:

> *Wherein ye greatly rejoice, though now for a season, if need be, ye are in heaviness through manifold temptations: That the trial of your faith, being much more precious than of gold that perisheth, though it be tried with fire, might be found unto praise and honour and glory at the appearing of Jesus Christ. Whom having not seen ye love; in whom, though now ye see him not, yet believing, ye rejoice with joy unspeakable and full of glory: Receiving the end of your faith even the salvation of your souls.*

Edwin pointed his finger at the warriors before him. "Some moments belong to King James."

"Glory!" shouted an old saint.

"These Scriptures describe what has happened to us, what is happening to some of you right now. We have been tested. We have been tried."

Jonathan blurted out, "And some have been fried!"

Edwin shook his head with a grin. "And some have been fried. Some deep fried. But what the devil didn't know was that God was using him to purify our faith. Satan tried to get us to lose faith in God. He tried to get us to focus on his power instead of God's power.

"He tried to destroy us with trials by fire. It didn't work. All he did was invest in the work of God. He sowed seeds, and the Bible says you reap what you sow. The devil sowed trials by fire. You know what he's going to get for his return?"

The congregation was on the edge of their seats—those who were still sitting. Edwin felt their hunger pulling at him. They wanted the word of the Lord. "The devil sowed trials *by* fire, and for his efforts he's going to get saints *on* fire."

The place went wild. When the praises finally died down enough so he could be heard, Edwin spoke again. "The church has been kicked around by the devil long enough. We've been on the defensive long enough. It's time to get aggressive. It's time to pick up the weapons of our warfare and fulfill the great commission." Edwin looked at Jonathan. "You know what else time it is? It's time to give the mic to Jonathan."

The congregation clapped for several minutes and Edwin rejoiced inside that he felt no envy.

"Believe it or not, I don't have a lot to say. At least not right now. This is Edwin's moment. What I do have to say is simply this: Edwin is right. Satan sowed trials by fire, and in return he's going to get saints on fire. He's already a nervous fella. By God's grace and power, we're going to put him on medication.

"We're going to invade every area of this city with saints on fire. We're going to take the flames of the Holy Ghost to places he thought we were too afraid to claim. We're going to come off the pews with mighty gifts of the Spirit. We're going to love as never before! We're going to pray as never before! We're going to fast as never before! We're going to forgive as never before! We're going to give as never before! We're going to live as never before! Are you ready?"

The congregation shouted, "Yeah!"

Jonathan handed the mic to Edwin.

"Are you really ready?" Edwin asked.

The loudest voice he heard came from behind him. It was Barbara screaming, "Yeah!" He turned and looked at her. "Come here, baby." She came. He hugged her and looked at the congregation. The rest of his family and Jonathan and Elizabeth huddled around him as he looked intently at his army. "We begin today."

The End

Go to EricMHill.com for Your Free

Spiritual Warfare Short Story

Let's Stay In Touch!

Join my newsletter at ericmhill.com/newsletter. Here's my contact info: Facebook.com/ericmhillauthor, ericmhillauthor@yahoo.com or Twitter.com/ericmhillatl. God bless you!

More On Next Page

Other Books by the Author

Spiritual Warfare Fiction

The Fire Series
Book 1: Bones of Fire
Book 2: Trial by Fire
Book 3: Saints on Fire

The Demon Strongholds Series
Book 1: The Spirit of Fear
Book 2: The Spirit of Rejection

Other Fiction

Out of Darkness Series
Book 1: The Runaway: Beginnings
Book 2: The Runaway: Endings

Non-Fiction

Deliverance from Demons and Diseases
What Preachers Never Tell You About Tithes & Offerings
You Can Get Answers to Your Prayers

Made in the USA
Middletown, DE
12 March 2024

51349802R00275